The Way Yo

CW01064210

Kiki Archer

Title: The Way You Smile
ID: 23578234
ISBN: 978-0-244-72622-5

K.A Books *Publishers*

www.kikiarcherbooks.com

Published by K.A Books 2018

Copyright © 2018 Kiki Archer

Editors: Jayne Fereday and Diana Simmonds

Cover: Daniela Di-Benedetto @designbydaniela

Author photograph: **Getty Images**

ISBN: 978-0-244-72622-5

For all of the mothers surviving.
I feel you.

CHAPTER ONE

Sitting in the slow-draining shower tray, Camila crossed her legs beneath herself. She'd angled the shower head towards the wall opposite and was watching the steaming water run down the tiles. Admittedly there wasn't anything fancy about her surroundings: a magnolia bathroom suite bought in a Wickes' sale over ten years ago, a shower tray with so many layers of sealant you could mistake it for a low-level shelf and a shower head that although clean (the threat of Legionnaires' disease should never be dismissed) was peeling badly. Still, this was her space where she could just be. Tilting her head backwards, Camila looked up. How chrome could peel was one of the subjects she'd addressed in a previous seated session, along with the debate about whether glass cleaning should be categorised as an actual art, because no matter which product you used and no matter how smooth your swipes your shower door would immediately betray your glass cleaning incompetence the second the steam started to rise. Even the mini window wiper tool she'd bought from the JML stand in Boots couldn't stop the evidence from appearing. Maybe it was all about the buff? She'd ask the men at the local hand carwash where they purchased their buffing cloths. Their buffing skills were always magnificent.

Camila stopped herself. Her life was more than this now. Or it was about to be. Yes she'd probably still cross her legs underneath herself after her early morning seated leg shave but now she'd have better things to debate. Work things. Career things. Posh friend things. Not that Julie Biggs from next door with her fountain of knowledge about Tesco vouchers should be sniffed at. In fact, Julie was a great source of information. She always knew when Next were doing their VIP sale and she'd alert you when the newspapers contained those half-price theme park entry vouchers. She could also tell you instantly what time and what channel the good programmes were on. But most importantly, Julie knew week on week which supermarket was selling the cheapest prosecco. (Asda at £4.99 a bottle this week.)

Camila focused on the silver razor. She should have used a new head. Today was a day for new heads. Yes, they were incredibly expensive, but if she couldn't treat herself today when could she? Running her fingers down her legs she nodded. Smooth enough. Maybe she'd change the head tomorrow to celebrate her successful return to the world of work. What was the title they'd given her? A mum returner? Camila laughed. She'd barely been there in the first place, unless she counted part-time jobs and that successful babysitting service she'd run in her teens, plus she was 'returning' somewhere she'd never actually been. Art and design was her major at university, not that she'd finished the course, yet here she was fifteen years later 'returning' to the world of market research, or market intelligence as it was now called.

Picking up the razor, she shrugged. How hard could it be? Once upon a time, back in the days when she'd stayed standing in the shower whilst shaving her legs, she'd used one of those pink disposable razors designed specifically for women. She thought for a second. When had that actually happened? That first time she decided to angle the shower head away and slide onto her bottom in the tray so she could shave her legs without having hair flopping in her face and blood rushing to her head? Was it before the kids or after? No, she'd definitely become the non-standing-to-shave woman post kids, just as she'd downgraded her hairdresser post kids and started to shop in the clothes section of Sainsbury's post kids. Either way, one glorious day she'd spotted Mick's silver razor on the side of the sink through the badly cleaned shower door, grabbed it, lathered up and shaved, and in that moment she'd shaved all her worries away. Smoothly, sleekly, enjoyably. No longer was she worrying about rust poisoning from the sharp piece of metal at the end of the pink plastic handle; now she had blades that were contoured, a head that bounced with some sort of suspension system, and a handle with a soft rubber grip, leading to silky legs that didn't immediately feel stubbly the second you stepped out of the shower and got goose bumps.

Turning the silver razor over in her hand, Camila nodded. Market research was all about substance over style. That's what she'd said in the interview and maybe that's what got her the job. Because while this three-bladed, double-suspensioned, masculine-looking silver razor might not aesthetically appeal to the traditional woman, by god could it shave your legs well, and not once would it give you one of those horrific cuts near your ankle like the pink plastic razor would, shearing off a section of your skin to the extent you believed you'd developed haemophilia because of the amount of blood that wouldn't stop flowing.

Putting the razor back down, Camila stood up. Focus. She needed to focus. She couldn't be this woman anymore, this woman who spent fifteen minutes in the shower tray on a daily basis debating life's big questions, no matter how attached she was to her single place of solace. Waving down at the slow-draining water, she spoke seriously. "It's been a wonderful fifteen years." She smiled and raised her voice, moving her gaze forward and trying her best to ignore the cleaning smears on the glass door. "But tomorrow, I'm a woman who stands in the shower to shave."

"What, Mum?" came the shout.

Turning off the water and stepping into the small en-suite, Camila reached for the pile of towels, grabbing the big one at the bottom and wrapping it around her body. It was one of seven different sizes that Julie had recommended on offer at The Range. "Pardon?" she shouted, now taking the third towel from the top and attempting to fasten it around her head. She cursed; it was too small. She tried the next towel down, lifting it in front of herself to assess its potential before wasting her time on another unsuccessful hair flick and towel swish manoeuvre. Again, too small. Working through the pile, she sighed. Great. There was pretty much one bath towel, one hand towel and five flannels of varying sizes. This was something else she'd have to stop: buying in to all of Julie Biggs' bargains. She needed to learn that they weren't, and never would be, either essential purchases or bargains. From now on she was going to be the woman who bought towels from Debenhams, or maybe even John Lewis.

"Mum!"

"What? Stop hollering at me. I'm in the bathroom." Camila reached for her trusty Kellogg's Special K towel, quickly wrapping it around her head.

"Straighteners. I need them for school."

"Wait!" Struggling to keep the big towel in place around her body due to its blanket size and her slight build, Camila opened the door from the en-suite just in time to see her teenage son reaching for her hair straighteners. "No! You can't take them."

"PE today."

"Michael, I need them!" They were the only implement capable of transforming her shoulder-length brown hair into any sort of style.

"Gym before school. Going early."

"Michael, I really do need them today."

"PE."

"And?"

"Meant to rain. Use Ethan's."

"His are always sticky with gel."

"Good job you love me hey, Mum." The tall boy grinned as he twisted the power cord around the appliance and backed away across his mother's small bedroom. He paused in the doorway. "Made you breakfast. Good luck breakfast."

Camila smiled, everything instantly forgiven. "Oh bless you, my darling."

"You'll be great."

Struggling to keep the towel in place as she moved towards him, Camila lifted a hand to her son's broad shoulders. "Have you got time to eat with me? I'll come down now."

"Already had my protein shake."

"Let me see you off then." Camila followed her son as he strode across the short landing and down the stairs. She smiled. The school portrait pictures were rattling on the wall beside her. Ten years of toothy grins moving more and more, year on year, as her sons got bigger and their stair stomps got heavier. "I'll be back in time to make tea as usual," she said.

"We're fine, Mum."

"If you're making me breakfast you obviously are. Is your bag in the kitchen?" Camila tiptoed across the hall's short section of laminate flooring wondering why no one had told her a decade ago when the plastic fake-wood-effect panels became such a craze that laminate flooring was actually a nightmare to clean. Mopping led to buckling, polishing led to broken necks and no implement sold on the JML stand at Boots ever did the job it was meant to do, so down she'd go on her knees, gently spraying and buffing, but still her hot shower footprints showed up, hence why she always danced as quickly as she could into the kitchen. Or wore slippers.

"Have you got my slippers? Are they in your room?" She turned to her son who'd followed her through. "You've destroyed so many pairs, crushing down the backs with those huge pontoons of yours."

"Pontoons?"

"You told me I couldn't call them barges. What about battleships? Shall we call them battleships, or how about U-boats?" She watched as her eldest child tucked the straighteners into his school bag before she noticed the bowl, spoon and cereal box on the counter.

The boy grinned. "What? That's what you have for breakfast."

Camila smiled. "It's perfect, my darling." Reaching out she squeezed his arm, wondering at what point the hair ruffle had changed to the bicep squeeze and when exactly her fingers had become unable to reach half way around the huge muscle.

"Thought you had someone in the shower with you this morning. Heard you talking."

Camila almost spat out her laughter.

"What? We don't mind. He's doing it. Why can't you?"

"Because I have morals." Camila quickly corrected herself. "Sorry. That was wrong."

"It's not. He's a tosser."

Camila let the words hang in the air before assessing her son's face in the silence. "You're a good man, Michael."

"Stop going on about me being only fifteen then."

5

"I stand by yesterday's discussion. In my day fifteen-year-olds didn't have full beards. Apart from Jennifer Langley. Thyroid issues."

"You're not funny, Mum."

"Says you, Mr Bigfoot." Camila reached out and hugged the muscles once more. "You're a *good man*, Michael."

The shout from the landing was loud. "He's Cassie Stevens' good man too!"

The tall boy slung his bag onto his shoulder and hollered. "Do one, Ethan."

The shouting continued. "Isn't that what you've been trying to do?"

"Boys!" Camila turned to the hall and angled her voice up the stairway. "Ethan, I need to borrow your straighteners."

"Broken. Got a curling wand if that helps?"

CHAPTER TWO

Closing the driver's door of her old-style Citroen Picasso, Camila adjusted her handbag and turned to walk across the H.I.P building's car park. Today she planned on keeping her head held high. Today she wouldn't worry about the absence of another Citroen Picasso in the car park. Who cared that it wasn't the row upon row of Renault Grand Scenics and Vauxhall Zafiras that greeted her at the supermarket? Did it really matter that most of these cars were hatchbacks or fashion 4x4s? She kept walking. It obviously didn't as she'd secured the job last week. Was that down to her outfit? Having tried on her university admissions suit, bought seventeen years ago, she'd quickly realised the boot-cut trousers and shapeless jacket wouldn't quite cut it; and why she'd kept them in her wardrobe for so long was an inexplicable mystery. Was it the nostalgia of a fond memory: university suit shopping with her mother? Or the pride it evoked when remembering she'd received the six unconditional offers whilst wearing it? Her and her boot-cut trousers had been wanted back then.

Well her and her new ankle-grazing capris and slim-fit blazer were wanted right now. Camila nodded. A brand new purchase from Next. Off the shelf and onto the counter, no VIP sale slots or end of season lines, simply supply and demand. They had it, she needed it, so she bought it. Camila laughed. Would this new job make that a regular occurrence? She laughed again. *Julie*, she'd say, *put those coupons away*. Walking across the tarmac to the beat she privately chanted the musing again. *Julie*, she'd say, *put those coupons away*. Again. *Julie*, she'd say, *put those coupons away*. Oh gosh, what was she doing? She was nervous. She needed to focus.

Lifting a hand to her hair, Camila checked the wand-curled strands she'd left deliberately loose from her bun. She nodded, they felt stylish; everything was on track. PICASSO, she screeched, internally, but loud. A Citroen Picasso! Camila waved at the slow-moving people carrier that had more windows than bodywork – essential for those inquisitive children who needed to be told 'horse' every time a horse was visible and 'train' every time a train could be seen. She waved again at the car. Why was she waving? She was almost at the building's entrance, the door to another world, another life, not her old life where it was essential you found a fellow frazzled mother and instantly made friends.

The woman in the Picasso buzzed down her window. "You can see I'm lost, can't you?"

Camila scuttled over as quickly as her new heels would allow. "Are you a mum returner?"

"I'm not dropping them off. Can you drop them off?"

Noticing the two children in car seats at the back, Camila frowned. "Here? They have a crèche?"

"Cheeky Monkeys."

"Oh, you're looking for the playcentre? You've come too far. It's first right on the roundabout back there. It's not one of the best though. The Funhouse in town's better."

"Yes, I've done that one to death."

"They let you drop off in Ikea."

"Really?"

"It's only a small play area but you can sign them in and sit in the café for a couple of hours."

"Oh, how wonderful. How old are yours?"

"Fourteen and fifteen, but I had five solid years of playcentre exploration."

"Fourteen and fifteen?"

"I've looked after my brother and sister's children on and off since then. Thirteen towns, three counties, I've covered it all."

"I meant your age."

Camila flushed. "Garden centres are good too; they often have little playpens. Then you've got the indoor parks at some of the big shopping centres. You'll know all this though."

The woman blew out a large puff of air. "Swap?"

"Nope, I've done my time and now I need to go." Standing up straight, Camila glanced at her watch. "Gosh, I really do need to go. Try KidzPlay, next motorway junction down. It has a proper coffee machine."

"You work here? At H.I.P Marketing? What's she like?"

"I've not met her yet." Camila stopped herself from getting drawn back to the open window. "I do need to go." It was going to be so hard to snap out of the 'I need to chat to everyone' mentality that had developed over years of child-only interaction. In the beginning when the boys were young there were times she'd only ever talk to the till lady at Tesco. That was until she'd discovered Sure Start centres and a whole breed of women just like her, desperate to talk without rhyming or singing or infantile explanations that were always followed by 'whys' and more 'but whys'. The fact most of the Sure Start activities, for example Rhyme Time, involved both singing and rhyming was by the by; other adults were in the mix and that was all that mattered. Obviously she'd make new friends here and hopefully they'd have better things to discuss than whether or not you should give your child the flu vaccine – which had in actual fact turned out to be one of the more interesting debates they'd had over the years, even though Patricia Goodyear – supermother of triplets – acted like a dictator, demanding they all sign up.

"Did you see her on TV last night?"

Pausing her walk, Camila glanced back. "Harriet?"

"Such an influential woman and so young. Thirty-two with nearly the same number of businesses."

"What channel?" Maybe she'd have time to watch it on her phone at lunch. Just as it had been essential to keep on top of the dates of the Argos 3-4-2 on toys, and the gossip about teachers from the school PTFA, now it would be essential to know exactly what was what in the world of Harriet Imogen Pearson, entrepreneur. If she was being honest, she'd had no clue the young businesswoman actually owned the posh H.I.P building she passed on the back route to Ikea. Yes, she'd seen Harriet on various business programmes, as instructed by Julie, but she'd not realised the woman actually owned bricks-and-mortar buildings like this one on the industrial estate just outside town, assuming instead that Harriet was simply the reality TV type. "Worth watching?" she asked.

"Did you know H.I.P stands for Harriet Imogen Pearson?"

"I did. I really have to go."

"Channel 4. Nice to meet you. Say hello to Harriet for me if your paths ever cross."

"Will do, will do." Camila increased her walking speed to a trot as she rolled her eyes at herself. No, she wouldn't. What would she say? Hi Harriet Imogen Pearson, a woman I befriended in your carpark because she had a car like mine, whose name I never actually found out, told me to say hi.

"I'm Wendy by the way." The shout carried across the car park. "Wendy Isabelle Newman. I could be the W.I.N to her H.I.P Marketing. She's hip, I'm a win-er."

Camila raised her hand in receipt of the shout but didn't turn. Gosh, it was happening already and she wasn't even in the building. Of course a successful business entrepreneur like Harriet had been gifted a great acronym by her parents. H.I.P. She's hip. Whether Wendy from the car park was indeed a winner would never be known, but at least her acronym was one to be proud of. Spotting the receptionist at the back of the foyer through the huge glass windows, Camila waved as she pressed the intercom button, repeating her name when requested. "Camila Moore."

Stepping into the huge modern space, Camila walked to the perfectly polished glass reception desk that was once again smear-free. It was something she'd noticed at her interview last week and wondered whether or not she should mention... but she hadn't and she wouldn't. Just like she wouldn't lie about her middle name. Obviously she'd thought about it but the people at H.I.P already had it down on her original application form and, yes, while she understood her mother's desire to pass on her own mother's first name, surely at some point one of her parents would have noticed, or commented? Camila smiled. No, they wouldn't. They were old-school elderly parents. The rudest acronym they'd have heard would've been something like B.U.T.T or B.U.M or possibly T.I.T; yes, definitely T.I.T. Camila thought back to that one Christmas where her father had used the word to describe one of the birds pecking heartily on a fatball on the feeder only to have his three children fall about laughing because it was the most obscene sentence they'd ever heard their father say.

Would either of her parents have had a problem passing on the name Uma? No, of course not. Was it a problem for her growing up? Yes, always. A boyfriend suggesting he buy her one of those lovely necklaces made from an outline of her initials. No thank you. C.U.M was not something she wanted dangling around her neck. Or the girls on their post A Level holiday suggesting they all get tattoos of their initials below their belly buttons. C.U.M wasn't something she wanted permanently above her pant line. Or her A Level art teacher suggesting they use their initials to create a mural of different fonts. No one wanted to see a mural of C.U.M and it certainly wouldn't be displayed at open evening alongside all the others.

"Hi, Camila, take a seat; we're just finalising your pass. You'll need to wear it at all times."

Camila looked at the piece of plastic clipped onto the receptionist's blazer. 'Helen Anna Howes.' The H.A.H embossed in the same font as the H.I.P branding. She nodded. "How wonderful."

CHAPTER THREE

Walking back towards the mustard-coloured sofas at the foyer entrance, Camila smiled at the woman sitting alone who happened to glance her way. Yes, she wouldn't usually make a bee-line for someone with dip-dyed pink and blonde hair, but this woman could be an employee and people like her were her people now. Sitting down she smiled again. "I like your ombre."

"Excuse me?"

"Your hair. It's called ombre, isn't it?" Camila was sure she'd read about it in a hairdressing magazine while having her standard cut and blow dry at her non-franchised hairdresser who probably performed a hundred shampoo and sets to every ombre, but would still know what it was if asked, as did she.

"Sombre." The woman picked up her phone from the high-gloss yellow table.

Camila waited.

"Sorry, can I help you?"

"Oh, I thought you were showing me something on your phone?"

The woman didn't reply.

Easing out of her eager forward lean, Camila turned to adjust one of the heavy gold cushions that had caught awkwardly underneath her bottom. She dared to glance at the woman again. Nope, there definitely wasn't anything coming back. Instead Camila turned her attention to the tall amber vase in the centre of the table. She'd noticed this last week. Lots of areas dotted around the building in varying shades of the same colour. This was the yellow waiting area in the foyer. There was a red coffee area to their right with additional seating, a green wellness area towards the back of the building with seating that actually looked quite comfortable, and an outdoor area with some light blue pod chairs and ocean-coloured rattan swing chairs.

"Sombre?" Camila couldn't help it. Whether it was the nerves or genuine intrigue she wasn't sure, but she needed to know. She'd need to have her finger on the pulse with all things modern if this was the world she'd now be living in.

The woman's sigh was notable. "Subtle ombre."

Camila looked at the bright pink and blonde hair.

The sigh sounded again. "Softer."

Camila continued to stare.

"But going beyond balayage."

Camila nodded. She had no clue what balayage was and the woman's two-tone hair was anything but subtle.

"You do know what balayage is, don't you?"

Camila nodded with force.

The woman raised her eyebrows. "What is it then?"

Camila stared. Who was this young punk? Quizzing her at 9.00 a.m. on a Monday morning as if she ran the joint. She nodded again. What if she did run the joint? What was that film she'd watched a couple of years ago about two older interns going to work at Google? They'd had no clue what they were doing but the boss turned out to be some nondescript guy they'd been nice to. *The Internship.* That was it. Damn. What if this woman with her non-sombre and definitely dip-dyed hair, because that garish pink and blonde certainly wasn't subtle or soft, turned out to be the building's boss, or one of the bosses? Should she confess or battle through? It was exactly like those times her sister's posh friends came to visit from university and told lots of in-jokes before quizzing her with ridicule because she'd laughed awkwardly alongside them.

The woman's expectant eyebrows were still raised. "Flamboyage?"

Oh this was getting ridiculous now. "I know how much a shampoo and set costs."

"Excuse me?"

"Cheaper than a cut and blow dry." Camila knew because she paid attention when her hairdresser's mostly old clientele were discussing how much it took out of their pensions.

"You think I should get a shampoo and set?"

"It might be the new frangipane."

The pink-haired woman swiped her phone from the table, rose from her seat and waltzed off towards the ladies toilets.

Camila raised her own eyebrows. She just so happened to know that the restroom had an orange theme and probably wouldn't calm the offence Miss Know-It-All had just taken. Grabbing her own phone from her bag, Camila Googled: *'Ombre sombre'* – there it was *balayage*: A French word meaning to sweep or to paint allowing for sun-kissed natural-looking hair colour, similar to what nature gives us as children. Catching a final glimpse of the bright pink hair before it disappeared behind the orange door, Camila stared. As if that colouring was slightly more than natural. She looked back to her phone and clicked. What was the other word? Fannylarge? No. There it was. *Flamboyage*: A hot new trend and low maintenance hair colour technique that achieves soft peek-a-boo highlights. Dropping her phone back into her bag, Camila huffed. Oh how ridiculous. As if highlights could be peek-a-boo. What would they do? Pounce out on you? Surprise you when you least expected it? That's what was wrong with all of this nonsense jargon – again something she'd said on her interview that might have got her the job. No nonsense was the way forward. That woman's hair was garishly dip-dyed, half pink and half blonde.

"You're here, thank goodness, come come."

Camila turned at the sound of the high-pitched voice, drawn first to the highly coiffured quiff and shaped eyebrows then to the incredibly slim build. She looked at the young man's name tag. Doug Oscar Gray. The D.O.G embossed heavily. Why on earth had no one mentioned to Harriet Imogen Pearson that just because something works for one person doesn't mean it should be rolled out to the masses before true thought and research had gone into all the possible repercussions? This young man was far from dog-like and if a dog breed had to be pinned to him then a Chihuahua would fit more than the font's heavily embossed Bulldog-type breed suggested.

"I'm Doug. You're the last one."

"I've been told to wait for my name tag."

"Come come, we can sort it in the room."

Grabbing her bag, Camila rose from the sofa and glanced towards the orange door. Her late-to-the-game discussion about peek-a-boo hair would have to wait. "Last one?" she queried.

"Yes yes come come."

Following the quick legs, Camila straightened the pussy bow tie neck of the black shirt she'd chosen to wear under her fitted blazer. She'd worn a green blouse on her interview having been told by the lady in Next that her black ankle grazing trousers and black blazer could be worn daily in an office environment as long as they were accessorised with brightly coloured tops and shoes. Little did the lady in Next know what a mishmash of colours the H.I.P building was and that green blouse days would leave her clashing at coffee time in the red area and blending into the background when relaxing in the wellness area hence why she'd decided to go for black today until she had time to pay more attention to the other employees' attire.

Adjusting the dangling material once more she debated her choice. A plain black button-down shirt would have looked too formal and there was a chance she could have been mistaken for a mime artist coming in to give a seminar on mime. She stopped herself; she was panicking; why would anyone come in to a market intelligence firm and give a seminar on mime? Either way she wouldn't be mistaken for a mime artist today because she had a beautiful pussy bow tie neck cascading down to her middle. She yanked on it. It was getting caught on her bag strap.

Looking up at Doug who was now a good four metres ahead, she took in his outfit. Tan trousers and tan shirt. Damn, that was right: tan was the one colour that matched everything. She thought back to H.A.H on reception: a tan dress. Why hadn't she noticed this on her interview? She knew why; she'd been too flustered and if she was honest most of the interview had been a bit of a blur, starting with the panic in the car park and judgement about non-people-carrier type people, followed by the forms she was asked to fill in whilst clashing in the coffee area. Forms that once again asked for her full name which then brought on the panic of her X-rated acronym.

Glancing back to the foyer, she looked around for another employee. What if tan was the uniform? What if tan was expected? No, surely someone would have told her… but then again no one had told her much about anything. She'd seen the job advertised online: *Market Insights Analyst* and was about to scroll past until she read: *ideal for a 'mum returner'*. Clicking on the mum returner phrase she'd then found a whole host of other jobs for women like her, but this was the closest to home and market insights did seem to have a link, no matter how tenuous, with art and design – that's what she'd said in her interview as well. Was that what had got her the job? She had no clue. She certainly hadn't been expecting the phone call to say she'd been successful, let alone the first call asking her to come in and discuss her application.

Maybe it was down to the green blouse? No, definitely not, but if the Jackson Pollock-esque artwork displayed in this never-ending foyer was anything to go by she'd do well to buy some colourful patterned shirts as that style worked well in this space. She could get something floral, or maybe even animal print, then at least part of her clothing would pick up and complement whichever area of the building she happened to be in. Catching up with Doug, who was now waiting by the huge mirrored wall she'd tried to avoid looking at because of the psychedelic nature of the foyer's clashing reflection, she realised she didn't even know where her base would be and she certainly hadn't noticed that there was a chrome lift in the centre of the mirrors. She'd simply arrived, filled in the forms, been walked around the ground floor by someone whose name she couldn't remember after the car park panic, the coffee clashing and the acronym angst, before Pamela from Insights – as that's how she'd introduced herself and spoken about herself when relating non-stop details of the hectic demands placed upon her – took her into a small side room for a chat. 'Pamela from Insights will do it,' the woman had said whilst recalling the demands, 'well Pamela from Insights needs some help,' she had announced, before concluding that 'Pamela from

Insights likes the look of you.' And it was at this point that Camila had stared around the empty room, aware that Pamela from Insights didn't have a particularly tough choice as she was the only one there.

Julie from next door had decided there would be hundreds going for the job because mum returner jobs were in such high demand; that's why she should wear the green blouse to make herself stand out. They'll call you the girl in the green shirt, she had said, before joking about the other things they'd call her: young mum, hot stuff, cute butt. The fact she didn't even get called these things when helping out on Julie's bacon butty van currently located next to a building site and frequented by many a cheeky workman didn't seem to matter. Julie was being kind, trying to give her a pre-interview boost.

Catching sight of herself in the dazzling lift doors, Camila noticed her bottom, visible thanks to the fashionable cut of the fitted blazer. She smiled. Not bad for a woman her age. Maybe *that's* why she got the job? Maybe she didn't fit the mould of the mum returner. Thirty-five, two teenage boys, a long term boyfriend – their father – who'd never proposed and was now living with Jackie from the gym. No, she hadn't gone into that much detail so that couldn't be the reason. Whatever the reason was, she was here and she was ready to work. Doing quite what she wasn't sure as the chat with Pamela from Insights had been very wordy, just like the online job description. Yes, Camila had started by introducing herself and giving her spiel on art, design, simple solutions, substance over style and the ridiculousness of nonsense jargon, but then Pamela had cut in with a lot of discussion about whether she'd be able to produce continuous reporting and ad hoc requests delivered in an accurate and timely manner. She'd nodded. Following this was the question about analysing multiple sets of data and creating outputs to help inform a business about market dynamics and competitive activity. She'd nodded again, before actually nodding with force when asked if she could create new and improved techniques and solutions for data collection, management, and usage. That had meant filing. This whole thing was probably about filing. Collecting the data, sorting the data, filing the data. She could do that, plus she was always finding fault with things and musing potential solutions – take this morning's brainwave about the hand car wash buffing cloths for instance – so if blue sky thinking was required then it shouldn't be a problem at all.

Bottom line was, she was here, in a lift, with Doug the DOG, rising up to a floor she didn't know existed. She eyeballed her own reflection. She just had to roll with it. Admittedly if this had happened on a university interview all those years ago she'd have been alert, aware and anticipating everything, but once you'd had children you quickly realised you had very little control over your life. You simply spent your parenting years stumbling from one issue to another. They're born, you try not to drop them or smother them. They start eating, you try not to choke them or poison them. They walk, you try not to trip over them or lose them. They use the toilet once, you think potty training's over, it's not. They climb out of the cot bed, you get door gates. They climb over the door gates, you secure all exits. They talk, you watch what you say. They start school, you field their homework, their projects, the horrific school PTFA, not to mention the friends, the mothers of the friends and the after-school activities. Then there are the sports clubs and the fixtures that intensify at secondary school. Plus, there's technology and the internet, and suddenly here are the girlfriends and the beards, and you're supposed to do all this with the support of your partner, but she'd had to do it alone. Mostly.

Okay, so Mick had been present, but only in the loosest of ways. No, that was wrong. He'd provided an income. He still did. Yes, it had been tight and they wouldn't have had the luxuries they'd had without her part time jobs here and there, but they were far from poor and she'd certainly not had a bad life, just a blurred life: non-stop, lived for others, barely time to breathe.

"Go go go, room five on the right. I'll be next door."

Camila stepped out of the lift. This was exactly like the time she'd been asked to help out last minute at the primary school Christmas nativity. She'd had no clue what was going on but had made herself useful. So now, if room five wanted her room five's where she would be.

CHAPTER FOUR

Glancing up and down the first floor corridor, Camila noticed an actual hubbub. People, presumably workers, were actually working. There were comings and goings from the multitude of numbered rooms feeding off the corridor on both sides, and what looked like a large open-plan call centre with numerous work stations at one end and a theatre set-up with big screen and stage at the other. It was as if the corridor was a pulsing vein connecting the beating heart and working brain. Stepping back, Camila made space for a woman marching past with a folder in her hand and a communication set on her head. There wasn't actually any need for her to retreat, the corridor wasn't narrow, but it felt appropriate given the woman's obvious importance and her own newbie status within the firm. Strange though that Pamela from Insights hadn't shown her the whole building. Maybe it was a security clearance thing? Maybe they were testing top secret products? Smiling and excited, Camila crossed the corridor to room five. To knock or not to knock? She lifted her hand but didn't get chance to decide.

"Get in here! I really don't like having to rely on new people, always late, they'll be here in a minute!"

Camila looked down at the hand that had ushered her into the room, now attached to her elbow and guiding her towards the spare seat at the large round table. "I was told to wait for my name tag."

"You do that in here, quickly." The hand moved to Camila's shoulder and encouraged her down onto the vacated chair.

Camila succumbed before looking up at the hand's owner, another Doug type, but this one more frantic. "Should I introduce myself?" she asked.

"What? No! Here…" Leaning across the table the man pulled the marker pen and roll of blank stickers towards Camila. "First name only."

Looking around the table, in the window-less box room, Camila felt awash with relief at the sight of the other hand-written stickers. Nine women, some tapping into phones, others sipping hot drinks and one rising from her seat, lipstick in hand, making her way towards the large mirror on the side wall, but all with just their first names on show, not a single acronym in sight.

"Ladies, will you please sit down! Phones away."

Lipstick woman laughed. "You're not usually this flappy."

"Huge clients, huge day."

"We've still got to be honest, right? And you always say the clients are huge."

"They are in my world. Just make sure you participate."

Lipstick woman turned to Camila. "That's why you're here, love. He might look all nervous but he'll fire you if he thinks you're just after free food."

The woman opposite Camila piped up. "I thought we were on fashion and design today?"

"You are!" squealed the man before morphing into a cool and collected individual who managed to stand up straighter yet looser as the door to the room swung open. "Welcome, hi, great to see you again," he said. "Do come in. Can I get you a drink? Ladies, would any of you like another drink?"

Camila looked at the new Doug, previously frantic, now charming. The distance between her position at the round table and his position at the door was too great to read his actual name tag, but whoever this person was he now seemed in stealth mode using that same hand, more gently this time, to guide the group of four men into the room whilst simultaneously popping a pod in the Nespresso machine and passing over a remote that looked like it might fire up the overhead projector and interactive screen at the front.

"Kevin, I know you liked the hot chocolate last time. I've got that on the go. Dave, anything for you?"

The man busy connecting his laptop to the sockets on the front table shook his head. "I'm okay thank you, Nigel."

Nigel? Camila looked at the new Doug. Nigel? Surely he wasn't old enough to be called Nigel? But then again Doug didn't seem old enough to be called Doug. Glancing around the enclosed room, which was pleasingly free from bright colours, Camila eyed the other women. She always found it fascinating to imagine someone's name and was often shocked to find out it was something totally different to her own initial judgement. And while it was obviously going to be something slightly different as she'd not been the person to christen the woman pushing her trolley at a snail's pace down the cat food aisle in Tesco, or the lady filling her car and staring into space at the petrol pump opposite her own, you could still often gauge a type of name. For example, lipstick woman looked like a Teri, somewhat cheap and probably quite viscous. Camila studied the name tag: Tina. Close enough. And the small woman opposite who'd piped up about the task for today; she looked like a Clare. Camila read the tag: Sharron. Nope, she'd got that one wrong, Clare and Sharron were in two completely different name group categories. The Clares were shy and mouse like, the Sharrons enjoyed a good drink.

Looking at the other women still tapping into their phones or sipping from their plastic cups, Camila deemed her quick assessment almost spot on. There was an Asha, a Chloe, an Ellie, a Kayla, a Megan and two she couldn't quite decipher behind folded arms, but they'd probably fall into the new name / shortened name / funky name category that rose in popularity during the late nineties, early noughties. In fact, all of these women were young. Surely this wasn't the new batch of mum returners? Camila corrected herself. No, of course not, they'd been here before and were clearly confident enough to ignore Nigel when he'd asked for phones away, plus that Tina woman had been downright rude to him... but maybe that was just in her name's nature?

Camila rose from her seat.

"What are you doing?" hissed Nigel, suddenly appearing alongside her with the stealth of a ninja as he removed the roll of stickers from the table.

"Getting a drink. You just asked if any of us wanted drinks. I haven't had one yet."

The hiss sounded again as the marker pen was swiped away too. "Too late, sit down and listen." The voice rose in volume, accompanied by a motivational fist bang on the table. "Ladies, let's do this." Nigel spun to the front with pointed finger. "Team Mesh-Up, it's over to you."

Sitting back down in confusion, Camila watched the women put their phones back in their bags and tuck themselves into the table, or in Clare, Asha and Chloe's case turn their chairs to face the men at the front. Maybe the table bang was the secret sign of commencement?

"And lights," cheered Nigel, materialising at the door and flicking the switch by himself.

Camila sat in the darkness. What the hell was happening? Where the hell was she? And why the hell were there no other Camilas like her?

"Ladies, we meet again."

Camila glanced around in the darkness, only able to see a slight shimmer from the large rectangular mirror to the right hand side of the room.

"And this time we have products."

Camila continued to stare. Where were the products? Were they glow-in-the-dark? It was definitely no-to-drinks-Dave talking, but who was he talking to and what was he showing?

"Are you excited?"

Camila jumped at a rather raucous whoop coming from Tina's side of the table.

"I said are you excited?"

Again another loud whoop, this time accompanied by a drum-rolling table hand bang. Surely that wasn't Sharron? Actually it probably was, because Sharron wasn't the quiet Clare type her mask had suggested; she was Sharron and her banging was loud.

"And one more time: ARE YOU EXCITED?"

Camila started to panic. It was like they were at the fun fair plunged into darkness on the waltzers, about to be spun until they were sick. Or worse, pinned to the barrel wall on the rotor with the floor disappearing as they spun round and round and round. Reaching into her handbag she found her phone and swiped up quickly. One touch and there was light.

"Who is that? Turn that off!"

Camila held up her mobile like a detective presenting their badge. Praise be for Steve Jobs and his torch app; everything in front of her was illuminated, including Nigel's swift retreat of hands from Tina's shoulders. Apart from that things looked normal. The four men were standing at the front and one of them had the remote poised in the air pointed towards the projector, clearly about to press play. Dammit, that's all they were doing, showing them something on the screen. This was Julie's fault, always passing on her *Take A Break* magazines where every other page was an alien abduction or a friends to enemies murder and there'd definitely been articles about deaths in the workplace.

"Who is that?" snapped Nigel once more.

Camila turned the light towards the voice. He was coming her way. She flashed the beam from left to right like a child making shapes with a sparkler. Maybe he'd think it was coming from someone else. She did a quick figure of eight. Everybody did a figure of eight when they had a sparkler.

"Is that you, Tanisha?"

Oh yes, Tanishas were naughty. She must have been one of the arms-folded women to her left.

"No, it ain't me, it's—"

"Ouch! Turn that light back on!"

The sound of Nigel crashing into the back of a chair masked the dull thud of Camila's now-switched-off phone as it dropped back into her bag.

"Shall I press play?" Dave's voice again.

"No, you need to build it up."

Was that Kevin with the hot chocolate? Camila squinted. She couldn't see, they were back to the pitch black and mirror shimmer.

"Are you excited?"

Tina tutted. "No. Not anymore."

"I'm sorry, gentlemen." Definitely Nigel. "Shall we start again?"

The funfair entertainer took a deep breath. "Are you excited?"

Camila dared to say: "Yeah!"

"I said: ARE YOU EXCITED?"

Camila tapped on the table in the darkness. "YEE-HAH!" She'd got away with torch-gate and was feeling liberated.

"One more time: ARE YOU EXCITED?!"

"HELL YES WE ARE!" Was anyone else whooping? Camila wasn't quite sure, but now she knew she wasn't about to get stabbed to death in the dark by men who drank hot chocolate, she could relax in the spirit of things.

"Then let's Mesh-Up!"

"*Mesh-It-Up, Mesh-It-Up, Mesh-It-Up Boom!*"

Nigel's voice was firm. "Tina, we spoke about this last time."

"What? I hope that's the soundtrack you've used?"

Fairground man's voice had fizzled out. "Sorry, this doesn't seem to be playing."

"*Mesh-It-Up, Mesh-It-Up, Mesh-It-Up Boom!*"

"Tina!"

"What?"

"Can someone turn the lights on?" Nigel was clapping. "Tanisha get your torch back out."

"It wasn't me!"

Dave's voice again. "Wait, I have it. Here we go."

"*Mesh-It-Up, Mesh-It-Up, Mesh-It-Up Boom!*"

"Tina!"

Kevin: "We're starting."

Camila let out a "HELL YEAH!" in the darkness. She couldn't help it. It was like all those times they used to play murder in the dark as children. The second the lights went out she'd get all giddy and caw like a bird. She let out another "YEE HAH!" at the exact moment the screen lit up. Shifting in her seat, Camila tried to ignore the stares and just concentrate. Not only was the room suddenly very bright but the volume of the clip showing at the front was incredibly loud, and while it wasn't Tina's *Mesh-It-Up, Mesh-It-Up, Mesh-It-Up Boom!* ditty, it was something quite similar. She focused. Women, working out. No, they were posing for photos. Wait, no, they were flirting with each other and pouting for more pictures. Hang on, they were jogging off into the sunset... and what the hell were they wearing?

Nigel turned the lights back on as the Mesh-Up logo filled the screen.

"So, ladies, what do you think?" It was funfair Dave, hands raised to the room. Kevin beside him was nodding. The two other men had now retreated to seats below the screen, tablets in hand.

Tina spoke first. "Love it."

Camila watched the general consensus of agreement from the women.

"Sexy," added Sharron.

"Catchy tune," contributed Tanisha.

"Outfits look great," said the woman to Camila's right who was wearing something similarly as scanty.

"Is it an app?" Camila felt the need to show worth.

Kevin halted the lifting of his hot chocolate and looked her way. "Excuse me?"

"On their phones?"

Nigel stepped in. "Sorry, she's new."

Kevin carried on, sipping from his cup with an accepting nod before swallowing. "Not to worry. So, logo? Visible enough?"

Camila spoke again. "The one at the end?"

Kevin nodded. "On the clothes too."

"Was it?"

The hot chocolate was placed firmly on the table at the front. "You didn't notice the logo?"

Camila shrugged. "I wasn't quite sure where I should be looking."

Tanisha cut in. "You just feel adverts like that."

Again, a general consensus of nods from the women.

"Well, I felt uncomfortable."

Nigel glared at Camila. One of the tablet men lifted his hand. "Go on, please," he encouraged.

"Well, they looked like they were wearing some sort of see-through underwear and flirting with each other."

Tanisha cut in again. "Fluidity's en-trend."

25

"But taking photos of it all?"

"They were just pouting."

"Why?"

"That's what you do at the gym."

"They were at the gym?"

Tablet man spoke again. "You didn't realise they were at the gym?"

Camila laughed. "No! What on earth were they wearing? You don't wear that to the gym. Okay, I got that they were lightly jogging, or sort of skipping off somewhere into the sunset at the end, but I thought the rest of it was about a photo filter or something?"

Dave reached into the big duffel bag that was sitting next to the laptop and dropped a selection of clothing onto the table. "Mesh-Up gym wear."

Camila laughed. "You've got to be joking?!"

CHAPTER FIVE

Standing in the small viewing room to the side of room five, Harriet Imogen Pearson turned to Doug and whispered. "Where in god's name did you find her?"

"I'm so sorry. I thought she'd been briefed."

Harriet lowered her voice. "No, this is wonderful. Look, she's going again."

Camila Moore's voice came through the speakers. *"These leggings look like the black lace curtains my mum put up when she was mourning my aunty."*

"Must have been a sexy aunty then." Tina was tutting on the other side of the mirror.

"There's nothing sexy about these leggings."

Harriet spoke again. "Why's Tina still here? I told you I wasn't happy with her last time."

"Nigel got rid of someone else instead. Said Tina was liked by the brands."

Discreetly signaling to the three men in their darkened room who were also observing through the one-way mirror, Harriet shook her head and lowered her voice. "I very much doubt any of us are liked by the Mesh-Up brand at the moment, but hey ho it's what they pay us for."

Camila's voice was loud and clear. *"Fat poking out of meshing isn't sexy. And why are the sports bras so push up?"*

Stepping closer to the mirror, Harriet watched the show that was occurring in the focus group with interest.

"And finally she gets it." Kevin, who'd left his hot chocolate to go cold, held up both thumbs. *"That's why we're called Mesh-Up."*

"It's more like a mess up if you ask me. Four men making gym wear for women. It's no wonder you've ended up with something so peek-a-boo. In fact, why don't you have the models wearing flamboyage hair?"

Harriet struggled to contain her laughter. This was awkward enough as it was for the men watching from her side of the mirror without her adding ridicule in this room too.

The confidence continued. *"You do know what flamboyage is, don't you? It's peek-a-boo. Hair's allowed to be peek-a-boo but anything housing a woman's thighs isn't."*

Harriet smiled as the criticising woman stood from her seat and started to pace.

"What's the purpose of the brand?" questioned Camila.

Dave was quick to jump in with an answer. *"To be worn by women at the gym."*

"Really?"

"Yes, and that's not a sports bra it's a top." Kevin was arms folded.

"Where's the rest of it?"

"That's it. Sports crop top, no need for a bra, it's all built in."

"Those women had underboob!" Camila was circling the table. *"Real women don't wear this stuff to the gym."*

Tina cut in. *"They do. This is our fourth session with Mesh-Up and we've already established demand."*

Camila ignored her. *"Ellie? Really? You'd wear something like this to the gym?"*

Harriet nodded to herself: clever, focus on the quietest member of the group.

Tina's voice was loud. *"You only chose her because she's chubby."*

"Ellie is far from chubby," continued Camila, *"she's simply female and most females struggle to zip up their jeans let alone squash themselves into a pair of mesh leggings like a sausage at a sausage factory. Plus, no one wants to get out of the car and walk to the gym in this 'top' with their mum tums and stretch marks on show."*

Ellie gasped. *"I haven't had children!"*

Tina jumped on the insult. *"She thinks you're just fat then!"*

"*Ladies!*" Nigel was doing his best to calm tempers. "*Camila, you're late to the game. This is niche gym wear for the eighteen to twenty-fives. The Instagramers. The women who post their progress on social media.*"

"*Oh, so they weren't flirting with each other?*"

Nigel spoke again. "*They were flirting with their phones.*"

Harriet and Camila laughed at the same time on either side of the mirror. "I'm sorry," said Harriet, turning her attention to the guests in the darkened room, "but this can happen in focus groups."

The tallest man spoke up. "Yes, but we've used H.I.P for the market analysis, product intelligence and competitive intelligence aspects of this project as well."

Harriet lifted her hands. "She's one voice."

"But she's our target market."

Doug cut in. "No, she isn't, look!"

Harriet turned back to the show. Nigel had his finger pointed towards the door. "*You're thirty-five?! What are you doing in here then?!*"

"*You invited me in.*"

"*Clearly a mistake. Out you go. Gentlemen, I'm so sorry. This explains a lot. Anyone for another hot chocolate before we resume with the correct audience?*"

"*So what am I meant to wear to the gym?*" Camila wasn't budging.

"*Not this!*"

Tina was now up from the table, standing by Nigel's side. "*I bet you don't even go to the gym.*"

"*I do Davina's DVD at home.*"

"*And what do you wear?*"

"*Pyjamas mostly. But doesn't that mean there's a market for people like me?*"

Nigel spoke again. "*The over thirty-fives? Yes, we have dealings with Sainsbury's. Mary Berry's brought out a new 'relax' range.*"

Camila's gasp was loud. "*For people gardening or bowling! I've seen that. That's not for me!*"

"*Well this isn't for you either.*" Nigel snatched a pair of leggings and top from the table and waggled them as he pointed towards the door.

Camila continued. "*All you'd need to do is lose some of the see-through meshing around the thighs. I get the idea that sportswear needs to breathe, but this is just gaping. Put it at the back of the knees or near the ankles if you have to, not that ankles breathe, but meshing's obviously important to you. Then you need to make the waist band thicker for those of us who've had children."*

Nigel gasped. *"You've had children?!"* He turned to the men in the room. *"Again, this explains so much. I'm so sorry, gentlemen, she isn't your target market."*

"Hey I could wear this if I wanted to!" Camila took the clothing from Nigel.

Tina piped up. *"You're old, with children. Mesh-Up wouldn't want you wearing their brand. That's the whole point. They want it worn by young, cool, child-less women like us who share pictures of themselves looking hot so other people notice their brand."*

"They're not going to be hot with all this meshing going on. It's like wearing a large-gaped black doily and two minutes ago you thought I was the target audience."

Tina folded her arms. *"Put it on then."*

"No."

"Why not? Because you're old with children?"

"I still work out."

"Put it on then."

"Fine I will."

Harriet watched open-mouthed as the woman on the other side of the mirror, who in actual fact looked more sexy and stylish than all the other women put together, returned to her seat before pulling off her trousers and pulling up the leggings. She watched on as the woman crouched in on herself, taking rather a long time untying what looked like quite a complex bow from around the neck of her shirt.

"Ta-dah!" announced Camila jumping up from her seat.

Tina pointed. *"You've still got your bra on and I can see your stretch marks."*

"I'm a tiger who's earned their stripes and guess what? I'm proud of them. But some women are more body conscious than I am; that's why I suggested the thicker waistband that could be rolled up or down. Also, as you can see from my white bra under this black mesh, your top simply isn't big enough. Anyone doing any actual exercise will be offering up two bouncing dumplings along with their sausage mesh legs if this is all the support they'll be getting."

"I don't think you look too bad," offered Dave.

"*Nor me*," added Kevin.

Harriet looked through the window at Camila. She looked sensational. A pocket rocket of confidence. She wasn't tall but she had a great figure and her brown hair that was secured in a loose-but-smart bun accentuated her pretty face and drew attention to her expressive eyes that showed off her soul as she spoke. Harriet smiled. The scene was one of the most naturally beautiful things she'd witnessed in a long time.

"*You're too old, sorry,*" said Nigel, still pointing to the door. "*Admittedly you don't look it, but this is the eighteen to twenty-five age range focus group.*"

"*Surely I have some worth?*"

"*Not in here you don't.*"

"*Right.*" Camila walked back to her chair. "*But just so you know, no one likes those pouting Instagram gym bunnies.*" She stood still in the silence. "*I'll just get changed shall I?*"

"*Change in the ladies outside. We need to crack on.*"

Harriet watched as the nearly naked woman who was currently being held together by black meshing gathered up her belongings from the floor. She turned to the men on her side of the mirror and nodded. "Gentlemen," she said, "you'll have to excuse me."

****

Closing the door to room five and entering the corridor, Camila looked down on herself. Her white bra was screaming out through the black mesh holes in the top and there was so much flesh on show it was criminal, not to mention the fact that her new pussy bow tie was dragging along the floor behind her. She smiled. At least she'd still got it. That ability to make women like Tina jealous and men like Kevin take note. She glanced up in search of the toilets. "Harriet Imogen Pearson!" she gasped, taken aback by the sight of the impeccably dressed woman standing in front of her. "What are you doing here?!"

"Me?" said Harriet. "I was hoping to ask you the same question."

CHAPTER SIX

"You look *absolutely* incredible."

Camila glanced over her shoulder to see who Harriet Imogen Pearson was talking to.

"You. Dressed in that Mesh-Up gear. You look incredible. I mean you'd look incredible without that Mesh-Up gear too." The follow-up was quick. "Not naked of course. I didn't mean naked. I meant in your suit, or a dress, or… or anything really."

Camila glanced back once more.

"Forgive me, I'm Harriet."

Returning her attention from the long corridor, Camila focused on the outstretched hand. Was Harriet Imogen Pearson holding that out for her? Well she couldn't shake it as she was arms-full of pussy bow tie shirt, trousers, blazer and bag.

"Sorry, let me help you with that. I see you're wearing your shoes."

Staring down, Camila studied her black glittered court heels. When paired with her plain black trousers and blazer they'd added the pizazz her outfit had needed. Again there'd been a worry that plain shoes were too mime-artisty, but the sparkle had offered the jazz that was missing. Now, however, when paired with her see-though mesh leggings, she looked like a hooker. "Sorry, I need those back." Camila nodded to her belongings now in Harriet's hands.

"I'll carry them. This way."

Having no choice but to follow the brisk walk, Camila wrapped her arms around her bare stomach trying her best not to look too awkward. Unfortunately, such a quick pace required a balanced posture and her contortionist's cover-up meant she had to walk with her head pushed forward to ensure the onward momentum: A bit like a child in a sports day sack race, bag clutched in on herself, top half of her body earnestly pushing on, about to topple any moment. She followed the fast feet. Where were they going? Would she shoot down this corridor like a glitzy black bullet exploding into the Mary Berry 'relax' range room? Surprise, grannies, I'm here!

"I think I should be in the Sainsbury's group."

Harriet Imogen Pearson suddenly halted her walk and spun round. "Don't be so ridiculous."

Camila couldn't stop herself, her sack race game had been too strong. She head-butted Harriet's shoulder like a bull's strike on matador, her arms instinctively releasing their grip of her own stomach and wrapping instead around Harriet's. "I'm sorry," she said, quickly trying to pull away from the embrace, realising that Harriet's arms had instinctively reached out to catch her and dropped all the clothes on the floor. "Sorry, could I just..." Camila tried to wriggle free once more.

"Right, sorry, there you go. Let me get those."

Camila stood awkwardly, moving her arms to her chest before crossing them over her stomach as well, trying to cover as much flesh as possible, which inadvertently led to a plumped up cleavage as if she was deliberately squeezing her assets out on show.

Harriet was staring as she rose back up with the belongings.

Glancing away from the eyes, Camila focused on the fast moving woman behind Harriet's shoulder who was marching down the corridor. Camila shuffled backwards. She expected the woman to stop and stare, or at least pass judgement, but the woman hurried on without comment.

"You're nothing new," said Harriet having followed Camila's gaze. "Well obviously you are as I've not seen anything quite like you before and I didn't mean it that way; I meant in this corridor, on this floor. She'd never have stared. Well she might have done if she'd noticed it was me, I'm not often in the building, but my point is we have all sorts going on: fancy dress costumes, toy testing, horror Halloween makeup and, like I said before, you look incredible, not that I'm comparing you to the horror Halloween makeup. Listen to me rattling on. You'd think it was me standing there half naked, if only I had your confidence, which is what I was saying, it's so refreshing and empowering." Harriet took a deep breath and paused to emphasise her words. "What I witnessed in there was one of the most beautiful things I've seen in a long time."

Camila stared at the stunningly gorgeous woman standing in front of her. She'd not been in the room had she? No, of course not. She'd have noticed her and assigned her a name. Would she though, as she'd instantly have recognised her as Harriet Imogen Pearson, owner of H.I.P Marketing, and she did look like a Harriet. She had an air of composure about her, or the Harriet on TV did; this woman was either chatting in a frenzied manner or staring in silence as she was again now. Camila stared back. She could be a Meredith, or possibly an Evelyn; someone with stature. She wasn't particularly tall, in fact Harriet was only slightly taller than she was, yet Harriet managed to hold herself in a way only certain women did. Well the Harriet on TV did; this woman was looser somehow and her gold-rimmed glasses, that gave her an air of importance on the big screen, suddenly looked like fashion frames designed to give stature as opposed to glasses worn because someone had stature, or needed them obviously.

"So I'm not in the Mary Berry group?" asked Camila finally.

"Good heavens, no! That's why we stopped, wasn't it? Sorry, I've rather ambushed you, haven't I?" The pile of Camila's gathered belongings were adjusted and the hand was sent out again. "I'm Harriet Imogen Pearson. I own the company."

Camila shook the soft fingers. "I recognised you. Do you want me to help you with that?" She signalled to her own clothes now clumped under Harriet's armpit.

"You did, didn't you? Sorry I'm in a bit of a flap, I just want to get off this floor. You shouldn't be on this floor."

"Too old?"

"Goodness no, look at you. I had no clue you weren't in the eighteen to twenty-five age range. They had no clue you weren't in the eighteen to twenty-five age range, and while I do appreciate who Mesh-Up's target market is there's nothing to say you can't wear their gear. You pull it off so well and the way you're proud of your body is admirable. I wish I could show such confidence."

Camila stared at the woman again. She was truly stunning, fashion glasses or not. She had glossy skin, glossy hair, full glossy lips, dark velvety eyelashes that enticed you through the gold frames into the dazzling blue eyes, and cheekbones that shimmered. Camila continued to stare. They were actually shimmering. It was as if Harriet Imogen Pearson had been filtered with the Wonder Woman snapchat filter, the one that gave you slightly bouffant, but perfectly styled dark hair. The only thing missing was the gold headband. Camila almost gasped. No! That was it, it was the gold rims of her glasses that made her look like Wonder Woman, as if her headband had slipped. But then again it was so much more than that; it was the whole shimmering package. "You'd look much better in it than me," she managed to say.

"Goodness, no, I'm thirty-two."

Camila laughed. "And I'm thirty-five!"

"I'm not sure if it's that fact or something else that's got me so lost for words!"

"This is you lost for words?"

Harriet paused. "Not the gabbling, obviously, I just mean…" She reached out to take Camila's hand. "Come on, I want you in the lift."

Camila let herself be led.

"I didn't mean like *that* obviously," said Harriet, releasing Camila's hand and waving her forward instead.

Camila watched on as Harriet struggled to tuck the clothing under her arm with one hand, using the other to press the lift's call button multiple times. "Like what?" she asked, moving to the side to avoid stepping on her own pussy bow tie neck that still dragged on the floor.

"Nothing. Get in. Up to floor five we go."

****

Sitting on the chair opposite Harriet's desk, Camila was thankful for the opportunity she'd had to change. A bathroom on floor five not far from Harriet's office had given her chance to breathe and take stock. It was one thing being okay rumbling along for fifteen years from situation to situation, never quite knowing what was coming next, but this was something else entirely. This was surreal. It wasn't surreal when you realised you'd left your breast pads at home, for example, and had to endure a shopping trip with two wet patches on show, a shopping trip where you happened to bump into everyone you'd ever met in your whole life. Situations like that were awkward and embarrassing and you just bumbled along. Similar to the time she'd been accosted by Michael's PE teacher at his first parents' evening at secondary school and been told her son had a body odour issue, only to panic that she'd not put on deodorant herself that day due to an ill-timed visit from the boiler man who'd turned off the hot water whilst trying to fix the fault and suddenly panicking that the PE Teacher would think it was a hereditary issue. Not to mention the fact she felt like an awful mother because she'd not realised her son could be at an age where body odour was a thing, which then sent her into a spiral of panic about where time was going. And while situations like those were all a bit blurred as you hazily battled your way through, you still knew they were happening.

This, however, sitting in Harriet Imogen Pearson's office on day one of work, felt completely unreal. The office was similar to something you'd see on an interior design show, in fact she was sure she'd seen Harriet filmed here for something or other, sitting, as she was now, behind the huge reclaimed-wood desk flanked on either side by two Japanese Fruticosa trees, and she only knew they were Japanese Fruticosa trees because Julie had seen them advertised on the shopping channel and suggested they both get them for beside their front doors, which being next to each other would make them look like ten and eleven Downing Street. That's what Julie had said anyway. The fact the shopping channel trees were artificial and only two-foot-tall didn't seem to matter to Julie, it was the idea that topiary held stature.

Looking around at the office, Camila had to accept that topiary did indeed hold stature; well, Harriet's topiary certainly did. Not only were the two tall trees either side of the desk real, there were two indoor topiary areas on the left and right hand sides of the room receiving light from two large lantern shaped roof windows so you entered the space like a bride about to walk down a rainforest aisle to the reclaimed-wood altar-desk at the front. That's what she'd felt like anyway and was relieved to be back in her pussy bow tie shirt and blazer as the mesh leggings and top simply wouldn't have cut it.

"This office. Be honest."

Was Harriet Imogen Pearson talking to her? Yes, of course she was; there was no one else in the room and as surreal as this felt, it was actually happening.

"I see you looking around. I'd like your thoughts."

Camila smiled. "It's fantastic. It makes me feel like I'm outside. You have lots of natural light coming in from those roof windows and I love how they're pitched up like lanterns adding even more height to the room. Your desk reminds me of the entrance to Narnia, for some reason, even though the trees are green. There's something imposing, yet magical about it, whether it's the runway to get here through the indoor planting I'm not sure, but this whole space is a cross between a garden centre and a film set. I see you've got a drinks and seating area on the other side of the plants and a conference desk area on that side and I actually like the idea that you have to walk around the topiary to get there. It's as if whatever you're doing and wherever you're going there's a reminder that life's out there."

Harriet was smiling. "You're just perfection."

"Am I?"

"You're absolutely perfect."

"For what?"

"For me." Harriet nodded. "For the business. But if I'm honest I was slightly unsure when you started that majorette routine with your phone torch."

"You saw that? You were there? Where were you?"

"Behind the mirror."

"You were standing behind the mirror?" Camila looked at the woman sitting behind the magical wooden desk in the magical botanical garden. Was she like David Blaine or something?

"There's a viewing room next door. It's a one-way mirror. You've done focus groups before?"

"Today's my first day."

"Didn't Doug draft you in from the agency? Most of the focus group women are agency, but we like to keep them on the books for continuity."

"Nope."

"Who are you then?"

"Camila Moore."

"And what are you doing here?"

"I'm not entirely sure."

Harriet laughed. "This makes it even better."

"It does?"

"Yes! The way you held court in there was wonderful. You picked up on the fact the brand was run by men. The parent company Work-Up caters solely for the male sportswear market and the idea to branch out into female gear is logical, but not with the same people in charge. I liked how you interacted with the other women, using the personal example of Ellie as to why the brand may have issues. You had absolutely no qualms in speaking your mind, which you continued to do outside of the room when talking to me. You made a joke about me being lost for words when I was rattling on. People never make jokes to me, or about me, especially when they've just met me."

"It wasn't a joke; it was a statement."

Harriet laughed. "Exactly. You're brutally honest, which is why I asked about the office. It splits opinion, but I like it."

"Isn't that all that matters?"

"Not in the world of market intelligence. That's why focus groups are so hated."

"They are?"

"Floor one is the lowest of the low. I had to get you out of there."

"You did?"

"You know the focus group is pretty much the F word in market intelligence, right? Ultimate power's given to people who like to hear themselves speak, or people just there for free food. Those women don't really know about sportswear and they probably don't really care about sportswear. Yes, they may be the target age range, but that's about it. So many design and strategy hours are wasted on the opinion of people who don't actually matter."

"They don't?"

"No. Focus groups kill innovation. As Steve Jobs said: true innovation comes from recognising an unmet need and designing a creative way to fill it."

Camila smiled. "That torch on the iPhone was needed."

"Exactly!" Harriet was laughing. "It wasn't what you said, Camila, it was how you said it. You were uninhibited in both thought and action. The balls it took to change in front of the group and parade yourself around like that, and you weren't doing it in a showy off way, just a fact finding way."

"I have children; it was no big deal."

"But they were grown men."

"My sons are bigger."

"Excuse me?"

"Taller I mean."

Harriet was still frowning. "Excuse me?"

"Michael and Ethan, my sons."

"Are taller than the Mesh-Up men?"

Camila nodded.

"Are they…"

"Fourteen and fifteen."

"Your children are fourteen and fifteen?! Well thank goodness for that! I was about to ask if they had a growth hormone issue."

"You weren't!"

"I was, but I didn't, as I, like a lot of people, worry about saying the wrong thing. You, however, have a natural honesty about you. I see it and I like it, but can we go back to the fact your children are fourteen and fifteen? You don't look a day past twenty yourself!"

"That's very kind of you."

"It's true!"

"They're the main reason I have no inhibitions. You can't with teenage boys around."

"No, it's more than that. There's something special about you and you shouldn't be working with the lowest of the low. Goodness, can you see why I wanted to get off that floor so quickly. Imagine if Market Research could hear me say that."

"Aren't you Market Research?"

"No. The company's Market Intelligence which is divided into four sections: Floor One – Market Research, home to the focus groups. Floor Two – Market analysis, slightly more important, where's the market going? Is it growing, is it in decline? Floor Three – Product Intelligence, exploring and predicting the trends. Floor Four – Competitive Intelligence, keeping clients abreast of their rivals' strategies."

"It all sounds the same to me."

"Ha! I love that! But it's not and you shouldn't be down there at the bottom."

"I'm not sure I'm even meant to be on floor one. I only got shown around the ground floor."

"By whom?"

"Pamela from Insights. I couldn't see her name tag as it was tucked into her jacket pocket, but that's how she referred to herself."

"No!"

Camila nodded. "I'm meant to be on the mum returner scheme."

"We don't have a mum returner scheme."

"Well I got the job."

"You got Pamela's job which is… which is…" Harriet rolled on her chair to the left hand side of her desk and tapped into her computer. "Bear with me a minute."

Camila watched on as Harriet fingered down the screen as if speed reading. "Everything okay?"

"I see what this is."

"What is it?"

"She gave you the job because…"

"Because what?"

"Because…" Harriet paused. "It doesn't matter. She found you and I want you."

"You do?"

"Up here with me on floor five."

"What happens on floor five?"

Harriet smiled. "This is where we expand the business."

"So there isn't a mum returner job on the ground floor?"

"Pamela obviously used that phrase because she knew it would get hundreds of responses."

"But I was the only one there."

"She cherry-picked you from your application form."

"Why?"

"She…" Harriet shrugged. "She obviously saw in you what I've just seen in you."

"From my CV? I've only worked part time at my friend Julie's bacon butty van for the past few years. I did a stint on the fish counter at Tesco before that but the hours were too long and I never liked putting my children into child care. My boys might be tall but that doesn't mean they're responsible. Well they are now, which is why I'm here and ready to work full time."

"Good, because I want you." Harriet nodded. "For the business."

"And Pamela doesn't?"

"Pamela can find someone else to do whatever bits and bobs she needs doing. Collating various responses to telesales questionnaires no doubt."

"Is that what I was meant to be doing on the ground floor? She did sound busy."

"She's quite infamous around here is Pamela. She chooses to work away from others in one of the small rooms down there."

Camila smiled. "So I've still got a job?"

Harriet nodded. "You, Camila Moore, have got a promotion."

CHAPTER SEVEN

"And as I left her office I could hear her on the phone summoning Pamela from Insights up to floor five." Camila was huddled on her lounge sofa, pyjamas and slippers on, next to Julie, also in dressing gown and slippers, both with flutes of prosecco in hand, even though it was barely past four p.m.

Julie was frowning. "Did she call her Pamela from Insights?"

Camila took a sip of the bubbles. "No. Pamela Simpson-Smith."

"And did you see what happened?"

"No, I got to come home early."

"Chars to that," cheered Julie, reaching across the sofa to chink their flutes together.

Camila smiled. This is why she loved Julie. Not only did she say chars instead of cheers because she thought it made herself sound posh, she always insisted on flutes for special occasions and had declared this a special occasion having dashed out of her house the second she saw Camila's car pull into the cul-de-sac. Julie had then listened briefly through the large Citroen Picasso's window before saying she'd be back with prosecco, flutes and PJs, giving Camila just five minutes to get in and changed so the debriefing and discussion would be fresh faced and hot off the press. And while Julie wasn't one to gossip in a malicious way she was certainly someone who seemed to know everything first. If you wanted the full story you only had to ask Julie from Number Eleven.

Camila tucked her feet tighter into herself on the sofa before lifting her glass in a toast. "So. I have a promotion from a job I didn't start, onto a floor I didn't know existed, with a multi-million-pound entrepreneur who seems to think I'm great."

"That's why we've got the bloody flutes out!" Julie did another cheers. "Do you think she'd let me park up in her car park?"

Twisting her body and glancing out of the bay window, Camila stared at the back end of Julie's pink-coloured bacon butty van and the ridiculous slogan that read: *Julie Biggs, She Sells Pigs.* Even though there was a picture of a bacon sandwich on the side of the vehicle, its shape and colour, combined with the large side window hatch, often saw it mistaken for an ice-cream van. "I'm not sure," she said. "I think they must get food brought in as I barely saw anyone on the ground floor and it was the same again today. Yes, there was that pink-haired punk who Doug obviously mistook me for, but there were tons of people on floor one and I'm assuming it's the same on floor two, three and four so they've either got catering facilities on those levels or there's a back entrance to the building. It's as if the ground floor's just a front for the whole show."

"It often is in places like that and I don't mind parking at a back entrance. The van doesn't take up much room."

Camila turned her attention to the window once more and stared at the pink vehicle blocking her view. Admittedly it was only a view of the next driveway in the curving cul-de-sac, but it was an eyesore all the same. "I can ask."

"No, you can't. Not yet anyway." Julie nodded. "Give it a day or two."

Camila laughed; her neighbour was such a wheeler dealer. The female equivalent of Del Boy from *Only Fools and Horses*, a programme her parents used to watch on repeat. Like Del Boy, Julie never meant any harm but, also like Del Boy, Julie never seemed to learn. There was always the next big thing. The venture that would turn her fortunes around. Thankfully she'd had her bacon butty van for over three years now and seemed settled into an enterprise that awarded her a steady income. Yes, she sometimes had little blips where she sourced the rashers of bacon from somewhere she shouldn't, or filled the van with smog producing fuel, but for the most part her current business was above board.

"How can Harriet know all her employees?" Julie was pouring more prosecco.

Camila held out her glass before taking another sip of bubbles. "What do you mean?"

"Well, she runs god knows how many businesses and you said there were loads of people on floors one, two, three and four."

"I only saw floor one."

"Still, you said the car park was full."

"The front car park. There might be a back car park too."

"Exactly. So how does Harriet know who Pamela from Insights is?"

Camila shrugged. "I don't know. Maybe that's how she's got to where she is now. She's clearly a people person."

"Because she was kind to you?"

"You think it was just kindness?"

"I don't know what it was, but you know me, Camila, I'll always give it you straight."

Camila smiled. Julie never gave it her straight. Julie would insist the wallpaper she'd recommended from the man at the market looked lovely even though the pattern didn't match up no matter how perfectly you placed it. She'd also insist the scented candles she'd bought in bulk and given as Christmas presents were indeed scented even though smoke was the only thing they gave off. Thankfully Camila had imposed a strict 'nothing that's on show' rule upon herself three years after becoming Julie's neighbour and getting sucked in to all of her bargains. Yes, the cheap bottles of bleach were fine as bleach was bleach and the nondescript, often foreign brand was hidden behind the back of the toilet. Likewise, expensive book sets when the boys were growing up were so much cheaper from Julie's source than the school book fayre or WH Smiths and they seemed of a similar standard, although produced on slightly thinner paper but again, no one apart from her and the boys had to see them.

Important things though, like carpets and wall paint, were a definite no-no. Camila had learnt that lesson within the first year of moving into the cul-de-sac. Julie had been such a wonderful neighbour from day one, offering to help the 'young couple', as she'd called them, get on their feet. It was very obvious from the set-up – a heavily pregnant nineteen-year-old with a boyfriend the same age and two sets of parents, one a lot more elderly than the other, working together to set up the soon-to-be-family in a small semi-detached on the cul-de-sac that was nice enough, but certainly not a reward – that none of this had been planned. Yes, they had a home, but they didn't have anything to put in it and that's where Julie had stepped in.

Camila smiled at the memory. Julie wasn't that much older than she was but she had Terry, who she called her 'old man' and who was indeed a lot older than them all, and he gave her standing – as if she'd been around the block once or twice – and to be fair to Julie, she probably had. She'd raised Terry's two children from a previous marriage, dealt with his various philandering's, seen off the odd issue with the police and kitted out most of the cul-de-sac in exotic delights. Thankfully, the interior of Camila's house now looked totally different to all of the others even though the exterior and interior layouts were identical. She remembered one year early on where all of the houses had the same solar panelled stick-in-the-grass stake lights, making the street look like some sort of airport landing strip. But now, even Julie's house, the semi that was attached next door, which was the exact mirror image of the one they were now sitting in, couldn't have been more different.

Camila's 'nothing that's on show' rule meant she'd eventually bought real wallpaper from Wickes, and yes while it wasn't designer it did stick to the walls as did the real paint she'd bought from B&Q, a far cry from the streaky oil-based stuff Julie had given her when she'd first moved in that was definitely responsible for the horrible chesty cough Michael couldn't get rid of in his first few months of life. Either way her house was now lovely. Yes, it had taken fifteen years and lots of scrimping and saving to get to this point, but she was proud of the cosy carpet that hadn't gone threadbare, and happy with the plush deep-cushioned sofa even though she'd had to pay in installments. Both were a dark grey that complemented the silvery theme of the lounge. Even the real Yankee candle sitting on the shelf below the television was a glittered grey. Reaching out, Camila pressed the switch on the free-standing lamp. It wasn't dark yet but the light drew attention to the pretty beaded crystals hanging from the shade.

"Can I give it you straight about your towel set first please?" said Camila, turning back to Julie. "One huge one, which was incredibly heavy, and six face flannels. It's a good job they're out of sight in my en-suite."

Julie laughed. "Oh, you're so bloody dramatic."

"That's something we both know I'm not." And it was true. Situations were just dealt with in both Camila and Julie's worlds.

"You're right. That's why I'm worried."

Camila drank more prosecco. "I promise you, I got a promotion."

"But why?"

"You think she felt sorry for me?"

"You were standing there in next to nothing having been kicked out of a focus group for being too old."

"She didn't have to come out of the viewing room."

"Of course she was going to come out of the bloody viewing room."

"Why?"

"Because you're standing there in next to nothing."

"What do you mean?"

"Camila, you might not be dramatic but you can be naïve."

"You said those towels were a Must Have!"

Julie laughed. "You are bloody funny."

Camila lifted her glass in a cheers gesture.

Julie leaned forward in her seat. "Tell me again what she said."

"She said lots."

"The gushing stuff."

"I don't think it was gushing."

"It sounded gushing."

"I don't think that's how she meant it to sound," Camila smiled, "but she said I was perfection."

"Mmm hmm."

"She said I looked incredible."

"Mmm hmm."

"She said I was refreshing and empowering, and she wished she had my confidence."

Julie banged on the arm of the sofa. "So. Harriet Imogen Pearson, that ball-busting business bitch off the telly, wants your confidence?"

"I had my stretch marks on show."

"They're barely scratches."

"She said she liked how direct I was."

"And then directly told you she wanted you."

"For the business. She made that clear."

"Camila. Take stock. What can you offer Harriet Imogen Pearson? The woman who's already got the business world in lockdown."

"I guess we'll find out tomorrow."

"Do I need to spell it out?"

"I.T." Camila laughed. Julie didn't. "What? The boys used to find that funny."

"She wants you."

"I know she does."

"No." Julie wiggled her body. "Like that."

"Like what?"

"Like," Julie wiggled her body again, "that."

"Nope, I'm not following. Do it again."

"Like," Julie paused, "oh you bloody cow."

Camila smiled. "I know she's a gay woman."

"Oh, you do?"

"Of course I do. It's brought up in almost every interview."

Julie lifted her glass and nodded. "Well then, I rest my case."

"Just because Harriet Imogen Pearson's a gay woman doesn't mean she wants every woman she gives praise to."

"But she wants you."

"For the business."

Julie gasped. "You help out in my bacon butty van! You've done part time bits and bobs here and there. What can you offer her apart from your hot body?"

"Stop being kind."

"I'm not, you're a bloody cracker!"

"I was being sarcastic. I have skills."

KIKI ARCHER

"And she wants to see them. Look at you, life's short, give it a whirl; I would if Terry would let me."

"Would you?"

"With her? God yeah, she's bloody gorgeous. Honestly, Camila, either way you're onto a winner."

"It wasn't like that."

"That's where you're naïve. She saw you. She fancied you. She's going to take you."

"Where?"

"Bloody heaven if the stories in *Take A Break* are true. Plus, fluidity's en-trend."

"You're the second person who's said that today."

"Was Harriet the first?"

"No!"

"Mum?" The shout was questioning.

"Shhh, that's Michael." Camila put her glass on the silver side table. "I'm in the lounge," she shouted. "Good day at school?"

"Oh."

"You okay?"

"Yeah."

Camila heard the front door close. "You want a drink?"

"No... I..."

"Snack?"

"No."

"Are you coming in?"

"No... I..."

"Michael?"

"Just going upstairs."

Camila heard the giggle from the hall before turning to look at Julie's raised eyebrows. Both women were thinking the same thing. "Michael?" she said, jumping up and opening the lounge door in time to spot a pair of female legs dashing up the stairs in front of her son. "He's got a girl up there!" she hissed, turning back to Julie.

"Leave him."

"I wasn't due back until six. He obviously thought he'd be home alone."

"Bloody well leave him."

"I can't! I don't know who it is. He's never brought a girl back before."

Julie patted the sofa. "Like mother like son."

"What?"

"Give it time, you bloody vixen, give it time."

CHAPTER EIGHT

Standing in the lift as it rose to floor five, Camila tucked her H.I.P pass into the inside breast pocket of her blazer. That's what Pamela from Insights had done on the interview day, plus the lanyard with its pattern of heavily embossed company logos was clearly visible around her neck, so hopefully that would be enough. Checking herself in the mirrored walls, Camila smiled. The afternoon and evening with Julie had been great fun. Gossipy, giggly and exactly what she'd needed to get her through the discovery that her eldest son was bringing girls home on the sly. No, that was wrong, she'd always been there in the afternoons so it wasn't a regular occurrence. That he'd done it at the first possible opportunity was a slight worry though, and it's not like she'd have said no to a girl coming round. But for him to usher her in and scuttle her upstairs unseen was disappointing. She had a good relationship with Michael, a great one in fact. Plus, they'd had the sex chat numerous times before so it wasn't like there was anything he should be embarrassed to talk about. "Mum, can I invite a girl round?" "Of course you can, son, but remember you're only fifteen." It was that easy.

The possible reason for his lack of openness became apparent just as Julie was leaving. Both Michael and his mystery woman were halfway down the stairs, creeping in socks, at the exact moment she and Julie had bustled out of the lounge, the prosecco all gone. The two teenagers had frozen, she'd smiled politely and Julie had screeched at the top of her lungs: "Cassie Stevens!"

It just so happened that Cassie Stevens was the head girl at Michael's secondary school, well known for dating the head boy, both of whom were eighteen. Julie knew this because the pair of them were often pictured in the local paper doing good here, there and everywhere. School power couple save scout hut. Head kids kiss on Mt. Kilimanjaro. Most people didn't read the local paper, shoving it straight in the recycling bin, but Julie did. She scoured it from top to toe looking for deals, bargains and any local occurrences she might not be abreast of – which were few and far between.

It turned out that Julie also knew Cassie Stevens' father. Her second screech of: "Your dad better bloody not find out about this," caused by the fact Bill Stevens was a reformed wheeler-dealer now running the (mostly legitimate) local boxing club. His daughter was his shining light. His beacon of pride. His proof that the Stevens family were now of good standing. Camila had obviously questioned Julie about her second screech once the two teenagers had left the house, slightly perplexed at the suggestion her son could bring the girl down in the social rankings. Julie had explained it was more of a loyalty thing. Bill Stevens being one of those people who didn't take kindly to liars and cheats, an interesting stance given his previous line of work.

The encounter had led them back into the lounge for a final bottle of bubbles where they decided Michael's simple explanation that he was helping Cassie with her maths work was actually the most logical. Michael was fifteen. Yes, he looked twenty-two, but he was fifteen. Cassie Stevens was eighteen. Plus Michael was well known as the maths whiz kid, the only one in school to be sitting his A Level exam two years early. This is where he'd have met the sixth former and this is where their platonic relationship would have begun. There'd been a chinking of flutes between Julie and Camila when this was decided and a swift return to their previous discussion about women who have sex with other women.

Camila laughed to herself in the lift as she remembered the conversation. Julie had been so blunt. She'd said the way to tell whether Harriet liked her was simple. She'd stare at her boobs. Lots. Camila's counter-argument that she didn't stare at a man's crotch if she liked him didn't seem to hold water with Julie, who insisted everyone did it. She'd said it was an evolution thing. An inbuilt mechanism to judge a potential pairing's suitability. She'd said it happened all over the animal kingdom, which then led on to Julie's next fact that homosexuality was found in over 1500 species while homophobia was found in just one, therefore proving which was the unnatural thing. Again there'd been another chinking of flutes because same sex attraction was indeed quite natural and should be cheered, even though it wasn't natural to her. Yes, Harriet was gorgeous. Yes, Harriet was smart. Yes, Harriet was a role model for women in all walks of life. But did that make her want to look at Harriet's boobs? No. Would Harriet, the gorgeously smart entrepreneur with it all, want to look at the boobs of a thirty-five-year-old mother of two with not much else? No.

Walking out of the lift and onto the corridor of floor five, Camila pulled down on her patterned shirt, accentuating the v-shaped neckline she'd chosen to wear. It wasn't deliberately booby, it just so happened to complement the Jackson Pollock-esque pictures on the ground floor. The fact that floor five was the same as floor one and very understated in its décor didn't matter, she and Harriet might end up in the red coffee area discussing this and that, or relaxing in the green wellness area reflecting on all their hard work.

Knocking on Harriet's large door, Camila waited, quickly adjusting her shirt once again. She stopped. She'd tuck it in instead. It would keep it in place and also emphasise her slim waistline. Sorting herself out, Camila cursed as her name tag swung free.

"Can I help you?"

Spinning around, Camila spoke quickly. "I'm here for Harriet."

The woman reached out and took hold of Camila's name tag before Camila had time to hide it back in her blazer pocket. "Oh yes," she said, "I know who you are."

"Is she around?"

"Harriet's not here."

"We're expanding the business."

The woman looked up at the ceiling and laughed. "Why does she do this to me?"

"Who?"

"Harriet."

Camila waited. She'd learnt from her experiences with her sister's university friends that the best thing to do when faced by possible ridicule was to stand still and stay silent. Don't give them any more ammunition, but likewise don't let on you've been knocked. What this woman was getting at, she had no clue, but her tone indicated a certain here-we-go-again annoyance.

"I'm Deana."

Camila shook the outstretched hand. There, whatever the issue was, it had passed.

"It's ridiculous that you're here."

Or maybe not.

"But here you are, so come this way."

Camila stood still. "I'm meant to be working with Harriet."

"Expanding the business? Right, I heard you. But Harriet's not here. She only comes in once a month."

Camila glanced down at her choice of shirt. "Oh."

"We see her a bit more now because of the show but she's never been a nine-to-fiver."

"The show?"

"Yes, the show. Surely you know about the show? That's what we're doing. You're part of the team whether we like it or not."

Camila stayed silent. Her one question had clearly annoyed further.

"Sorry. It's just…" The woman sighed. "Harriet can be frustrating. So many ideas. So many…" she gestured at Camila, "projects."

Camila continued to wait.

"And I'm sure this isn't your fault, but I'm always left to pick up the pieces."

Camila stood still.

"When the project fails…" The woman filled more silence. "Which it always inevitably does. But you're here now and I've been told to welcome you."

Camila nodded. "Count me as welcomed." Positivity always helped in situations like these. Just like the first time Mick said he needed some space. Even then she'd managed to smile and tell him in the politest of fashions to do what he needed to do. Shouting and reacting never helped anyone. Likewise, if someone confronted you with something, you should take it at face value and accept that those were the feelings they held. Trying to make them see sense or debate the validity of their feelings just wasn't worth it. This woman was clearly pissed off and no amount of discussion about the gushing Harriet had sent her way would change that. Plus, jealousy was always in the mix. That was almost always the main reason for meanness. Maybe she was stepping on this Deana woman's toes?

Camila followed the brisk walk down the corridor. Mick had been jealous of Julie's old man, Terry. The way he was free to come and go as he pleased. The way he could unofficially see other women. Mick had seen that and wanted it for himself. He hadn't set out to be mean. The fact he'd met Jackie from the gym and chosen to move in with her didn't quite follow Terry's M.O but, still, no amount of confrontation would have helped.

"Right, we're based here, at the end."

Camila nodded. Already the woman's tone had changed. Sometimes people just needed to let off steam, say their piece and move on. Not that she ever did. Not on a personal level anyway. Debating, discussing and criticising products was one thing, but not people; she'd never do that with people. She'd always avoid the dramatics and simply be there when needed. And that didn't make her a doormat, it made her consistent, and consistency was the one thing she'd promised her baby when he was born. She'd chosen to bring him into the world, the least she could do was figure out how to be mature. The fact that another little brother had come along so quickly the year after hadn't exactly shown maturity, but again it had happened and she'd been there for them both. Always.

Noticing more large doors as they passed, Camila realised this top floor was reserved for the exec. There was a silver sign on one door for the Managing Director, another for the Chief Executive Officer, three more for the Board of Directors, various Chiefs of Legal, Finance and Personnel and the one they were passing now read, "Deana DuBeck – Chief Strategist".

"Oooh, is that you?" said Camila, deciding it made perfect sense. The woman with her robust personality and matching robust appearance was clearly important.

"Yes, but we're working at the end."

Camila knew not to say more even though she desperately wanted to ask what Harriet's official title actually was. If Camila was remembering correctly, Harriet's office door simply displayed her name with H.I.P Marketing written underneath. Was Harriet just the owner? Or a shareholder? She certainly couldn't be too hands-on if she was only in once a month. But that made sense given that she had numerous other businesses and was on TV all the time. Glancing down at her shirt, Camila felt slightly disappointed. She'd been looking forward to seeing Harriet today.

"Right, as you can see this floor is predominantly offices, but at the end here we have our open-plan workspace. This is where the team's based. We have—" Deana gasped. "Harriet!"

Camila looked up to see Harriet Imogen Pearson in all of her Wonder Woman glory standing in the centre of the workspace flanked by a cameraman whose camera was pointed their way.

Harriet smiled widely. "Goodness, I love your shirt, Camila. Come, come you need to make your show debut."

Camila stepped forward, noticing the four work pods on the left of the room, two occupied by middle-aged men, the other two vacant. Next she noticed the cosy area on the right, complete with a screen, soft seating and some formal tables and chairs, all of which were empty. She looked back to the camera and smiled. "Oh, how wonderful," she managed to say, once again unsure where she was or quite what was expected.

CHAPTER NINE

Adjusting to the bright light lasering her vision from the top of the camera, Camila tried to half smile. She'd had a very in-depth discussion with Julie one evening about what the other half of a presenting double act did when not reading the cue card. They were still visible on screen but you weren't meant to be watching them, you were meant to be focusing on whatever link the speaking presenter happened to be introducing. Ant and Dec. Holly and Phil. Claudia and Tess. It happened all the time. For a huge chunk of the segments, one of the presenters was just standing there and you didn't really notice them... until you did, and from that point on all you'd be able to focus on was that non-speaking presenter because it was fascinating. She and Julie had discovered the non-speaking presenter performed three moves in rotation. The half-smile – the one she was doing right now, staring straight into the camera, lips turned slightly at the corners, head completely still. Then the turn to co-presenter and nod at a point well made, and then the micro-expressions, again performed face-on to the camera without the loss of eye contact. A tiny raised eyebrow at a particularly controversial point, wide eyes when something shocking was said, a small frown at something sad, a slightly bigger frown at something confusing, a puckered mouth at intrigue. That's where she'd rotated, to the puckered mouth because Harriet had turned to camera and posed the question: "Who is this, I hear you cry? A ringer brought in at the last minute?"

Camila continued to pucker.

"A secret weapon kept under wraps until the live show?"

Camila opened up the pucker into an O-shaped lip query.

"Is she my trump card?"

Camila did a micro frown, the use of "trump" hadn't been used in a positive manner since the 2016 American elections.

"Has she been up my sleeve?"

Camila raised her eyebrows.

"Is she the ace in my hole?"

Camila bared her teeth and widened her eyes.

"Stop!" shouted the woman standing next to the cameraman, her arms now in the air. "I'm going to have to stop you!" She pointed at Camila. "What's going on with your face?"

Camila blinked as the camera was lowered and the light dropped away. "Me?"

"Yes, you're in shot!"

"I know."

"So what are you doing?"

Camila looked to Harriet. "I should have thrown in a turn to co-presenter, shouldn't I?"

Harriet laughed. "Are you channeling Ant and Dec?"

"We're short enough."

"Ha! Speak for yourself."

Camila glanced down. "Says your high heels."

"Ladies! We need to film this. Go again, but you've got to stay still."

Camila frowned at the finger pointed her way. "For the whole segment?"

"Yes."

"Right." Camila nodded as the camera was lifted back onto the cameraman's shoulder, the bright light illuminating her face once again. Focusing, she listened as Harriet started her spiel. It was strange to just stare at the lens with no emotion, but that's what she'd been told to do. She lifted her lips into a half smile, she couldn't help it, too long looking emotionless would make those beady-eyed viewers who were aware of the fascination of the non-speaking co-presenter think she was a novice and, yes, while she'd never been in front of a camera like this before she'd certainly watched a lot of TV and knew what looked good.

Thinking back to a programme she'd seen a while ago on a condition called imposter syndrome, Camila smiled once more. The syndrome was categorised as a persistent fear of being exposed as a fraud. It was all about a person's inability to internalise their accomplishments. People who'd achieved success but didn't believe they deserved success. It had seemed ridiculous back then and rather self-indulgent of the supposed imposters and now the scenario she found herself in confirmed her initial judgement. Everyone was an imposter until they actually stepped into the room, but once they'd crossed that threshold they became a member of the room. It didn't matter if there were people in it who'd been there for years, you were all now there together. Yes, she'd queried in yesterday's seated shower session the reasons why she'd got the job, but not to the extent that she'd ended up asking the company or debated whether or not to come in. Life threw all sorts at you and you just needed to smile and battle through with gusto. She'd never been a presenter before, but here she was presenting. She turned the corners of her lips even higher.

"Stop!" shouted the woman. "You're smiling like a Cheshire cat!"

"I'm happy to be here."

"You need to be deadpan until you're introduced!"

Camila shook her head. "The co-presenter's always half-smiling when they're not talking."

"You're not a co-presenter!"

Harriet cut in. "You could be though. I like your work. I can sense your positivity next to me."

Camila nodded. "Why thank you."

"What are you two doing?" continued the woman, before seemingly remembering who she was addressing. "Sorry, Harriet, but we need to get this segment filmed. I'm heading over to Barry Maddison's next."

Camila gasped. "Barry Maddison's taking part in this?"

Harriet nodded. "As is—"

"Ladies, please!"

"I'll fill you in in a bit." Harriet smiled. "Let's get this right then we can go sit over there and discuss."

The idea of a personal tête-à-tête with the boss sounded wonderful, not only so she'd be able to know what the hell was going on, but also because Deana was now head down and working in one of the pods on the other side of the room. "You want me deadpan?"

Harriet laughed. "Can you even do deadpan? I've never seen eyes as expressive."

"Really?"

The woman sharply interrupted the connection. "You'll be out of shot until you're introduced." She nodded. "And we're filming."

Camila watched as Harriet returned her gaze to the camera, marvelling as she reeled off the same nonsense for the third time running but with as much enthusiasm as if it were her first.

"She's Camila Moore and she's my new woman."

Camila continued to stare.

"Camila, why don't you introduce yourself?" Harriet was smiling. "Tell us your secrets."

Camila realised she was still gazing agog at Harriet. She spun to the camera. "Right, I'm Camila Moore… and I'm Harriet's new woman." That's what the co-presenter did when they weren't sure what was going on, they repeated. "And I'm *so* full of secrets."

Harriet nodded. "Are you really?"

"I sure am," said Camila with a 'let's go' fist thrust in front of her body.

"Well, don't give them away just yet, we want to win this thing."

"We sure do," said Camila, firmly adding her input even though she still had no clue what this thing was.

Harriet focused back on the lens. "What I can tell you is this. Camila's the puzzle piece we've been missing. The key to our box. The cherry on our bun."

"I'm more of an iced finger type woman if I'm being honest." Camila had no clue where that joke had come from but there it was all the same.

Harriet laughed. "As long as you're not a fan of cream pie."

The shout was sharp. "Ladies! We're stopping."

Harriet frowned. "That was good, wasn't it?"

"Just outline Camila's role. Quickly. Come on, Harriet, you're the one who asked us to come in this morning. We'll keep rolling."

Harriet raised her hands contritely before continuing. "Camila here is sharp as a tack. A blue sky thinker. A real breath of fresh air. If anyone can invent an invention, this inventor's the one."

Camila turned to camera, her deadpan expression suddenly spot-on.

CHAPTER TEN

"Okay, so questions," said Harriet. "You must have lots."

"I have no clue what's happening." Camila was seated on a sofa in the open-plan area, watching as the film crew of two re-positioned themselves by the work pods. "I mean, I'm good at playing catch-up, I've been doing it my whole life and as far as I'm concerned imposter syndrome's self-indulgent. You put me in front of that camera so you must think I'm worthy of being in front of that camera, so I did my stuff in front of that camera."

Harriet laughed. "You sure did."

"But why's there even a camera? It's not live, is it?"

"No, the show's not airing for another three weeks. It's the same with all reality things: loads of footage and only a fraction will make the final cut. It's playing over a weekend. A pre-recorded show on the Friday and Saturday nights, and the live final on the Sunday." Harriet pointed to the camera. "I think that footage will go out on the Saturday show, basically the one where we're all in the thick of it."

"The thick of what? And who's 'all'? And why's the camera pointed our way again?"

"They'll be getting a long shot of our work in progress – me over here getting you up to speed."

"As I invent something? I'm not an inventor, Harriet. What's made you think I'm an inventor. They can't hear me can they?"

"No, footage like this always has a voice-over." Harriet put on a Geordie accent. "Harriet's secret weapon shows Harriet her skills."

"I haven't got any skills."

"You have. You just held your own on TV."

"Talking waffle about waffle. I said we wanted to win this thing. I even did a fist thrust."

"I particularly liked the fist thrust."

"But I have no clue what this thing is."

"Can you do the fist thrust again?"

"No."

The Geordie accent returned. "Harriet's ace up her sleeve thrusts her fist in the air in triumph."

"Why are the voice-overs always Geordie?"

"They just are. Please? Do it for me?"

Camila looked at the smiling lips. "Fine," she said, clenching her fist in front of her, unable to stop her own mouth from curving up at the corners.

"You have a good fist thrust."

"I know I do."

Harriet laughed. "You really are a pocket rocket aren't you? I could put you in any situation and you'd take it in your stride. Little strides admittedly, with those little legs of yours, but you would, wouldn't you?"

"You're about a centimetre taller than me!"

"But my heels are higher."

"Right, I'm going to wear platform shoes tomorrow."

"I'll wear my stilettos."

Camila looked down at Harriet's high heels, her eyes moving up the shapely legs that were crossed at the knee. "Red ones?" she asked.

"If you like?"

Unable to identify the sudden charge in the atmosphere, Camila felt her cheeks redden. Yes, it was banter, but there was something else as well. Teasing? An intrigue? A connection that a new employee shouldn't necessarily have with their boss within one day of meeting. Were they friends? No, of course not. She decided to focus. "Can you fill me in please?"

"If you like."

Camila laughed.

Harriet shrugged innocently. "What?"

"I don't know. You make me laugh."

"You make me laugh too."

"Laugh nervously. I'm here to do a good job, Harriet."

"You will."

"But doing what?"

Harriet nodded. "Inventing."

"Inventing what?"

"An invention."

"For what?"

"For anything." Harriet pointed back at the camera. "What you did just then was great. It showed me you're able to fake it until you make it and so much of this is PR." She smiled. "But now I need you to focus."

"I can focus."

"Is that your focusing face?"

"It's my ready-to-absorb face. Go. I've got this."

Harriet nodded. "Okay. We're taking part in a new programme called *Budding Businesses*. That woman's one of the producers, Lydia. There are four of them but she usually works with us. The other producers are attached to the other entrepreneurs who are our competition: Barry Maddison from Maddison Computers, Oliver James from the restaurant chain and Jill Masters from Jill's Gyms."

"Wow."

The Geordie accent returned. "Four entrepreneurs all competing on the show that shows start-up success."

"You're starting a new business?"

"Correct. The rules say we can expand on a current business if we want to, but it has to have an entirely new USP."

"Unique selling point."

"Good. I've heard on the grapevine that Jill's starting a cosmetic treatments spa… it's an expansion on the gym theme but a totally new business if you see what I mean?"

"I do. What's Barry Maddison doing? He's huge? Why's he taking part? In fact, why are you taking part? You've successfully started loads of businesses already."

"Eight."

"I thought it was thirty-odd?"

"I'm a shareholder in a lot of businesses, but I've started eight from scratch."

"Why do it again?"

"Why not?"

Camila paused. "I don't know." She smiled. "Maybe because you don't have to?"

"I want to."

"Why?"

"It's a challenge."

"And you get to be on TV."

"I'm not a narcissist."

Camila laughed. "I didn't say you were."

"My businesses don't need me. I set them up with the executive infrastructure in place so I can step away. Not completely. Not a big step anyway."

"Well, you wouldn't with those little legs of yours, would you."

"Oh touché, Miss Moore, touché."

"Sorry."

"It's fine, I deserved that." Harriet smiled. "I'm still at the board meetings and I do hold a lot of the power, but I put the right people in place so I'm free to move on to the next big thing."

"Which is this?"

"For the moment, yes. I love the challenge of a start-up and it'll be interesting for people to see how it all works. Plus, there's the challenge of winning. Three weeks from now all our new businesses will be judged by a panel of experts to see which is the best. The winners will obviously get great exposure."

"And they'll win."

"I'm not a megalomaniac."

"I didn't say you were." Camila laughed again. "So what's the business?"

"Well obviously at H.I.P Marketing we work with companies and brands developing projects and ideas… but what about the individual with an idea? Where do they go? There are currently only three reputable, and I say reputable in the loosest of ways, but there are three main invention-to-production companies out there, and none of them are leading the market, none of them are well known." She lifted her hands to Camila. "If you had an idea where would you go?"

"I don't know."

"Exactly, well you'd come to us at H.I.Pvention."

Camila stared at her boss. "Do all of your businesses have your initials in their name?"

"I'm not an egomaniac."

"I didn't say you were. Sorry, go on. H.I.Pvention."

"So we—"

"Wait." Camila shook her head. "I have to say it. It makes me think of a cushion or something that will stop someone breaking their hip. The prevention of hip breakage."

"No, it's invention, with me, Harriet Imogen Pearson."

"Right."

"So, H.I.Pvention becomes the market-leading design and innovation firm for individual inventors. You have an idea, you come to us at H.I.Pvention. We take you on a five step journey from idea to prototype."

"Five steps?"

"One: feasibility assessment. Is the idea worth pursuing? What will the costs be? How easy will it be to produce? Two: patent search. Is the idea unique? Has it been patented before? You know what a patent is?"

Camila nodded. "A patent is something that stops others from making, using or selling your invention?"

"Good."

"I watch *Dragon's Den.*"

"They asked me to be a Dragon."

"They didn't!"

"They did."

"Why aren't you?"

Harriet shrugged. "I'm thinking about it."

"Oh, how exciting!"

"I need to wrap this up first."

"Wrap this up? Aren't we still at the gift-buying stage?"

"We. I like that."

"You do?"

"Yes." Harriet continued. "Step Three: concept development, using sketches and computer-aided design to flesh out the idea. Step Four: patent drawings necessary for the patent application. Step Five: prototyping."

"Wow! Where are all these people?"

"Here."

Camila looked to the four work pods across the room. Deana was sitting in one, one was empty and the other two were filled by two tired looking men. "Three people?"

"Four including you." Harriet smiled. "It's a business model."

"So you're not actually starting the business?"

"Oh we are, but we need to show how it'll work. Brett over there's our designer. The bald guy. Wait, let me introduce you properly."

"To the bald guy?"

Harriet laughed. "I won't phrase it like that. Follow me. I'll introduce you to the ginger guy as well."

Camila rose and tried to compose herself. Surely Harriet couldn't joke like that in this day and age. It was the same yesterday when she was calling the focus groups on floor one the lowest of the low. "Will I be the short dwarf?"

Harriet halted. "You can't say things like that on camera."

"Oh right, sorry, I thought…"

"I'm teasing. They're packing up. Come on, penguin."

"Penguin?"

"Little legs."

"Don't penguins waddle?"

"The little ones are cute though."

"You think I'm cute?"

"You're thirty-five, Camila."

Camila flushed. "Right, yes, sorry."

"I'm teasing! It's going to be so much fun working with you."

"You're part of the team?"

"Not really, but I'll be in and out. Right, ladies and gents, this is Camila. I briefed you yesterday and here she is in all her glory."

Camila looked around at the unimpressed faces, aware that the camera was now pointing her way. "Hi guys!"

Harriet continued. "We have Brett over here. He's our designer working on concept development and patent drawings. Geoff's our engineer, again working on concept development but majorly focused on prototyping. Deana you've met, she's in charge of research, assessing the feasibility of ideas and checking for patents. That leaves this pod for you, Camila, our new ideas inventor."

Camila did a fist thrust. "Let me at it."

"We're not rolling," said producer Lydia. "You can stop all that now."

"Still, let me at it." Camila maintained her forced smile.

Lydia turned to Harriet. "We've got enough for today; like I said I'm needed over at Barry's. Big announcement apparently. The whole crew are there."

Deana spoke up. "He's getting special treatment."

"He's not. You all get the same air time in the end."

Harriet placed her hand on Deana's shoulder. "It's fine, we've got this."

Camila watched as the pod people appeared to hold their composure while Lydia and her cameraman said their goodbyes and headed off down the corridor.

Deana broke first, hissing her words. "We've not got this."

Brett spoke next as he rubbed his hand over his bald head. "Yesterday was fruitless and I'm out of ideas today."

"And fake it until you make it is okay to a point," added Geoff, "but we're at that point now. I honestly think we need to contact inventors."

"Stop." Harriet was hands in the air. "How much more impressive will our presentation be if our new business can showcase an in-house design that was seen through from idea conception to patented product invention? Plus, we can't offer our services to the public until the show goes live on the Sunday night."

Deana crossed her arms over her body. "But our ideas are shit and any half decent ones have been done."

"Helloooo," said Camila, waving her hand.

"Oh god," gasped Deana, swivelling on her chair. "Mistake one, believing all of Harriet's fluff. Are you an inventor? No. Just like I'm not a researcher and, yes, while Brett and Geoff may have had designer and engineer in their job titles here at H.I.P Marketing they're not qualified to design and create something brand spanking new."

"This is small scale," said Harriet. "Getting the real people in place as we expand will be easy, as are details such as premises and websites; that's all happening in the background. Trust me, I know what I'm doing. Stick to the format. Come on, you're the nucleus of H.I.Pvention."

"You're staying to watch?" asked Deana.

"Yes, follow the format I set. Everyone to the sofas. Camila, this is how each day starts until we have our Eureka moment."

Camila crossed the room with Harriet, glancing back at the others who were traipsing behind them having taken odds and sods of paperwork from their desks.

"Right, sit down everyone." Harriet remained standing until they were settled before positioning herself at the more formal seating to the side of the sofas. "Camila, this is what we do. Yes, I've given you the title of lead inventor, but if I'm honest we're all lead inventors. We all thrash out our ideas first thing in the morning. You need at least five a day but I'm really wanting twenty, thirty, forty. Right, Geoff, you go first. What have you got for us today? No idea's a bad idea."

Geoff coughed as he fingered his paperwork. "Okay. So how about little umbrellas that fit over your shoes?"

CHAPTER ELEVEN

Seated in an awkward perching position on the edge of a sofa in the open-plan area at the end of floor five, Camila couldn't hide that she was totally aghast. Ideas had been thrown into the session for a hat with hair attached so you didn't appear bald – one of Brett's; a gym work-out headband that said: No one knows I'm a ginger – one of Geoff's; a kitchen scale for nuts and seeds that converted portion weight into calorific value – one of Deana's; and a stiletto shoe with remote control adjustable heel height – one of Harriet's. And now the group had come full circle and were seriously discussing the idea of umbrellas for shoes.

"You've bought a nice new pair of loafers," said Geoff.

Brett cut in. "Loafers aren't nice."

"The ones with the tassels are," continued Geoff. "Anyway, you've bought these tasseled loafers and they're suede."

"Suede tasselled loafers? No." Brett was shaking his head.

"It doesn't matter what shoes they are. Clogs then. You've bought some new clogs."

Brett squealed. "Who buys clogs?!"

"Whatever. You've bought some posh new shoes."

"Clogs are never posh."

"You have posh shoes; it starts to rain. Your umbrella keeps your head dry but not your shoes. Why not have a compartment inside your umbrella that appears when you open it and hey presto, inside are two miniature umbrellas that you clip over your toes."

Camila had to speak up, she couldn't help it. "Does the apartment have an en-suite?"

Deana snapped. "We're brain-storming. No idea's a bad idea."

"This one is." Shunting even further forward on the sofa, Camila lifted her hands. "Not only would two miniature umbrellas sticking up from the ends of your shoes look ridiculous, but it's raining so there'll be puddles and your shoes will get wet anyway."

"Ah ha." Brett was pointing his finger. "Could the shoe umbrellas be the all-encompassing ones that go out and down all the way to the floor?"

Geoff nodded. "Clear though, so you can still see your posh clogs."

"Hmm." Deana was frowning. "What about people with different sized feet?"

Camila shook her head; this was ridiculous. "Just yank a shoe cover over your shoes if you're that bothered."

Harriet stood up, having taken a back seat to watch proceedings. "Camila's right. A shoe cover could work."

"I'm not saying it would work." Camila turned to her boss. "People only use those things when they're looking around a show home or walking onto a crime scene. Have you ever seen people wearing them around town?"

Harriet raised her eyebrows. "Gap in the market then?"

"But what are we patenting?" Camila laughed. "A plastic bag?"

"We'll find out, won't we." Harriet nodded. "This is stage two of the day. Whatever idea we've chosen to focus on is then researched by Deana, and now you as well, while Brett and Geoff start the drawings and prototyping."

"Which we always have to stop the second Deana tells us it's already been done," added Brett.

"In this case we already know it's been done – you only have to watch CSI or Midsomer Murders to know that." Camila knew she sounded as exasperated as she felt.

Harriet shook her head. "But it gets us into the habit of working through the system stages. The bottom line is we don't actually need an invention to present to the panel on the live show. We can showcase our business model as it is before offering our services to the public who'll no doubt have inventions they've been developing for years. You'll be the heads of your own departments, all with two people working underneath you, two researchers, two designers, two engineers." Harriet paused. "But how much more spectacular if we can show them we've already developed a product internally. Individual inventors are much more likely to use the services of a start-up if they can see it's already successful."

Camila put up her hand. "So an in-house inventor won't actually be needed when H.I.Pvention goes live?"

Deana snorted. "You're not needed now."

Harriet stepped forward. "She is. She's the one who came up with the shoe bag idea."

"I didn't," said Camila, not wanting any association with the ridiculousness.

Deana stood up. "So I'm researching patents for shoe coverings, right?"

Harriet nodded. "Yes, and umbrellas with compartments."

"I like that," said Geoff, also standing from the sofas. "It starts raining, you pop open your umbrella, what else would be handy to pop out? Apart from the shoe coverings obviously?"

Brett nodded. "A hat with hair underneath so the see-through umbrella doesn't highlight your forehead shine."

"You've not got a forehead shine, mate," added Geoff, "you've got a full flashing beacon up there."

"Says you, ginger nuts."

Camila stayed seated as the three walked away to the pods. She forced her best smile as Harriet sat next to her on the sofa.

"I've not seen that smile before."

Camila frowned. "What smile?"

"That one. The one accessorised by those sad eyes. You have eyes that tell a story, Camila. I noticed it yesterday."

Camila stared into her boss's piercing blue eyes, framed by the gold glasses, pieces of art in their own right. "I'd rather have eyes like yours."

"Ha! Is that a compliment?"

"Of course. Your eyes are gorgeous."

"Do you always say what you feel?"

"Never actually, not on a personal level at any rate, but you started this mutual eye congratulations." Camila held the connection before feeling her cheeks redden. She turned away. "What I meant to say was that I'd never tell Deana she was snappy and self-protecting."

"But you'll tell her her ideas are shit?"

Camila laughed. "I didn't say that, did I?"

"Your eyes did. You've got concerns, I can see them. Come on, let it all out."

Checking that everyone was head down and working in the pods, Camila whispered. "They just don't look like they want to be here, and the idea that they'll be department heads in a new business seems wrong to me. They should be excited and bubbly and thrilled to be part of such a wonderful adventure."

"Your face hasn't looked thrilled during this session."

"Because the ideas are poor, but to be part of something like this at the start is momentous. They should be buzzing."

"They won't remain as H.I.Pvention business heads unless they choose to. They'll return to their positions here at H.I.P Marketing and Deana will continue to be my Chief Strategist in whatever direction I take next. So much of early doors business is smoke and mirrors, Camila. Plus this is a reality TV show, a competition, anything goes, and it may be that I don't even take the new business any further once the show finishes."

"Oh no, you must! It's a great idea!"

Harriet smiled. "It is, isn't it? I have a separate team scouting for locations, and a team sourcing the designers and engineers." She paused. "They'll obviously work on agency daily rates to start with until we establish the viability of the whole thing. But my web design team are working wonders on the online stuff. It's the website that's the main showcase for our services and that's looking incredible. I guess the set-up's a bit like *The Apprentice*. Do you ever watch that?"

"I love it," said Camila.

"Their tasks are similar… design this, create this, start up this. They're showing how things would work, but so much of it is fake it 'til you make it."

Camila shook her head. "You need to stop saying that. You have to believe this is a legitimate business that'll make you money."

"Oh, it will. We'll charge the inventors a fee for each stage of the process. Plus, there's the option of waiving those fees and opting for shares in the patent and prototype for any ideas we think are credible."

"The shoe bag idea's not credible."

"No, but it gives us practice when searching for patents and designing the products."

Deana hollered from the pods. "Shoe umbrellas have already been done. Patent filed October 2014. We also have a shoe-covering rain umbrella that's tied to the leg, patent filed April 2013. Says here in the abstract that the market prospect is high."

Harriet shouted back. "Move on to umbrellas with compartments."

Camila watched as Brett turned his sheet of A3 paper to the group with a rough sketch of tiny umbrellas attached to the toes of large clogs. He ripped it in half.

Camila whispered to Harriet. "A high market prospect?"

"Listen, it's true what they say: no idea's a bad idea. You've got to think of the novelty shops, the tourists in London, the online market place. Almost everything you fancy can be found online." Harriet paused before laughing.

"What?" Camila smiled. "I didn't say anything."

"You're going to be trouble, aren't you?"

"I hope not."

"Really?"

"Of course."

"Right." Harriet coughed. "Okay, so I want you to go and help Deana with the patent searches; she'll explain it all. When that's done I want you to individually research and brainstorm more ideas that'll be discussed tomorrow."

"And what happens in three weeks when the business goes live?"

"Who knows where we'll be in three weeks."

"Will there be a job for me here? I mean what am I? Am I a market researcher, or an inventor, or a mum returner?"

"You're one of my women." Harriet paused before laughing again.

"What?" Camila frowned. "I didn't say anything."

"Don't worry, I look after my women." Harriet pointed. "There! That's why I'm laughing! Your eyes gave me a look!"

Camila smiled. "They didn't!"

Harriet reached out and squeezed Camila's shoulder. "Listen, Camila, life's an adventure. This is going to be one hell of a ride."

"I'm more of a practical person."

"Well get over there and get going." Harriet rose from the sofa, offering her hand to help Camila up.

Camila let herself be led, slightly conscious of the way Deana clocked the physical contact. She wiggled out of the grip. "Thank you, right, I'll make a start."

Harriet nodded. "Meet me for coffee this afternoon? Fill me in on your progress? Say three, during your afternoon break?"

"In the red coffee area on the ground floor?"

"Goodness, no," said Harriet, walking away. "My office, other end of the corridor. Where we were yesterday."

Camila nodded as Harriet disappeared before taking her seat and tucking herself into the work pod next to Deana.

Deana pushed her chair back and swivelled around. "She used to be like that with me, you know."

Camila nodded but didn't look at Deana. "And you've not done too badly out of it, have you?"

CHAPTER TWELVE

Knocking for the third time on the door to Harriet's office, Camila debated whether she should try the handle and go in. It was three o'clock. Harriet said coffee in her office at three.

"She does this too," said the now familiar voice.

Camila turned to see Deana walking towards her.

"Talks the talk, makes elaborate plans… until the next shiny thing comes along and steals her interest."

"She might be on a call or in a meeting?"

"No, she'll have forgotten. Hot Harriet will be off somewhere with somebody else."

Camila studied the woman she'd spent the past few hours beside. She'd naively thought they'd been making some progress. "Does she know you talk about her like this? Harriet told me very few people have the nerve to joke with her."

"Oh, I'm not joking, she's an absolute nightmare. She's obviously hot, but she's also very hard to handle. She gets away with it though because she's a genius who makes an awful lot of money for an awful lot of people. The general consensus is to let Harriet do what she does." Deana shrugged. "Come on, this isn't your fault. Let me take you to the snack bar. It's on floor two, everyone goes there. Warm pastries, muffins, fruit if fruit's your thing which looking at that tiny little waist of yours, I'm guessing it is?"

Camila paused, unsure if that was a compliment or an insult.

Deana continued. "I obviously go for the pastries. They have all sorts. My favourite are the salted caramel croissants. Come on, let me take you."

Camila smiled. Deana's guard was definitely dropping. And, yes, while Deana hadn't invited her to the snack bar at lunch time but instead disappeared with Brett and Geoff the second she'd nipped to the toilet, leaving her to work through lunch in case they came back and got her, which they didn't, she was being okay now. "I think I should give Harriet another minute," she chose to say.

Deana shrugged. "Your choice, but you'll be wasting your time."

"She definitely said three." Camila held the connection until Deana shrugged again and turned towards the lift. In normal circumstances Camila would have welcomed the invitation. It was important to accept the olive branch… and the atmosphere between them had definitely improved as the day had gone on, whether that was because she'd quickly understood how to perform a patent search, or because she'd made a couple of rounds of tea without being asked, she wasn't sure, but Deana's demeanour had certainly softened. Even so, a coffee with Harriet trumped any sort of early bond Deana may or may not be offering.

Camila knocked once more before trying the handle. Locked. Turning around she glanced down the corridor. Their open-plan work space was just about visible at the end. Brett and Geoff had gone onto the balcony for a cigarette, Deana had obviously gone to the snack bar, and here she was, loitering like a loser. Maybe Harriet was in with one of the exec? Camila tried a casual slow walk past the large office doors, angling her head at each one she passed. Harriet's voice was distinctive. Posher than most, with an intriguing edge: cheeky somehow. Camila stopped herself. Why was she smiling at that thought? Harriet's voice didn't sound cheeky on television, it sounded serious and formal, but there'd definitely been a teasing tone as they'd talked. Shaking her head, Camila made her way to the lift. She couldn't get drawn in to something that wasn't there. If Harriet wanted coffee at three she should have been there for a coffee at three.

Entering the lift, Camila pressed the button for the ground floor. She'd grab a drink from the red coffee area in reception to avoid Deana who'd no doubt be smug that she'd been right about Harriet's haphazardness… and haphazardness was the correct word; it certainly

THE WAY YOU SMILE

wasn't anything more sinister like deliberately building someone up just so you could knock them down again hours later. Camila looked at her own reflection. It probably wasn't even haphazardness. It was probably just the stress of running thirty-odd businesses and being pulled in all sorts of directions. Not that Harriet came across as stressed. Plus there was the fact she'd said she was free to come and go as she pleased. Camila's sigh briefly fogged the mirror. It didn't matter, either way they wouldn't be catching up about the day.

Leaving the lift, she made her way down the long foyer past the crazily-coloured paintings before turning to smile at H.A.H sitting behind the glass reception desk in what she now noticed was an incredibly uncomfortable-looking, almost upright, chair. It transpired that employees did in fact enter through the main doors, their passes giving them access as Helen Anna Howes had explained. The other interesting fact was that the front car park was the only car park, meaning people must either get in really early, or the hubbub on floor one was unique to floor one as again there'd been no one milling around when she'd arrived and there was no one milling around now. Camila's hours were nine to five, so she'd got in at nine, but maybe this was the type of place where you were expected to give extra?

Camila decided she'd check that with Helen once she'd made herself a coffee. Actually, she'd see if Helen wanted one now. The receptionist had been kind to her, apologising for yesterday's mistake before congratulating her on her new position. Harriet had no doubt filled her in just as she had with her three colleagues on floor five. Camila smiled to herself. That sounded strange. The idea she had colleagues. Deana was obviously the most senior of the group, but there didn't appear to be a strict line of command between them all. It was more of a team type set up: all of them working under the same remit. And that remit was more than expanding the business, it was building a new business entirely.

Turning back to the reception desk, Camila smiled. She could handle a bit of sniffiness from Deana if it meant being in the mix of something so wonderful. "Helen," she said quietly, conscious that everything echoed in the large open space, "can I make you a drink?"

"Me?"

"Yes. Can I make you a coffee? Tea?"

"Really?"

Camila nodded. "Of course."

Helen rose, or more accurately, leapt from her chair. "Oh, how lovely. No one ever comes down here and offers to make me a drink. Are you going to have it over there? I think I'll join you."

"Yes, shall we—" Camila stopped at the loud clipping sound of fast-moving high heels. It was Harriet, dashing at break-neck speed from the other side of the reception area that housed, among other things, the green wellness room and blue outdoor space.

"Harriet!" she shouted, no longer worried about the echo.

The clipping halted.

"Over here!" Camila waved like a lunatic.

"You're here!" said Harriet, immediately changing her direction. "I was just on my way to..." The voice paused as her eyes were drawn to Helen. "Oh, are you two...?"

Camila shook her head. "We're just grabbing a coffee. I thought I'd missed you."

"No no, I was..."

The receptionist spun around. "Sorry, Camila, I actually need to get on with my work. Next time though, thank you."

"You're sure?" queried Camila, watching Helen walk away before turning to address her boss instead. "Harriet? Do you have time for a coffee?"

"Please stay if you like," said Harriet to the receptionist who was already back at her desk.

"She's already gone."

"Did I leave it too late?"

Camila laughed. "You spoke too softly as well. She'd never have heard you."

"Oh, that's a shame." Harriet was smiling. "I was dashing back up to my office for you. For our meeting. For our chat."

"Did you forget?"

"No! Of course not! I was speaking to Pamela from Insights about... oh it doesn't matter, I was dashing back for you, but here you are." The laugh was loud. "Goodness, you didn't wait long did you! And you got yourself new company as well!"

Camila ignored the teasing. "Shall we sit down over there on the red chairs? I'm not sure about the length of my afternoon break and by the time we get back upstairs—"

"You're here for as long as I want you." Harriet paused. "The coffee I mean, not in general. I'll get Helen to update your contract so you've got nothing to worry about."

"What might I be worried about?"

"Oh, I don't know."

Camila laughed. "Do I need to sit down?"

"Yes, what are you having?"

"I can't let you make my coffee, I'll do it."

"It's only popping a pod in a machine. Go on, sit down."

"A latte then, if you insist." Taking a seat in front of the windows, Camila watched as the owner of the company made her a drink. Again, Harriet had been a bit flappy, such a contrast to the person she portrayed to the press, or maybe the way she was currently behaving was an act, a distraction, a test. Maybe this whole thing was some kind of set-up? Camila straightened in her seat. No. Imposter syndrome. She'd never let herself succumb.

"So, Harriet," she said as her boss sat down next to her with two steaming mugs, "what exactly am I supposed to be scared of?"

Harriet laughed. "So direct."

"You said I should be worried."

"No, I said there was no need to be worried."

"I'm not worried."

"I can tell. Here, have your latte."

"What have you gone for?"

"I'm a black coffee type woman." Harriet lifted the mug to her lips.

"Strong, rich and potent?"

"Ha! And you and your latte are lovely, velvety and… and…"

"I'm not velvety."

"You look velvety."

Camila raised her eyebrows. "What's your third word?"

"Let's chat for a bit and see if I can find one?" Harriet was blowing gently on her coffee. "You really are quite something."

"You don't know me."

"And you don't know me, but here we are chit-chatting away. Okay, let me start; how's the day gone so far?"

"Good actually." Camila took a sip of her drink before relaxing into her seat. "I see your vision. I understand what you're trying to do. And if I'm honest I see now why the three of them aren't as buzzing as I assumed they should be. If they've been on this for a while I can appreciate how it might have got somewhat frustrating."

"And it's at this point that most people give up. But I'm not most."

"And I've got fresh eyes."

"You're going to invent the invention aren't you?"

"I'm going to try."

Harriet moved her mug towards Camila's in a cheers motion. "Right, that's business done, now how about pleasure? I want to get to know you, Camila."

Camila laughed. "Can I ask why?"

"You intrigue me."

"In one day?"

"In one moment. Watching you through that mirror yesterday was one of the most memorable things I've had happen in a long time."

"That can't be true. If the press reports are to be believed you've done it all. My friend Julie told me about an article in *Take A Break* magazine where you were abseiling down a waterfall into an alligator-infested swamp."

"Correct."

"So quite what you think I'm going to offer you is rather perplexing."

"I don't want anything from you, that's where the rumours begin."

"I've not heard any rumours."

"Yes, you have."

"I haven't." Camila took another sip of her drink before meeting Harriet's eyes. "But I get the impression you want to discuss these rumours with me?"

"I'm not solipsistic."

"I didn't say you were and I'm not even sure what that means."

"I was called it once on a show. They were being rude, trying to say I believed only me and my mind existed."

"You do seem to be quite the one woman show."

"Ha! You've definitely not heard the rumours then!"

"What are you alluding to? I know you're a gay woman and what you get up to is nobody's business but your own. Plus, I always take people on face value and you've been nothing but kind to me."

"Aren't you questioning why? Don't you worry that I could have ulterior motives?"

"Wouldn't that make me the egocentric?" Camila shrugged. "What an over-inflated sense of Me I must have to believe you fancy me just because you're gay and I'm female."

Harriet ran her fingers through her hair. "Hallelujah! I knew I was right about you! Such a fresh-thinking clear head."

"So you don't fancy me then?"

"Well obviously I do, but you shouldn't assume it."

Camila laughed. "You're the character, Harriet, not me."

"Says you, Miss: I'm happy to tease my new boss."

Taking a sip of her latte, Camila paused before speaking. "Do you have many friends?"

"Of course I do. What a strange question. Do you?"

"One. Julie Biggs, my next door neighbour."

"I'd like to meet Julie Biggs, your next door neighbour."

"No, you wouldn't!" Camila squealed. "Oh, you do make me laugh."

"And you make me laugh with your straight-to-the-point questions and if I'm honest, most of my friends are fair weather." Harriet fingered the gold rims of her glasses. "I've not got that one woman I share everything with."

"So you're single?"

"In the friendship stakes and I guess officially in the romance stakes." Harriet paused. "The lines can blur somewhat when you're gay. That's what causes the rumours."

"Never worry about what people think."

"It's hard when you're in the public eye."

"People still talk about you when you're not in the public eye. You wouldn't believe the gossip I heard when I fell pregnant."

"Try multiplying that by a million."

"It doesn't matter if there's one person talking about you or one hundred, it still hurts to the same extent."

"Goodness, I am being solipsistic, aren't I?"

"I've still got no clue what that means."

Harriet sat back, crossing her legs at the knee. "Tell me more about you."

Camila shrugged. "I was pregnant at nineteen, then again at twenty. Their dad, Mick, he's been around for most of it, in the loosest of fashions."

"He's not around now?"

"Not currently."

"You never married?"

"He never asked."

"And if he did?"

"Now? I'm not entirely sure."

"And there's no one else?"

"There's Julie."

"Who I'm going to meet later."

Camila laughed. "This is a fresh start for me. It's something new, and I'm happy."

"I can tell."

"So am I a project?"

Harriet gasped. "You *have* heard the rumours!"

"Just the odd comment."

"Right, let's clear this up. This is what I've been angling the conversation towards." Harriet nodded. "I see things in people. I like to bring them out of their shells."

"You think I'm a tortoise?"

"You're not a tortoise, no."

"So what do you see in me?"

"Something I've never seen before."

"Intriguing."

Harriet took a sip of her coffee. "Isn't it just."

"Are you going to build me up like Deana?"

"Oh goodness, what's she been saying?"

"Nothing and I'm not sure I need building up."

Harriet laughed. "You're right, I think it's you who's going to be teaching me a thing or two."

"I don't know how to abseil into a crocodile-infested lake."

"It was an alligator-infested swamp."

Camila moved her hand to her face to block the light that suddenly started to stream through the glass fronted building. "Lake, swamp. Why even do it in the first place?"

Harriet shrugged. "I completed my bucket list by the time I was twenty-five, so I made another... which I completed by thirty."

"And now? Crikey it's bright in here when the sun comes out."

"Now I don't have one. Shall we move?"

Camila peered out at the sky. "It's fine, the cloud's coming back." She smiled. "I've got a bucket list."

"And what's on yours?"

"Lots."

"Give me an example."

"Okay, I want to eat Thai food. I also want to skydive."

"You've never eaten Thai food?"

Camila shook her head.

"Tonight. We'll do both."

"What?"

"This evening. Tonight. I'll take you for Thai, then we'll go to iFly the indoor skydiving place."

"I can't."

"Why not."

"I've got to feed the boys."

"Making tea for two teenagers? I've never done that before. Maybe I've got the first entry on my new bucket list."

"Don't be ridiculous."

"I'm not. It'll be fun. I'll help you complete your list; you help me complete mine."

"Why?"

"Why not?"

"Because you're my boss and I only met you yesterday and I can't afford Thai food, let alone skydiving, even if it's indoors."

"Think of it as staff training."

"This is silly." Camila held on to her mug and stood up. "I'm going back to the umbrellas on shoes. It makes much more sense than this. Plus, my break's over."

"My office at five," said Harriet. "You only live once."

"No, thank you."

"You'll be there."

"I won't."

Harriet smiled. "We'll see."

CHAPTER THIRTEEN

"She said she wanted to test my boundaries!" squealed Camila towards her car's passenger seat where her mobile phone was lying on loud speaker.

Julie's voice was gasping from the other end of the connection. "Where is she?"

"Behind me! In her Lamborghini!" Looking in the rear-view mirror, Camila debated how they'd got to this point, where her boss was following her home in her sleek Lamborghini sports car as she bumped along in her banger. She looked away. She knew how they'd got to this point. Harriet had been right: she'd said yes. She'd gone to the office at the end of the corridor at five and said yes. Why had she said yes?

"Why did you say yes?!"

"I don't know." Camila gripped the steering wheel even tighter. "Why not?"

"Because it's bloody weird!"

"It is, isn't it?"

"Totally!"

Camila shook her head. "Quickly go and let yourself in. Make sure it's tidy."

"Your house is always bloody tidy!"

"Just go in, light the candle on the fireplace. Make sure it smells nice. Make sure the boys' bags aren't strewn all around the hall. Make sure—"

"Camila, I've got this. This is what friends are for."

"We're literally five minutes away."

"Five bloody minutes?! I'm going!"

Camila heard the phone cut off and looked once more in the mirror at the vision behind her. Harriet had switched her gold-rimmed glasses for dark shades and the evening sun was shining through the Lamborghini's low windscreen like a magical beam, illuminating Harriet as if she were the goddess of light. Camila gasped. What had she been thinking? It was one thing giving as good as she got in a bantering conversation, or fronting up to people in the world of work, but this was real life, this was her life and her life wasn't appropriate for the likes of Harriet or Harriet's Lamborghini.

Maybe she could nip upstairs when she got home and pretend one of the boys had an issue. An illness? Some homework that needed her help? But what if they weren't there? Was it their gym night tonight? Probably; it was always their gym night even if it had been their gym morning. Fine. Her washing machine had broken down. Or maybe the dishwasher? There was flooding in the kitchen. No. Harriet might offer to come and take a look. Keep the lie simple. She'd double-booked herself. Reaching down to the passenger seat, Camila clicked to redial Julie. She'd ask her to come round. Julie could pretend they were going out to the bingo. No, Harriet might want to join them. Julie had an AA meeting. No one would offer to join in with that.

Cursing, Camila squeezed the steering wheel as the phone went to voicemail. "Julie! It's weird! I don't want to go! Well, I do want to go, but it's too soon, which makes it weird, so when you see me pull in, you dash round and pretend we're going to an AA meeting, for you obviously not me, and I know you're not an alcoholic, well you might be, we probably both are, but pretend you've got a meeting and I've offered to come along for support, that way I can be all gutted that I've doubled-booked, but obviously my friend's AA meeting would take priority over a night out. Please, Julie. Make something up. A doctor's appointment that I've got to come along to? Just something. Please. Literally come over the second you see my car. I'm going. I'm almost home."

Hanging up, Camila took a deep breath. This was definitely the best solution. She should never have said yes; it was inappropriate if nothing else. Or was it? One woman being kind to another. One woman wanting to give experiences to the other. And it certainly wasn't the lesbian issue that was causing the trepidation. Sexuality didn't matter. Or did it? Was it clouding the issue to some extent? Or was it that she was Harriet's employee? Or the fact they'd only known each other a day? Yes, they seemed to get on, yes they were a similar age, and yes she'd always wanted to eat Thai and skydive, but not in the same evening and not on a whim. Things like this should be saved for, and built up, before you counted down to the big day and appreciated everything in its entirety. She shook her head. She actually had the chance to eat Thai and skydive. When would she realistically get the opportunity to do that again?

Pressing redial, she called Julie. "Dammit!" she shouted, as the phone went to voicemail. "Scratch that last message. I'm going. I'm just nervous. I've never been offered something so casually before. It just threw me. But I'm fine. I should go. You stay at home. I've got this." Nodding, she hung up. This was how life should be lived. You grab the bull by the horns. You say yes to adventure. You live each moment like it's your last. Glancing again in the rear-view mirror, Camila gasped: but doing it with Harriet made it so much more hair-raising. Not in a horrifying way. Yes, there was panic and slight agitation but not because of something bad. It was more a mixture of nerves, adrenaline and excitement. Butterflies. That's what it was. She had butterflies, and butterflies were meant to be good.

Turning into the cul-de-sac, Camila held her breath. This was it. There was no going back. Harriet was about to see who she really was: modest house, modest life, modest person, and if Harriet didn't like that, there was nothing she could do. Pulling into her driveway, Camila cursed at the bulk of Julie's bacon butty van. It was as if she was seeing it for the first time, and it truly was a clapped-out old eyesore. Oh well, she decided, as she pulled the key out of the ignition and got out of the car, this was her patch and she was proud of it. Or was she? Camila's eyes widened. Julie, or a dolled-up, off-on-a-hunt, jolly hockey sticks, country-bumpkin version of Julie, had just waltzed into the road.

Camila watched as her next door neighbour, now with arms in the air, guided Harriet's Lamborghini onto the pavement. All of the driveways could only accommodate one car and Harriet had been doing a good job of parking on the curving street, but Julie had taken it upon herself to act as if Harriet was landing a BA flight from JFK, directing the Lamborghini with flamboyant hand gestures. It wasn't this, however, that was causing the most shock. It was Julie's attire. She was dressed head to toe in tweed. All tweed. A tweed blazer buttoned up to the top, a tweed skirt that came to rest just below the knee and Burberry ankle boots that were no doubt fake – either way their tweed was yellow and clashed with the green tweed of the suit. The boots did however match the off-white silk gloves Julie was also sporting.

"Julie!" hissed Camila under her breath. "What are you doing? What are you wearing?"

Julie ignored her, moving instead to the driver's door of the Lamborghini. "Welcome," she said with a bow, before looking around for a clasp that would open the door.

"Stand back," mouthed Harriet through the window.

"What?" shouted Julie.

Camila dashed over to her crazed friend. "You have to stand back. It's a Lamborghini. I saw her getting into it earlier."

The pair watched as the scissor door rose like the wing of an insect. Julie moved in first with her hand outstretched. "Here, let me help you. That's very low down isn't it? I'm Julie. Could I have a picture please?"

Camila gasped. "Julie!"

"It's fine," said Harriet, pulling herself up from the seat. "Where do you want me?"

"No, I meant of the car. Do you mind if I sit in it?"

Camila gasped again. "Don't you dare!"

Julie continued. "If I sit down here in the driver's seat could you stand next to me, Harriet?" Pulling her phone from her tweed pocket, Julie passed it to Camila. "You take it. I'm getting in. Oh, this is wonderful. Camila take a picture! Quick! Look at me! Stand by the car, Harriet, so you're in the shot as well."

Camila looked at Harriet in apology.

"It's fine," Harriet was smiling, "take the picture."

Camila held up the phone and snapped.

"More than bloody one!" demanded Julie, now raising her gloved hands to the steering wheel as if she was driving the car at speed.

Camila snapped once more. "I'm so sorry about this. This is my friend Julie."

"We've met. Isn't she wonderful?" Harriet tapped on the roof of the car. "Julie, why don't you sit on the bonnet?"

The squeal was loud. "Can I?"

"It makes a good shot. Here, let me lift up both doors."

Julie got out of the car. "Incredible! It looks like a winged eagle!"

Camila watched the exchange open-mouthed. What on earth was going on? Her friend was lolling about on the bonnet, legs and arms akimbo. It looked like a tweed catalogue shoot gone wrong. That, or the start of a low-budget porn film.

"Don't just stand there! Take the picture!" Julie was laughing. "Look at us! It's me and Harriet Imogen Pearson off the telly. We're sprawled over her Lamborghini! Harriet, sprawl a bit more. Cock your leg up like me! That's it. Camila, quick take the picture!"

Camila slowly lifted the phone before clicking once. "Harriet, I really am sorry."

"It's fine!" said Harriet. "Right, shall we go in?"

"Follow me!" squealed Julie, hauling herself off the car and trotting straight towards Camila's front door.

Camila turned again to Harriet. "I really am—"

"Stop it. I love meeting new people and Julie's great fun." Clicking her car locked, Harriet continued. "And I don't mind having my picture taken." She paused. "But my leg wasn't too cocked was it? I have to be careful what gets shared out there."

"You looked fine. Julie was the one spread eagle." Camila turned to the house and her hallway that was now visible with the front door wide open, the boys' bags strewn all over the floor. "Julie!" she snapped, as her friend picked them up quickly.

"Is Julie your cleaner?" Harriet was frowning.

Julie cut in. "She bloody wishes! No, Camila asked me to have a straighten-up before you arrived. Come in, it's fine now."

Camila flushed. "I just asked for a quick check." She turned to her neighbour. "But I see you used the time to play dress-up instead."

Julie feigned offence. "I've been wearing this all day."

"Tweed?" said Camila. "In your bacon butty van?"

"I have a very posh customer."

"News to me. What are they called?"

"Figgy."

Camila tried not to laugh. "Stop being so silly." She turned to Harriet. "Please do come through. We'll go in the kitchen because I very much doubt my nice scented candle has been lit in the lounge."

"It hasn't," said Julie, "but Figgy's real. She comes to the van with her friend Queenie."

Camila led them into the kitchen. "Figgy and Queenie? And what do they order?"

"Fried bread, with a Fanta."

Camila couldn't help but laugh. "Which they eat in their tweed? Harriet, I'm sorry, please ignore this nonsense and sit down."

"Jodhpurs actually."

Harriet joined in. "It's fascinating. You're making me feel right at home. I knew a Figgy once."

Julie laughed. "I bet you did."

"Right," said Camila, turning to her friend. "Thank you very much for popping in but I think I can take it from here."

"Could I have my phone back please?"

Camila passed over the mobile.

Julie stayed where she was. "Wait, I've got messages."

Camila shared another apologetic look with Harriet before moving back into the hallway and shouting up the stairs to the boys announcing, if they hadn't heard already, that she was home. It was at this point that the sheer dread hit her. She could hear Julie's phone from where she was. The automated voicemail had just announced that Julie had two messages. "Julie!" she screamed.

"Mum?!"

"Wait, Michael!" gasped Camila, dashing back into the kitchen.

"Mum," said Michael coming down the stairs, "it's important. Cassie's here and we wondered—"

"Michael, wait!" Camila reached out and grabbed Julie's phone from its position in the crook of Julie's neck. It wasn't on speakerphone but the volume was loud enough to clearly relay the words of message. *"Julie! It's weird!"* she was saying, *"I don't want to go!"*

"What are you doing?" squealed Julie, standing up and grabbing the phone back.

"Turn it off," said Camila, trying to jab at the handset but accidentally clicking the loudspeaker button as Julie yanked it back, sending it slipping through her silk gloves and under the section of kitchen counter that was missing a baseboard.

The panicked voice was even louder. *"...dash round and pretend we're going to an AA meeting—"*

"Please don't listen to this!" gasped Camila, now on all fours.

"...pretend you've got a meeting and I've offered to come along and support, that way I can be all gutted that I've doubled booked—"

"La-la-la-la-la," Camila was shouting. "Michael! Quick! Come in here! Your arms are longer than mine; quick, reach down and get the phone!"

"Please, Julie. Make something up. A doctor's appointment that I've got to come along to? Just something. Please."

"I'm not an alcoholic!" gasped Julie to the occupants of the kitchen.

"I can't get it, Mum."

"Just reach, Michael, reach!"

"I'm not an alcoholic, Harriet." Julie was shaking her head. "I don't know why Camila would say that. I know I didn't come and clean her house like she asked me to but this is taking it too far."

"I think I've got it," winced Michael, now on his stomach on the kitchen floor. "Where don't you want to go, Mum?" he said, pulling the phone out and handing it over.

Camila stabbed the button to end the call.

"Mum?"

"Just shush," whispered Camila before turning around to the room. "Harriet," she nodded, "this is my eldest son, Michael."

Michael smiled. "Oh wow! Can I have a selfie?" He sprinted into the hall and yelled, "Cassie! Quick! Come and get a selfie. Bring my phone."

"Who's having selfies?" asked Ethan, walking into the kitchen and looking up from his iPad. "Neat!" he screamed. "It's you! Can I have a selfie as well?"

CHAPTER FOURTEEN

Closing the front door behind Julie, Camila heard giggles from upstairs. The boys and Cassie were no doubt excitedly poring over the selfies that Harriet had graciously posed for. Realistically, Harriet should have simply walked out. She'd heard the whole message. Everyone had heard the whole message and it was wholeheartedly embarrassing for each person involved. Apart from Julie. Julie didn't seem bothered at all. Camila shook her head. What had Julie said on the phone? *"That's what friends are for."* Yet she hadn't done what she had been asked to do. She'd used the time to dress up like a demented aristocrat and invent ridiculous stories about Figgy and her penchant for Fanta to ingratiate herself with a woman she'd moments before said was weird and full-on.

Taking a deep breath, Camila walked back into the kitchen. "There was a second message," she said, lifting her hands, ready to explain.

Harriet shrugged. "It doesn't matter."

"It does. I changed my mind. I said I *did* want to go. It's just been a hectic day and I was confused and frazzled and Julie wasn't helping."

"Julie seems to like me."

"Tell me about it!" Camila reached for a chair and sat down. "Forgive me. I'm a novice."

"A novice what? A novice friend? A novice socialiser? A novice with gay women?"

"It's not that."

"It obviously is. You'd never second guess a straight woman. You'd never debate whether to go somewhere or not."

"I probably would."

"You wouldn't."

Remembering all of the times she'd made fast friends with the women at playgroup, Camila looked away. They'd meet up the next day, sometimes the same afternoon. They'd slot into each other's calendars without a care in the world, just glad of the company, never once questioning whether it was peculiar to suddenly spend so much time with a stranger. Angling her chair so she was face on to Harriet, Camila nodded. "You're my boss."

"Not day-in-day-out and the set-up's not like that. Look, it doesn't matter. The last thing I want is to make you feel uncomfortable. I'm not weird. At all. I'm just someone who gives. I'm too giving in fact."

"I'm an idiot, aren't I?" Camila shook her head.

"It's fine. I've been here before."

"But I'm different."

"I thought you were."

Watching the eyes, Camila cursed herself. The connection was undeniable. What that connection was, she had no clue, and whether the general public would class it as strange, or too soon shouldn't matter; they had a bond; they were on the same level somehow. "I'm not a charity case."

"Where did that come from? I never said you were."

"Sorry, I didn't mean to say that. I was actually thinking that we should ignore what people say and just do what makes us happy."

"I'm not asking you to marry me, Camila! Honestly, this is getting too confusing even for me. I'm just a woman you've made a connection with, a connection I rightly or wrongly believed would bring us both some fun."

"But what am I adding to the pot?"

"This! Your neighbour. Your boys. They're such fun. Plus, we agreed you'd help me complete my new bucket list."

"Making tea for two teenagers?"

"And one of their girlfriends it seems." Harriet stood up. "So where do I start?"

"She's not his girlfriend. They're study buddies."

"You're sure about that? Do you have eggs?"

"Harriet, sit down, I can't have you making my children's tea."

"Yes, you can. Go and get changed. You can't wear your work suit for iFly. You need something comfortable. Trousers and top. Lace up shoes. When you're changed I want you to take a seat in the lounge. Light that infamous scented candle of yours. Just relax. I've got this."

"Have you got clothes to change in to?"

Harriet smiled. "So we're still going then?"

"If you'll still have me?"

Harriet opened the fridge door. "I was thinking of asking Julie if I could borrow some of her clothes. She's got my style spot on. And it doesn't look like you've got eggs."

Camila studied her boss's attire and laughed. There was nothing faux-aristocratic about her. She simply had style. A statement gold necklace that was accessorising a fitted black dress, heels that were clearly expensive and a longer length tailored jacket with simple collar that pulled the whole outfit together. The sight of her leaning into the small white fridge was quite something. "There's food in the freezer. Honestly, let me do it."

"No. Go. It's on my bucket list and I always achieve my bucket lists." Harriet smiled. "That's what you can do when you're changed. Sit in the lounge and write down ten things you'd like to achieve. I'll do the same in here. We can share our lists and discuss them en-route to Thai Rainbow."

"Thai Rainbow?" Camila smiled. Thai Rainbow was the posh restaurant she'd noticed in the upmarket shopping place in town, home to the likes of Harvey Nichols and Malmaison. The luxury complex had been pitched as a lifestyle destination and was somewhere she'd gone once, by accident, fast concluding it wasn't the place for her. All it had taken was a glance in a few windows and she was out of there. But it was the small restaurant, Thai Rainbow, where her gaze had lingered that little bit longer. The aromas spilling out of the open doors had been heavenly and the beautifully carved teak interior that was visible through pretty arched windows had looked other-worldly. Well, she had decided it must look like Thailand with its dainty flowers and intricate sculptures – one in particular of a mermaid and a swan still vivid in her memory. Either way the prices on the menu were ridiculous so she'd returned to her car and the retail park she'd intended to visit that housed a huge Primark, two H&Ms and three Greggs bakeries amongst the Poundlands and discount stores.

Giving in to Harriet's insistence, Camila made her way upstairs, pausing to listen outside Michael's room. It was quiet. Too quiet. She lifted her hand to knock but stopped herself. What if they were mid sum? She dropped her hand. But what if that sum was multiplication? Knocking quickly, she shouted. "All okay in there? Tea in half an hour." She had no clue what Harriet was cooking, but if she opted for freezer food then half an hour was about right. The door opened quickly and her son signalled her in.

"Everything okay?" she asked.

"Shhhh!" said Michael closing the door behind her.

"What?"

"That's Harriet Imogen Pearson!"

"I know."

"Shhhh!"

"What?"

"I hope you've apologised!"

"It was a misunderstanding, Michael."

Cassie got up from the bed. "Do you think she'd come to school and give a talk about her achievements? She's an incredible woman."

"That you insulted!" added Michael.

Camila looked at the route Cassie had taken. She'd risen from her seated position on the bed – that was covered in books – over the carpet, that was covered in folders, to their position at the door next to Michael's desk – that was strewn with stationary. It was fine, she concluded, nothing untoward was happening here. "Pardon?" she said, focusing back on the pair.

"You insulted her! She's Harriet Imogen Pearson."

"You knew I was working for her."

"I knew you were working at H.I.P but I didn't think she'd be there and I definitely didn't think she'd be in our house! She's amazing, Mum."

Camila couldn't help the squeak of disbelief her voice box emitted. It was the most animated she'd seen her son in a long time.

"What?" he huffed.

"That's the longest sentence you've said so far this year." She smiled. "What did you want me for earlier?"

"Oh. Cassie. Can she have tea?"

Camila turned to the pretty girl. "Of course you can. Harriet's cooking."

Michael spoke up again. "No way! Cassie, quick, add that to the Snapchat, this is so epic! Mum, you have to make friends. You've officially got the chance to be cool."

"Have I now?" said Camila, shaking her head as she questioned why she'd been the only person with any doubt in her mind. Julie had jumped on the Harriet bandwagon as had all of the kids and it sounded like most of Snapchat had too. "Well we're going out tonight. You'll be okay on your own?"

"Thank god she forgave you! Don't screw it up, Mum."

"Language!"

"What?"

Camila turned to Cassie. "Make sure your parents know where you are."

"They do. They're following the Snapchat story. My dad's asked if Harriet can come into the boxing club and give a talk about motivation and drive. And Jacob, the head boy—"

"Your boyfriend."

"Right, well, umm, he's the one who suggested she comes into school."

Camila watched her son turn and walk back to the bed. "I'll see what I can do," she said. "I'll get Julie to pop in and see how you are later on."

Michael sat down heavily, jolting the books on the duvet cover. "Ethan needs that, I don't."

"Either way she'll be in and out. I'll see you downstairs in a bit."

Exiting the bedroom, Camila tapped on the door opposite. "Ethan, can I come in?"

Her youngest son's arms reached out and yanked her into the room that was much tidier and not as musty smelling. "What are you doing up here?!" The hiss was disbelieving. "You can't leave her downstairs on her own. She *is* still here, isn't she? You haven't mucked it up even more have you, Mum? You do know who she is, don't you? This will get me huge cred at school. My selfie's already had fifty likes."

"I'm just checking I'm okay to go out tonight?"

"With her? Of course! Take loads of pictures. Send them to me. I'll Instagram them. You might even make it into the papers!"

"Why would I want to make it into the papers?"

"She's a star! You could be a star too!"

"Thanks a lot." Camila tutted. "I remember when you used to call me the brightest star in the sky? Remember? I used to call you my little twinkle star and you used to say—"

"Yeah alright, Mum, out you go."

Camila stepped back as her son forcibly removed her from the room. She turned to look at both doors that were now closed. "Right," she nodded, "I'll jump on that bandwagon as well."

CHAPTER FIFTEEN

Camila wasn't sure whether to laugh or cry at the way Harriet was driving her car. Harriet had declared it the second point on her new bucket list: drive a car that has traditional gears, something she claimed she'd not done since passing her driving test fifteen years ago. Camila chose to laugh. She couldn't help it. She'd been laughing from the moment she'd re-entered the kitchen on Harriet's call that "dinner was served." First of all, no one in their house called it dinner; it was tea. Teatime. Dinner gave the illusion it would be a posh meal and if Camila was honest, Harriet's concoction wouldn't even pass for an on-the-run, cobbled-together, end-of-the-week, eat-up-what's-left tea, of which she and her boys had eaten plenty. It was more of a – I've forgotten how old the children are and I've also forgotten the vegetables type tea. There had been three plates showcasing three identical food-faces. Four fish fingers made up the spiky hair, two faggots were the eyes, there was a sliced faggot for the nose and a Findus crispy pancake for a smiling mouth. Camila had burst out laughing when she'd walked in, quickly hoping that Harriet's responding look of hurt wasn't genuine. Either way the boys and Cassie had buoyed the atmosphere, reacting to the meal with cheers of excitement and more selfie snapping, leaving Camila to question whether in fact she'd become the mother who cooked boring teas.

"What are you are laughing at?" asked Harriet.

"Keep your eyes on the road! There's another speed bump!"

"I'm so high up I can't see them. It's like I'm driving a minibus."

"A minibus that has gears, remember."

"I'm used to pulling a paddle. This thing's an actual wooden stick. I haven't had a car with a clutch for so long." Harriet dropped down a gear with a crunch. "There she goes."

Camila laughed again. "I don't know why I'm laughing, this isn't funny. I can't afford a new gearstick."

"Gearbox?"

"I don't know, just whatever you're destroying with your driving. And watch that bump! The suspension!" Camila held on to the corners of her seat. "Seriously, Harriet, I can't afford a new car."

"I'm trying! I'm not doing it deliberately, just like I didn't deliberately put so many of those faggoty things on their plates. Well I did because I needed two eyes and a nose, but I didn't know there was a two faggot rule or that there was minced beef inside those Findus crispy pancakes as well making the whole thing rather meat heavy."

Camila laughed again but in reality none of this was funny; she still wasn't sure whether Harriet was taking her for a fool. Here she was driving her old Citroen Picasso whilst wearing a velour tracksuit from Tesco. Camila decided to address it. "I just said faggots are one meal, as are fish fingers and Findus crispy pancakes. You used three night's worth of meals in one sitting."

"I thought it was fun."

"It was, and this is, as long as you're not taking the Mickey. My shopping bills are expensive enough as it is and there were vegetables that needed eating today."

"Kids don't like vegetables! They like faggot faces!"

"Stop it," laughed Camila. "I'm being serious."

"So am I! Didn't you see how they wolfed down those balls of meat. I'm adding that to my bucket list. Number eleven: eat a faggot-based meal. I bet you can put them in the slow cooker and make a faggot casserole. And the aroma coming from those minced beef and onion pancakes, well."

"You're treading a fine line, Harriet."

"What do you mean?"

"This chat. And look at you! You're dressed in my Tesco tracksuit."

"It's velour. It could be mistaken for Juicy Couture."

"But why are you wearing it?"

"Because you came downstairs in that lovely shirt and jeans and asked if it was too formal for skydiving, to which I asked what else you had and you replied: a Tesco tracksuit or some leggings which you felt would be too *informal* for Thai Rainbow, but which I then added onto my bucket list: Wear some supermarket clothing."

"But that's taking the Mickey out of me!"

"It's not! It's doing things I've never done before and I think I look good!"

Camila studied the driver of the car. Harriet did look good; she looked fantastic in fact. She'd kept her statement gold necklace on and her high heels, transforming the £7 outfit into something a pop star might wear at an RnB award show and pairing that with her wonder woman hair and made up face she looked red carpet ready. "You said we needed lace-up shoes for skydiving."

"I can borrow yours. We go in separately."

"Are we the same size?"

Harriet nodded. "I checked your shoes in the hall. That means you can borrow my red stilettos too."

"The ones you're wearing tomorrow?"

"Oooh, do I notice a cheeky tone in your voice? Right. I never need to be dared twice."

Camila continued. "Let me guess, swapping shoes with another woman is on your bucket list too?"

Harriet's face screwed up in mock disbelief. "Of course I've swapped shoes with another woman before!"

"I didn't know."

"It's a lesbian must! Morph into the person you're dating with immediate effect. Share outfits, share shoes—"

"Share beds."

"Ha! Where did that come from?"

"So let's get this straight—"

"Another good one." Harriet was laughing.

"You've already achieved three of the things on your new bucket list. Your bucket list that's about half an hour old. Cook, car, clothes."

"Correct. And your list's about to get started as well." Harriet nodded. "Because the valet parking's just here. Eating Thai food, we're a-go."

****

Camila was cringing. How ridiculous that they'd asked a valet to park their car. Their Citroen Picasso with its wooden gearstick. And he'd definitely given them a look. It wasn't quite a sneer, more of a smirk. She turned back and watched her car being driven away.

"I'm telling you he didn't give us a look," said Harriet, reaching out for Camila's arm, guiding them towards the arched entrance that was glittering with fairy lights. "I can see you're still stewing."

"I'm not."

"What are you thinking about then?"

"We could have used the normal car park."

"The valet's easier. We're right here at the entrance."

"It's more expensive."

Harriet halted their walk. "And now you're taking the Mickey out of me."

"Of course I'm not!"

"Exactly. You do things one way, I do things another and neither of us are used to each other's way of doing things. When you're with me I'll get the bill."

"What and when you're with me you get to wear crap clothes? It hardly feels like a fair exchange."

"You think I look crap?"

"No, you look great! Incredible in fact."

"Exactly and I'd have never known about the wonders of supermarket clothing if it wasn't for you."

"You're teasing me."

"I'm not!"

"But you're not going to start wearing £7 tracksuits now are you?"

"And you're not going to start using the valet parking. Look, we can go back if you want to. We don't have to do any of this, I just thought it would be fun."

"It is."

"So stop over-analysing everything!" Harriet yanked on the arm and re-started their walk under the archway and through to the posh shopping destination's concourse. "Life's short, you should live it."

"That's what I'm trying to do."

"So say yes in the future, say yes to everything."

Camila raised her eyebrows. "Everything?"

"Oooh, you've got a naughty streak in you, madame."

"Are bosses allowed to call employees *madame*?"

"I didn't put *that* much tone on it! And it's not like I'm directly your boss. Fine, I'll stop that as well if you like."

Camila smiled. "No. I think I can handle your flirting."

"My flirting?"

"Yes. You're the gay woman."

"Who doesn't fancy every woman I see."

"Oh."

"See! It's you!"

Camila laughed. "You're right, this is fun. Come on, Thai Rainbow's this way."

"Hmm, you know the way? I think you're much more in-tune than you're letting on."

"Laaaaaa!" Camila sang the pitch perfect note with gusto before smiling at her partner in crime. "I'm in tune. Did you get it? Tell me you got it?"

CHAPTER SIXTEEN

Taking in the opulence of their surroundings, Camila squeezed the arm that was linked into her own. She could see Thai Rainbow tucked away in the corner of the concourse next to a pillared walkway that led on to one of the posh hotels. It could be suggested that opulence wasn't the right word to describe what was essentially a shopping centre, but when the shops consisted of jewellers with big glittering displays in their windows and fashion boutiques whose frontages looked like the gateway to Paris or Milan, you'd be forgiven for buying into the promotional spiel that the 'lifestyle destination' was indeed an 'oasis of luxury.'

Camila squeezed again. She was excited, excited to be with her partner in crime. She paused her thought; why was that phrase jumping to the forefront of her mind? Yes, opulence was there to describe their location, possibly because it was a buzz word she'd heard associated with the place… but her and Harriet? Partners in crime? Where had that come from? She smiled. It had come from her stomach. The butterflies. The excitement. The feeling that she was sixteen all over again, off on some illicit adventure. She laughed. How sad must her life be if a trip to a restaurant could be such a thrill?

"What's funny?" asked Harriet.

"Excitement levels are high."

"Really? Oh, Camila, you are incredibly sweet."

"I think I'm a bit of a dork. I can't stop smiling."

"It's the company."

"You might be right." Camila couldn't help it. Yes, she should probably play it cool with Harriet: one because she was her boss, two because Harriet was a gay woman and as much as she said that didn't matter, it would be wise not to give her the wrong impression, and three because they'd only just met; but there was something about their connection that made her want to be open and honest. She was enjoying herself. She was excited. She was feeling like a teenager all over again. "Are you sure I look smart enough?"

"I'm the one wearing the tracksuit."

"I think that tracksuit's wearing you. That's what they say about couture clothing, isn't it? The clothing wears you?"

"If I'm honest, it's started to get a bit static."

Camila laughed.

"No, I'm serious, look. It's sticking to me. Like suction wrapping."

Glancing down, Camila couldn't help but notice the outline of Harriet's strong thighs as she walked. She was about to comment when her eyes were drawn to the outline of Harriet's intimate area.

"Stop looking! I can feel it getting sucked right in there!"

Glancing away, Camila tried not to blush.

"And these shoes are making me trot like a camel too!"

Camila kept her eyes forward. "Do camel's trot? They have toes don't they? I don't think toes trot."

"Very funny." Harriet yanked the clinging velour fabric from between her legs, aerating it with a couple of puffs before letting it go. "Dammit! It's just pinged right back in there!"

"Can I help?"

"Yes, Camila, pick it out and pull me along like it's a lead."

"Really?"

"No!" Harriet paused. "Do you have any hairspray? It stops the static."

"There's a Boots back there."

"Perfect." Harriet spun them around before quickening their pace. "We'll just use a tester can."

"Hairspray doesn't come in tester cans."

"Everything does! Can't you remember going into Boots before school and putting on a whole face of makeup for free?"

"No!"

"You really haven't lived, have you?"

"It appears not."

"Come on then, you could do with a bit more blusher if I'm honest."

"Won't people recognise you?"

Harriet halted their walk and lifted her arms to their surroundings. "There's no one here."

"Well there is." Camila signalled to the few lazy shoppers moving in and out of the boutiques and nodded at the couple who were laughingly pulling their suitcases towards the hotel's walkway. Admittedly everyone's pace was leisurely, a far cry from the frantic march you'd see at most shopping centres, as if the people who could afford to come here didn't have a care in the world.

Harriet continued. "I'm like Deborah Meaden from *Dragon's Den*. I'm not cool enough to be stopped in the street."

"You're far from Deborah Meaden-like. My kids couldn't take enough snaps of you!"

"Because I was there. They wouldn't chase me down if they saw me here."

"They've never been here."

"Okay, here's an example. I go and give a talk in a school and they all want pictures. The same kids then see me in the street and ignore me."

"Because they've already got the pictures."

"No. I'm not a pop star or an actress. People are only interested in pop stars and actresses."

"You're a reality star."

"Ouch!"

Camila nudged Harriet's arm. "Because you're such a great business woman." She nodded towards the blue and white sign of the pharmacy. "Come on. And I didn't mean the cheap and tacky reality shows, but you're on TV and you're known for being on TV."

"Because I'm a business woman."

"Yes."

"Good." Harriet shrugged. "People do recognise me sometimes and they do come up and chat but it's not something that stops me doing what I want. Plus, this is Boots. No one's ever approached me in Boots."

"I'd approach you in Boots."

"Would you?"

"Actually no, but I might follow you a bit to see what you're buying and then gossip about it with Julie."

"I'm not buying anything, I'm using the testers. Come on."

Following Harriet into the store, Camila smiled. This was exciting. Not simply because she was hanging out with Harriet Imogen Pearson, but because she was going on a girly outing to Boots. Yes, times had changed and her boys probably had just as many products as any daughters might have had, but the boys didn't seem to take joy in choosing the products and they didn't want to choose the products with their mother, or discuss them, or try them on.

Harriet pointed. "Here we go, hairspray."

Camila watched as Harriet reached for the green can on the top shelf. "What are you going to do?"

Harriet pulled back the waistband of her tracksuit bottoms and sprayed.

"You can't do that!"

"I know." Harriet shook her head. "I can't get them back far enough. It's just gone all over my fingers. I need to spray it on the inside front legs of the fabric."

"Can't you just put the can down there?"

"It's huge! They'll think I'm shoplifting. What's that down your trousers, Miss Pearson? Oh, just a supersized can of four hundred mil Silvikrin shine and hold hairspray."

Camila tried not to laugh. "Can I help?"

"Yes, pull my trousers back as far as you can."

"I can't!"

"You can. Just yank at the waistband on three. Quickly, you'll need to get your fingers down there."

Camila glanced up and down the hair products aisle. The shop seemed to be empty. "With two hands?"

"All of your fingers inside the hem, yank back and I'll blast it."

Reaching out to the tracksuit bottoms, Camila pulled gently on the drawstring.

"Just get your fingers in there! I'll need two hands to hold onto this big boy! Ready? One, two…"

Camila slid her fingers inside the velour fabric, making contact with the soft skin of Harriet's stomach. She paused. Harriet was silent. "Are you going to say three?"

"In a minute."

Laughing, Camila looked up at the pretty blue eyes made even more beautiful by the gold framing of the glasses. "You're teasing me."

"You're the one with your hands down my trousers."

"Right, I'm stopping."

"No! Yank back, on three. Three."

Camila laughed again. "I can't."

"Get your fingers in there and yank!"

"I'm laughing. You lose all your strength when you're laughing."

"You're not even trying!"

"I am!" Pulling back on the bottoms, Camila's laugh morphed into a high-pitched giggle at the underwear that came into view. Black fabric and see-through. Sexy, and certainly not from a supermarket. And while a giggle wasn't the appropriate response when faced with such lingerie, she was glad she'd emitted a giggle and not a gasp.

"Further back."

Camila yanked again, bringing Harriet's strong thighs into view.

"That's it! Now let me spray this bad boy."

"EXCUSE ME, ladies!"

Camila released her grasp pinging the trousers back into place, which in turn knocked the large can of hairspray from Harriet's hands.

"WHY is there a can of hairspray down your trousers?"

Camila stared at the woman before turning slowly to see the outline of the supersize can of shine and hold hairspray where it had slid down to a resting position just above Harriet's right knee.

Harriet lifted her hands to her hips and adjusted her stance. "Pardon?"

Camila watched the can slide down to the ankle.

"There is a CAN of HAIRSPRAY down your trousers."

"Oh right." Harriet bent down in an attempt to pull it out next to her high heel. "I'm terribly sorry."

Camila watched as Harriet struggled with the hem.

"This tracksuit's quite tight at the ankle, would you mind giving me a hand, Patricia."

"Patricia?" Camila looked to the shop assistant's name tag. It read: Anne.

"Yes, *Patricia*, would you mind giving me a hand?"

Camila cottoned on. "Oh right. Yes. No problem... Gretel."

Harriet spluttered. "Gretel?"

Crouching in front of Harriet, Camila couldn't stop her shakes of laughter. "I like the name, Gretel," she whispered, unsure whether Harriet could hear through her own giggles.

"I can't... get it... out!" Harriet was gasping.

Camila tried to tug on the tight ankle band, but her strength was limited by the effort of suppressing her laughs.

Harriet took hold of Camila's hand and looked her in the eye. "You're going to have to go in from the top, Patricia."

"LADIES! Please!"

"Me?" gasped Camila.

"Yes you, Patricia." Harriet yanked open the waistband. Camila rose from the floor and stared at the see-through knickers once more.

The shop assistant clapped her hands. "I know you, Gretel. I'm sure I know you from somewhere. Have you been caught shoplifting before? I never forget a face."

Using the slight distraction, Camila dived forwards and down, reaching into the tracksuit bottoms, trying her best to ignore that her face was rubbing against the silky lingerie and warm tummy.

"Oooo Patricia, be careful," said Harriet with a giggle, "you're breathing on me."

Camila pulled out the can. "I am not." She turned to the lady. "I'm so sorry, here you go."

Harriet nodded. "It fell down there. Complete accident. Come on, Patricia, let's go and try on some blusher."

Camila coughed. "Gretel, I think my cheeks are flushed enough as they are."

"You're right, my dear Pat-A-Cake-Poo, shall we make hay while we can?"

"WAIT! I do know you."

"Toodle-oo," continued Harriet, grabbing Camila by the hand and trotting her out of the store.

"Pat-A-Cake-Poo?" gasped Camila, glancing over her shoulder at the shop assistant who was holding the can of hairspray at arm's length as she cursed their departure.

"It's endearing. You're Patricia, my little Pat-A-Cake-Poo." Harriet quickened their pace. "You, however, with an unlimited choice of names at your fingertips opted for Gretel. Do I look like a Gretel? Do you think of me as a Gretel?"

"She knows you!"

"She doesn't."

"What about CCTV!"

"You were the one in the compromising position." Harriet pointed ahead. "Come on, look, Thai Rainbow are opening their doors." She nodded. "And you'll be pleased to know my cling issues have gone, along with the camel toe."

Camila didn't follow the finger that was pointed towards the intricately carved wooden doors of the restaurant, instead she glanced at Harriet's crotch. "Well worth it then."

"That's what they all say."

Camila shook her head. "You're trouble aren't you?"

"Says you."

"What?"

"You gave me clothing that clings. Was it deliberate? Did you want to see my outline?"

"I saw more than your outline, old Gretel."

"Is that what you thought when you saw it? Old Gretel?"

Camila laughed loudly.

"Shush! We're going in, they do actually know me in here."

"They know you in Boots now as well."

"Shush!"

Camila looked towards the doors that were now wide open, the aromas from the restaurant already wafting their way. "Why are they all just standing there?"

"Shush," said Harriet guiding them past the sculpture of the mermaid and the swan and into the beautifully decorated restaurant.

Camila froze as the group of employees burst into a rapturous applause. Why were they clapping? Who were they clapping? She glanced around; she and Harriet were the only ones there. She smiled. They were still clapping. Should she bow? What was Harriet doing? Harriet was curtsying! She should curtsy! Lowering her head, Camila extended her right leg behind her left, bending at the knee as she lifted an invisible skirt.

"What are you doing?" hissed Harriet.

"I'm curtsying because you curtsied."

"I was adjusting these trousers. The ankle's still not right after you went fishing around down there."

"You didn't curtsy?"

"No, I didn't curtsy!"

Camila looked around at all the smiling faces, the hands still clapping with force. "Why are they clapping?" she whispered. "Did they see our show in Boots?"

"The restaurant's just opened."

"And?"

"You've never been clapped at before?"

"Not like this."

"It's a thing."

"Where?"

"Here, and when you're on holiday, you know, they open the restaurant and you're the first ones there so they clap."

"That doesn't happen at Butlin's Bognor Regis." Camila smiled awkwardly as she glanced around. "Do we just stand here?"

"No, I told you we need to shush. They won't interrupt us while we're talking."

Camila stayed quiet and waited for the clapping to die down.

"Harriet, good to see you again. Do come though."

"Thank you, Kasem, it's good to be back."

Following the lead, Camila suddenly jumped at the sea of hands that swished together in the same direction, signalling them into the restaurant. She curtsied automatically. She couldn't help it.

CHAPTER SEVENTEEN

Playing with the stem of her wine glass as she looked at the menu, Camila felt herself drawn more to the colourful border that intertwined beautiful dancing women with bejewelled elephants than the list of dishes on offer. If she were honest, the idea of scantily clad women using elephants' trunks as skipping ropes made more sense than the words on display. There was: Por Pia, Thung Thong, Tom Yung, Plar Gung and there wasn't a single explanation in sight. Taking a sip of her wine, Camila nodded before swallowing. "They sound like wrestlers."

Harriet laughed. "What?"

"Gai Yang. Oh, that could be you! Gai Yang takes on Moo Pad." Camila pointed with her glass back towards the restaurant's entrance. "Moo Pad could be that woman from Boots."

"I'd beat her."

"Yes, then you'd take on me. Pla Chu-Chee."

"No, I think you're down here." Harriet tapped on the menu. "Plain noodles."

"Oh wow! It actually says plain noodles. I'll take the plain noodles."

"No, you won't."

"I will. I don't know what anything else is. You can always tell if it's a posh restaurant because it doesn't have an English translation which keeps riff raff like me away."

"You're scared of the menu?"

"Terrified."

"You're not."

"If I came here alone I'd quickly realise this wasn't for me and head back over to Boots for a sandwich deal. You know the one with the packet of crisps and a drink."

"You'd rather have a sandwich deal than eat here?"

"You're right, this is on my bucket list. I'm doing this. But could you order for me? And my wrestling name wouldn't be plain noodles. It would be…" Camila scanned the menu once more. "Oooh: Crying Tiger."

"You'd be a crying kitten if you got in the ring with me."

"Can I have the Crying Tiger please?"

Harriet pushed up her glasses and continued to read. "No it's just a steak with tamarind sauce and chips, I've had it before. I want you to experience traditional Thai food. Couldn't you tell from the name that Crying Tiger would be the one gimmick on the menu?"

Camila nodded slowly before saying: "Noooo."

Harriet laughed. "You're very funny, do you know that?"

"I'm not trying to be funny."

"Well you are. Right, shall we order?" With a tiny movement of her head, Harriet had Kasem's attention once again. "Thank you, we'll have two Tom Yums to start with, chicken please, not prawn."

Camila smiled in support of the choice.

"And we'll also have the Rainbow Platter of canapés. Then we'll have a Gaeng Khiew Wan and a Gaeng Daeng, again both with chicken, and one portion of Khao Ma-Praw and Pad Khee-Mao Gai."

"Certainly, and more wine?"

Harriet nodded. "Yes, this is lovely; a bottle please."

Camila smiled as the waiter walked away before turning her attention to Harriet. "Aren't you driving?"

"I can have one."

"You've had one."

"No, I'm having one. I still have half a glass left, but it's always nice to have the bottle."

"You're going to get me drunk, make me eat gay food and throw me out of an aeroplane aren't you?"

"What do you mean gay food? Thai food's not fancy."

"No! Gay-Deng, Gay-Weng, Gay-Mauw-Chow."

"Mauw-Chow? Now that *could* be gay." Harriet was smiling. "There are absolutely no planes involved with indoor skydiving."

"But we're still doing it on a stomach full of Thai food and wine?"

"I like to live life."

Camila laughed. "I can see you do, and I'm only teasing you about... you know."

"My drinking problem?"

"No! The gay jokes. Do you have a drinking problem?"

"Of course not!" Harriet was laughing. "And I like that you tease me about my sexuality."

"I'm not sure I'm teasing you. I'm just going for the easy laughs."

"They're actually quite funny, and no one does it anymore. Maybe they're too scared of who I am, or maybe it's political correctness?"

"Oh, I hope I haven't crossed a line?"

"Of course not, you're funny." Harriet smiled. "I find you funny. There's something about the way you smile, Camila. There's a naughtiness in you. A cheekiness. It's like you've got a secret smile, but I see it; it's like you're sharing it with me."

"Hmmm, well no one's ever called me funny before."

"It's in your top three. You're funny, cute and intelligent."

"In that order?"

"Yes."

Camila paused for a second. "Okay, I'll take that."

"So would I."

"But what happened to velvety?" Camila raised her eyebrows and smiled over the rim of her wine glass as she studied her dinner companion. "Okay, you're... right, let me see."

"Why are you looking all sexily at me over your glass of wine?"

"Just being me."

"Ha! See! You're hilarious."

"Hilarious didn't make my top three though, did it? Right, Harriet Imogen Pearson, you're complex, you're intriguing and you're..."

"Give me a pretty, or a beautiful."

"I don't tend to categorise women like that, but okay, you're stunning."

115

"Oooh, I like that, but just so you know, I'm not particularly complex."

"You are!" Camila gasped and returned her glass to the table. "You're here with me when you could be anywhere with anyone. I have no clue what's going on."

"That's the simplest choice I've made all week."

"Oh, that's nice."

"I am nice."

Sitting up straighter, Camila felt emboldened by the wine. "Okay then, and I'm only asking it because you alluded to it, but are you a player? With women?"

"Yes."

"Ha! Where's the denial?"

"I always respond to an honest question with an honest answer."

Camila nodded. "I know what we can do. Let's play never have I ever."

"Why?"

"Because this is fun and I feel like I'm reliving my youth."

Harriet shook her head. "Never have I ever is too limiting. Let's just take it in turns to ask each other questions that we have to answer openly and honestly."

"Deal. You go first."

Harriet lifted her glass and twisted the stem between her fingers. "Right. Why did you say you don't categorise women based on appearance?"

"I categorise them based on name. The Harriet's are quite haughty."

"Are we?"

"The name is, yes."

Harriet smiled. "I was actually asking why you feel uncomfortable gifting another woman with the beautiful or gorgeous tag?"

"I'm not sure I do feel uncomfortable about it."

"You find women attractive then?"

"I didn't say that and how many questions is this?"

"Okay, sorry, your go."

"Right. What was your first impression of me?"

Harriet took a sip of wine before responding. "Honestly?"

"Of course honestly."

Another sip was taken before the glass was returned to the table. "I watched you in that focus group and I fell in love."

"You did not!"

"Not in the traditional sense of the word admittedly, I just knew there was something special about you." Harriet smiled with her eyes. "I knew I had to follow you out. I knew I had to get to know you. I knew I had to invite you for dinner. I haven't got to where I am today by missing moments. I trust my gut. I go on the adventure. I live life."

"So you had a plan?"

"I just trust my instinct, Camila. People are so hung up nowadays on what they should say, how they should say it, what they should do, who they should do it with. I like to *not think* sometimes and be the person who *doesn't worry* if they double text, or makes the first move," she smiled, "or says more than they should."

"See! This is so intriguing and it *is* complex!"

"It's not. The complex people are the ones who second guess. The ones who debate the ins and outs of friendships, like you and that spiel on the phone."

"But I'm here."

"So there's hope for you yet."

Camila laughed. "And what do you hope for me?"

"Is that an official question?"

"Yes."

"I hope we have fun. That's what life's all about."

"Is it?"

"Yes." Harriet shrugged. "What do you think life's all about? What's your life motto?"

"Crikey, all this before starters. Pass me the wine, I need a top up."

Harriet filled both glasses. "Shall we get a car for the rest of the evening? I'll send someone to collect yours."

"Said like it's the easiest thing in the world."

"It is."

Camila nodded. "Fine, we're living your life tonight, so let it be."

"I like that song." Harriet gently rocked her body as she sung the line quietly. "It's so simple, yet so profound. What do you think Paul McCartney was meaning? Let it be. Just let it be."

"Is that a question?"

"It can be and it'll probably give me your answer to my previous question as well."

Camila lifted her glass and peered into it. "You're too smart for me. I'm lost already."

"Okay, let me re-phrase. Do you accept what's what in life and just let it be, or do you strike out on your own and live the life you want… the life you make?"

"I think it's a mixture of both. But I do believe you should leave your problems in the past and move on with things, which is what that song's actually about."

"Do we have a secret Beatles fan?"

"No, I read it in Julie's *Take A Break* magazine once. There was an article on mis-heard lyrics and the true meaning of songs. His mum died and it was about that."

"Wow. You just taught me something. I didn't know that."

"It's hardly momentous."

"I think you're going to teach me a lot, Camila."

"Don't tease me."

"I'm not! We're going to be good for each another."

Camila smiled. "Fine. Well guess what. You want more knowledge? The lyric wasn't: *We built this city on sausage rolls.*"

Harriet burst out laughing.

"That was a joke by the way."

"I know it was! Oh, Camila, you really are great."

"And you're easy to please."

"Was that your first impression of me?" Pushing back and crossing her legs, Harriet re-positioned herself on her side of the table. "In fact what *was* your first impression of me? My question."

"That you're easy to please."

Harriet laughed again.

"It's true. I've just been myself and here you are lapping it up."

"Should I tone it down?"

"No, I'm flattered. It's fun."

"See. The true meaning of life."

"Easy to do after the bills are paid."

"Well, yes, but…"

"But nothing." Camila turned her attention to the sculpture of the mermaid and the swan. They were still the only couple in the restaurant and she could hear the water trickling down the structure as it changed colour over the glittering lights. She shrugged. "It's much easier to have fun when you don't have any worries, you have to admit that."

"Everyone has worries, they're just different for each person."

Camila returned her eyes to Harriet. "Hmmm, should I get the limo to pick me up or the Jag?"

"Hey, we agreed we're not allowed to tease each other's lifestyles while we live them."

"Sorry." Camila sat up and spoke with a smile. "So, my last question before the starter arrives, which I can see over your shoulder is on its way, is…" she waited until the platter was just above Harriet's shoulder before leaning forward and whispering: "Have you ever had sex with a straight girl?"

"Camila!" Harriet lurched backwards and almost knocked the platter out of the waiter's hand.

"What?" said Camila, smiling before shrugging. "I think Julie wants to give it a whirl."

✳✳✳✳

"Julie?" Harriet was still shaking her head as she passed the proper soup spoon over to Camila. "Julie? You tease."

"It's not this silver spoon?" Camila was frowning at the cutlery.

"No, that's the dessert spoon; you use this spoon for the soup. It's like a small ceramic ladle. Watch." Harriet picked up her own implement. "You scoop up some soup, then you can use your fork for the chicken," she paused as she stabbed into the spoon before chewing the small chunk of meat and swallowing, "and then if you want you can lift the spoon and sip the normal way… or," Harriet turned the spoon's handle to her mouth and tipped backwards, "the Thai way. Did you see how the soup ran down the handle? It's got a groove in it like the banks of a river."

"That can't be right. What if a piece of chicken rolls down and hits you in the face?"

"You've already eaten the chicken from the spoon with your fork."

"They don't have chopsticks?"

"Not in a Thai restaurant, no." Harriet laughed. "You're good with chopsticks but you're worrying about a spoon?"

"You're sure you do it like that?"

"You're changing the subject; we're talking about Julie." Harriet nodded. "Go on, just try it."

Scooping some of the clear aromatic liquid into the deep spoon, Camila made sure she avoided the chicken, she wanted to taste the soup first, plus it would be easier to eat the chicken from the bottom of the bowl instead of jabbing a spoonful of soup with a fork that was bound to cause splashage. She looked up. Harriet was watching her. "Carry on with yours."

"I want to experience your first taste of Thai with you."

"I'm only sipping some soup."

"Down the handle."

Camila looked at the grooved run, it looked plausible. She lifted it to her lips. "Don't watch."

"I'm watching."

She tipped the spoon backwards.

Harriet nodded. "I'm imagining Julie."

Laughing as she gulped, Camila choked on the chilli infused liquid as it hit the back of her throat, inhaling the spicy hot fumes before swallowing awkwardly. She gasped. She couldn't breathe.

"Are you okay?"

Camila tried to inhale, her windpipe reacting in self defence to stop any more of the ridiculously spicy soup entering her system. She sucked in a tiny bit of air.

"You sound like Darth Vader."

Camila shook her head; she honestly couldn't breathe.

"Here, have some wine."

She wheezed again, her eyes now watering with the fumes. She was half laughing, half dying, but it wasn't funny at all. The tiny amounts of air being drawn in were all that were keeping her alive.

"Shall I feed it to you?" Harriet lifted the glass.

Camila shook her head as she held on to the table. She just needed to focus, and relax. She made another Darth Vader noise.

"That sounded promising."

"Stop... it," she managed between constricted, now laughing, gasps, trying her best not to draw employee attention their way. Yes, she was choking, but it would subside soon, it was only a bit of clear liquid after all.

"It's quite spicy isn't it?"

"It just..." wheeze, "went down..." wheeze, "the wrong..." wheeze, "way."

"Have a good cough."

Camila was now having to deal with a fit of the giggles as well as no air. She angled her chair away from the table. She needed to compose herself.

"Breathe through your nose."

Camila shook her head, there were spicy fumes up there too. She focused, managing to take in a bit more air. She focused again, her windpipe gradually relaxing. Managing to clear her throat as best she could, she nodded as she turned back to the table. "All... better," she croaked.

"You sound like Joe Pasquale."

Camila coughed again. "Thank you... for your... help."

Harriet smiled. "I'm sorry, are you okay? It is quite spicy isn't it? You don't have to eat it if you don't like it."

"Rather... embarrassing," said Camila, relieved that her voice was almost sounding back to normal.

"You styled it out well."

"Let me try it again." Camila coughed. "I didn't actually manage to taste it that time."

"Maybe just sip from the spoon. It does tend to shoot down the handle quite quickly doesn't it?"

Camila gasped as she saw Harriet sipping her soup normally. "Did you…" she coughed, "do that… deliberately!"

"I didn't think you'd choke."

Camila cleared her throat. "It was your Julie comment!"

"Well your comment to me nearly knocked the platter out of the waiter's hands. Now we're even."

Camila managed a proper sounding laugh. "Oh you're childish, aren't you?"

"The best people are."

Scooping up some more liquid, Camila paused before sipping carefully and swallowing slowly. She nodded. "Spicy and hot… but lovely."

"Julie?"

"Enough! Don't tease me when I'm eating this. I need to concentrate."

"So would I if I was with Julie."

"Harriet, seriously."

"Sorry, she's your friend. I wouldn't anyway. She's not my type. She's too horsey."

"She's never usually horsey. I've never seen that outfit before."

"That's what happens. People think they need to change for me." Harriet reached out for a satay stick that was poking up like a peacock's tail from the platter of canapés. "They think they have to impress me or alter who they are for me to be interested in them. That's why I like you. You're just doing you." She took a bite and smiled. "And I'd do you too if that's what your original question was asking?"

"It wasn't!"

"Really?"

"I just wanted to know if you'd…"

"If I'd ever been with a straight girl? Of course I have, and I don't actually believe anyone's exclusively straight anymore. Labels are bad. They box people off. Most women are intrigued. You said it yourself that you are."

"Intrigued by you, not by the thought of having sex with you!"

"Mmm hmm."

Camila laughed. "You don't believe me?"

"Of course not."

"Because you're so irresistible?"

"No, because most women would if they could. Not with me, but with someone of the same sex, especially if they knew they'd never get found out, if they knew there wouldn't be any repercussions," she smiled, "if they knew their secret was safe."

"I don't believe that."

"Fine. My question to you then. How often do you let your mind wander to women? In a sexual way?"

"Never!"

"Oh, stop it!"

"Honestly never."

"Really?"

"One hundred percent. I've never even thought about it."

Harriet signalled for Camila to try something from the platter. "These are good. Okay, so who do you imagine?"

"When?" Camila reached for a carved flower.

"That's a raw potato. Put that back."

"It's not a watermelon?"

"No, it's a potato. Try one of these fish cakes."

"Pretty potato."

"Focus. Who do you imagine when you're… you know?"

"No one!"

Harriet bit into a spring roll. "Oh, Camila, please."

"What?"

"So for the whole of your sex life you've only ever focused on the person you're with?" She swallowed quickly. "You've never pretended they're someone else?"

"I've only ever been with Mick."

"Well Mick must be a total stallion then."

Camila tried to hold on to her laughter as she returned to her soup.

"No?"

She stabbed at the chicken at the bottom of the bowl. "Mick's fine."

"You're uncomfortable aren't you? I'm sorry. I'm not your go-to sex gossip woman yet."

"I don't have a go-to sex gossip woman."

"Everyone does!"

Camila shrugged before chewing. "I don't. Sex isn't a huge part of my life."

"But it must have been at some point?"

"Obviously I do it. Well, I did it."

Harriet smiled. "With Mick."

Camila nodded.

Harriet smiled again. "The stallion."

Resting her spoon in her bowl, Camila shook her head. "Sex isn't as important as everyone makes out. It's not that big of a deal."

Harriet whistled under her breath. "Oh, I do feel sorry for you straight women."

"Why? Fine. My question to you. How important is sex in your life?"

"Hugely. Massively. It's second on the list to fun. And sex isn't a rude word. It's about intimacy. Feeling that other person in their entirety. Going there with them. Taking it to the next level. Seeing what your potential is together."

"Julie's a right goer."

"Ha! Good re-direction. Okay so what *do* you get passionate about? What do you gush about? What gets you feeling all the feels?"

"I'm not sure I really gush about anything. Choking on that soup's the most excitement I've had in a while." Camila picked up her spoon and tried again.

"Oh, Camila, you have so much potential."

"For what?"

"For life!"

"I'm living my life."

"But you could be so much more."

"And that's where it starts to get a bit offensive." Camila blew gently on the clear liquid. "You're saying my life isn't enough. I love my life. I love my boys. I'm happy."

Harriet reached out for Camila's arm, squeezing the elbow. "I'm sorry. I didn't mean it like that. I just want you to remember who you are."

Taking a moment to reply, Camila shrugged. "I'm not sure I ever actually had the time to find out who I truly am. I'm a young mum who's been playing catch up ever since."

"Play it with me?"

"Smooth."

"I'm serious. This is your time. That's all I'm saying." Harriet squeezed the arm once more. "Have fun with me."

"I'm not sleeping with you."

Harriet smiled.

"I'm not!"

"Did I say anything?"

"Your smile did."

"And what did it say?"

Camila leaned across the table. It said: "Mmm hmm."

CHAPTER EIGHTEEN

Climbing into the black limousine, Camila giggled as she sank into the soft leather and saw the fully stocked bar. The whole evening had been such a mish-mash of elegance like this paired with childish nonsense like the drive over and the mishap in Boots; their conversations degenerating in much the same way after each subsequent glass of wine. Watching Harriet pull herself into the vehicle, Camila patted the leather seat beside her. "I can't believe you've just given a uniformed chauffeur the keys to my car."

"Well I wasn't going to give them to old Moo Pad in Boots now was I?"

"Ha! We're intoxicated, aren't we?"

Harriet reached into the display cabinet for two tall glasses. "Let's open one last bottle. I've told him to drive the long way home."

"We're definitely not doing iFly?"

"You still want to do iFly?"

"I think I'm too tipsy."

"We are. That's what we decided. We'll do it this weekend. I'll book it in. Sorted. I'll let you know what time, but definitely this weekend. Right. One last glass. You're okay going the long way home? In fact, he won't stop until I tap on the window."

Camila pulled back the cuff of her shirt to look at her watch but the hands were too fuzzy and she couldn't read the dial. "Plenty of time. This is fun. Will he take your car too?"

"The other chauffeur? Yes. He'll drop yours off, collect mine, take mine to mine, then call for a lift back to the chauffeur place where the chauffeurs sit and wait for the chauffeur call outs. We have a different chauffeur driving us now. Two chauffeurs came. I guess chauffeurs are a bit like firemen sitting and waiting for work."

Camila laughed. "Look at that. I wait all my life for a chauffeur and two turn up at once."

"You've been in a limousine before?"

The action of shaking her head took Camila slightly longer than usual.

"Never? Wow. You get to lie down!"

Camila watched as Harriet clumsily kicked off her high heels and lay on her stomach across the leather seats, her chin propped up as she rested on her elbows, her tracksuit sticking tightly to the outline of her bottom.

"There's space your way too. Do it. We can chat face to face."

Glancing out of the window, Camila could see they'd set off, even though it didn't feel like they were moving. "Shouldn't I wear a seatbelt?"

"The window's up, he can't see us or hear us."

"But we're still in a car and we're still on a road."

"You're right." Harriet pulled herself up and buckled herself in next to Camila. "But now it's like we're sitting together on the bus."

"No, this is much smoother. Plus, this bus has booze." Camila leaned forwards. "You're strapped in, I'll do it. Is Pol Roger nice?"

"It'll do. Fill us to the brim."

Popping the cork and doing the honours, Camila handed over the glasses before moving into the seat in the corner and nodding. "If I sit here we're on an angle. Move up one so we can talk nicely knee to knee."

Harriet passed the glasses back before unstrapping and re-strapping. "Ooo nice position, what shall we talk about?"

Camila took a sip of the bubbles. "Never have I ever. Let's do it."

"You're obsessed with that game!"

"I never ever got to play it properly."

"Good one. Okay I'll start." Harriet swigged heartily. "Sex on the beach?"

"The drink?"

"No! The act."

Camila shook her head. "No. You?"

"Yes." Harriet continued. "Sex in a car?"

"No. You?"

"Yes. Sex in a cinema?"

Camila squealed. "No! Surely not?"

"Yes. Sex—"

"Stop asking about sex!"

"That's what never have I ever is! It's all about the rude stuff."

Looking out of the window into the darkness, Camila shrugged. "Fine. Touch yourself in the shower?"

Harriet burst out laughing. "Oh, bless your little soul."

"What? I do it sometimes. There's other stuff too."

"Shall we just drink and sing songs?" Harriet hollered loudly. "*We built this city on sausage rolls.*"

Camila sighed. "I'm not interesting enough for you, am I?"

"You're fascinating." Harriet nodded. "Because you're pure."

"That's not what my mother, father and brilliantly fantastic older siblings said when I got pregnant at nineteen."

"So you've had sex once then?"

"Twice actually."

Harriet laughed. "Do you get embarrassed talking about sex?"

"Well obviously not as here we are."

"Green light. Okay. Let's continue. What turns you on?"

Looking down at the bubbles fizzing in her glass, Camila could feel her cheeks flushing. She'd never been asked that before, by anyone, but her answer was easy. She smiled. "Feeling like they really want me." She returned her attention to Harriet. "Like they're really into me. You know what I mean? It's that look in their eye. It doesn't happen very often, but when it's there it makes you feel so wanted."

"Oh, darling, and the rest of the time he just pokes it in there?" Harriet shook her head. "You deserve so much better."

"He's fine! Or he was fine. Busy gifting his gifts to Jackie from the gym now though."

"Old Mick, the stallion."

Camila took a big gulp of bubbles. "I can live without it. There's no way I care enough to go out and look for it."

Harriet winked. "You have your shower."

"Don't you?"

"Shower? Yes, I shower."

Camila laughed. "So you'll pry, but you won't fess up?"

"You can ask me anything." Harriet paused. "But on a serious note, you don't find love, Camila; love finds you, through fate."

"I thought you forged your own path in life? That's what you said, wasn't it?"

"Yes, but people get drawn together for a reason. Look at us."

Lifting her glass, Camila clinked it against Harriet's. "Chars to that."

"Chars?"

"It's what Julie says. It's a posh cheers."

"You think she'll let me inside when we pull up and I knock on her door?"

"Honestly? I think Julie would run a mile."

Harriet nodded. "I do too. It's always the loud bolshy ones who talk the talk but never walk the walk."

"And the quiet ones?"

"They're the ones that need watching."

Camila smiled. "Are you watching me?"

Harriet took off her glasses. "I can't see a thing."

"Give them here! Let me try them on." Taking hold of the gold frames, Camila studied them before focusing on the brand name that was engraved on the inside arm, it was either too small or she was too tipsy to read it. "Designer?" she asked.

"Expensive. Pass them back please."

"You find that don't you," said Camila, continuing to play with the glasses. "Really cheap stuff hides their brand, like the plain white t-shirt from Tesco. The mid-range stuff shouts out their brand, like the Adidas t-shirt with the large logo. Designer stuff will quietly signal their brand, like the small horse on the Ralph Lauren t-shirt and the truly truly truly expensive stuff hide their brand again."

"So you're saying my glasses could be Tesco?"

"Or Poundland. Poundland do a good range of reading glasses."

"They're not reading glasses." Harriet held out her hand. "Could I have them back please?"

Ignoring the request, Camila pushed the frames onto the bridge of her nose before gasping. "They're clear lenses?! They're fashion glasses?! Harriet, you're a fraud!"

"A tad harsh."

"I mean they're fake!" Camila lifted them up and down between her first finger and thumb. "They're clear lenses!"

"And?"

"And why do you wear them?"

"I like them."

"You're hiding, aren't you! They're a front! A security system."

"They're not." Harriet shifted in her seat. "Could I have them back please?"

"No! I'm going to ask you more questions."

"Please, Camila."

"No. Right." Camila peered over the top of the frames. "Who are you really, now I've unmasked you?"

Harriet looked away. "I just like them."

"Do you ever not wear them?"

"Sometimes. When I'm at home on my own."

"Why aren't you looking at me?"

"Could I just have them back please?"

"No, this is interesting. Are they your front?"

Harriet leaned forward. "I'll snatch them off you."

Camila laughed before focusing on the piercing stare, quickly realising the threat was serious. Removing the glasses, she handed them over. "I'm sorry, here you go."

"Thank you."

Watching Harriet re-position the gold frames, Camila shrugged. "You're beautiful without them, but obviously you're still beautiful with them. I just mean you don't need them, they don't add anything." She paused. "Do they hide something?"

"Of course not."

"So why are you on edge?"

"It's intrusive."

"Says you, asking about all the sex stuff!"

"Taking someone's glasses off is different." Harriet looked out of the window. "But there's no issue. Maybe it's just my persona. Harriet Imogen Pearson's a brand, characterised by many things, and one thing is the glasses."

"You could just take them off?"

"I could."

"But you don't want to?"

"I don't know. Maybe they are my front. But I'm not hiding behind them, I just feel empowered when I wear them."

"Like Wonder Woman."

"What?"

"Nothing." Camila smiled. "You don't have to wear them when you're with me."

"I like them."

"Mmm hmm."

Harriet returned her gaze and laughed. "Don't you start with that. Fine, maybe I do feel more confident when I wear them."

"Because you're the brand, and people don't mess with the brand."

"It's just easier to be the ball-buster."

"So you don't like showing your vulnerability?"

"Does anyone?"

"It can bring you closer to a person." Camila smiled before noticing the bright lights of the football stadium. She recognised where they were; the driver was definitely doing loops meaning Harriet could end this whenever she wanted. She took a deep breath. "Do you trust me?"

The look was puzzled. "Ummm."

Camila continued. "Let's try something. I know I'm pushing you, but let's go there."

"I like the sound of this."

"You won't. What I want you to do is answer these questions. First with the glasses on, and then with them off."

Harriet laughed. "Good on you trying to push the boundaries. Let me finish this drink first then I'm with you."

Camila watched as Harriet necked the remainder of her glass. "Okay, stay as you are with the glasses on. Now tell me. Are you happy?"

Harriet nodded. "Of course I am. Can I have a refill please?"

"Wait. Take the glasses off."

"Let me just top myself up. You want any more?"

Camila shook her head as Harriet faffed around with the bottle. "Cheers."

"Ready?"

"No."

"Glasses off."

"Really?"

"Yes, do it."

"Can't I just nudge them to the end of my nose?"

"No, completely off. Come on, Harriet, this will be fun."

Harriet laughed. "I think you and I have different definitions of fun."

"For me then? Do it for me."

The sigh was notable. "Okay, fine, they're off."

Camila smiled. "Thank you. Now look at me." Camila waited until the piercing eyes were connected with hers. She smiled again. "Are *you* happy? *You.*"

The nod was forceful. "Yes."

"Truly?"

"Yes," Harriet smiled, "mostly. Oh, Camila, you're gooooood."

"See! Right, next one. Glasses back on. Are you a player with women?"

Harriet adjusted herself before nodding. "Yes."

"Now, glasses off. That's it. Look at me. Keep looking. Crikey your eyes really are beautiful, Harriet. Sorry, I was distracted for a moment there. Right. *You.* Are *you* a player with women?"

Harriet smiled. "Not really. I'm just... I'm not sure anyone gets close to the real me."

"Because you don't let them. You let Harriet Imogen Pearson take the lead."

"But I am Harriet Imogen Pearson."

"Yes, she's a part of you, but she's definitely your front."

The laugh was loud. "Are you a secret psychologist?"

"No, I just see you." Camila waited for the eyes to return. "I see you."

Breaking the connection, Harriet put her glasses back on. "Right, my turn. Never have I ever deliberately tried to get inside someone's mind."

"I'm not doing that."

"Really?"

"No, I'm just chatting. We're just chatting. We're bonding. We're getting close. It's what people do."

"A day after meeting?"

"You're the one who invited me here!"

"Because you're hot."

Camila gasped. "That's the only reason? Oh you meany! Thankfully I see your glasses are on so I know it's your glasses doing the talking." Camila lifted her drink. "And I'm not talking about the ten or so of these glasses we've consumed."

Harriet shook her head. "I think we should stop. This could end up going one of two ways. But I apologise for what I said. This isn't about you being hot."

"Oh, well damn it."

The laugh was genuine. "You know you are though."

"No one has ever called me hot before so whoever's calling it, and whatever their reason, I'm taking it and not questioning it." Camila nodded. "I'm hot."

"And then some."

"You wouldn't say that if your glasses were off, would you?"

"Let's not go back there." Harriet finished her drink and nodded. "Reach up and tap that window would you?"

"We're done?"

"Like I said, this could go one of two ways."

"I'm not sleeping with you."

"That wasn't one of the ways."

"It wasn't? Oh." Camila reached out and knocked loudly. "You're right though. I might end up talking crap and embarrassing myself."

"End up?"

"Oh you tease." Camila knocked again. "Home, James."

"What was that?"

"It's what they say. In the movies. To the driver."

"He's called Peter."

Camila nodded. "Pull us in, Peter."

Harriet laughed. "And he will. Look, your cul-de-sac's just up here. I didn't realise we were so close."

"Yes, you did and you didn't want him doing another loop." Camila squinted out of the window into the darkness, wondering if she should suggest stopping at the end of the road to avoid causing a scene, but then again Julie would have already told the whole neighbourhood about Harriet's visit and while returning home in a limousine was rather full-on, it felt quite nice to showboat for once. She nodded. "Look. My car's back and your car's gone. Wait. Who's that in my drive? Isn't that the other chauffeur? Or is it Julie wearing another weird outfit?"

Harriet leaned forward in her seat. "No, Julie's over there in a dressing gown."

"Where?"

"Next to her bacon butty van and, look, police. Two of them."

Camila unbuckled herself as the car pulled in, yanking on the door handle the second it stopped. "Are the boys okay?" she gasped, bursting out of the limo in a frenzy of panic.

"Mrs Moore?"

Camila dashed to the policeman. "Miss. It's Miss. Miss Moore. Camila. The boys? What's happened?"

"Is everything okay?" asked Harriet, right behind.

Camila was shaking her head. "The boys?"

"They're fine," snapped Julie. "The coppers think I've nicked her bloody car, don't they?"

"We didn't say that," said the same policeman.

Harriet turned to the empty space where her Lamborghini had been parked. "My car?"

"So the boys are okay?" Camila was breathing deeply.

"They're fine!" shouted Julie. "Her car's the one that's gone awol."

Harriet turned to the second chauffeur. "What's happened?"

The chauffeur shrugged. "It looks like it's been taken."

"Taken where?"

Julie muttered. "On a joyride probably. Bloody ridiculous leaving it here anyway."

Harriet frowned. "What do you mean?"

"You were asking for trouble. And look at you in that limo." Julie pulled her pink dressing gown tighter around herself. "Really, Camila."

Harriet scanned the street. "You've stolen my car?"

"Don't you start blaming me as well!"

"Your people?" Harriet turned to the small crowd that had started to form. "These people? They've stolen my car?"

"Ooooh *these people*." Julie was mimicking.

Harriet gasped. "You've STOLEN my LAMBORGHINI?!"

CHAPTER NINETEEN

Your people. That's what Harriet had said. *Your people. These people.* Stepping out of the lift onto the fifth floor of the H.I.P building, Camila shook her head. Harriet hadn't meant it the way Julie had assumed. Harriet was simply making reference to the group of people who'd inevitably started to gather to watch the scene, and while that wasn't great, she wasn't necessarily lumping Julie in with that bunch. Agreed, Harriet had left rather abruptly in the limousine, but wouldn't you if your car had been stolen? And it didn't mean she was waltzing away, never to return again, as Julie had declared; it was just late, and the evening had come to an end. Admittedly, it might have been nice for Harriet to pop in for a nightcap, but her car had been stolen, of course she'd want to get off.

Camila nodded, it was fine. Harriet would have insurance, in fact Harriet would probably have numerous cars; not that it made the crime any less important. Camila gasped. Crime. Who was she kidding? It was awful. A crime on her doorstep. What impression must Harriet have of her now? Passing Deana's office as she continued down the corridor towards the open plan area, Camila realised she was about to find out.

"Morning, Camila," said Deana.

Geoff raised his head from his work pod. "Morning."

"Same from me too," added Brett.

"Morning," replied Camila, scanning the space from left to right. Harriet wasn't at the pods and the soft seating in front of the screen was empty, as was the formal seating and the coffee area near the coat rack. Camila looked towards the balcony. Harriet didn't smoke but she might be getting some air.

"All okay?" Deana was suddenly blocking her view.

"Fine, fine, yes. I'm not late, am I? Do you start earlier?" It had been extra hard hauling herself out of bed after the boozy evening, but she'd deliberately set her alarm half an hour early and stood under the shower on cold and hard for that little bit longer than was comfortable, but it cleared her head... a bit.

"It's nine o'clock; you're bang on schedule. Over to the sofas please everyone."

Geoff rose from his seat at the pod. "We get in early to think of our ideas for the show and tell."

"Speak for yourself," said Brett. "I do my homework at home like I'm supposed to."

"So that list I've just seen you frantically scribbling isn't what you're about to read out?"

"Of course not!"

"Can I make you a drink before we begin?" asked Deana.

Camila focused on the woman. Why was she being so nice? "A latte would be lovely, thank you." It was good. It would give her time to think up some inventions because with all of last night's excitement she'd totally forgotten she was actually required to do some work here.

"She doesn't offer to make us drinks," said Geoff with a laugh. "How much are you paying her?"

Camila tried to smile and nod as she dropped her bag at her work pod before taking her coat to the rack on the wall. She wanted to be polite but she didn't have time to get into a conversation; she needed to think of an invention. Returning to her desk and taking her notebook from her bag, she cursed. She'd been so wrapped up in Harriet and the fun they'd been having that she hadn't even thought to prepare anything for today. Smiling at Deana, already at her side with her drink, Camila reached for a pen and followed the group to the sofas. Hopefully Harriet would arrive soon and let her off the hook. But no, that would show favouritism and it certainly wasn't the impression she wanted to make. Plus, Harriet might still be cross about the car and if Julie was right Harriet had also been tarring her with the *"these people"* brush.

"So," said Deana, "who wants to begin?"

Camila glanced around. "Shouldn't we wait for Harriet?"

"Harriet's already been in this week." Deana nodded. "Brett?"

Camila continued. "I thought she said she'd be here more often now we're in the thick of it all?"

Brett laughed. "You begin then, Camila, seeing as we're in the thick of it all together."

Deana's voice was sharp. "Brett."

The bald man shook his head. "Sorry, I'm snappy. My ideas are crap this morning. I've only managed to find seven."

Camila swallowed. She hadn't even found one. She was good at thinking on her feet though, like the time Ethan had walked in on her and Mick making love. She'd spotted him out of the corner of her eye and loudly declared: "Silly, Mick! You've fallen on top of me! Can't you get up? You've tried twice, try again now!" Mick, having glanced over his shoulder and cottoned on, had played along; the fact he was still fully clothed and had indeed flopped into position before pushing up and down a couple of times made the ruse rather believable.

"A device that alerts parents to children entering their bedroom," said Camila, opening her notebook and pretending to read.

"Wouldn't you just see them or hear them?" asked Brett.

Geoff shrugged. "Not if you were asleep."

"Surely they'd come over and shake you on the shoulder." Brett was frowning.

"You're meaning when parents are having adult time, right, Camila?"

Camila looked at Deana who was nodding supportively. Why was she being so nice this morning? "Yes."

Brett huffed. "It could work for burglars as well I guess. They've disarmed the main alarm but you have a laser beam across your bedroom door."

"Battery powered," added Geoff, "avoiding the faff of hooking it up to the electrics."

"And portable," said Deana, "so you could move it into different rooms."

Brett winked. "Wherever the moods takes you, is it, Deana?"

"But a bloke's not going to bother about it." Geoff was shaking his head. "In the heat of the moment the last thing he's going to think is: oooh, I must get my portable laser beam out and stick it to the doorway."

Brett laughed. "Ai ai."

"Women would," said Camila. "Especially women with young children."

Deana smiled. "Good start, Camila, well done, we'll look into that one."

"Shame Harriet's not around to hear it," said Brett.

Camila noticed the tone. "I actually think she's due in." There was no need to play one-upmanship, but Brett had been sniping and Harriet *had* said she'd be in today. She'd be in wearing her red heels. Her red stilettos. Camila smiled to herself. Wearing them would be their secret sign. Their in-joke. Something only she and Harriet were privy to.

Deana spoke loudly. "I spoke to Harriet last night; she won't be in until we film again next week."

Deana's statement snapped Camila out of her daydream. "What?"

"Geoff, let's have your first one."

Camila continued. "Harriet won't be in until next week? I'm sure she will. She said—"

"I spoke to her last night, sweetie."

Camila looked at the hand that had reached out for her knee. *Sweetie?* Deana was only a couple of years older than she was and while her tone wasn't condescending, her "sweetie" word choice and action were. Camila suddenly got it. Deana felt sorry for her, that's why she was being so nice. "You spoke to her last night?"

"We need to move on. Geoff?"

Unable to focus on Geoff's rambling idea, Camila stared down at her notebook. Harriet and Deana had spoken last night? It must have been after their evening out as Harriet hadn't taken any calls; in fact, both of their phones had stayed out of sight all evening. So was Deana Harriet's go-to gossip woman? Or her go-to drama woman? Or the woman she turned to in a crisis? Either way, Harriet had chosen to speak to Deana and now Deana was more in the know than she was. Camila stopped herself. Deana was Harriet's second-in-command, of course they spoke all the time, and Harriet's absence was probably something to do with one of the other businesses. Camila suddenly had an idea. She knew how to flush out the truth.

Waiting for Geoff to finish his spiel about shoes with soles that adjusted to different surfaces, Camila spoke up. "What about a car alarm that actually works for once?"

She watched carefully. Deana reached for her mug, clearly trying to hide her smirk as she took a sip of her drink, Geoff outright laughed and Brett muttered something under his breath.

"Pardon?" said Camila.

"Apt," said Brett, more audibly.

Feeling her cheeks flare, Camila looked away. They knew. They all knew. Each and every one of them.

CHAPTER TWENTY

Curling herself even tighter into her work pod, Camila glanced around. The head-height screen separating her space from Deana's was mottled like bathroom glass, clear enough to let the light through, but private enough to protect your modesty… and while Camila wasn't planning on stripping off, she *was* baring her soul on her computer screen. She continued to type. It hadn't dawned on her that she didn't have Harriet's number. She'd planned on sending a simple text, apologising once more for last night, before nonchalantly asking when Harriet would next be around, because as far as Deana was concerned it wouldn't be until next week, but Deana didn't know they'd rearranged iFly for this weekend. Harriet had promised.

Camila re-read the words of her email. *You promised we'd do iFly.* It sounded too needy. She deleted quickly and stared at the screen, her subject header: *Hi,* and Harriet's email address: *hip@hipmarketing.com* now the only sections filled in. She glanced left once more before starting slowly. *Hi, Harriet.* Good. Not too pally, but not too formal either. *I realise we didn't exchange numbers.* Factual. *I've spent the morning searching for your email address online,* much to my frustration *but obviously you don't let any old hoity toity email you.* Wise. *Luckily I'm not any old hoity toity.* Factual. *I'm an employee and I have access to your company's intranet where I found your address.* Sneaky, but showing initiative. *I also got to know you intimately in the limousine last night.* Ish.

Camila paused. Was it too stalkerish? She read again. No, it was light hearted and fun. She continued to type, adding in that she'd come up with a few good invention ideas this morning so Harriet wouldn't think she'd wasted all her time trying to contact her. Admittedly she'd wasted a fair bit of time getting this phrasing correct, but it was important to set the right tone. It needed to be noncommittal and slightly standoffish. Harriet had been the one pushing things from the start, not her. *I'm really looking forward to iFly this weekend, let me know the details as soon as you can.* Not standoffish at all. *If you still want to.* Better. *I don't mind either way.* Noncommittal. *Well I do, because I was really looking forward to it last night, but understandably neither of us were in any sort of fit state to skydive, so give me a buzz on: 07184670201 or reply to me here or even pop in during the afternoon break today. Your red stilettos are calling me.* Too much?

"Camila, what have you found on the laser?"

Quickly minimising her email, Camila pushed back on her chair and addressed Deana, whose head was peering around into her work pod. "It's quite complex. Lasers are heavily patented."

"That wasn't a personal email was it?"

"Pardon?"

"Sorry, you're probably emailing about a patent query. I'm struggling to adjust to the lack of bossing around required in this role. Are we okay to regroup in five?"

Camila nodded. "Ten? I'm almost there."

"I'll make the drinks."

Geoff spoke up from the other side of the station. "And Deana making the drinks was unheard of in ALL her previous roles. Mine's a hot chocolate, please."

"Black coffee for me," added Brett. "She was my direct line manager once. Beastly."

Camila wasn't sure if Brett was talking to her but she offered a: "Ha," angled over the screen to the back of her computer just in case. She watched Deana at the coffee machine. She felt bad. The woman was being so nice. It clearly was a personal email from her Hotmail account, but Deana had chosen to handle it in the politest of ways with a quiet comment that she quickly retracted.

Clicking the email back to life, Camila prayed Deana hadn't noticed the addressee. Scanning briefly, she signed off and pressed send; it would have to do. Moving her mouse back to the patents portal, Camila scrolled down the list of inventions. Optical laser security systems, photoelectric light detectors, modulated beams of coherent light, reflective mirror beams, laser perimeter intrusion detection, it went on and on. She typed quickly: *Battery powered laser beam security.* A list of portable laser devices came up, mostly related to alignment tasks. She scanned down. Workmen's tools possibly? Getting that shelf straight? Or maybe measuring the length of a room? She paused. It was difficult sometimes to understand the jargon. *Laser pool guard.* There it was. The same principle. The first patent cited by the California Crime Technology back in 1972! And here they were, almost forty years later, thinking it was the best idea of the morning. Camila continued to read. There had been numerous other patents cited along the same lines: swimming pool safety alarm: 1988, alert alarm responsive to an unaccompanied child: 1990, entry alert guard: 2000, solar powered lighting alert: 2003, and here it was: portable alarm system for passageways: 2015.

"Is that you sighing, Camila? Do I need to rip up this drawing?"

Camila peered to the side of her pod to see Brett's bald head doing the same thing. "Yep, it's already been done."

The bushy eyebrows were raised. "You feeling the frustration?"

"Yep."

"You're on day two."

Camila nodded. "Yep."

"So you want to apologise because we've been feeling the frustration for so many more months than you have?"

"Brett, that's enough," Deana was back at the pods with the tray of drinks. "Let's go to the sofas and re-group."

Brett shrugged. "I don't have any more ideas."

"Camila, you said you had plenty." Deana was nodding. "Let's discuss some more of yours."

Camila pushed herself away from her work pod and stood up. This whole thing was about bullshit. It was all about bullshit. The more you bullshitted the more bullshit you encouraged; like a group of drunk girls discussing the meaning of life. One person would say something bollocksy but through the excitable energy it would snowball into something profound and before you knew it you'd solved the origins of the universe and discovered a new theory of evolution. The only difference here was the energy. It wasn't excitable, it was panicked, but it had the same effect: people latching onto daft ideas in the vain hope they'd provide the answers.

Camila took a seat on the sofa opposite Brett and Geoff. "What about an inhaler that can be kept in your bag for an emergency choking situation?" She waited, watching carefully for people's reactions. Deana sat down but left her drink where it was on the tray, Brett stayed silent and Geoff's shoulders shrugged.

"Do inhalers help when choking?" he asked.

Camila continued to observe, focusing particularly on Deana who lifted her mug but didn't sip. Camila spoke again. "You know, when something goes down the wrong way, or catches in your throat but it's not blocking your airways." She paused. Still no reaction from Deana. There was no way Deana knew about her mishap with the Thai soup, meaning Deana wasn't Harriet's go-to gossip woman as last night's gasping episode had been something that would definitely be shared between friends.

"Aren't you meant to get whatever you're choking on out, instead of sucking it in?" Brett was leaning forwards, finally contributing to the conversation.

"She means when your airways suddenly contract, like when you've swallowed sea water, don't you, Camila?" Deana was nodding.

Brett tutted. "If you're in the sea you're not going to have an inhaler with you."

"Make a waterproof one?" suggested Geoff.

Camila continued. "I was thinking more if you'd eaten something spicy and your throat suddenly tightens. Wouldn't the same principle as an asthma inhaler apply?"

Brett tutted again. "You'd need a prescription."

"You don't need prescriptions for all muscle relaxants," said Deana.

"Ai ai," laughed Brett.

Deana ignored him. "The medication in an asthma inhaler simply relaxes the muscles in the airways so they become less constricted."

"That's what I was talking about," said Camila.

"But how often do you choke like that?"

Camila replied to Brett's scoffing question. "How often do you use the rape alarm that you keep in your handbag?"

"Me? You think I have a handbag? You think I need a—"

"Oh, stop being so snappy, Brett." Deana was nodding. "This is good, we're brainstorming, and Camila's right, women keep so many things in their handbags just in case."

"And men? Don't men choke?"

"Of course you do," continued Deana, "and we can invent a man bag for you to keep your choking inhaler in as well."

Camila laughed. "We can't call it a choking inhaler."

"Oh, sweetie, we're nowhere near that stage yet." Deana paused. "Wait, let's do that stage now; we've not done it for weeks."

Camila frowned. "What stage?"

"Well, on the odd occasion where we actually manage to think of an idea that hasn't been patented we take it down to the focus groups for discussion and development."

Brett stood up. "And we quickly realise that it hasn't been patented because it's a crap idea."

"Where are you going?" Deana was now arms raised.

"I'm phoning floor one. Yes, the choking inhaler doesn't have much mileage but I'd discuss just about anything right now for a change of scenery."

"We could give it an extension cable so it has more mileage," offered Geoff.

Deana's groan was pained. "Was that meant to be funny?"

"But what if it's already been patented?" Camila was confused.

"Oh, sweetie, it probably has and even if it hasn't it's not a universal enough product for us to take into the launch show. Plus there are the medical and legal issues. It's just good to keep all the processes in place so when we finally have our eureka moment we can flow smoothly through each stage."

Looking to the hand that was back on her knee, Camila lowered her voice and tried to angle her body away from Geoff who was still sitting on the sofa opposite. "Can I ask why you keep calling me sweetie?"

The hand was quickly removed. "Sorry, I was just being friendly."

"Right," said Camila. "It's just... I'm not sure..." She couldn't find the words. "It's nothing else is it?"

"Like what?" Deana's brow was furrowed. "Oh, you think I...?"

"No! I just..."

"Oh for god's sake, you two," Geoff was on his feet. "Deana knows you're another one of Harriet's casualties. She's being nice to you because she knows what's coming next."

"And what is coming next?" asked Camila calmly.

"Next we're going down to floor one," said Brett, back in the sofa area having only caught the tail end of the conversation. "Doug and Nigel's 18-to-25 focus group have had a cancellation. They're free right now and happy to help."

Camila looked up. "The 18-to-25s? Well my day gets better and better."

CHAPTER TWENTY ONE

Standing in the lift as it descended to floor one, Camila didn't know what to say or how to behave. Clearly Deana, Geoff and Brett had been having a good old gossip, dissecting whatever information Harriet had passed on to whomever last night. Had Harriet told them to fire her? No, she was still here, and anyway she'd signed her new contract with Helen at the reception desk last night. But maybe Harriet had simply been mouthing off that she was done with her latest project due to her latest project's criminal ties? No, Harriet had said she wasn't a project. She'd said she was different. Special. Could this all just be speculation and sour grapes on Deana and co's part based on the women who'd allegedly preceded her? Quite possibly.

"Life's wonderful when you've got Harriet's attention, isn't it? But when she drops you, well."

Camila turned to Deana whose voice, even though lowered, was still audible to both Geoff and Brett in the lift. Camila knew she had no other option but to address it. "Deana, if you, or any of you for that matter, have something you'd like to say to me, then please just say it."

"Fine. You shouldn't be here." Brett wasn't shy about jumping in first.

"You said a nice hello this morning, Brett. You were being quite friendly."

"I thought you'd be hauled out straight away, but now it's the afternoon and you're still here."

"And where do you want me to go?"

"Wherever she moves the rest of the women like you."

Deana patted Camila's arm. "Sweetie, this isn't your fault."

Brett continued. "But you're definitely on your way out if your mate went and nicked her car."

"Who told you that?"

Deana coughed. "Sweetie, I'm her chief strategist; I know everything that goes on."

Camila thought back to the choking incident. "You don't actually, and it wasn't my mate, and Harriet is coming in."

"Sweetie she isn't, and I do, and if it wasn't your friend it was someone else on your street."

"Which would have nothing to do with me."

"Guilty by association." Brett was smirking as he leant against the lift's chrome interior. "She got rid of one woman she'd been nurturing because she found out she never washed her hands after using the bathroom."

Geoff spoke up. "Was that Sarah?"

"No, she got rid of Sarah because Sarah kept saying Jiminy Cricket."

Deana smiled. "Oh I remember her! If something went wrong it was: '*Jiminy Cricket*', or if something surprised her it was: '*Jiminy Cricket*', or if something upset her it was…"

The two men joined in with a chorus of: "*Jiminy Cricket.*"

Camila looked at her three colleagues. "What's wrong with you? Harriet would be devastated to hear you talking like this."

"She wouldn't," said Brett. "She laughs at the rumours and she's actually quite open about her women."

"Don't forget the odd man," added Geoff. "Remember Dominic? He got the chop for vaping."

Deana spoke up. "I think it was because he vaped really weird flavours like rhubarb and custard."

Geoff was shaking his head. "No, it was because he blew vape smoke rings. Harriet said it was ridiculous."

"And all these people went to an employment tribunal, right?" said Camila, having had just about enough. "Because you can't just get rid of people."

"Oh no, she promotes them, but into one of the companies where she's not needed. She's very clever is our Harriet."

"Not if she employed you three." Camila couldn't help it.

The shocked silence that descended on the trio had a charge that felt new to Camila. Yes, she'd upset Mick and the boys in the past by saying the wrong thing or lashing out with her actions, but this was different. This was awkward. This was embarrassing. Were her colleagues furious, or gobsmacked? Or were they about to lynch her like a scene from a photo story in one of Julie's *Take A Break* magazines: *I got set upon in a lift and thrown down the lift shaft.*

The ping that announced the end of their journey jolted them all back into action, as did the hubbub on the corridor of floor one, visible as the lift doors opened. A group of old-aged pensioners were streaming past on three-wheeled hover boards, blocking their exit.

"Close that again," demanded Deana.

Geoff did as instructed.

"I'm sorry," said Camila, in an attempt to halt the imminent onset of lift shaft crime. "I just don't know what I've done wrong. I've come up with just as many ideas as you lot have, not to mention that we've selected a number of mine for the patent searches. I've arrived on time every day. I've made the teas. I've followed instructions and I actually think I've fitted in quite well."

"But why?" Brett was arms folded. "Why are you here?"

"Because Harriet saw me in a focus group and said I had potential."

Brett continued. "Do you know how many others there have been? And the only real success story I can think of is Deana, which makes all these 'projects' of Harriet's, who are now in positions of power, a kick in the teeth for the hard workers like Geoff and myself who've slogged our butts off to get where we are now."

Camila was confused. "So they're successful? These people? These women?"

Deana spoke up. "But they're no longer in Harriet's direct circle."

"Well, that's a sign of good leadership then." Camila was nodding. "Spot potential and move them on."

"You're suggesting she chooses to keep an eye on me?"

"I didn't say that."

Geoff smiled. "Ooooh, Deana, does the latest project have a point?"

"I don't want to have a point. I just want to do the job I'm here to do."

Brett pressed the button to open the lift doors. "Here's your chance then. Go and show us your stuff."

"No problem, I will." Walking along the corridor, Camila was relieved to see the group of OAPs on their trike-like hover-boards at the far end, freeing her path to room five. Knocking once, she entered with gusto.

The tall and perfectly coiffured D.O.G Doug, still dressed in tan, was the first to turn. "Whoops-a-daisy, there you go again, wrong room."

Doppelganger Nigel spoke next. "Have you brought back the Mesh-Up clothing?"

Camila smiled politely as she walked past the two men, positioning herself at the front of the round table and nodding at the group of seated women, noticing the addition of the pink hair punk from the other morning. "Hi, I'm Camila Moore and I'm working with the H.I.Pvention team on floor five." She turned to her three colleagues who were loitering in the doorway. "Thank you for seeing us at such short notice. We'd like to talk to you about a new product idea."

Tina rose from her seat. "Nigel! You said I'd be the next one promoted from this group! She's on floor five? What's she doing on floor five?!"

Camila's voice was calm. "I was never meant to be in this group and I'm sure your promotion will come, Tina."

"Only if you get the boss onside," muttered Brett, audibly enough for the occupants of the room to hear.

"I have been," gasped Tina, now bashing Nigel's bony shoulder.

"Wrong boss," said Brett with a laugh.

"What have you got that I haven't got?" demanded Tina, turning her attack on Camila. "You were just that old woman with all the crap ideas about waist bands for stretch marks who got kicked out, weren't you?"

Camila heard someone behind her sniggering. She didn't need to turn; it could be any one of her so-called colleagues. She took a deep breath. In situations like these she knew what she had to do. She had to ask directly for help. People were more than happy to stand around and laugh, or watch someone suffer, until they were called out on it, but the second they were their actions would often change for the better. Like the group of boys at the skate park filming a fight, all jeering and goading until she marched over and told them to take a long hard look at themselves, the majority then choosing to lower their phones and help break up the scuffle. Or the people sitting on the bus, pretending not to notice the old man who'd just got on, choosing to stare out of the window instead of giving up their seats, until she'd politely tapped them on the shoulder to make them 'aware' of his presence, whereupon they'd jumped up as if it was their plan all along. Camila nodded. Now was one of those times. "Who's getting the ball rolling? Nigel, isn't it your job to call order? Deana? Geoff? Brett? Are we presenting this thing together?"

Nigel turned to Deana for confirmation that Camila was indeed where she was meant to be before ushering Tina back to her seat. "Ladies," he said, "it seems we need to pay attention to what's going on." He banged on the table. "Focusing faces forward please. Deana, are you heading this up?"

Deana stepped forwards. "No, Camila's the lead on this one, but we're all here to discuss."

"I'll type up the notes," said Brett, tapping on his tablet and moving to the seats against the front wall.

Camila smiled. This was good. Deana and Geoff were by her side, Brett had chosen a role that wasn't at all supportive but was needed all the same and Tina had piped down, for the moment. "Okay," said Camila, eager to show her ability to engineer discussions, if nothing else. "How many of you have choked on a liquid before?"

Silence.

"Or coughed as you breathed in and started to choke?"

More silence.

"Or, you know, you're eating something and you suddenly laugh and it's not the food you're choking on, it's your gasp that goes down the wrong way?"

Camila stared at the blank faces at the round table. "Spicy soup? You slurp it too quickly and your throat suddenly constricts?" She nodded; it was that asking for help time again. "Come on, ladies, aren't you here to interact? To participate?"

Ellie spoke first. "You called me fat."

"Yeah and you got me in trouble with your phone torch," added Tanisha.

"And you lost me a day's pay," said the pink-haired punk. "Because I hear it was you who stole my place in the group."

Tina stood up. "And I could definitely do whatever promotion you've got," she snapped.

Camila looked around at the women, suddenly wondering how the fight-filming boys might respond if the scuffling children were in fact nasty bullies, or the people on the bus recognised the old man for the dirty Peeping Tom that he was. These women didn't owe her anything. These women were happy to watch as she failed. She turned to Deana and Geoff who'd taken a notable step backwards. "I'll carry on, shall I?" she said, to no reply.

Brett spoke up, tapping in an exaggerated fashion on his tablet. "So. So far no one recognises the need for the product."

Turning to the remaining women in the group who Camila didn't think she'd offended, she started again. "All I'm asking is whether or not you can imagine this happening? Your airway contracting due to a cough or an awkward swallow? Can you at least imagine it?" It was a technique she'd used when Michael and Ethan were growing up, when they didn't want to admit to something, but they didn't want to sound stupid either. *Yes, Mummy, I can imagine my teeth dropping out.* "That's all I'm asking," she would say. "Imagine your teeth dropping out. Now, tell me again, did you eat all the sweeties?"

"I think I might have choked once when I was drinking a Coke and I laughed suddenly."

"Good!" said Camila, focusing on the woman sitting next to Ellie. "And did you find it hard to breathe?"

"For a bit."

"Were you gasping?"

"For a bit maybe."

"Okay, imagine you had an inhaler in your bag."

"I don't have asthma."

"No, a choking inhaler."

Tina was still standing. "A choking inhaler? Ha! Another crap idea from the crap ideas woman!"

Brett continued his over-the-top note taking. "When imagining a demand, the focus group still think the idea's crap."

Camila stepped forward and tried again. "How many of you have a rape alarm in your handbag?"

Silence.

"When you're out jogging?"

Silence.

"Strange, I thought you were the fit and active target group for Mesh-Up gym wear?"

A woman beside Tina spoke up. "I have one."

"Wonderful!" said Camila. "And how many times have you used it?"

"Never."

"Good, but you take it anyway. So now, can you imagine how the same principle might apply here? You probably won't choke, but you'll take the device just in case."

"What device?"

"The choking inhaler."

"CRAP name!" Tina was still standing.

The woman spoke again. "But I wouldn't pay for one. I only have a rape alarm because I got it free at my university fresher's fayre."

Brett tapped loudly. "No one would buy it anyway."

"You wouldn't pay five pounds say, for something that would stop the embarrassment of choking and spluttering for breath?"

Silence.

Camila nodded. "Okay ladies, not to worry. Thank you very much for your time."

"I could do that!" snapped Tina to Nigel. "Is that all she had to do? What's so special about what she's just done?"

Camila left the room, heading back to the lift, unaware of Doug's chastisement of everyone in the room.

"She's just held her own in the cesspit," he said. "And your time here, Tina, is done."

CHAPTER TWENTY TWO

Jabbing the button for floor five, Camila willed the doors closed. Embarrassed, shown up, mocked, unsupported, defeated, those were all understatements for how she was feeling right now. Ridiculous seeing as it was Deana's idea to go down to the focus group and Brett's idea to arrange it so quickly. She jabbed again. Had she been set up? Was it planned? Why even go ahead with an idea that had no real mileage? Yes, Deana had said it was good to keep all systems in place, but no one had helped her, they'd all just watched as she drowned, apart from Brett, who'd tried to hold her under. Keeping her finger on the button, she felt alone, which was silly seeing as she'd spent the best part of fifteen years alone, overcoming challenges all by herself, being both mother and father when she had to be, and cleaner and cook, not to mention taxi-driver and homework helper and personal shopper and first-aider, the list was endless... but the difference was easy, she did it for people who cared, for her children who were her world.

Sighing as the lift doors finally started to close, Camila questioned who she was doing this current job for, because it certainly wasn't bringing the empowerment and personal independence she'd originally hoped. A stint on Julie's bacon butty van was ten times as rewarding as this, the sheer joy and appreciation always visible on the customers' faces the second they took their first bite of whatever greasy snack they'd chosen. Even looking after her brother and sister's children at a playcentre seemed more appealing than this right now.

"Camila!" shouted Deana, shoving her foot in between the lift doors as they closed.

Camila looked down at the solo shoe, hoping it would be pulled out so she could continue her journey alone. She turned away as the chrome doors re-opened.

"Camila," Deana was panting. "Brett, Geoff and I… come on, men," she said, keeping the door open as she flagged them from the corridor. "Brett, Geoff and I, and in fact Nigel and Doug… Doug in particular, we wanted to say—"

"Deana! Sorry! Wait! Let me just jump in there! They said you were down here." A woman with short, spiky hair who was clutching a sheet of paper joined the crowd in the lift but shoved her bottom against the frame to keep the doors open. "I'll show Doug and Nigel next but, Brett, you're going to love this one! Listen up." She fanned her face with the email print off before reciting: *"Hi, Harriet. I've spent the morning searching for your email address online, but obviously you don't let any old hoity toity email you. Luckily I'm not any old hoity toity. La la la la la. I got to know you intimately in the limousine last night."*

"Ai ai," cheered Brett.

"La la la la la. *Your red stilettos are calling me."* The woman squealed as she flapped the paper again! "What a weirdo! This one's claiming to work with you lot."

Deana's cough was loud but the yapping continued unabashed.

"I think she beats the woman who said she was Harriet's long lost soulmate. Remember her? Deloris, I think she was called. Said she lived in the bushes in Harriet's office."

Deana's staged cough was even louder, and now accompanied by a violent head shake, but the spiky-haired woman was oblivious.

"Obviously this is all bollocks; it's from a Hotmail address. She does talk about the company's intranet though, but honestly the lengths people go to to make contact with Harriet. How stupid to think this is her actual email address? H.I.P at H.I.P Marketing." The woman laughed. "Of course it's going to go through a P.A first."

Bowing her head and drawing her shoulders in tight, Camila edged her way from the back of the lift and squeezed past her colleagues and the spiky-haired woman without saying a word, her pace quickening at the whoops and giggles that erupted behind her and chased her down the corridor until she turned and folded in on herself in the stairwell. Grabbing hold of the metal handrail, Camila clung on tightly as chilled wind whipped up the stairs. She shuddered. She had to get out; she had to get home. Who had she been kidding that she could do something like this? Halting her descent, she suddenly stopped. What about her bag and her keys? She paused for a second before recommencing her downward flight. She knew she couldn't go back. They were laughing at her, all of them, and she felt like an idiot. She *was* an idiot. She'd ask Helen to nip up and get her things. Helen had been nice, in fact Helen had been the only nice person she'd come across so far.

Thankful for the cool draught as she made her final descent of the stairwell, Camila fanned her cheeks just to be sure before straightening her blazer and checking her hair, exiting through the heavy door and into the foyer with as much poise as she could muster. She glanced around. Why was it so busy? The one day she wanted to sneak about unseen and suddenly the place was heaving with people. Was there a fire alarm? No, she'd have heard it. A tour of the building then? Whatever it was she needed to get to the glass desk and ask for a favour.

"Helen," she said, aware that the receptionist looked unusually frazzled. "I need... Oh no! What's happened here?" Her attention was taken by Helen's work surface. "It's covered in smears!"

"Tell me about it. People have been leaning all over it to write their name tags as there's no room left in the red or yellow areas."

"Who are they?"

"They're you."

"They're me? What? Replacing me? Well that didn't take long, did it?!"

"Your old job. Pamela from Insights said she didn't have time to re-advertise but Harriet said she had to do it properly. That's what Harriet was doing down here the other morning. Pamela told me. She's always huffing and puffing about on this floor moaning to me about everyone, Pamela that is, which is ridiculous seeing as she's meant to be on floor three."

"What do you mean do it properly?"

"Oh you know she can't just call in the person who'll steal her Christmas Crown."

Camila shook her head. "I'm lost."

"Pamela Simpson-Smith. She wins it every year. That's why she hides herself down here."

"Wins what?"

"The Christmas Crown, the Christmas Trophy. It's hush hush but it gets voted for and given out on the sly."

"Still lost."

"The award for the crappest acronym. She's won it for the past seven years. Won in the loosest of terms obviously."

"Pamela from Insights?"

"Yes, Pamela Simpson-Smith." Helen lowered her voice. "Pamela Isabelle Simpson-Smith."

Camila looked to Helen's name tag, staring at the heavily embossed H.A.H that matched the company's logo. She gasped, realisation suddenly dawning on her. P.I.S.S. Pamela from Insights was P.I.S.S. The woman had been ridiculed for being P.I.S.S for the past seven years and now wanted someone else to take the attention. Feeling for the name tag that was tucked into her own blazer, Camila pulled it out roughly. So that's why C.U.M had been given the job.

CHAPTER TWENTY THREE

Scuttling out of the H.I.P building's foyer, coat, bag and car keys finally back in her possession, Camila dashed across the car park towards her car. It was raining. Typical. Just when she thought today's shittiness couldn't get any worse, the weather decided to piss on her parade as well. Forcefully shoving the key into the slot, she cursed as her thumb nail snapped. "Oh well bloody hell," she gasped, turning to rest her back against the unopened car door as she shook her once pretty nail in the air. Breathing in deeply, Camila tilted her head back, allowing the cold rain to hit her face hard before attempting to exhale all of her tensions away.

Keeping her eyes closed, Camila tried to imagine that the pain of the almost freezing droplets now smashing into her eye sockets, and the slow damp seeping through her clothing, to be some sort of therapeutic spa treatment. They did that didn't they? At spas? Blast you with fire hoses, or douse you with buckets of cold water? At least she was getting this for free. Standing still and letting herself shiver, she tried to ignore the warm droplets sliding down her cheeks. Camila shook her head. She'd failed. She'd walked away from a challenge. She'd even forced Helen from reception to go back up and face the music. Not that anyone had been there on floor five frantically mourning her disappearance. The receptionist had said the workspace was empty. Camila exhaled again. They were probably still in that lift, laughing at her, laughing at her make-believe connection with Harriet. A connection that was definitely imagined, or certainly exaggerated, as they'd been right: Harriet hadn't come in today. With a final deep breath, Camila nodded into the rain, decision made. Walking away was the wisest move she could make.

Yanking the car door open and sliding into the driver's seat, Camila kept her head down as she started the ignition. She didn't notice the chauffer-driven sedan pull in front of the H.I.P building, or the woman who emerged from the backseat under an umbrella, or the woman's red stilettos that danced over the puddles before dashing through the glass doors of the foyer and heading towards the lift that would rise to floor five.

****

Much of the journey home was a blur for Camila, one of those times where you arrived at your destination with no clue how you'd got there. The journey from the H.I.P building wasn't far, but there were numerous sets of traffic lights, three roundabouts and tons of speed bumps, yet she couldn't remember manoeuvring through, around or over any of them. Had the lights been green? She couldn't remember. All she recalled were the noisy windscreen wipers and the fact she'd been deep in thought, replaying the day and reaffirming her decision to leave. Obviously she hadn't officially quit, but her contract was nine to five and it was only three thirty in the afternoon, yet here she was, turning into her road. Three thirty. Afternoon break in the office. She cursed herself. Why was she bothered? She'd only be sitting on her own, or possibly creeping along the corridor to see if she could hear Harriet's voice in any of the offices. And why care about Harriet? The woman had clearly tarred her with the criminal brush and decided to end their friendship, which was all incredibly fickle and rather unfair.

Plus a few days ago she didn't even know who Harriet Imogen Pearson was, not really anyway, so why should Harriet Imogen Pearson suddenly occupy so much of her head space? She shouldn't, but Camila knew why it was happening. Harriet had put herself there, in her consciousness, with her compliments and kind gestures. No one had called her hot before and it had been an incredibly long time since anyone had been so desperate for her company; and desperate *was* the right word. Harriet had been eager, yet now, all of a sudden, there was nothing. And it wasn't the fact she'd lost Harriet, it was the fact Harriet shouldn't have presented herself as someone willing to be found.

Pulling into her driveway, Camila turned off the ignition and sat for a moment, the rain immediately blotting the windscreen. What if it wasn't about the stolen car after all? What if she'd pushed the boundaries too far with her glasses-off game? Admittedly it was quite intrusive and she'd never have dared be so forward in her questioning had she not drunk so much, but Harriet had been driving that too, the "let loose and have fun" mentality. Yes, it couldn't have been much fun being told your fake glasses were a front for your fake persona, which was in essence what she'd concluded, but it was light-hearted, just like the rest of the evening had been. But maybe that wasn't enough for Harriet? Maybe Harriet *had* wanted more and her response to Harriet's question about how many times she'd thought of women in a sexual manner had dampened any planned progression of their friendship. Camila shrugged. She wasn't going to lie though. She'd never thought of women that way, but then again she'd never thought about women this way either, analysing every motive, every action, every non-action.

Camila closed her eyes. Would she ever actually go there? With a woman? With Harriet? Listening to the sound of the rain as it drummed against her car roof, Camila pictured the final scene in *Four Weddings and a Funeral*: Hugh Grant kissing Andie MacDowell in a torrential downpour. She'd always viewed it as one of the most romantic movie moments ever, the idea you were so consumed with someone, so lost in their kiss, that you'd say: "Is it still raining? I hadn't noticed." And obviously life wasn't like that and spontaneous romantic gestures never really happened, but it would be nice to think there'd be a time where she might lose herself in one moment of madness.

Keeping her eyes closed, Camila pictured Harriet standing in the rain, staring at her, calling her hot, calling her perfect, calling her her little pocket rocket. She paused. Would Harriet call her that in the moment? Probably not. Would she like Harriet to call her that in the moment? Well, she'd liked it when Harriet had said it before; it was cute and endearing. Camila refocused. So the rain would lash down.

Harriet would call her a little pocket rocket, a hot little pocket rocket, before moving forward with an outstretched hand that would reach up and wipe the rain from her cheeks. They would stare into each other's eyes before Harriet's lips, slightly parted, would advance, kissing the rain into her mouth.

Imagining the moment, Camila quivered. Kissing a woman. What would it actually be like? Would the kiss be hard or soft? Would they moan? Would their breasts push together? Would Harriet's hands start to wander? Where would they go? Would they reach behind her waist and pull her in tight? Would their legs part? Would Harriet's sexy black underwear that she'd had her face pressed against when retrieving the can of hairspray become damp, and not from the rain but from the kiss, the kiss that was heated and searching and—

Camila jumped at the loud bang on the bonnet. "Julie!" she gasped, seeing the fuzzy outline of the pink dressing gown and large golfing umbrella through the now steamed up windscreen. "What are you doing?"

"Hurry up!" said Julie, pulling open the driver's door. "It's bloody pissing it down out here!"

Camila unbuckled herself and grabbed her bag from the front seat, tucking under Julie's umbrella as Julie guided them both towards Camila's front door. "Why are you in your dressing gown?" she said, over the noise of the lashing rain, even though Julie in her dressing gown wasn't an unusual sight, but three-thirty was rather early, or rather late, even for Julie depending on which way you looked at it.

"Terry's back. Well he was. He's gone again now. Bought me a load of Champagne, the real stuff. Shall I bring a bottle round? Why are you back? I saw you sitting out here. Quick, get in the bloody house would you?"

Stepping into the hallway, Camila noticed the shoes first. A pair of female moccasins placed neatly next to her eldest son's huge pontoons that had obviously been kicked off and left to lie on their sides with their muddied soles in full view. Her attention turned to the portrait pictures on her stairwell wall. They were rattling, gently.

"Get in the bloody house would you!" gasped Julie, shoving Camila forward with her bottom as she struggled to get the large and soaking wet umbrella through the doorway.

"Shush!"

"What? It's bloody pissing it down out here!"

"Shush!" repeated Camila, silently signalling towards the school portraits.

"What?" mouthed Julie, finally closing her umbrella and staring at the scene.

Camila whispered. "The pictures!"

Julie stared. "What about the pictures?"

"They were moving."

"Well they're not now. Shall I get the Champagne? Do you have another promotion? Is that why you're back early?"

"They were moving. And keep your voice down. Look at the shoes, she's here again. There's no way they should be back so soon, plus the walls shouldn't be rattling." Camila slid off her heels and crept up the stairs before shouting: "Michael," willing to give a one second warning before she blasted her way into his room. "Why aren't you at school?" she said, throwing open his door as she winced, unsure what she was expecting to see.

"Mum?"

"Yes, it's Mum. What are you doing?" She surveyed the room. Just as she thought. Her eldest son and Cassie Stevens were standing by the bed, red-cheeked. Had they just jumped up? She studied their attire. His tie was off and his school shirt was loose from his trousers. She looked at the older girl: An easy access jumper dress that was rolled up at the sleeves, and ankle socks, not tights.

"We're working on a maths project."

"In school time?"

"School's finished."

"Fifteen minutes ago, you can't get home that quickly."

"Maths is last lesson. They let us home early to start work on our project."

"Oh, Michael, do you think I was born yesterday?"

163

The pretty girl spoke up. "It's true. We're manipulating Newton's theory of gravity."

Camila looked to her flushed son. "You're manipulating it? With your tie off and your shirt out?"

"It's hard work. Look." The boy picked up a large ball of elastic bands from his desk before moving back to the bed and stepping onto the duvet. "Ready, Cassie?"

The girl took her phone from the pillow and nodded.

Camila watched as her son dropped the ball from waist height as he jumped off the bed. "Careful! You'll go through the floorboards!"

"It's an experiment."

"Wait. Do it again." Camila held the bedroom door open as she looked towards the stairwell and portrait pictures. The frames rattled noisily. "They weren't moving like that," she said, her focus back in the room.

"What weren't?"

"The pictures on the wall."

"Cassie's been jumping, she's lighter than me."

Camila looked at the red-cheeked pair. "Do you think I'm stupid?"

The girl spoke again. "Of course not. We're trying to prove that mass attracts every other mass in the universe and that the gravitational force between two bodies is proportional to the product of their masses and inversely proportional to the square of the distance between them." She smiled. "You know how Newton demonstrated the universality of the force of gravity with his cannonball thought experiment? The one where he imagined a cannon on top of a mountain? Without gravity, the cannonball should move in a straight line. If gravity is present, then its path will depend on its velocity. If it's slow, then it will fall straight down. If it reaches the orbital velocity where the gravitational force equals the centripetal force then it will orbit the Earth in a circle or ellipse. If it's faster than the escape velocity when the kinetic energy is equal to the gravitational potential energy then it will leave the Earth's orbit."

Camila stared. "Right."

"You can go now, Mum."

"Right."

"Go on then."

Camila coughed. "Does your father know you're here, Cassie?"

"Yes, and he's really keen for you to use your links with Harriet to promote his new boxing outreach scheme."

"I'll have to get back to you on that one," said Camila, leaving the room more flustered and perplexed than when she'd arrived. Descending the stairs, she watched as the pictures rattled once more. It was definitely a different rattle.

"Are they fucking?" asked Julie, looking up from her position in the damp hallway.

"Of course not! And as if they'd carry on the second I left!"

"What are they doing then?"

"Manipulating Newton's theory of gravity."

Julie burst out laughing. "Ha! That's better than the one I got from Terry's youngest. She said she was practicing first aid on her boyfriend. You know what I said to her? I said you don't blow air up there, my love!" Julie paused. "And isn't it Einstein's theory of gravity anyway?"

"As if I'm meant to know."

"And they know you don't know."

"Should I go back up?"

"Don't be daft! Think about what you were getting up to at their age. They're only kids."

"Exactly!"

"Do you trust him?"

"Yes."

"So trust him."

Camila stood still on the bottom step. "Should I trust him?"

"No bloody way!"

"Oh, Julie, what would you do?"

"I'd crack open a bottle of champers and say chars to the fact I had a kid bright enough to bluff me with a load of old bollocks about gravity."

"This only started because I took that damn job. The second I turn my back and they're off the rails."

"He's upstairs with the head girl. He's hardly under a bridge taking meth."

"Julie!"

"What? Lighten up. Let me bring round some champers. Terry got me a load of new shoes as well. Jimmy Choos. The ones with the red soles. You can buy a pair if you want? I'll have to charge you full price though as they're the real deal, not like those ones from the market; remember them? Soles painted with red poster paint, left footprints whenever they got wet."

Camila took off her blazer and hung it over the bannister. "Why's Terry so flush?"

"Oh I don't know, some deal's come good. Come on, get in your PJs, I'll be back with the booze."

"I'd rather just have a cup of tea?"

"You okay?"

"Not really."

"You're not still pissed off with me about that bloody car business are you?"

"Did you have anything to do with that car business?"

"I didn't, no."

"But you know who did?"

Julie shook her head in disbelief. "Has she taken it out on you? I knew she couldn't be trusted. They never can, those self-serving rich bitches. Go on, go and get changed. I'll put the kettle on."

"No, honestly—"

"Go."

Not having the energy to argue, Camila turned back to the stairs. If she was honest she wasn't entirely sure she wanted Julie in her house, let alone making the teas or offering up comfort, as there was a high possibility that it was Terry, suddenly flush, who'd taken Harriet's car, and yes while that wasn't directly Julie's fault someone had told him it was here, and he'd been working away, so his coincidental reappearance was hard to ignore. Pausing on the middle step, she turned back to her neighbour.

Julie was still standing there, smiling and nodding in support. "Go on, I've got this. This is what friends are for."

Camila laughed, her resolve suddenly broken. She'd heard that sentence on so many occasions before where Julie had been there to save the day after some disaster that was more often than not of her own doing. Particular highlights included the time Julie had managed to source a continental adaptor on Christmas Day for a distraught nine and ten-year-old Ethan and Michael whose eager and excitable unwrapping had quickly turned into tears on the discovery that the game console, secretly sourced by Julie, turned out to have foreign plugs. "That's what friends are for," she'd said with a smile. Or the time she'd driven Mick, and a number of other guests who'd eaten the prawns at Mick's birthday gathering, to the hospital, having supplied the buffet herself. "That's what friends are for," she had said after blaming the hoo-ha on a bug that was going around. Camila stared at the woman standing there in her pink dressing gown. "Oh bloody hell, Julie, go and get the champers instead."

****

Lighting her grey glittery scented candle, Camila took the glass of Champagne from the shelf below her television and settled on the sofa, reaching out to pull the cord on the free-standing lamp so the pretty beaded crystals danced light all around the room.

"Sorted?" asked Julie, taking a sip of her drink, already in position on the other side of the soft grey cushions.

Camila tucked her feet under herself and pulled her dressing gown in tight. "Remember when you gave me that cherry hair dye?"

Julie laughed. "Not this again."

"It ran in the rain, staining my skin and ruining the new jumper my mum bought me."

"That jumper was horrible. Long haired and itchy."

"It was white. And remember how Michael and Ethan were just babies? They were totally freaked out whenever they saw me because the streaks looked like blood running down my neck."

Julie laughed and lifted her glass. "Chars chars. Good times."

"You offered me your umbrella."

"Of course I did."

"Because, no matter how many times I washed it, it still managed to run in the rain."

"What's your point?"

"And remember those light bulbs? Everyone on the street had them? They buzzed. Loudly."

"Was that the time I got the job lot of ear plugs? They were great, tucked right inside your ears, couldn't even see them."

"But you supplied the buzzing light bulbs."

"At half the price of the normal ones."

"And that DVD you gave Ethan last week, it's in Chinese."

"I've got an app that can translate it in real time. That film's not due out for another month."

"You're missing my point." Camila lifted her glass. "This Champagne? What's this for?"

"Because you've obviously had a bloody crap day."

"But why?"

"I don't know, you're about to tell me."

Camila sighed. "Fine. Harriet didn't come in."

"Was she meant to?"

"Yes, wearing her red stilettos."

"And this has upset you?"

"Yes, well no, it's not just that, that wasn't the final straw, the final straw was horrible." Camila paused, suddenly realising that her whole journey home and subsequent sit on the drive had been occupied by thoughts of Harriet, not thoughts of the email in the lift, or Tina in the focus group, or Pamela passing on her trophy. She shook her head. "Do you want to know why I got the job? The first job?"

"Because you're bloody good at what you do?"

"No, because Pamela from Insights is actually called Pamela Isabelle Simpson-Smith. P.I.S.S. She gets awarded with the company's crappest acronym trophy every year and she wanted to pass on the mantle and move away the unwanted attention. I'm C.U.M, Camila Uma Moore. C.U.M tops P.I.S.S every day of the week."

"Bloody hell." Julie tried not to laugh. "That's the only reason?"

"That's the only reason."

"I thought Harriet saw something in you?"

"Yes, my tits. You were right."

Julie leant over the sofa and rubbed Camila on the knee. "Oh bless you, you little good-titted orgasm."

"It's not funny."

"I know it's not, but if I'm honest you've lasted longer than I thought you would."

"Two days?"

"I gave you one." Julie took another sip of bubbles. "Women like us don't live in their world. We're the honest grafters."

Camila was now the one trying not to laugh; honest grafter was the least likely accolade she'd gift to Julie.

"What? We are. We look after our kids. We do the jobs no one else wants to do. We live the real life, not some showy-off car with wings, big-bollocked red-stilettoed world."

"She wasn't showing off in her car."

"You only buy cars like that to show off."

"So you wouldn't have something sporty if you could afford it?"

Julie lifted her glass. "No, I'd sell the car to buy important stuff like Champagne."

"I do hope you're joking because I feel upset enough as it is."

"That you lost your job?"

"No, that she didn't come in today, and I haven't lost my job, I walked out."

"You walked out because Harriet didn't come in? That's a bit bloody dramatic isn't it?"

"I thought I walked out because people were being mean and, you know me, I'm not usually bothered by that, I've put up with so much stick in my time, which makes me realise it must have been the fact that Harriet didn't come in that was the deciding factor. I was wrong about her and that upset me. I feel genuinely upset."

"Why?"

"I don't know. You know when someone gets inside your head."

"Camila, this sounds dangerous. *Take A Break* are always talking about people who play mind games. Gaslighting's the big thing at the moment."

"I don't think she meant to play mind games, and if I'm honest I liked the idea she thought I was special." Camila sighed. "But how I performed at work today shows I'm not special at all which must mean she was saying kind things because she was in actual fact after more than my mind, just like you said."

Julie was nodding seriously. "You've had a lucky escape. Tomorrow you can do a stint with me on the bacon butty van. We'll soon have you remembering who you are."

"And who am I?"

"You're the average everyday woman who doesn't get thoughts above her station."

"Really?"

"Yes. You're normal. Basic even, in the nicest of ways."

"Right."

"Tomorrow on the van, I'll make you feel back at home."

CHAPTER TWENTY FOUR

Sitting in the slow-draining shower tray with only a pool of lukewarm water for company, Camila tucked her knees into her chest and hugged herself tightly. She'd turned the shower off five minutes ago but instead of getting out she'd slid down the wall and slumped onto her bottom. She wasn't bothering to shave her legs so there wasn't any need to be down there, but likewise there wasn't any need for her to be anywhere else. The boys had taken themselves off to school half an hour ago and Julie wasn't leaving until ten. Not that a shift on the van was anything to get geed up about. Camila cursed herself. When had she become so precious? A few days in the world of work and here she was hating her real life, something that risked shunting her onto a dangerously slippery slope of despair... and that wasn't like her. This was her lot and she'd been foolish for thinking she was worth more. She mothered, she picked up the odd shift here and there, she helped out with her young nieces and nephews, and she cleaned. Yes, she thought, standing back up and reaching for the loofah that was hanging behind her so she could wipe a stray blob of conditioner from the wall, she cleaned.

Stepping out of the shower and finding her trusty Special K towel, Camila took a moment to wrap her hair into a turban before staring at her reflection in the small cabinet mirror. She never looked too bad with her hair pulled back from her face, the few wrinkles that had started to form disappeared with the tight wrapping. She nodded, she'd pull her hair into an Essex facelift today, a tight top pony that wouldn't need to be dried... and that wasn't being lazy, it just got hot on the van, plus she never liked to put too much effort in or dress in a way that might encourage any comments from the workmen. She'd also wear her tracksuit, her Tesco one. Camila felt her breath catch as she watched her own reaction in the mirror. There'd been a look of decision, followed by a look of realisation, followed by a look of pain. She couldn't wear the tracksuit because Harriet still had it, and that thought hurt. It was that look of pain that had led to the gasp. Obviously she wasn't hurt at the loss of the tracksuit, she was hurt at the loss of Harriet.

Camila dried herself with another towel before walking out of the bathroom, straight to her bed and tucking herself back under the duvet. The curtains were open, but it wasn't a bright day, in fact it was dull and miserable, just like her life. Sitting up and pressing her back against the cushioned headboard, Camila knew she had to snap out of it. She needed to focus. She knew she had to take stock and assess all she'd achieved. She was a mother of two good and healthy boys. She ran a home. She seemed fairly well liked by the people who met her.

Camila gave up and slid back beneath the duvet. She didn't really have a network of friends and her house wasn't that special. She didn't have a flash car or exotic holidays. She didn't do spa days or pamper herself. She didn't have adventures, unless you counted that one time Mick had taken her on the ferry from Hull for a day trip to Bruges. He'd pitched it as a weekend cruise. A cruise liner, he'd said, with shows and restaurants and a cinema. But it turned out to be an old tub that had actually caught fire in the North Sea two years earlier. "The Pride of Hull" it was called and it stank of alcohol and regret, hen and stag dos, men and women on their last bid for freedom before they became shackled to a life they didn't want to live.

Camila cursed herself again. This wasn't like her. She was upbeat, her glass was always half full. Half full of water admittedly, as she couldn't afford anything stronger. Harriet's glass however would be full of Martinis, or Margaritas or Long Island Ice Tea, definitely something exotic, something expensive because she'd picked up the bill in the Thai restaurant without giving it a second glance. She hadn't even looked at the receipt, she'd just paid and moved on. Oh, how to live life like Harriet. The glamour of the parties and the photo shoots, the choice of cars that never broke down, the choice of women. Camila paused at that thought. Harriet was someone who'd have sex on tap. She'd have a whole list in her phone that she could call up for some fun, most of them probably just grateful to hear from her again, taking all they could get whilst they could get it. Camila closed her eyes. She could have been one of those people. But what did she want to get? Was it the lifestyle? Or the friendship? If it was friendship. Or was it Harriet herself? Did she honestly want her? Another woman? For what? For the jokes? For the laughs? For the romance?

Camila felt herself drawn back to the *Four Weddings* rain scene, but again it was Harriet who was standing there in the street. She opened her eyes, she needed to concentrate, she needed to process. It had been the same when Mick had first left her, a constant toing and froing in her mind, wondering if she was to blame, wondering if she actually cared, wondering if it was anger or relief that she felt. She'd done the same back then: tucked herself into bed and just processed. She'd asked herself all the hard questions and tried to be honest with her answers, concluding that the over-riding feeling was one of *c'est la vie*. These things happened. People had affairs. Relationships broke down. Was she even that bothered? She'd decided no, and since that realisation she'd been able to move on without the internal debates about what she'd done wrong, or what she hadn't been able to offer him that had forced him elsewhere. She'd also decided she didn't need to hand out blame because no damage had actually been done. Yes, she felt a bit stupid, but she didn't feel hurt or betrayed, similar to the boys who just assumed their dad was a cock. Had she been too blasé in her conclusions? The fact that she and the boys had been able to move on with very little altering in their lives signalled no. It was what it was.

She closed her eyes again, and this was what this was. A confusion based on feelings she'd never felt before. A confusion based on a situation she'd never been in before. A hot, successful, powerful woman liked her. Or more correctly, a hot, successful powerful woman liked her then apparently didn't. So why was she bothered? Was it infatuation? Or did she want to be Harriet's confidante... or her lover? Camila slid further under the covers at that thought, wondering what it would be like to just go there. To just say yes. To experience a woman's body on her own. Would the sex be hard or soft? Would there even be a final sexual act? How lovely to think there'd be no agenda, no quick warm-up for the grand finale, a finale that was rarely grand and actually only pleasured the man because as much as the final thrusting was sexual, it didn't technically induce much pleasure, not for her anyway.

Camila paused her thought. Men definitely viewed sex as something they *got* from a woman. Would lesbians view sex as something they *gave* to a woman? Strange, given the different technicalities of the male and female anatomy, but plausible given the way women gifted themselves to their man with sex, often using it as a bribe, or a reward, or simply something you owed him because it had been a week or so since he'd last had it. Did that mean a woman would want to give herself to another woman for the pleasure she could gift, or the pleasure she could receive? That must be it. It must be a 100% mutual decision. If two women were going to have sex, both women must want to have sex, you couldn't just lie there and take it like you could with a man. Camila smiled, and she wouldn't want to just lie there. She'd want to feel the soft skin. To feel Harriet's soft skin.

Slipping even further under the covers, Camila imagined what she'd do first, given the opportunity. First she'd take off Harriet's glasses. She'd look straight into Harriet's eyes as she let her fingers run slowly up Harriet's body. She'd want to see the reaction she was causing. She'd like to watch Harriet's lips part as she traced her fingers over her stomach, as she moved up the curve of her breast. Camila swallowed. Would Harriet's nipples be as sensitive as hers were? Would they want to be teased before being touched? She'd tease her anyway. She'd trace over the curve of her breast and around her hard nipples, but she wouldn't touch them. She'd do everything she'd want someone to do to her. Take their time. Build up the action. Tease. She'd like Harriet to reach down and tell her to spread her legs before touching the inside of her thighs. Both of them letting their fingers wander, but never going where they were needed the most because they'd know that everywhere felt good in the build-up.

Everywhere brought pleasure. Harriet would get that. She'd play on that.

Harriet would understand how a woman liked to imagine. To imagine their nipples being squeezed, to imagine slow fingers being pushed deep inside. She'd understand how this imagination could bring you so close to the edge. Wanting what you weren't quite getting. Desperate to be touched properly. Kissed properly. Harriet would take control. She'd build everything up. Harriet would kiss the inside of her thighs. She'd pause on her lips. She'd take her time. She'd use her fingers to bring pleasure elsewhere, finally going there and grazing her nipples.

Camila let her hand run over her own chest. Harriet would touch her before gently squeezing her, then she'd pull the nipple up into her mouth. She'd then look up with her big blue eyes. She'd tease the nipple with her tongue, knowing she was on show. She'd move her hand back to the thighs. She'd push the legs wider. Camila slid her own legs apart in the bed. Harriet would be gentle and exploring before plunging straight in there, fucking her as deeply as she could, her fingers wet with the build-up. Camila pulled on her own nipple and touched herself properly. Harriet would fuck her with force. She'd get on top of her. She'd kiss her as she fucked her. She'd make her come quickly. She'd make her come hard.

Camila turned her head into the pillow, muffling her own cry of pleasure.

CHAPTER TWENTY FIVE

"You're late," said Julie, handing over a can of Fanta. "You look like you've just got out of bed. Why are your cheeks so red? Have you been running?"

Camila hauled herself the final way into the rickety pink van, slamming the heavy door shut. "I don't want Fanta."

"You always have Fanta."

"You always give me Fanta because it never sells."

"It's only a month out of date. Here, take it."

"I thought Figgy drank it?"

"Who?"

"Figgy and Queenie, the infamous Fanta drinking jodhpur-wearing new customers."

Julie throttled the ignition. "There she goes. She might be old but she's certainly trusty."

"Figgy?"

"Oh bloody hell, Camila, I wondered how long it would take you before you started rattling on about Harriet again."

"I haven't said anything about Harriet and the only thing rattling's this van."

"She's vintage."

"No, she's converted ice cream."

Julie heaved on the huge steering wheel. "I'm a good friend. We can talk about her if you want to."

"The van? Okay, she looks like a pink metal rust bucket and smells of fat."

"Oooo, you're feisty this morning. It matches your slick-back hair and your council estate clothing."

"Julie!" Camila reached up to grab her seatbelt. "You gave me these leggings."

"They're not leggings they're tights."

"They stop at the ankle!"

"They're footless tights. Haven't you noticed how see-through they are?"

Camila looked down. She'd spent rather too long in bed before grabbing the comfiest thing she could find second to her missing Tesco tracksuit. Plus the weather was dingy and there hadn't been much sunlight coming into the room, added to the fact she hadn't turned the bedroom light on as she was still enjoying the slightly illicit atmosphere. But now, sitting in the bucket seat of Julie's bacon butty van with the sun suddenly streaming in from behind the clouds she could see that her 'leggings' were indeed totally see-through. "You one hundred percent said they were leggings!"

"To be worn under a shirt dress or something, not as the main player with a waist length cricket jumper."

"It's not a cricket jumper; yes, it's white and loose knit, but it's not cricket."

"It looks cricket and it exposes your bottom." Julie pulled the van in at the end of the cul-de-sac. "I'm stopping. You need to sit up."

"Why?"

"Oh bloody hell, I can see them from here. You've got white pants on. Big ones."

"I like to be comfy on the van."

"Didn't you check yourself before you stepped outside?"

"You were honking me."

"Well, you're going to get honked at all day in that get up." Julie revved the engine and pulled into the road. "You might not actually, because your hair looks so slick."

"Aren't we going back?"

"We haven't got time to go back, plus your hair will distract from your two denier stockings."

"*You* gave them to me, Julie!"

"It's fine, you can wear the long apron." Julie revved again.

"The one that fell in the grease trough and never cleaned up properly? Thanks."

"That's what friends are for. Whoah! Who the bloody hell is that!"

Camila looked down at the car that had swerved onto the pavement on the other side of the road, horn beeping and lights flashing. "You pulled out onto their side, Julie!"

"They were going too fast! And look, another rich bitch in a sporty Merc. Ha, it's not Harriet, is it? OH BLOODY HELL IT IS HARRIET!"

Camila stared at the woman now getting out of the Mercedes. "It's Harriet! Drive, Julie! Just drive!" she screeched, ducking as far down in her seat as she could.

"She's already seen you."

"I don't care! You need to drive!"

"She's waving at you."

"JUST BLOODY DRIVE!"

Julie revved the engine. "If that's what my friend wants, that's what my friend will get." Julie shunted herself in her seat as if gee-ing the lumbering vehicle along. "She's a bit of a slow starter; maybe jump in the back in case she comes to the door."

Camila released her seatbelt and clambered through the gap between the broken-leather bucket chairs, suddenly plunging forward with arms and legs spread as the vehicle lurched into life. "Julie!" she screeched from her face first position on the floor, remnants of grease and floor bits scuffing her cheek like an oil-based face scrub. "My jumper!" Camila sat up and stared down at the once white wool. "It's filthy! And my face!" She used the back of her hand to wipe away the grit. "When did you last clean this floor?"

"I'm going to have to speed up, she's got back in her car."

"Just let me sit—" It was too late, the van jolted ahead, sending Camila into an awkward forward roll, accelerating her towards the rickety double doors at the back of the van and even Camila didn't need Cassie Stevens' knowledge of gravitational velocity to know she was about to burst out onto the street. "Turn!" she hollered trying to grab anything that would stop her momentum, the only thing in reach being the dirty pedal bin.

"What?"

"TURN!" The pedal bin slipped through her fingers.

"Left?"

"JUST TURN!" Camila hit the side of the grease trough that collected the fat from the griddle. It hadn't been emptied, just like the pedal bin, but at least she was at the cupboard under the front hatch now and not smashing through the double doors at the back. She lifted her hand to her head. The thick congealed layer on top of the grease trough must have cracked, allowing the cold liquid fat to surge out of the gully and onto her shoulder. She rubbed her pony tail. Damn, it had sloshed onto that as well.

"Where now?" asked Julie.

"What?" managed Camila, pulling herself back into a crouched position and daring to peep forward.

"You told me to turn left. We're in next door's cul-de-sac. Sinclair Street."

"WHAT?!"

"And she's behind me."

"Turn!"

"I'm going to have to three point it. I got my angles wrong."

"Oh god, Julie, please just get us out of here."

"She's parking."

"I don't want to see her."

"Why not?"

"Look at me!" Camila hauled herself up and lifted her arms to the side as Julie turned in her seat.

"Oh my fucking god! You look like a tramp! A tramp with transparent leggings and huge white fucking knickers!"

"She can't see me like this!"

"Your hair's literally dripping with fucking grease!"

"You didn't clean the grease trough! The fat cracked!"

"Oh god, she's coming."

"Please, Julie, just drive."

Julie honked the horn loudly. "Get out of here," she growled, as if scramming a cat from the road.

"You can't talk to her like that."

"Make your bloody mind up, would you!" snapped Julie, crunching the van into reverse. "I'll back out," she said, rocking in her seat to get the vehicle moving.

Camila peeped towards the front windscreen. "She's just standing there."

"Of course she's just standing there. She's probably thinking what the hell's Julie's pink bacon butty van doing in a car chase with a fucking greasy tramp held hostage in the back."

"Stop swearing!"

"I have every right to swear. You need to tell me what's going on!"

"I like her."

"WHAT?"

"I like her! I can't let her see me like this."

Julie slammed on the brakes, causing Camila to fall onto her knees, the thin fabric of the leggings ripping on impact. "You like her?! Like lesbian like her?!"

Groaning as she rolled onto her bottom, Camila rubbed her scuffed skin. "Ouch."

"You're in lesbians with her? Right. I'm not having anything to do with this. Out you go."

"I just…"

"Go on. Your lesbian lover's waiting for you." Julie shouted out the window: "THE BACK DOOR'S OPEN. YOU CAN LET HER OUT."

"No! Julie, please!"

Julie turned in her seat. "What about poor Mick?"

"You said you'd go there with her!"

"I was testing you! I never thought you'd actually…. with a woman?? Oh, Camila."

"Nothing's happened!"

"And it's not going to after she sees you looking like that. YES!" she shouted. "GO AND LIFT THE CATCH ON THE BACK DOORS!"

Camila sat still, stunned like a half squashed rabbit in the headlights as the van's back doors were thrown open. Harriet stood there, arms wide apart, the pale sunlight behind her giving her a Jesus type silhouette. "Oh hi, Harriet," she managed to say.

Harriet jumped into the van and down onto her knees. "Are you okay? What's happened? You're bleeding."

Camila looked to her now exposed left arm, a knit on her jumper must have caught and untangled. "No, I think that's tomato ketchup."

"But that's not ketchup on your knee. You're definitely bleeding. Are you okay? What's happened? You've got some grit in there too, we need to get it cleaned up. Julie, do you have a first aid kit?"

"What do you think this is, a bloody ambulance?"

Harriet turned her attention back to Camila. "Here, reach up to my shoulders, I'll help you out."

"Your suit. It's designer."

"I don't care about my suit. Come on, let me help you up."

Julie piped up again. "You won't get that grease out."

"Julie, is she okay? She looks a bit dazed."

Julie tutted. "She must be a bit bloody dazed if she's got feelings for you."

"Feelings for me?"

Camila groaned as Harriet hauled her upright. "I haven't got feelings for you."

"Stop groaning then," shouted Julie.

"You haven't?" Harriet was looking down on her patient with wide eyes.

"I… will you just take me home?"

Harriet smiled. "Of course I will. Here let me help you to my car."

"I can't get in your car, I'm filthy."

"It's fine, come on, it doesn't matter."

Julie tutted again. "Oh look at you two lovebirds. Isn't this sweet. Shut that door tight when you get out, in fact why don't you carry her as you exit over the threshold."

Camila turned back to her friend. "I'm sorry for the mess, Julie."

Julie whistled. "Things are going to get A LOT messier than this."

CHAPTER TWENTY SIX

Lowering herself into the Mercedes, Camila tried to inhabit as little of the passenger seat as she could. "Don't you have a blanket or something for me to sit on?" she asked.

"Stop fussing, it's just a car."

"But you've been avoiding me because your last car got stolen."

"Avoiding you? I've not been avoiding you. I came into work yesterday – in my red stilettos – to discover you'd walked out."

"Your red stilettos?"

"Yes, my red stilettos, which I then realised was rather ridiculous given that you'd decided to jump ship." Harriet stared at her passenger before starting the engine. "Camila, what on earth's happened to you? Why aren't you at work and why are you wearing a pair of tights? Where's your skirt gone? And why's your whole body so slippery?"

"I fell over. The grease trough cracked on me."

"And your skirt?"

"I forgot it."

"You were headed to work though, right?"

Camila paused. This all sounded so ridiculous. There was no way she could sugar coat any of it. "I left," she said, staring Harriet straight in the eye. What she'd learnt in life was that she had to be honest. She had to lay all her cards on the table and tell the truth. That's what she'd done with her parents when she'd found out she was pregnant. Yes, she'd wondered about the possibility of disappearing for nine months before returning with an adopted baby, or maybe just pretending she was getting fat until finding a baby in the park, or even just saying she had no clue how it had happened. Surely some boys released semen when they were swimming? Maybe the friction coming down the waterslide at the local pool had caused them to ejaculate and then she'd happened to slide down after them and her legs had opened with the force of the water and that's how it had happened. Or maybe a boy had used the girls' toilets and she'd sat on the seat where he'd accidentally left some sperm. Or maybe a boy had used the wrong showers at school and got carried away with the soap which she'd then used.

Camila squirmed in her seat at the memory. Aside from being implausible, all of those options had one major pitfall: she didn't want her baby taken away. This baby was hers, hers and Mick's, and that's what she had to say to her parents.

"I walked out because of you," she suddenly announced.

"Excuse me?"

Camila turned to Harriet. "Okay, I could blame the fact that I felt embarrassed that I only got the job because my initials are C.U.M."

"Camila—"

"Don't, it's true. Or I could say I was mortified when your PA read out the email I wrote you in the lift in front of the whole team."

"What email? You wrote me an email in the lift?"

"No, she read it in the lift. It doesn't matter. What I'm saying is that I could also suggest it was because I've had no good invention ideas."

"You've had some great invention ideas."

"I haven't, but let me finish. You've got inside my head, Harriet. I touched myself this morning. I was thinking about you." There. The whole deck of cards had just been slapped face up on the table.

Harriet was smiling.

"What? You don't think that's weird?"

"I think it's weird that you'd choose to revert to a skirt-less greasy spoon shift girl instead of confronting your attraction."

"You don't like my new look?"

Both Harriet and Camila smiled before Camila continued slowly. "I didn't say it was an attraction."

"You said you never thought of anyone apart from Stallion Mick."

"When I'm having sex."

"Oh right! I see! But you're a solo sex fantasist are you?"

"I didn't say that either."

Harriet started the car. "I need to get you home. We need to explore this further."

Camila glanced out of the window. "Where are we going? Why have you turned left? My house is just there on the right."

"I'm taking you home. My home."

"No! I need to get changed. I need to shower."

"I have a shower. I have clothes."

"I need my clothes."

"I have your tracksuit."

"We can't go to your house."

"Why not?"

"Because I should be at work."

"Where? On the van? In the office? What do you want, Camila?"

"I don't know."

Harriet was smiling. "You thought about me?"

"Stop it. I shouldn't have said that."

"You said it."

"I know."

"Why?"

"You tell me. Maybe I'm just some woman having a mid-life crisis? I suddenly think I can do a new job, then I think I can chat up the boss, then—"

"You've been chatting me up?"

"I don't know what I've been doing."

"You want to stop?"

Camila smiled. "No."

****

Climbing out of the car, Camila hadn't been sure what to expect. A huge country pile perhaps? Or a modern Grand Designs house? A gated driveway at the very least. But here they were, in an underground car park beneath an apartment complex. Yes, there had been security at the barrier but there were other cars. Lots of them. Camila gasped for a second. "Wait. These aren't all yours are they?!"

"Of course not."

"So where are we?"

"Home."

"You live in an apartment? With other people living in the building?"

"You sound disappointed."

"I just…"

"It's nice. Follow me."

Camila walked with one hand in front of her legs and one hand behind, doing her best to hide the now off-white knickers.

"It's fine. I've seen you already."

"Oh. Right."

"And remember I saw you dressed in that see-through mesh outfit too."

"Oh yes, you did, didn't you?"

"I've not seen you looking quite as slick though. You might need a hand in the shower."

Camila stopped. What was she doing? Why was she here? It was one thing to close your eyes and imagine another woman, but something else entirely to actually go there. To shower together? On a Thursday morning? That didn't happen. Or did it? Was there a whole world of excitement out there that she'd never experienced? Well of course there was. There were holidays and ski trips and adventure sports. Could sex in the shower with Harriet be likened to an adventure sport? Quite possibly.

"I'm joking!" said Harriet, holding open the door that led out of the car park.

"Right," said Camila, continuing her self-protecting forward shuffle.

"Unless you want to of course?"

Camila stopped again. "You have to stop doing this."

"Doing what?"

"Getting into my head. These might be little throw away comments to you, but now I'm standing here seriously considering the possibility of getting in the shower with you."

"Is it on your bucket list?"

"It wasn't, no."

"Do you want it to be?"

"Again, said in the most flippant of fashions."

"Sex doesn't always have to be serious, Camila. You can just have it."

"And then what?"

"And then if it's good you might have it again."

"Oh no! Now there's the pressure of a poor performance."

"Camila. Can you please just take twenty steps back."

Camila glanced behind her.

"Not literally! Just chill out. Calm down. You need to get clean. That's all that's happening here."

"It is?" said Camila, not believing a single word.

CHAPTER TWENTY SEVEN

Showering for the second time that day, Camila marvelled at the difference in her surroundings. Yes, Harriet didn't live in a huge house but she did live in a rather swanky apartment. Swanky in terms of its open plan and minimalistic decor. It wasn't massive, but it gave the illusion of space. This shower for instance, in the corner of the fully tiled bathroom, no shower screen or glass cube boxing you in, just a powerful shower head, with space to move around. Camila sluiced the water through her hair and thought: Harriet would definitely have sex in here. She checked the bathroom door: still locked. Harriet wouldn't be having sex in here today. Camila smiled. Had she really contemplated leaving it unlocked? Maybe for a millisecond before sensible reasoning kicked in. She and Harriet couldn't have sex. It just wasn't right. Not in terms of the moral aspect, which didn't exist, or even the boss and employee aspect, which did exist but could be got around, but more the – why on earth would they? aspect.

But at the same time, why on earth was she even here? Why had Harriet come to find her? Why had Harriet insisted on bringing her home? There were so many questions she wanted to ask but their conversation always took them elsewhere, as if the real attraction, the real draw, was simply talking to one another. When they'd walked into the apartment, for example, she should have gone straight into the shower, but instead they'd ended up on a tour of the space, despite her greasy, grubby state and the apartment's pristine appearance. Harriet had insisted on throwing a towelling dressing gown around her and walking her through the rooms, showing as little material regard for her home as she had for the Mercedes, which was strange given her reaction to the missing Lamborghini.

Camila knew she'd have to address it, but under the warmth of the shower it was easier to focus on all the positives. Take Harriet's office for example, actually the cosiest and most personal area of the place. There was row upon row of books ranging from fine art to ancient literature and few of the typical business publications you'd expect to find in the home of someone like Harriet Imogen Pearson. What also surprised her was Harriet's confirmation that this was it; it was the only property she owned. There was no chalet in the French Alps, or cottage in the Lake District. No villa in Spain or condo in Florida. This was where Harriet spent her time. Obviously she said she travelled a lot and spent time in hotels, but in terms of worldly possessions, this seemed to be it.

Camila smiled to herself. That Harriet continued to surprise her seemed to ignite her feelings of intrigue further. She'd been expecting glitz and glam and maybe even a whole host of framed accolades on a wall, but there'd been beautiful paintings instead, some that were clearly originals, but a lot that were simply well known prints. A row of Georgia O'Keeffe's, for example, lined the wall that led from the open-plan lounge into a bedroom, the brilliant colours of the magnified flowers becoming more intimate with the last one at the bedroom door being her famously sexual *Grey line, with Black, Blue and Yellow*. This had led on to an interesting discussion about the artists they both liked. Harriet had been engaging and thoughtful, and seemed to have very similar taste to her own.

Having glanced through the bedroom door, however, Camila realised they had very different taste in bedroom décor. The room, even from the doorway, appeared to contain only a large bed adorned with silky gold sheets and walls that were dark crimson. Definitely a sex room. Camila tutted at herself before squeezing more body wash into her hands. Why was she thinking about sex again? Maybe that was the guest bedroom? There were a number of rooms they hadn't been in so maybe the room that Harriet chose to sleep in was more like her office? Personalised and thoughtful. Camila rubbed the soapy liquid into her skin. Where would be the best place to have sex? In a personalised and thoughtful room that had soft throws and pretty cushions, or under those silky gold sex sheets?

Frantically foaming up the bubbles, Camila shook her head. Why did she keep having these sex thoughts? She and Harriet were colleagues, friends maybe. That was all. Yes, Harriet was a gay woman, but she wasn't. She was straight. She fancied men. Yet here she was finding herself increasingly attracted to Harriet. Why? Was it that Harriet didn't have a huge television taking up a whole wall in her living space? The only screen visible being the small one in the office that Harriet said she used to watch the news whilst she was working. But why was that endearing? Just like the row of cookbooks in the kitchen. They'd managed to warm her heart too, maybe because she'd imagined Harriet as someone who would always eat out, or at least have a private chef, but the image of her with music on, preparing food from scratch as she sipped on a glass of wine was appealing somehow.

Maybe this whole thing was just the excitement of getting to know someone new? Camila rubbed a particularly stubborn smear of grease from her left shoulder. Who was she kidding? This thing with Harriet was layered. It was an excitement she'd not felt in a very long time, perhaps ever before. A chemistry that she couldn't quite place. An illicitness that when you looked at it in its purest form wasn't illicit at all. She was technically a free agent and Harriet appeared to be a free agent too. So why not just go there? Well, she wasn't even sure if Harriet actually wanted to go there, and if Harriet did want to go there would she actually let her, because if Harriet went there it would mean she'd have to go there too. Reaching for the razor blade that was resting on the shelf next to the toiletries, Camila changed the head and decided to shave just in case. She'd put the head she was using in the bin and pop Harriet's back on. Girls shared things. It would be fine. Plus, Harriet wouldn't want to feel her leg stubble.

But why would Harriet even be feeling her stubble? Why would it even get that far? Camila gently swiped the razor up from her ankle, careful to avoid her cut knee. Better to be safe than sorry.

"Are you okay in there?" came the shout.

"I'm good," said Camila, honestly meaning it. She was cleaning up nicely and she felt confident, such a far cry from the wallowing of last night. Strange how the actions of one person could change her demeanour completely, meaning the whole period of despair must have been predominantly about Harriet after all. She could handle Pamela from Insights and the bitching on floor five, but what she hadn't been able to handle was the distance from Harriet, the idea that the connection was all in her mind. It was similar to that quote she'd seen on Facebook once: Sometimes I feel like we're friends, sometimes I feel like we're more than friends and sometimes I feel like I don't know you at all. "Can I ask you something?" she shouted, before angling the shower head towards the wall so she could hear Harriet more clearly.

"Fire away," came the reply.

"Why didn't you come in yesterday?"

"I did. In my red stilettos."

"What time?"

"Just gone three-ish." The pause was long. "Why?"

Camila shook her head. How could she explain this? How could she even justify this to herself? If only she'd been patient. If only she'd trusted Harriet's word that she'd be in. Harriet was a few hours late and meanwhile she'd morphed into a psychotic single white female. Camila corrected herself, no, it was the fact that Deana had been claiming to know Harriet's schedule. Deana had said she definitely wasn't coming in.

Turning the water off, Camila slid down the tiled wall next to the door. The wet room was warm with steam and it was nothing new for her to sit naked on the floor of a shower, only this time she wasn't squashed into a plastic tray and this time she had proper things she needed to debate, things that actually mattered. "How come you told Deana about the car?" she asked. "The Lamborghini."

"She deals with the leasing firm. Deana can't actually drive. I think it's her vicarious thrill to have me fulfilling her fantasies. It's harmless... so far."

Camila leaned her forehead against the door. "Is this your way of telling me you have history?"

"We don't. Not like that anyway. I own the Merc, that's why I don't mind it getting dirty but Deana thinks I should be seen in something more jazzy... again probably because she likes me driving her around in something flash."

"Do you drive her around a lot?"

"No, and this isn't about that. She's my number two, we go to the odd meeting together, but that's why I was angry about the Lamborghini. It didn't belong to me and it's important to look after other people's things."

"I'm sorry it got stolen."

"Obviously it's not great, but the leasing company has insurance for that sort of thing. Deana had to know because she's in charge of the cars."

"Did you say anything else to Deana?" Camila knew she had to be careful. There was a fine line between natural curiosity and psycho suspicion.

"What is there to say?"

Camila let the silence hang in the air, before voicing her query as nonchalantly as she could. "She just mentioned that you might not be in for a while."

"Ignore Deana, she's always trying to organise me. What was this email about? The one from the lift?"

"Oh, I just tried to get hold of you. I wanted to know about iFly. I realised I hadn't got your number."

"I said I'd be in."

"I know."

"But you walked out."

"I know."

"Are you coming back?"

"If you'll have me?"

"I'll have you."

Camila smiled at the tone.

Harriet continued. "I got called to an emergency meeting yesterday morning. I have a lot of commitments. But if I say I'm doing something, I do it."

"Right." Camila shook her head. She felt utterly foolish. "So it wasn't about me pushing you with my questioning in the limo?"

"Was that you pushing me?"

"Ignore me," said Camila before whispering to herself: "*I have no life.*" How could she have failed to understand the huge life Harriet led? She clearly had lots of things going on. She was clearly someone who had a schedule that wouldn't allow time for stewing or analysing or maybe even taking things personally. The last thing she'd want was a needy idiot trying to attract her attention.

Harriet spoke first. "Okay, maybe it was. Just a little bit. But that's not why I was late yesterday. Yes, I cut our ride short because I felt you were getting too close to my truth but then all this has happened and I haven't had time to think about any of that."

"What's your truth, Harriet?"

The voice was quiet. "You get me. You see me."

Camila smiled on her side of the door. "I unmasked you."

"I think you did. Or you were trying to, and I felt vulnerable. Maybe my glasses are a bit of a disguise? A protection of sorts, but you saw straight through me." Harriet spoke again only louder this time. "But I see you too and I know people were mean but you can't run away from things. I heard you held your own in the focus group. Doug, Deana and the team were really impressed."

Camila straightened her back against the wall. As much as she'd love to delve deeper into Harriet's admission it was obvious from her surroundings that Harriet was so much more than the front she presented. "They were?" she said instead.

"And that Tina's gone."

"She has?"

"Things move fast. You can't look away for a second. You also can't pick up shifts on your friend's bacon butty van when you're meant to be inventing the next invention."

"I'm not an inventor."

"You're a blue sky thinker. You have a secret smile. There's a real depth to you, Camila."

Again, like the hot comments, whatever Harriet's motivation was Camila decided she was going to take the praise with both hands.

"And you don't need to worry about work. I got to the bottom of everything yesterday. I spoke to Helen. I told the team what you'd discovered about your initials and that you were rightly taking a moment to take stock. But remember, Camila, like I said to them all, I hired you because of what I saw in that first focus group, and Deana and the team agreed yesterday. Deana said she chased after you to tell you."

Camila realised that Deana would never let on to Harriet that people read and laughed about her personal emails so she'd obviously omitted that part of the story which was probably a saving grace for them all. "So you know about the acronym awards?"

"I do."

"You don't try and stop it?"

"I've stopped it. Admittedly it went on for too long without me realising but we're in the age of #MeToo. It's not appropriate for you or Pamela Isabelle Simpon Smith or Alan Simon Stevens or Sally Lucy Ulrika Tonks to have those initials on show."

Camila gasped and laughed. "There is *not* a Sally Lucy Ulrika Tonks!"

"There is, and, yes, childishly I used to find it quite funny too, as did the other fair-weathered acronymed employees, but I know it's cruel. We're overhauling the whole system. I think Pamela wanted to pass over the mantle before it was scrapped entirely." Harriet sighed. "Listen, Camila, I understand it must have hurt your feelings but you have a job to do. I want this new business to succeed. To win. You're going to be instrumental in that. You're a special person, Camila. That's why I came to get you today. Although I must admit I was disappointed you didn't come in to work this morning. My gut was telling me you would... maybe not for the business, but possibly for me."

"I didn't think you'd be there."

"I'm here. In fact, I'm just the other side of the door."

"Give me five." Camila stood up and turned the water back on, giving her hair a final rinse before replacing the head of the razor and returning it to its original position. Wrapping her body in a super soft towel, Camila used another to soak the moisture from her hair then combed out the tangles. Unlocking the door, she stepped into the hallway to find Harriet patiently leaning on the wall, arms folded. "And now I'm on this side of the door with you."

CHAPTER TWENTY EIGHT

"Was that meant to be some sort of coming out metaphor?" Harriet was kneeling on the floor next to the sofa, opening up a first aid kit. "The bit about you being on my side of the door?"

Camila clamped her knees together, all confidence lost. Here she was in just a towel with the stunningly gorgeous Harriet Imogen Pearson on the floor seeing to her injuries. "I was just announcing my departure from the bathroom," she managed.

"Do you usually do that?"

"I don't usually do any of this."

"What? Have someone see to your wounds?" Harriet gently parted Camila's legs.

Camila's eyes fluttered at the contact. Harriet was focusing on her left knee, carefully rubbing in antiseptic cream before applying a gauze dressing. It was similar to the time she'd had to go for physiotherapy for her broken elbow three years ago. A silly slip in the snow leading to eight weeks in a cast to set her arm at a right angle. It was the physiotherapist's job to re-straighten it once the cast was off, meaning twelve weeks of manipulation and strengthening sessions designed to restore full movement, a difficult task given that she couldn't straighten her arm even halfway. But she'd found herself enjoying those sessions immensely and looking forward to them week on week because of the physical contact she was receiving. The physiotherapist was roughly her age and reasonably pretty, but it wasn't about who she was, it was about what she was doing. Her fingers pulling and rubbing, using her strength to gently manipulate the arm.

Camila guessed it was similar to the one-minute head massage you got at the hairdressers when your head was over the sink with the conditioner on: probing fingers eliciting a physical reaction. That's what Harriet was doing now. Whether she meant it to or not, her gentle smoothing touch around the gauze was having the same effect. Camila let herself close her eyes for a second. How sad that the most arousing touch she'd experienced in a very long time came because of a fall in Julie's bacon butty van. She didn't mind though. It was just nice to be cared for. Being a mother to two teenage boys was hard. They didn't hug back properly anymore and they certainly didn't stroke your cheek or hold your hand like they used to and she missed that contact. Of course it wasn't arousing, just like this wasn't arousing, it was just tender and caring.

"I want to fuck you, Camila."

Fuck. She was aroused. Keeping her eyes closed, Camila contemplated staying still until it all went away. But did she want it all to go away? She didn't know. All she knew was that Harriet had parted her legs further and was now kneeling in between them. And how did she know this? Well she could feel Harriet's hands on the base of her bottom pulling their bodies together and connecting them both at the waist. Camila knew if she opened her eyes Harriet would be there, directly in front of her, eye level in her kneeling position. What should she do? Her towel was still covering her modesty but one movement and it would fall to the sides, exposing everything. When was the last time she exposed everything? She had a good body but she hadn't used it sexually in a very long time. Would Harriet want her to use it sexually? And what would she want her to do? Mick used to like a dirty lap dance. He'd be in his jeans but she had to be naked, grinding on top of him. Camila cringed.

"Sorry, you don't want this." Harriet moved out of her position, turning her attention back to the first aid kit. "But please don't cringe."

Camila flashed open her eyes and looked down at the scene. "No, it wasn't you."

"You're not going to say: *It wasn't you, it was me*, are you?"

"It was Mick."

"Mick?"

"Ignore me. Come back."

Harriet was smiling. "You want me to come back between your legs?"

"I don't know what I want. I want time to make up my mind. Come back and let me decide." Camila re-closed her eyes as she felt Harriet move back into position. She could smell her perfume. She could sense her presence. This was the moment where she had to decide. Would she be able to treat it like those other occasions in her life where she'd been frivolous? Like that time she'd let the hairdresser take three inches off her hair instead of one. She'd not planned it, she'd simply said yes when asked, and it was a big change; three inches made an awful lot of difference. Then there was the time she'd switched her broadband on the doorstep. A cold caller. She never said yes to cold callers, but that time she'd just given it a go; she wasn't sure what had convinced her, she'd just felt like acting out. Was this acting out? Could this even be categorised in the same manner? Her hair grew back and she'd returned to having just the one inch cut off, and in regards to her broadband she'd ending up returning to the original supplier after twelve months. Could she let Harriet fuck her and then return to her life if she wanted?

The thought of letting Harriet fuck her sent another quiver down her spine.

"You clearly don't want this," said Harriet moving back out of her position. "I saw you shudder again."

"No, that was a good quiver, that was an anticipatory shiver."

Harriet rose back up on her knees. "And what are you anticipating?"

"You fucking me," said Camila, reaching out for Harriet's glasses.

"What do you want me to do?"

"Whatever you want." There, she'd said it. She wanted this, or she wanted to try it at the very least. Life was short, that's what she'd learnt recently. Life was also very boring, that's what she'd learnt over the course of the past fifteen years to the extent that she potentially believed that life was actually taken away from you the second you gave life to another. Maybe this was finally her time. A new job. A new love interest. She felt Harriet's lips move to her neck. A new sensation entirely.

"I really want to fuck you," whispered Harriet. "I want to make you feel things you've never felt before."

Camila turned her lips towards Harriet's cheek, enjoying the soft sensation of their faces together. "What will you do?"

"I'll make you come, so hard, and so many times."

Camila groaned. Harriet's words were spoken so gently but they had such an edge, and it wasn't an edge like Mick's words when he'd growl: *Give me a blowjob*, or *Suck me harder*. This was about her and her pleasure. She cursed herself. She needed to stop thinking about Mick. She needed to stop comparing this. She needed— Harriet's lips were suddenly on hers, Harriet's tongue gently pushing into her mouth. Camila moaned, she needed to just go with this, as this was so incredibly good. Pushing into the kiss, Camila found her hands at the back of Harriet's neck, pulling her closer, forcing more of her into her mouth. The kiss had morphed from a gentle connection of lips to a frantic, moaning, all-encompassing snog. She was snogging Harriet Imogen Pearson. She was snogging her really hard.

"Slow down," said Harriet, pulling out of the embrace. "Come with me."

Camila let herself be led from the sofa, using her spare hand to keep her towel in place.

"And you can leave that there if you like."

Camila dropped the towel. She gasped at herself. She'd dropped the fucking towel. Deliberately. She was naked, being led by Harriet Imogen Pearson into one of the bedrooms.

"You continue to surprise me, Camila."

Camila didn't answer. She was in shock at the way she was continuing to surprise herself. Where had this come from? This confidence? This sod it and see attitude? This sweary sod it and see attitude? Was it because she actually wasn't that invested in Harriet or this situation, or was it because she was head over heels invested in this situation and wanted to give it her best shot? Harriet had said she could leave the towel there so she'd left it there.

"You have an incredible body," continued Harriet, pulling Camila into one of the rooms they'd not yet explored.

Camila looked around. It was a bedroom positioned in the centre of the apartment with no windows, just a gentle pink haze glowing out from a small pink lamp on the bedside table.

Harriet followed Camila's gaze. "I turned it on when you were in the shower."

"So this is your sex bedroom?"

"It's just a bedroom with good walls." Harriet closed the door and pushed Camila against one of them. "No pictures." Harriet parted Camila's legs with her own before grabbing Camila's wrists and pinning them above her head. "No need to worry about anything falling when I fuck you."

"You're going to fuck me against this wall?"

"I'm going to fuck you everywhere."

Camila could feel herself getting wetter. Harriet had only kissed her once but her direct statements were turning her on. She had imagined lesbian sex to be all flowers and chocolates. Gentle stroking and kissing, not this full-on, foul-mouthed fucking. "What are you going to fuck me with?"

"My fingers. My mouth. My words."

Camila groaned again as Harriet's lips returned to her neck. "I like you talking," she whispered, remembering how Mick had always been so silent during sex, barring the times he demanded something, or grunted in completion. Harriet's soft voice, however, was adding to the anticipation, making her want all the things on offer.

"I want you to let yourself go," said Harriet.

Camila whispered into her ear. "Look at me. I'm naked and spread eagled against the wall."

"That's too good an invitation," said Harriet, keeping the wrists in position but stepping backwards.

Camila watched as Harriet appraised her from top to toe, her eyes definitely pausing on her chest and the area between her legs. "What do you like best?" she asked.

"I like your neck," said Harriet, stepping back in and kissing it gently. "And I like how your collar bone protrudes just here," she continued, teasing the area with her tongue. "And I like your nipples," she said, sliding Camila's wrists lower down the wall before taking a nipple completely in her mouth.

Camila cried out at the contact. Harriet's tongue was circling one of the most tender areas on her body and her teeth were nipping at the hardness. It was all so forward and fast. She closed her eyes and moaned again, conscious she could very easily get carried away, and while that was obviously what she'd expected to happen, she wanted to savour every second and enjoy every moment of this surreal, yet so real, situation.

"Let me see you," she managed, before pushing against Harriet's grasp and switching their positions against the wall. She smiled at the look of surprise on Harriet's face. "What? I like to give as good as I get." Camila released Harriet's hands and moved her fingers to the small buttons on Harriet's work shirt. It was like she was unwrapping a present she'd not been expecting. Those were often the best kind. The complete surprises, just like the course of the morning. She popped the third button down and Harriet's black lace bra and ample breast came into view.

"Kiss me," said Harriet, lifting her hands to Camila's face.

Camila continued to stare at the cleavage. "I want to see more of you," she said, undoing the final buttons and sliding the shirt over Harriet's shoulders to drop to the floor. Next she reached around to the back of the bra, unclasping the catch and slipping the lace straps down Harriet's arms. The feeling that shot through her body was one of raw desire. Harriet's breasts were magnificent, so full, with nipples that were so hard.

"Kiss me," said Harriet again.

Camila reached for a breast as she pushed her body into Harriet's, their nipples pressing hard into each other. She kissed Harriet's lips with force and moaned into her mouth as her thumb made contact with Harriet's nipple. She circled it gently. Harriet's tongue responded, circling her own deep inside her mouth. Camila groaned, this was so hot and so sexy. She felt sexy. She felt like she was as much in control as being controlled. This thing was mutual, they were both getting off on each other. She moaned again. Harriet's hand had come to join her own, working on her breast, on her nipple. Camila pressed her leg in between Harriet's. "I want to feel all of you," she said.

"So take my trousers off," came the whispered reply.

Camila continued to kiss Harriet's mouth as her fingers found the button and the zip. She glanced down; Harriet's trousers were now around her ankles and her black lace knickers were on show. Camila rolled at the material on either side of Harriet's hips before gingerly dropping to her knees and pulling down the knickers, managing not to flinch as her injured leg made contact with the ground. And, yes, while she was at waist level to help Harriet step out of her trousers and underwear, she was also down there to look. She wanted to see Harriet. To stare at the area between her legs. It looked so smooth and enticing, and it was just there. Camila paused momentarily. It was now or never: Like the call to dance at a wedding. The longer you left it the harder it was to get up and join in. The best course of action was giving it your all from the start, and small side-steps around a handbag wouldn't do, you had to get down there and floor slap to *Oops Upside Your Head.* Camila re-focused. If that dance floor called you, you went. Bringing her mouth forward, she made contact with the smooth skin.

"Oh my god, Camila," came the cry from above her. "This should be me, not you."

Camila pressed her face deeper between Harriet's legs, slowly parting the area with her tongue. She'd always been one of those people who had to do things properly. This is what lesbians did, so this is what she'd do and the fact that Harriet tasted so good made it even more pleasurable than she'd imagined. There were no sweaty bollocks or long stringy hairs to contend with and there certainly wasn't a hand on the back of her head making her take more. She was simply free to kiss and explore as she pleased. Moving her hands around the back of Harriet's bottom, Camila pulled herself closer. What she hadn't been expecting was Harriet's leg to rise and lift onto her shoulder. Suddenly everything was right there. A moisture and a wetness and a place to push her tongue deep inside.

Harriet cried out again. "Fucking hell, Camila, I need you on the bed."

Camila looked up. Harriet was flushed and her eyes wide with surprise and pleasure. "I'm happy where I am," Camila said with a smile.

"I'm meant to be the one fucking you!"

"Trust me, this is pleasurable," said Camila, before giving in and letting herself be led. She gasped as Harriet pushed her down onto the bed and gasped again as Harriet straddled her waist and pinned her arms. She'd expected everything to be so tender and thoughtful. The idea that a woman could be rough with another woman hadn't occurred to her, but it was mesmerising because it was a different kind of aggression. It was safer somehow because of the slight size of Harriet's body, but that didn't stop it from being powerful. It was the idea that it was powerful more than the power of the actual act that made the whole being dominated thing really quite a turn-on. Plus, Harriet was now above her grinding herself on her waist, her breasts gently moving with the action.

"I want you to watch me," said Harriet. "I want you to see how I'm using your body to get myself off."

Camila swallowed hard, Harriet was pushing backwards and forwards with her bottom. She could feel Harriet's hard clit just above her own. It was as if Harriet was riding something that wasn't there. Camila moaned, but there didn't need to be anything there as this was the most arousing vision she'd ever witnessed. A gorgeous woman sitting on top of her, pinning her arms out to the side as she writhed around in pleasure, her full breasts there for the viewing.

Harriet leaned forward and kissed Camila deeply before rolling them both over and switching their positions. "I want you to do that on me," she said with a smile.

Straddling Harriet's waist, Camila held onto the wrists and started to move her pelvis in small circles. It felt good. It felt empowering. Using Harriet's body for her own pleasure. She looked down at Harriet; she was staring, this was pleasuring her too. Women were so visual. So easy to look at. So easy to watch. Releasing one wrist,

Camila brought her hand up to her own breast before gently squeezing her nipple between her finger and her thumb.

"Fuck me, Camila."

"Isn't that what I'm doing?"

"No, it's what I'm doing," said Harriet, breaking her other arm free and pulling up on Camila's bottom, shunting her further up her body.

Camila worked her way up with her knees, coming to a rest either side of Harriet's head before screaming out in pleasure as Harriet suddenly lifted her mouth and kissed deeply right between her legs. Camila cried out again, Harriet's hands were parting her from behind, her fingers were finding their way in, they were pushing further inside her as her tongue expertly circled her clit. Camila felt herself moving with the rhythm, unsure if anything had ever felt as good. She screamed out; it was getting better, Harriet had moved a hand up to her nipples, taking it in turns to rub them and squeeze them as her other hand continued to fuck between her legs from behind and her tongue continued to work its magic. Throwing her head back in ecstasy, Camila knew this experience would change her life completely.

CHAPTER TWENTY NINE

"And I thought that would be the pinnacle of it all, but fuck me, Julie, it wasn't. We did so much stuff after that and—"

Julie interrupted her. "What's with the gutter mouth? You've been swearing like an East End whore since you started your bloody story."

"So you *do* still have a problem with it!" Camila flopped back onto the sofa. That evening, Julie had been the one who'd come round with prosecco. Julie had been the one who'd apologised. Julie had been the one begging for details, and yes it had been against her better judgement to tell her, but she'd insisted. She'd blamed jealousy for her outburst in the van. A worry that she was going to lose her best friend and next door neighbour because apparently lesbians immediately moved in with each other on their second date.

"Tell me more. I don't have a problem with it and I'm happy for you as long as you know what this is and as long as you don't get hurt."

"It hurt when she tugged on my nipples, but in a gorgeous pleasure pain way."

"Camila!"

"What? Do you want the details or not?"

"This isn't you."

"What do you mean?"

"You're just Camila."

"And who is just Camila?"

"She's my lovely, sweet next door neighbour."

"Maybe I don't want to be lovely and sweet anymore. Maybe I want to be Harriet's hot bitch."

"Camila!"

"What? I feel alive. For the first time in a very long time I feel like I've got something to look forward to."

"And that something's hot lesbian sex, is it?"

"Yes, hot sex. Very hot sex. And a connection. We have a genuine connection. And obviously I had to come home because of the boys, but we could have stayed in bed all day. We were chatting and cuddling and..." Camila smiled, "connecting. She's fascinating, Julie. There's so much more to her than you'd imagine. Do you know about her charity work? She gives over fifty percent of her earnings away."

Julie laughed. "And she told you that, did she?"

"I got it out of her."

"Okay."

"What?"

"I just think you need be careful."

"Why?"

"Look at you. You're a fresh-faced lesbian virgin in awe of her superstar boss."

"I'm not a lesbian virgin anymore and she's not really my boss."

Julie wrinkled her nose as she nodded towards the area between Camila's legs. "So what exactly did she put up there?"

Camila took a sip of her drink before smiling in remembrance. "Life."

****

Putting the finishing touches to her homemade spaghetti Bolognese, Camila wondered how much concern she should award Julie's behaviour. Julie would usually stay in the lounge while she was cooking, choosing to watch some afternoon TV instead of helping out before joining her and the boys for tea. Today, however, she'd made her excuses and left. Maybe it was just a bit of casual homophobia? How had Harriet put it? All mouth and no action? Maybe that was Julie. Playing the "yes, I'd like to try it" card, but being absolutely horrified when someone actually did. Just like

Gemma Stubbs from school. She'd told everyone she smoked twenty cigarettes a day before ratting to the teachers about the group outside the sports hall at the end of year leaving party who were enjoying a celebratory smoke. Or maybe Julie had issues with her continuing this? Maybe in Julie's eyes it was okay to try it as a one off, as an experience, but as a lifestyle choice it was a definite no. Camila stirred the sauce. Could this be a lifestyle choice? Whatever that meant. She shook her head. They'd agreed to go on a date, that was all. Julie had asked what was next, so she'd told her: Harriet was going to romance her the old-fashioned way.

The way Harriet had asked her was incredibly sweet. She'd said she wanted to take things slowly as it wasn't like her to jump into bed with someone she really liked. Camila smiled. Harriet really liked her. She liked her so much that she wanted to play it all old school love story. A dinner date tomorrow night at a very posh cocktail restaurant where they served dishes like beef cheeks and lobster thermidor, and she knew this because it was the first thing she'd Googled once she'd got home: Jungle Fung. Admittedly it sounded a bit like a playcentre she'd take her nieces and nephews to, but the website was impressively chic. She stirred the sauce again. What would she wear? Harriet had said she would pick her up and drop her off and conduct herself in the manner in which one should conduct themselves on a first date... a stolen kiss goodnight on the doorstep the only aim of the evening, alongside getting to know one another better of course.

Camila smiled and, yes, while she'd love to see Harriet's naked body again, the idea of a date sounded incredibly appealing. The no-more-than-a-kiss rule meant she could wear her Spanx which in turn would allow her to squeeze into her one designer dress. An impulse buy a few years ago when she'd won on the Grand National. She didn't usually bet but she'd been given a tip from Patricia Goodyear, super-mother to triplets, and Patricia knew everything about everything so if she said Jolly Jackman was going to win at 60-1 then Jolly Jackman would win at 60-1, which he did and her incredibly frivolous £10 bet that she'd surreptitiously placed in the betting shop gave her a return of £600 plus her original £10 and even though excitement levels were high, there was no way she could tell Mick she'd placed a £10 bet… which obviously meant she had to keep her winnings a secret. Julie knew and had suggested a splash-out girls' shopping trip where she'd encouraged the spending of the whole £600 on one little black dress. And it was little, it was tiny, hence the Spanx.

Camila sighed. She'd had some great times with Julie. That shopping trip included. She had thought Julie might not agree with spending the money on herself but Julie had been generous in her gushing about how Camila needed to spoil herself every once in a while. Yes, Julie may have taken things too far in urging that the tighter the dress the better, but they'd had fun and she'd ended up with her first proper piece of designer clothing. The fact she'd had little occasion to wear it wasn't the point. She owned a designer dress. A real designer dress, not just French Connection or Zara level – even though she'd only ever bought one of those in the past as well. A Caroline Castigliano.

The first time she'd worn *the dress* she'd expected the Spanish Inquisition from Mick and had spent the whole day making up a story about how she'd borrowed it from one of the rich school mums, but Mick hadn't even batted an eyelid. He might have muttered, "you look nice", but that was about it. Reaching out for the salt and pepper grinders, Camila wondered how Harriet might react? Would she know immediately that it was designer? Would she gasp? Would she want to rip it off there and then? Twisting the head of the salt grinder, Camila felt her body quiver in remembrance. She could still feel where Harriet's tongue had been, where her fingers had ventured, where the ripping orgasm had taken her. It had honestly been next level pleasure and she'd been so loud. She'd always been conscious of coming with Mick mainly because she often faked it, and it transpired that her faking it sound was quite different from the real deal – which she had to keep a lid on the odd occasion it did actually happen so Mick didn't spot a difference, not that he ever would.

Camila put the salt down. She needed to stop being so hard on Mick. They'd had their good times. Ish. She smiled. She genuinely did wish him luck with Jackie from the gym as he'd been a good catch back in the day and Jackie might be able to restore him to his former glory. Times changed though and this was her time to restore herself, or even just explore who she truly was. Could it be that she actually was a designer dress-wearing sex whore? Camila smiled. Who cared if she was? Women had all sorts of mid-life crises, they had surgery – that seemed to be the big thing at the moment. A dramatic facelift with lip and cheek fillers that made everyone look like puffy clones. A bit of lesbian sex seemed tame in comparison. Camila smiled again, she'd never have guessed she'd be so comfortable with it, but then again she'd taken to spiralising vegetables quickly too – something she thought she'd never do, but when a spiraliser came into her possession there had been no stopping her.

Dropping the spiralised carrots into the sauce, Camila shouted over her shoulder, "Five minutes till tea." The traditionally grated, now spiralised, carrots were the last thing in the dish, adding a sweetness to her Bolognese sauce the boys always claimed was one of their favourites. The fact that Michael and Ethan had devoured whatever she'd put in front of them from an early age didn't seem to matter, they raved over her spaghetti Bolognese and it was heartening to see them eat so well.

"Do you need a hand, Camila?"

Camila turned quickly, smiling at the sixth form girl. "Cassie, hi, I didn't know you were here."

"Am I okay to stay for tea?"

"Of course, of course. Where's Michael?"

"He's just finishing off some work."

Camila smiled politely. Michael would never let a love interest loose in the kitchen alone with his mother, not that there'd been any other love interests, but she knew her son. "Everything okay?" she asked.

"Fine thanks. Shall I lay the table?"

Camila smiled again. Maybe this was just girls? Yes, Michael and Ethan were domesticated but they'd rarely pop down for a chat. "How's the manipulation project going?"

Cassie laughed.

"Didn't you say you were manipulating the laws of gravity?"

"Oh, yes."

"Weren't you?"

"Yes."

Camila pointed to the top drawer. "The cutlery's in there."

The pretty girl paused with a handful of forks. "Can I ask you something?"

Camila held her breath. "Yep." This was it. How was Cassie going to phrase it? – How do I tell my boyfriend, the sixth form head boy, that I'm seeing your son? How do I tell my dad, the reformed criminal owner of a boxing club, that I'm seeing your son? How do I explain to the world that I'm seeing your son who's only fifteen?

"What made you keep Michael?"

Camila gasped.

"You were only nineteen weren't you?"

Camila tried to panic breathe through her nose.

"I'm just interested."

Holding onto the kitchen counter, Camila tried to steady her voice before she spoke. "Ummm."

"It's an RE project on ethics and morality."

"An RE project? Oh! Right! Okay! Hang on... you think I'm immoral?"

"Of course not, I just want to know how you came to that decision."

Camila coughed. Why was she suddenly the one being judged? Surely Cassie had come down to find out how she could sell her story of cradle-snatching without being judged?

"Was it a hard decision?"

Camila coughed again. Why was she on the spot and why was this girl so self-assured? This girl was having dangerous liaisons with her son, by all accounts, yet here she was asking about the ethics and morality of a grown woman's teenage pregnancy.

"I mean you're obviously a great mum, you're so good with the boys and they've turned out so well, you clearly all respect each other and get along brilliantly. The way you talk to each other is so friendly and kind, but did you have doubts and—"

"Hi Ethan!" said Camila with great enthusiasm as her second son entered the kitchen, before noticing he was face first in his iPad. "Will you turn that bloody thing off!"

CHAPTER THIRTY

Clambering out of her car, Camila stared at the H.I.P building. This was it. She had to show her face and carry on. Just like those Monday mornings at school after those weekend house parties when you were fifteen and you'd snogged every boy invited. You knew the gossip would be spreading like wild fire but you just had to grin and bear it. Camila smiled at the memory. It was always fine because there was always someone who'd done something far worse than you and the panic was short-lived once you'd actually shown up and remembered that gossip happens then life goes on. This was the same, she reasoned. Life went on. Yes, she'd thrown her dummy out of the pram and taken a day off, but she was back and ready to work. Nodding to herself, Camila wondered why her legs weren't moving and why she wasn't striding straight into the building? Was it the nerves of seeing Harriet again after their sex fest? They'd finished the afternoon agreeably with a cup of tea and biscuits – again something she hadn't been expecting – but it had been sweetly charming and there'd been no panic then about what they'd done so why should there be panic now? Harriet wouldn't be panicking; she was a pro at all this.

"Camila!" Harriet's voice was unmistakable. "I wanted to see you before you got inside. I've been panicking that my lust face will give the game away!"

Turning around, Camila saw Harriet tottering towards her in red stilettos.

"I've been waiting for you," she continued. "What are you doing just standing there?"

Camila laughed. "Panicking that my lust face will give the game away."

"Show me your lust face."

Camila narrowed her eyes and pouted.

"No, they'll just think you've got conjunctivitis."

"Harriet!"

"What? Come here."

Camila stood still as Harriet wrapped her arms around her before kissing her on the cheek.

"I just wanted to say good morning properly."

Camila continued to stand with her hands by her sides, rooted to the spot.

"And I'm glad that I did because your response was more than I'd hoped for."

Camila laughed. "We're in the car park. Isn't this even more conspicuous?" She nodded towards the building. "Now we're going to have to walk in together."

"It's fine, the others are all upstairs. I've briefed them already so you shouldn't have any problems today. I'll head to my office and join you all later."

"And what are we doing today?"

"At some point we're fucking."

"Harriet!"

"What? We've agreed we're not fucking tonight. I'm wining and dining you properly then I'm dropping you home so I'm going to have to have you at some point today."

"Isn't that wholly unprofessional?"

"It's my building."

"And it's my reputation."

"I'm not planning on getting flyers made up and inviting the exec to come along for the show."

Camila shook her head. "I'm not comfortable with this."

"I'm joking!"

"Good. So we're not…?"

"Getting flyers, no. But I'm telling you, you won't be able to keep your hands off me."

"Harriet, I will. I'm here to do a job."

"Why are you standing in the car park then?"

Camila laughed. "You're trouble."

"Me? You were the one paddling my—"

"Enough! We need to go in."

Harriet nodded and started their walk. "See, we couldn't have said all this during the morning inventions brainstorming session."

"Oh dammit," gasped Camila. "I haven't even thought of any."

"So your professionalism's not really that important to you then, is it?"

"I've been occupied."

"And sulking."

"Oh, Harriet, don't say that. Do they think I've been sulking?" Camila entered the building and walked towards the lift. "The team? Are they angry?"

"No. They, like I, think you've rightly taken a day off to get your head around Pamela from Insights' inexcusable actions. Honestly, Camila, they all said you conducted yourself really well in the focus group."

"But the choking inhaler idea was awful." Camila sighed as they clipped across the open space. "We still haven't got a genuinely good product to take forward to the live show."

"I have faith in you."

"That makes it even worse! And there certainly won't be time for any funny business if I've got to re-invent the wheel."

"We'll see."

"We won't see."

"You're back!" said Helen Anna Howes, sporting a huge smile as she stepped out from behind the polished desk before gifting Camila with a huge hug. "I'm so happy you're back!"

Harriet stared at the connection.

"Sorry, back to it," said the receptionist, dashing back to her desk.

"You're popular," said Harriet under her breath as she ushered Camila towards the lift.

"Are you jealous?"

Harriet pressed the chrome button. "Genuinely? No. It's heartening to see how much Helen likes you. Helen doesn't like anyone."

"She said I was the only person to ever come down and make her a coffee."

"Because you're special. I've been telling you that."

"I don't think that makes me special. That's makes me normal."

Harriet waited for the lift doors to close before turning to Camila. "You're far from normal. There's something about the way you smile. It gives a glimpse of your secret."

"You've said that before and I don't have a secret, or at least I didn't until now."

"Maybe not your secret then, maybe it's a glimpse of your secret sparkle or your secret soul. There's just so much more to you than meets the eye, Camila."

Camila looked at Harriet's smile. "And I think you have a way with words. You have a way of making people feel special."

"You are special."

Camila held her gaze. No one had ever called her special before. Ever. Not even her own mother, and as much as she wanted to keep her guard up and see Harriet for who she most likely was, it was too tempting to get pulled into the romance of whatever was happening between them. Was it just wordplay, or friendship, or attraction? Or could it really be something deeper than that? There was a definite spark and interest but there was also a passionate tug, pulling her into Harriet like their hearts wanted to hold one another. Camila glanced down. Their bodies had connected. Harriet's hands were resting gently around her waist and Harriet's lips were pressing softly against her own.

"I really like you, Camila," whispered Harriet, drawing away from the embrace as the lift reached its destination.

Camila opened her eyes and spoke quietly. "What are you doing to me?"

"Giving you inspiration for a good morning?" Harriet squeezed Camila's hand before releasing their connection and stepping out into the corridor. "Now go and show them your stuff." She grinned happily before turning left and walking towards her office.

Camila watched Harriet before nodding with confidence and striding towards her pod with gusto. The boss liked her. The boss more than liked her. So what if her colleagues were jealous? In its simplest form she had nothing to lose. This job was new and completely unexpected so if it did fall apart then so what? She'd find something else. It made sense to live every second of this while it lasted. Live life. That's what she was doing. Imposter syndrome, schimposter pindrome. Camila smiled at herself. She was such a dork, but she was a cute dork, or more accurately as it had transpired, quite a rampantly hot dork who'd said yes to everything Harriet had requested.

As Camila covered the final yards to the workspace she shook her head; she couldn't keep reliving the sex, it was distracting and really rather knee-buckling. "Hello!" she said to the office with a bit too much vigour.

Deana was the first to stand. "Camila, I'm so sorry about Wednesday. You were great in the focus group and I can only apologise for what happened in the lift."

"Yep, soz," muttered Brett.

"I'm sorry too," said Geoff, standing up and coming round to talk to Camila properly. "Can I take your coat? Get you a coffee?"

"I'm fine. I just want you to know that I do want to be here and I'm going to do my best to make H.I.Pvention a success."

"You have ideas?" said Brett, still not standing but at least leaning sideways on his chair to look her straight in the eye.

"I thought we could all look at it differently this morning. How about we sit down and moan."

Deana laughed. "What do you mean, moan?"

"Let's all talk about our past twenty-four hours – about anything and everything that's made us moan or niggled us." Camila suddenly felt herself blushing. Harriet's tongue had made her moan in the last twenty-four hours, as had Harriet's fingers and the sex toy Harriet had whipped out of her bedside drawer. Snapping herself out of it, Camila signalled towards the sofas. "Shall we start?"

"I'll make the drinks," said Geoff.

"And I'll take the notes," added Brett, finally standing up.

"I like this idea," said Deana with genuine warmth.

Camila took off her coat and smiled. Everything was going to be a-okay. She hoped.

****

"So a productive morning then?" asked Harriet from her position behind her reclaimed-wood desk in her large topiary-filled office.

Camila nodded from her seat between the pots of lush greenery. "It was actually. We have a few leads."

"For example?"

"Why do I feel like I'm being interviewed all over again with you way over there and me sitting amongst your bushes."

"You're always welcome amongst my bushes."

"I don't recall you having any bushes."

"Focus. We're at work."

Camila laughed. "Me? You started it. Fine. We discussed the things we'd been moaning about," she paused. "Don't laugh, even though that's where my mind went too, but the things that had me moaning *in annoyance* over the past twenty-four hours were those see-through leggings, the fact I had to sit down in the shower to shave my legs, the way my boys never seal the top of the cereal bag, the fact we still seem unable to create a carton of juice that's easy to open, the fact my car smells, the fact that no matter how well I do my makeup my foundation always looks horrific in the natural light, the fact that I never actually know if my breath smells after I've had a coffee."

Harriet laughed. "I'm stopping you there. Your car doesn't smell, nor does your breath and your makeup's always perfect." She nodded. "So we're inventing a new juice carton are we?"

"No, Brett had a lot more moans."

"I bet he did."

"We all did, hence my first statement that we have some good leads to be working on." Camila glanced at the clock on the wall. "And on that note, I think my break time's over."

"Back at school, are you?"

"No, I'm at work."

"Just come here a minute."

"No, I need to go. Brett and Geoff only went onto the balcony for a cigarette and Deana said she wouldn't be too long in the canteen."

"One minute."

Camila stood up and made her way to Harriet's side of the desk.

"Now sit down."

"Where?"

"On my desk."

"I'm not sitting on your desk."

Harriet stood up and pulled Camila in close, kissing her passionately before guiding Camila's hips down into a seated position on the surface. "How long do you have really?" she whispered.

Camila smiled. "Three minutes."

"That's long enough," said Harriet, returning to her chair.

"What are you doing down there? I thought you were going to kiss me?"

Harriet wheeled herself in between Camila's legs. "I am," she said with a smile. "Good choice putting your skirt on today."

Camila glanced behind her at the Narnia-esque entrance aisle from Harriet's office door. Yes, the door was shut but anyone could walk in. Throwing her head back she moaned. It was too late, Harriet's mouth was already there, between her legs, her fingers had pushed her skirt up before pulling her thong to the side. Camila praised the fact that she'd worn the skirt, which had by consequence led to the thong. Camila gasped at the fast movement of Harriet's mouth and tongue. She had taken all of her, all at once, kissing her roughly.

Leaning back on her hands, Camila tilted her hips forward allowing Harriet's tongue access to where it really wanted to go. She gasped again. It was so intrusive and rampant. Camila groaned at the pleasure. Harriet was fucking her pussy with her mouth. Really fucking it. Camila cried out in satisfaction; and she was quite happy to let her.

CHAPTER THIRTY ONE

"I don't know, Julie, I really have to question my behaviour. It's like that thing with George Michael. You know when he went into all those public toilets and propositioned strangers. Of course they were going to know who he was. And of course he was eventually going to get caught. But he said he knew this. It was as if on a subconscious level he played dangerously because he wanted to get found out."

"You're not George bloody Michael, Camila."

"I'm just saying I don't understand my behaviour. And I want to understand my behaviour. I want to understand how a normal mother of two who's led a very boring life to date can suddenly straddle her female boss on her female boss's desk and serve up dinner to her face."

"Camila!" Julie was grimacing. "I'm more interested in where your bloody gutter mouth has come from! This just isn't you."

"What if it is? It turned out to be George Michael after all. Once he got busted he came out as gay."

"If you're a bloody lesbian, Camila, you don't need to put on a show for the whole bloody workforce just to get that fact out there. No one cares anymore."

"You care."

"Because I know you, and this isn't you."

"What if I want it to be me?"

"Do you?"

"I don't know." Camila shook her head. "I honestly don't know."

Julie took a sip of her drink before nodding thoughtfully. "We should go on a girly holiday to Magaluf. That's what most middle-aged women do when they want to let their hair down. Or we should go and watch the Chippendales live or something? Or how about a new haircut?"

"I don't want a new haircut."

Julie clapped her hands together. "I know! Let's go and get you some fillers or a nice bit of Botox. The earlier you start the better."

"I'd rather just have hot lesbian sex with my boss."

Julie gasped. "Listen to yourself, Camila! You have morals!"

"I clearly don't, just look at this dress! It's much tighter than I remembered."

"I approve of your Caroline Castigliano dress, but your bloody behaviour leaves a lot to be desired."

"We're opposite then because this dress is borderline pornographic whereas my behaviour's one hundred percent normal."

"It's not pornographic! It's designer! Real designer. You look amazing. I'm totally bloody jealous. There's absolutely nothing to you."

"That's the Spanx. I'm wearing an all-in-one knee-length Spanx just to doubly firm up my stomach."

"She's not getting access tonight then!"

"Exactly. We're slowing things down. We're getting to know each other properly."

"You're going about all this the wrong way round."

"And what is the right way to go about something like this, Julie? Maybe I'm just happy to not know. To not care, in a way. What will be will be. Why can't I just act frivolously for once?"

"Go shopping if you want to act frivolously."

"Julie, I just don't understand the problem you've got with it."

"I don't have a problem with it. I just want you to be careful."

"I know what I'm doing."

"Do you?"

"Well, no. Not at all. But that makes it exciting and fun and I can't remember the last time I felt excited or like I was having real, genuine fun. This is fun. Yes, it's incredibly naughty fun, but so what?"

Julie shrugged. "Your life."

"You're my friend. Be happy for me."

"It's going to implode as fast as it's exploded."

"So be my friend when that happens?"

Julie lifted her glass. "Chars. I can do that."

"Wonderful," said Camila with a nod before glancing out of her lounge window for the umpteenth time that evening. She'd got ready ridiculously early after work and was actually quite thankful when Julie popped round with another bottle of her posh Champagne as it had momentarily stopped her from pacing in too-tall heels which she'd subsequently taken off and switched for a more sensible pair. She'd been anxiously questioning her outfit choice, her makeup, her hairstyle – which she'd decided to wear up in the end, believing it tamed down the dress somewhat. Something her mother had said was that people judged you on your hair and your shoes. It didn't matter what you were wearing in between, as long as your hair was good and your shoes were good, you were good to go. Pulling down on the tight dress, Camila wondered how anyone would be able to see past the outfit even if the shoes and hair were magnificent. "Which shoes, Julie?" she said, tapping in the slightly smaller heels she'd switched into before pointing her toe towards the pair discarded by the sofa.

"No one's going to be looking at your heels when you're in that dress, but the tall ones, they make you look sexy."

"I was going for glamorous." Kicking off the heels, Camila returned to her original pair. "Be honest. Am I more Julia Roberts pre-Richard Gere or post-Richard Gere?"

"You mean hooker outfit or polo party?"

"Not polo party, that was a spotty summer dress. I mean glamorous get-on-a-private-jet outfit."

"You're just you, but dressed up a bit."

"Right."

"You're fine."

"Okay." Camila frowned. "Just fine? Really?"

"What do you want me to say? I'm not going to tell you that you look fit. I don't want you getting the wrong impression."

"Oh, Julie! How long have we known each other? I'm not going to suddenly start fancying you!"

"I don't want to take that chance. You look good, but not bloody fuckable."

"Wonderful," said Camila, "and on that note someone who does want to fuck me has just arrived."

Julie jumped up from the sofa. "Another limo? Oh god, this is far too *Pretty Woman* already." She tutted. "And he was only after one thing as well, wasn't he?"

"Feel free to let yourself out."

"And what the bloody hell is she wearing?!"

Camila turned back to the window. All she could see was the smile.

****

Sitting across a table that was tucked away in the corner of the chic restaurant, Camila was still focused on Harriet's smile. It had been one of those times, walking from the limo towards the doors of the restaurant, where she had to force herself to glance down and check what Harriet was wearing, because until that point she'd had absolutely no idea. She'd watched a television programme on it once. A show that had girlfriends nipping out at various intervals during their dates to get changed to see if their boyfriends noticed. And a huge majority of them didn't, and while the conclusion had been that the men were unperceptive and ignorant, Camila now realised they were possibly just completely enamoured by their partner. That's exactly how she'd felt when opening the front door to Harriet. A mixture of nervous excitement that found her so totally enveloped in Harriet's presence and words that she'd been oblivious to everything else around them, including Harriet's beautiful black jumpsuit accessorised with a gorgeous diamond choker and matching diamond bracelet. Her heels were also black and eye wateringly high, adorned with sparkling gems around the ankle straps. In summary, Harriet looked regal, but in a funky kind of way.

Most of the journey to the restaurant had been a blur too. There had been immediate frantic kissing the second they were in the limo, with Harriet even straddling her for a moment, before they calmed down and put on their seatbelts. Camila had honestly felt like she was sixteen again with raging hormones and a total disregard for appropriate behaviour. They were meant to be taking things slowly, getting to know one another properly. She smiled across the table. They'd ordered their food and were currently enjoying a rather expensive glass of wine. "So," said Camila, "do you believe in life after death?"

Harriet laughed into her glass. "Interesting question."

"We're getting to know each other. There's no better way than finding out someone's thoughts on evolution, god, the planets and so on."

"Oh, Camila."

"What?"

"You're so sweet."

"Sweet?"

"I don't know? You're just innocent, which makes you really rather magical."

"You weren't calling me innocent yesterday."

"And that was a surprise too! You're a remarkably layered person."

Camila shook her head. "No, I'm not." She shook her head again. "Definitely not."

"You are. Look at that dress. I recognized it as a Caroline Castigliano straight away and your hair's so sophisticated. You look like you come to this kind of place on a nightly basis."

"I'm not sure I'd want to," she glanced around, "don't get me wrong, it is lovely." She smiled. "But answer my question."

Harriet shrugged. "Is there a god? No. My mother lost twin boys during labour five years before I came along."

"Oh Harriet, I didn't know."

"I don't speak about it in interviews but it's out there. Basically I wasn't them and no matter how much I tried to be them or live up to them, I just wasn't, and I don't think I was ever enough for her."

"I'm sure you were."

"You weren't there."

"I wasn't, no. But your dad? How was he?"

"They're both still here. They're both on the scene, but it's functional. It always has been."

"Is that why you shy away from love?"

Harriet laughed. "Don't try and psychoanalyse me. I pay a therapist for that."

"You're in therapy?"

"Not currently."

Camila smiled. "I'll continue then. Was it because you wanted to show your mother you were worth just as much as her boys that you became a lesbian?"

Harriet laughed loudly. "Oh goodness, Camila, don't give up your day job. You don't just become a lesbian; you either are one or you aren't."

"I might become one."

"No, you might embrace your fluidity or accept the possibility you could be bisexual, but you're not a lesbian."

"I could become one just like I became a member of the neighbourhood watch."

Harriet laughed again. "How can you make that comparison?"

"Easily. Just like I wasn't a mother until I was."

"Hmmmm. Okay, instead of me trying to unwrap that, how about you just dive straight in with your thoughts on god instead, they might make more sense."

Camila nodded. "Okay, so the idea of a greater being is feasible. But not in the religious sense. There's no great creator wanting you to bow down and worship him, but we're all definitely here for a reason which means there must be something, or some source, or some grand scheme in charge of that reason." She took a sip of her wine before continuing. "I think there's a high possibility this whole thing could be some sort of computer game."

Harriet laughed loudly. "This is meant to help us bond? What if I end up thinking you're a crackpot?"

"Do you?"

"Not yet, but tell me your thoughts on evolution."

"Hundred percent didn't happen."

Harriet laughed again.

Camila continued. "Evolution doesn't explain how life first appeared on earth."

"But you're saying it wasn't god?"

"Not in the traditional sense of the word, no." Camila shrugged. "Do you have any clue how many planets are out there?"

"I'm not an astronomer."

"There are more planets out there than grains of sand on our beaches."

"Are you a geologist too?"

"Trillions. Billions of trillions."

"And….?"

"Don't you think that's fascinating? Don't you have to accept there must be something else out there? That we must be part of something greater?"

"If I'm honest, I'm a little bit too busy to get into all that." Camila smiled.

Harriet continued. "Why are you looking at me like that?"

"It's telling. I think you're head down, racing through life."

"Aren't you?"

"I have been, yes, but I've always been interested in the what ifs."

Harriet nodded. "What if we go to the toilets for a snog?"

Camila laughed. "You don't like this line of conversation?"

"I guess you're making me feel a bit like you did the other night when you were taking off my glasses and telling me I wasn't being true to who I really was."

"I didn't say it like that!"

Harriet shrugged. "I know life's short, Camila, and I know it's fascinating. I know there are lots of questions to ask, but sometimes keeping yourself busy is a good way of stopping you from having to ask those questions."

"And what would you question?"

"My life." Harriet lifted her hand. "No partner. No offspring. My family's distant. Sometimes work's the only thing that makes sense. Work and fun maybe?" She smiled. "Come on, let's go to the toilets."

"You could kiss me here?"

"I could, but I want more."

"To shut me up?"

"Yes."

"Dinner will be here any minute," Camila glanced up at the approaching waiter as she spoke. "And that's not appropriate behaviour on our old-school wooing date."

"I'm sorry, ladies," said the man who was serving their table. "There will be a slight delay on your starters, may I refill your glasses?"

Harriet looked at the bottle of red sitting on the table and their glasses that were both still over half full. "We're okay, thank you. I think we'll have a wander in the gardens."

"Certainly," said the waiter, pulling back Harriet's chair before moving around to Camila's side of the table.

"We'll take our glasses with us," said Harriet, signalling for Camila to do the same.

"They have gardens?" asked Camila, following Harriet's gentle weave between the tables that actually didn't need to be woven between due to the large distance separating the diners. "Should we collect our coats? Now this is romantic. Is there a maze? There's always that bit in costume dramas where the betrothed couple go for a walk in a maze."

Harriet turned a corner, guiding them towards the outdoor seating and garden area visible through large leaded windows. It was lit by sparkly fairy lighting and tall glowing patio heaters.

"Oh, how lovely," said Camila, "there's no one else out there." She paused before following Harriet past the door that would have taken them outside. "Where are we going?" she said, confused, until Harriet's hand slipped into her own and pulled her through a door to the left. "No, not the toilets, it looks beautiful out there." Camila stopped. "Wait, oh wow, it's even more beautiful in here."

"Restrooms. Not toilets. Obviously there are toilets just there but here's the chaise longue, and the perfume stand, and the mints, and the sweets and—"

"And the open door," whispered Camila as another diner entered the space.

Harriet nodded at the woman before the woman closed the door on a cubicle. "There's a changing room just here," she whispered.

Camila let the hand lead her once more. "Why would there be a changing room?"

"Same reason there's that wicker basket full of cotton slippers. The restaurant's often used as a wedding reception venue, guests come and get changed," she signalled to the slippers, "and they take their heels off."

"But guests don't come in here and kiss," said Camila as Harriet closed the door to the room where there was another velvet chaise longue as well as several mirrors.

"Trust me, they do."

"Wait, you do this a lot?"

"Everyone has a past."

"That's on a cycle?"

"What do you mean?"

"Am I simply your latest bit of fun?"

"You want to be more than that?"

Camila paused for a moment as the feeling of what the hell am I doing washed over her once again. "I have no clue."

Harriet laughed. "If you'd have said yes then I might have taken seriously the idea that you'd become a lesbian, because that's what they do: jump from meet to married in milliseconds."

"Right."

"Come here," said Harriet, clicking the lock on the door as she pushed Camila against the wall. "I want to kiss you."

As the soft lips met her own and the hands rose to her waist, Camila felt every shadow of doubt disappearing as if Harriet was the sun shining out from the clouds. She moaned into the soft mouth as Harriet's hands travelled up the side of her body towards the curve of her breast. "We only have two minutes," she managed to whisper.

"I only need two minutes," said Harriet, spinning Camila round roughly so she was face first against the wall.

"Harriet."

"Shhh."

Camila tried to speak once more but Harriet's teeth were grazing her neck and both Harriet's hands were cupping her breasts. Camila tried to focus. How could she tell Harriet about the Spanx? She groaned as Harriet's hands slipped into her dress from the top. It might be okay, she reasoned, the design of the Spanx was such that her bra was out on show as normal, the tight material of the hold-everything-in one piece curved down around her stomach.

"I love your nipples," whispered Harriet into Camila's ear.

Camila groaned again as the fingers slipped inside her bra and squeezed her hardness. Her dress was tight fitting but elasticated, a bit like shrink wrapping that easily loses its suction once the air gets in there. Maybe if she slid the straps off her shoulders that would be enough for Harriet. Carefully she moved her hand up and out of the material, repeating the action on the other side.

Harriet moaned in satisfaction, pushing Camila forward before suddenly pulling down on the cups of the bra, pressing Camila's bare breasts against the cold wall. "You're so intoxicating," she whispered.

"Kiss me then," said Camila, turning her head to the side.

Harriet spun Camila back around, taking hold of her hands as she kissed the lips deeply.

Camila could feel the silkiness of Harriet's jumpsuit pressing against her nipples. She kept her eyes closed. She didn't want to look down knowing her boobs were just there, out on display. She cursed herself. She'd done that. She'd offered them up like an aperitif. It was as if she was constantly finding herself in these situations that *she'd* got herself into only to be shocked that she was there. It was as if Harriet was her drug and she lost all sense of real-world normality when she was in her presence. That woman from the rest room could be out there right now hearing all of this bumping and pinging. Damn. What was that ping? Camila glanced down, Harriet had yanked on her dress but it had slapped back against her thighs. "Wait," she gasped, mind back on the Spanx.

Harriet kissed her harder before moving her mouth to the nipples.

Camila stopped thinking about the Spanx.

"I want to take you, Camila."

Camila moaned again before pulling herself back from the brink of total entrancement. "Wait, I'm wearing—"

It was too late, Harriet was back at her mouth kissing her deeper, her hands on her breasts, pushing her against the wall. Kissing was fine. Feeling was fine. Moaning was fine. But what was Harriet doing now? Shit! She'd stepped backwards. She'd grabbed the sides of the dress. "Harriet!" she gasped. No! With one swift yank the dress was down. "I…"

"What the bloody hell are you wearing?!"

Camila felt the dress slide to her ankles. She might as well just step out of it now. She had nothing left to hide, or lose. She decided she'd just have to own it. "It's my Spanx," she said, bending over and giving a little wiggle.

"I can see that!" said Harriet. "But you don't need Spanx!"

"Thanks," said Camila, choosing to wander around the small changing area in the hope that she'd find an angle where the mirrors weren't relaying the vision of herself trussed up like a piece of pork. She found herself awkwardly leaning on the back of the chaise longue.

"What am I meant to do with your Spanx?"

Camila shrugged as she slid down onto the velvet chair. "Well, there is a little hole just here."

Harriet stared at the legs that were now up and parted. "Bloody hell, Camila, is there no end to your madness?

Camila shook her head. "Possibly not."

CHAPTER THIRTY TWO

Placing the pile of bacon sandwiches she'd made for breakfast onto the kitchen table, Camila re-lived the moment from the restaurant's changing room. It had happened over two weeks ago now although the memory was as clear in her mind as if it were yesterday. And, yes, while there had been an awful lot more crazily wild and highly inappropriate sex since, reminiscing about the legs spread, chaise longue, easy-access Spanx was still one of her favourites. Who knew that's what the hole in the gusset was designed for?

"You're smiling again, Mum," said Michael.

"Am I?" laughed Camila, turning to her eldest son as he entered the kitchen before giving him a half hug, half bicep squeeze.

"Yep. You've been smiling all week."

"It's been a good week. Come and sit down."

"You invented the invention?" asked Michael, still standing.

Camila sighed, it was the only thing getting her down at the moment. The idea that she was failing Harriet professionally. Yes, she hadn't asked for the job, or pitched herself as an inventor, just like she hadn't offered one iota of promise that she'd be able to invent the invention, but Harriet seemed to have this belief… that was starting to wane. Camila stopped herself. She wasn't going to let herself fall into that trap of over-analysis. Harriet had been fine with her. A little short at work sometimes, but that was in the team environment after yet another day of no progress. She wasn't going to let herself worry that Harriet's slightly altered behaviour was down to her disappointment with her professionally. They were just entering a new phase of their relationship where there was more discussion and slightly less sex. Only slightly. Plus it was lovely to get to know her more deeply. It was fast becoming apparent that Harriet was quite an introverted soul despite all the extroverted sex, enjoying evenings in and quiet trips out to galleries and parks. Yes, they'd got round to doing iFly, which had been hilarious, blown around in a tube of pressurised air with goggles and what looked like a swimming cap on, and they'd had lots of laughs go-karting and zorbing, but things seemed to be slowing down slightly.

Camila stopped herself again. They weren't. There was just more of the other stuff going on. The day-to-day stuff. The coupley stuff. The cooking for each other and the sitting quietly whilst the other one worked. Camila smiled. Everything was fine. She'd been able to force herself to stop questioning her actions over their frantic style of sex, so she'd have to treat this in the same manner: sit back and go with it, accept things for what they were. She still had nothing to lose and this was still all amazing fun. She paused. But was it still fun for Harriet? She'd been quieter, or more subdued, which probably had absolutely nothing to do with anything other than the stresses of the new business. Camila nodded. She'd have to invent the invention. "I haven't invented it yet," she said to her son. "How's Cassie?"

"She's good. Right. School."

"Wait, Michael, I've made you some bacon sandwiches."

The deep voice shouted from the hallway as he disappeared through the front door. "Had a protein shake. Julie's here. See ya, Mum."

"Oooh, are you serving breakfast?" asked her next door neighbour, waltzing into the house like a member of the family.

Camila looked at Michael's place setting. "Bacon sandwiches?"

"See! You do miss my bloody van! When are you coming back? Debbie from two doors down is doing my bloody head in. All health and safety this, health and safety that. Plus, she's no good for a gossip. She's not got a rampant lesbian sex life like you, in fact she doesn't even have sex with her old man. Says he's impotent. Says it just lollops there like a—"

"Morning, Ethan!" said Camila with a smile as her youngest son appeared behind Julie, her smile disappearing the second she noticed the illuminated screen of the iPad. "Will you PLEASE turn that thing OFF!"

Julie grinned innocently. "Have your bits and bobs gone all lollopy too? Sounds like you need a good sha—"

"Julie!"

"You alright, Mum?" asked Ethan, taking his seat at the table.

"Sorry, I'm just a little bit stressed at work."

"You've still not invented the invention then?"

Julie spoke up. "Oh god, that's one of Harriet's phrases." She put on a whiney voice. "She's going to invent the invention, this one. She's my little inventor. She's my pocket rocket of ideas."

"Harriet doesn't speak like that."

Ethan spoke up. "She does, Mum, and I think she likes you."

Julie badly stifled her laughter.

Camila coughed. She knew the conversation with her sons was coming, but around the table eating bacon sandwiches with Julie on a Tuesday morning was not the time she'd choose to tell one son that she was indeed having something with Harriet, and what that something was she still wasn't sure, so any announcement would be premature. If she was honest, she'd toyed with the idea of telling them everything from the start: how it had happened, why it had happened, the fact that she was enjoying it happening, but then she realised she wouldn't have gone into that much detail had Harriet been a man. She'd have kept her private life private from her sons until the time came when she knew it was serious enough to invite him over. The fact they'd met Harriet on numerous occasions already was simply an offshoot of her being female. A female friend. "She's just a female friend," said Camila. "But if she does like me I'd be flattered."

"Would you go there, Mum?"

Camila nodded. "Yes, Ethan, I think I would."

"Cool."

Julie didn't disguise her look of confusion. "Wait. That's it?"

Camila ignored her. Her son was eating his sandwich as if they hadn't just had the exchange, which was heartening in a way, but also made her question why she'd not told both sons sooner. The non-stop madness between her and Harriet had been going on for over three weeks now. Did she owe the boys an insight into her behaviour? She paused for a moment, remembering some of that behaviour. There was no way they needed that insight.

Julie piped up again. "Well anyway, she won't want to go there for much longer if you don't give her a bloody invention."

"I'm trying."

"Just figure out what pisses you off."

Camila resisted the urge to say: you. You, Julie, with your bad language in front of my son. You, Julie, with your digs about homosexuality. You, Julie, as you sit and eat the bacon sandwich I made for my eldest.

"You're pissed off with him," continued her neighbour.

"I am not," said Camila, reaching out to ruffle her youngest son's hair.

"Stop it, Mum."

"He's always on his bloody tablet."

"He's fourteen. For the past two years I've let them both decide how much time they spend on it."

"And how's that working out for you?"

"It's the world they live in. You want me to invent an invention that bans technology?"

Julie shrugged. "Something that shows you how much time they've spent on it. Good for younger kids too."

Camila bit into her sandwich. "That's not..." She put the sandwich back down. "Wait..."

Julie carried on. "Allow kids a certain number of hours a day – all dependent on their age and whatnot, and they choose how and when they have it."

Ethan spoke up. "You did that already. That reward chart. Remember."

Julie laughed. "Bloody shit that was. Your mum's chart didn't work at all. You'd need something technical."

Camila got up from the table and started to pace. "I had to clock watch didn't I, and then I'd forget, or I'd go off to do something and they'd say they'd had an hour but—"

"We always had much longer than an hour," interrupted Ethan.

Camila waved her hands. "Yes, because there was no real way of keeping a check. Not a way that wasn't a pain or a faff." She nodded quickly. "A box? A box that stores hand-held technology. iPads, mobiles, PS Vitas, your Nintendo DS. When you take the gadget out of the box a timer's triggered."

Julie laughed. "And you're going to invent that are you? Too bloody complicated."

Camila paced faster, her hands waving harder. "It's not. You'd just need a small microchip sticker. You stick that sticker onto the device. Here, give me your iPad, Ethan." Camila took the screen. "Imagine a little sticker just here, or wherever really. But this sticker, with its microchip, senses when the thing is taken, I don't know, say a metre away from the box, and sets off the timer. The box has a screen on top with each child's name and each child's piece of technology and will show you how long each piece of technology has been out of the box."

Ethan took another bite of his sandwich. "I'd just sit next to the box and go on it."

"Fine, five centimetres away from the box then."

Julie shrugged. "Wouldn't work."

"Why not?"

"You're not a microchip engineer."

"No, but other people are. Think about security tags. The ones on those expensive men's razor blades. They're just stickers. It's a sticker with a whirling metal thing in it. The cashier forgets to deactivate it and it sets off the alarm as you're trying to leave."

"So?"

"So basically that technology's not difficult, or expensive. You break the distance connection between the technology and the box and the timer starts. You put the technology back in the box and it stops. The screen on top of the box has a running timer showing each child and each child's technology."

Ethan took another bite of sandwich. "There's a problem. If your technology's in the box all the time it'll run out of batteries."

Camila clapped her hands together. "It'll have a power adapter inside, like a big adaptor plug. Your chargers stay in there." She nodded frantically. "That solves the problem of chargers lying all over the place too. Your technology's charging in the box, you take it out and go on it, it tracks how long you've been on it until you return it to the box."

Ethan spoke again. "What about the xBox and the Wii?"

"They're in the lounge. It's easier to keep track of the time your kids are watching TV or playing on big consoles. What's hard is the hand-held stuff that they take into their bedrooms." She turned to her neighbour. "Julie, why are you so quiet."

Julie shrugged. "Might work, I guess."

"Bloody hell, Julie, it would bloody work! It would fast become a staple in every bloody household!"

"Mum!"

"Sorry, Ethan, but THIS IS IT! The Technology Box!"

Julie tutted. "You'd need a better name than that."

"No. It does exactly what it says on the tin. The Technology Box. Every household would have one! It contains your chargers and charges your stuff, it keeps a log on how long the technology's been away from the box. It would work. It would be incredible. I'd buy one. Everyone would buy one. I need to go." Camila squealed loudly. "I need to bloody well go!"

****

Camila hadn't remembered the drive to the office, or where she'd parked her car. She couldn't even remember if Helen had replied to her hello as she'd dashed into the building before pounding on the button to call the lift. What she could remember was spending the entire ride bouncing on her tip toes before flinging herself out onto the corridor and dashing towards the team's area. She'd arrived earlier than usual but they were all there, Harriet included. She had toyed with the idea of calling Harriet on her hands-free in the car but she'd spent the time finalising the vision of the Technology Box in her head so she could articulate her idea with confidence and credibility, and now, looking around at the faces of Deana, Brett, Geoff and Harriet, she was glad she had. There was a spark of excitement in their eyes and Harriet had a smile that was knowing. She smiled back. This was a good idea. Everyone knew this was a good idea.

Harriet spoke first. "Deana, patent search. Brett, drawings. Geoff, engineering. Camila, come to my office."

Camila watched as her three colleagues rushed back to their pods before following Harriet's fast march out of the area. "You think it's a good idea?" she said, trotting as quickly as she could after her boss.

"Shush."

Camila upped her pace. "It's a good idea."

"Shush," said Harriet again, now almost at a run.

"What are you doing?" laughed Camila, now having to run to keep up.

"Stop laughing," said Harriet, pumping her arms to propel herself along faster before lunging at the door handle to her office and charging inside. She turned to yank Camila into the office with her. "Now laugh!" wailed Harriet, slamming the door shut.

Camila felt herself enveloped in Harriet's tight hug. Harriet was jumping them both up and down. They were jumping and laughing, and kissing and groping, and stumbling towards the conference table at the side of Harriet's office.

"You did it," cheered Harriet. "You've done it."

"But the patent," muttered Camila between the heated contact.

Harriet continued to kiss. "It's a new idea. I just know it is."

Camila let herself be manhandled towards the table top. "You like it?"

"I love it. It's incredible. It's incredible like you. I love it like you."

Camila felt herself groan with desire. Whether Harriet meant it romantically or professionally, or even sexually she didn't at this exact moment care as Harriet had flipped her around and was now bending her over the table, riding her dress up as she pulled down on her knickers.

"I fucking love you," said Harriet once more.

"So fuck me," gasped Camila, spreading her hands out across the table as Harriet reached up to her shoulder, holding it tight before forcing Camila's body back onto her fingers. Camila cried out in pleasure.

Harriet brought her mouth down to Camila's ear as she continued to thrust. She bit on the lobe before whispering. "And I'm going to fuck you for the rest of your life."

CHAPTER THIRTY THREE

Sipping on her second coffee of the morning, Camila prayed the caffeine would kick in quickly. The past twenty-four hours had been frantic, with very little sleep; mostly because of all the sex, but also because of the fast-paced nature of the invention advancements. Camila repeated the phrase in her head: invention advancements. Maybe if she hadn't stayed awake after a day of frenzied work in the office she wouldn't be on her third take with producer Lydia. Camila said it out loud: "Invention advancements."

"Do you want me to say that bit?" asked Harriet from her co-presenter position beside Camila.

"No, I've got it." She nodded. "There have been so many invention advancements over the past twenty-four hours."

"Perfect," said Lydia, "and then, Harriet, I want you to go into more detail."

Camila placed her coffee on the table they were standing behind before smiling as the camera was raised. She was glad she only had to get that phrase out. Harriet had a much harder job, catching viewers up with all of the latest goings-on. And a lot had been happening. An initial patent search had shown the idea was unique. The feasibility assessment had shown the idea was worth pursuing. Geoff's concept development was now in full swing with Brett's patent drawings running alongside this. A team of engineers were in the office working on the prototype and a marketing team was there too working on ads and promotion. Camila smiled. It was so similar to an episode of *The Apprentice*: people split off into subgroups, all with the aim of bringing the Technology Box to fruition. She smiled again. Her idea. So many people working on her idea. It was thrilling, and even if she hadn't been up having sex with Harriet all night she knew she wouldn't have slept much anyway.

Camila had phoned her older sister at lunchtime the day before, explaining as quickly as she could the need to get the patent application in to the Intellectual Property Office, meaning it was all hands on deck and she'd be really grateful if her sister could come round and stay with the boys in case she didn't make it home that evening. Polly had unfortunately claimed to be busy even after a number of pointed reminders from Camila about the numerous times she'd stepped in to look after her nieces and nephews. Nothing, however, could convince her sister to change her mind. Camila ended the conversation seriously considering the possibility that Polly was jealous. Admittedly they'd not spoken much over the past few weeks and she probably felt out of the loop, but this was a crisis. Camila stopped herself. It hadn't ended up being a crisis as they'd all left the office at ten and Julie had stayed over, so she'd been free to spend an entire night at Harriet's.

Camila coughed as the camera was lowered for a lighting tweak. She picked up her coffee and sipped. Bless Julie. She'd been the one to call her yesterday to ask if they needed any help, even offering to bring a batch of bacon butties to the office from her van. This had led onto the childcare question with Julie simply saying "consider it done" without even a query. She'd then stayed on the phone taking a real interest: what was happening, had the idea been patented, how long until the idea was officially confirmed as theirs and so on and so forth. She was interested, she cared and, for all her faults, Julie was a good friend. Camila glanced at Harriet. Julie had enabled the sexfest that was last night.

Holding her blink for a moment too long, Camila shuddered at the memory. Not only had the whole evening been super-hot with no time, volume or space constraints, but it had been super romantic with Harriet opening up about her feelings. Camila had accepted that Harriet's frantic declaration of love yesterday morning over the conference desk was more an explosion of emotion than a real life feeling. Harriet had been overwhelmed by the Technology Box idea, she'd been thrilled that her protégé had come through, she'd been high on adrenaline and triumph… she hadn't meant to say that she loved her. Camila glanced at Harriet again. They hadn't actually addressed it last night and this was all her own speculation, but Harriet had opened up about being slightly quieter than usual, saying she'd been processing her thoughts and feelings about Camila. She'd said she was hooked. That was the word she had used: hooked. Overly enamoured. Lost in her. Content. She'd said Camila was special. One of a kind. A magical soul. The whole thing had been romantic and really rather moving, but Harriet hadn't said she was in love, which was actually quite a relief for Camila.

Turning to her boss once again, Camila smiled. There was definitely something between them. A connection that went deeper than sex. A feeling that went further than lust. An awareness that they did have a future. But after all the years with the same man, Camila wasn't sure she was ready to declare her love for a woman so soon. She continued to stare. There was a high chance she *was* falling in love with Harriet, but putting the tag infatuated or obsessed on things made it easier at this point. Plus, she was having fun. Adding an emotional label might suddenly make matters more serious and she'd had so many years of serious; this was her time to let loose and love life. Yes, she currently didn't want to do that with anyone other than Harriet, but right now everything was just perfect.

Harriet adjusted her glasses. "You're smiling at me."

"I'm just happy. Everything's so great."

"Isn't it just," said Harriet, before turning to Lydia. "How much longer please? We've got a lot to do."

"Sorry, there's a problem with the lighting. Two minutes."

"There's so much I want to say," whispered Harriet, her focus back on Camila.

"Don't we have to be careful until the patent confirmation comes back?"

"I didn't mean that, but yes in general conversation with people we do, but not on camera as this episode won't get shown until Saturday and by that time our patent will be filed. The whole process to get the full patent can take years, but it matters who filed first;

however, we can't file until we have all the patent drawings and concept details, hence the frantic rush with all hands on deck."

"You can put your hands on my deck any day of the week," whispered Camila.

"I plan on doing that every day of the week," returned Harriet.

Lydia interrupted them. "Ladies, we're good to go."

Camila returned her coffee to the table and smiled at the camera, starting her short monologue on Lydia's command. "We're absolutely thrilled to announce that we have our invention and as you can see from the hubbub going on around us, there are non-stop invention advancements occurring minute on minute."

Harriet took over. "The Technology Box that Brett's drawings outlined earlier will fast become a staple in every household with young children. It charges the technology and it also keeps a check on the time children have spent on that technology. Obviously it's up to each parent or carer to decide how long their children are allowed on the various devices, but at a reasonable price point there's very little reason not to invest, even if just as a storage box to contain the growing numbers of handheld devices and chargers."

Camila cut in. "Nothing worse than having cables lying around everywhere, then losing the cables, then arguing about the cables." She nodded. "The cables are in the Technology Box. You'll be able to choose the pattern on your Technology Box to fit in with the style of your room, a bit like those credit cards where you can upload a personal photo."

"You see," continued Harriet, to the camera. "This one's full of ideas. Have you literally just thought of that?"

Camila smiled. "Yes."

Harriet turned and hollered at the web design team across the room. "When you order online make sure there's a section for the buyer to personalise the design of the box." She returned her focus. "You see; it's go, go, go here. However, we must remember that the most important thing isn't actually the new invention, as amazing and innovative as it is. It's the fact that we here at H.I.Pvention can get your design from idea creation to patented prototype with absolute ease. H.I.Pvention will fast become the number one go-to design and innovation firm for the individual inventor. There's a huge market for the new business, and now, thanks to this lady sitting beside me, I'm confident we're going to win the *Budding Businesses* show."

Camila smiled. "The Technology Box *was* my idea, and I'm really glad."

"But it's been more than your idea," continued Harriet. "You've breathed a breath of fresh air into the team." She smiled. "You've breathed a breath of fresh air into me."

Camila channelled co-presenter micro-nod harder than she'd channelled it before. She didn't want to burst into a Cheshire cat grin, but she had to accept the compliment. She half-smiled at the camera but Harriet wasn't stopping.

"You've made me remember what life's all about. You've made me happy." Harriet reached out for Camila's hand and lifted it into the air. "Yes, this lady here is making me very happy, and I never usually open up about my personal life but I'm not sure I can keep this one in; in fact I don't want to keep it in. Not only is Camila my lead inventor, she's my soulmate and I've fallen head over heels in wild, passionate love with her." She turned to Camila. "I love you, Camila, and I want the whole world to know."

Camila swallowed hard before exhibiting a co-presenter expression she didn't realise had been in her repertoire.

CHAPTER THIRTY FOUR

Camila remained frozen with the same shocked, perplexed, half angry and half enamoured look on her face as the camera was finally lowered.

"We'll go and do some filming at the pods," announced Lydia.

Camila stayed silent.

"Well say something then," whispered Harriet as the film crew moved away. "And she'll want a response from you. I've never known her let something lie so easily. She's clearly aware of the tension."

Camila dropped her gaze to her mug of coffee. There was a small ripple on the surface of the brown liquid, minor in comparison to the tsunami of emotion welling up inside her right now.

"I just wanted to say it properly." Harriet found Camila's hand once more. "I wanted to make a grand gesture. And I know what you're thinking, you're thinking it's about the ratings and the dramatics, but it's not." Harriet paused before continuing. "I know I said she'll want a response, but I want a response too; that's the most important thing."

Camila was aware of the fingers wrapped around her own, just as she was aware of the hubbub in the office, but she wasn't entirely aware of herself or her feelings. Was this really happening? Had Harriet Imogen Pearson, famous entrepreneur, honestly just declared her love in front of the nation? Camila gasped, snapped out of the daze like a patient resuscitated from CPR. "It's okay! It's not live!"

Harriet frowned. "It's not, but this segment will most likely go out on the Saturday show."

"It can't!"

Harriet released the fingers. "You don't feel the same?"

"I feel... I feel..." Camila was glancing around at the busy network of people who were completely oblivious to her panic.

"You feel what?"

She turned her attention to Harriet. "I feel totally and utterly ambushed."

"But I love you. I'm in love with you."

"And?"

"What do you mean and?"

"And why are you telling me this now?"

"I told you yesterday."

"In the heat of the moment."

"Exactly and I wanted you to know I wasn't joking."

"Why would you be joking? This isn't funny, Harriet. None of this is funny. This can't go out live."

"It's not going out live. It's going out on Saturday before the live final on Sunday."

"Exactly!"

"What? It's not live."

Camila shook her head. "I'm not one of your possessions that you can just wave in front of the cameras."

"I never wave my possessions in front of the cameras."

"Well I'm not a trophy."

"Why would you think you're a trophy?"

"Because you're lifting me up and shouting about me in front of everyone."

"You deserve to be shouted about."

"I'm not ready to be shouted about."

"You're not?"

"No! My boys don't know. Their dad doesn't know. My family don't know."

Harriet was smiling. "So there *is* something to know?"

"Is this a game to you?"

"Of course not. I just don't understand why you're so angry?"

Camila laughed in shock. "You're one of the smartest women I've met. You know full well why I'm angry."

"Okay, so it puts you on the spot."

"And why would you want to put me on the spot?"

"Because I want you."

"You have me!"

"Do I?"

"Well you did until that little stunt." Camila didn't want the smile to form on her lips, but there it was curling at the corners of her mouth all the same. "And that really was quite the stunt."

"I'll tell Lydia to cut it." Harriet paused. "If you want it cut, that is?"

Camila smiled again, her eyes widening. "You're telling the world that you love me?"

"They can cut it."

"Wait."

"What?" said Harriet.

"I can't help it if you love me."

"You can't."

"And who am I to stop you shouting about it?"

"Really?"

"Really."

"Right then, well: I LOVE YOU!" yelled Harriet to the office, causing a momentary raised head from one or two people before the hubbub continued, seemingly unaffected.

"Harriet!"

"What?"

"You're behaving like a child."

"You make me feel like a child. A sixteen-plus child obviously, but a frivolous, carefree child all the same."

"But I can't be frivolous or carefree as I have actual children to look after and an actual family to think of."

"You're in love. What's the big deal?"

Camila paused. She hadn't actually said she was in love and she wasn't entirely sure she was in love. Yes, she'd loved the past few weeks, yes she'd been acting frivolous and carefree, and, yes, Harriet was indeed very loveable, but did she actually feel that emotion of love? She looked down at her mug of coffee. The surface was motionless.

"You're not, are you?" Harriet shook her head. "That's what this is about. It's too soon for you. Goodness. I'm an idiot." Pushing the rims of her glasses further up her nose, Harriet nodded. "Right. I really am sorry, Camila. I'll make sure Lydia doesn't use that section."

Camila's voice was quiet. "It's just... I think that's maybe for the best."

"I understand." Harriet clapped her hands. "I've galloped into this without checking you're even saddled up. Right. Come on then. Let's move on."

"It's that easy?"

"We have work to do. I'm a big girl, Camila. It's all good." Harriet clapped her hands once more. "Right, let's go and work on our pitch."

"Wait, what?" Camila frowned, almost as thrown as she had been at the love outburst. "What do you mean our pitch?"

"Sunday night. I want you in front of the panel."

"On the live show?"

"On the live show."

"I can't!"

"You can."

Camila threw her hands to her mouth. "I'd rather tell you I loved you!"

****

Pulling into her driveway, Camila was surprised to see Julie's van still parked next door. It was lunchtime and Julie never missed a lunchtime shift. Stepping out of her car, she jumped at the hand that grabbed hold of her arm.

"Have you seen her?" shouted Debbie, her neighbour from two doors down. "She's said I'm on my final warning. I can't lose this job. My old man doesn't need any more stress what with his issues!"

Camila looked at the bedraggled woman.

"Have you heard about Roy's issues?" continued Debbie, slightly less shouty. "He doesn't need any more upset. He's been a bit emotional recently. The docs think it's a cause of his impotence. You do know about his impotence, don't you? It's led to a few problems and, anyway, like I was saying I don't want to add to these problems by losing my job on the van."

"Isn't she answering her door?"

"No, I saw her and her old man Terry leaving in a posh car this morning."

"Terry's back?"

"All dressed up they were."

"Have you tried calling her? Wait, what time was this?" Camila remembered her morning phone call with Julie. She'd said the boys had been fine overnight before offering – for the second day running – to bring butties into the office.

"Dead early it was. I was awake because my old man wanted to give this new suction machine he'd got off the internet a whirl, from China I think it was, all plastic and a bit tacky, but it didn't work anyway and I was looking out the window so I didn't have to see how sad his face got every time he popped the machine off and his—"

"Debbie, stop. If Julie's not at work, then you can't be at work. I wouldn't worry about it."

"Really?"

"Really. Go home and spend some time with your husband."

"Oh no, I can't bear to look at it anymore, all limp and shrivelled it is, like one of those little grubs the kids put on the end of their fishing lines."

"Maybe if you didn't stare at it all the time it might take some pressure off him."

"You think?"

"I don't know, Debbie. I'm not great with men either."

"I know. I saw your Mick with that Jackie from the gym. They weren't hiding it at all."

"They don't have to." Camila pulled her shoulders back. "In fact, I've got someone new too."

"Julie told me. That rich bitch Hillary. It's just a phase. We all would if we could. In fact, I might if he doesn't sort his lolloping knob out."

"She's called Harriet and it's not a phase and I think it's one thing to say it, but to actually go there with a woman, well." Camila stopped. She had no clue where she was going with this.

"Well, I would. For her money if I'm honest. Is that why you're with her? Fair play I say."

"I'm not with her for her money, Debbie, I'm with her because I love her." Camila nodded. There, that's where she'd gone. Admittedly it was only to Debbie from two doors down who no one properly listened to because of her constant droning on. Plus it was more of a test as opposed to an actual declaration of love, a trial in a way, to see how it rolled off her tongue, to see if it sounded right, to see if it felt right.

"My old man says he loves me, but how can he if he just lollops there all limp and—"

"Debbie, I don't think it's as simple as that." She stared at the woman who'd gone straight back to her impotence chat without even a raised eyebrow at the apparent declaration of lesbian love. "Anyway, I need to get on." Turning towards her front door, Camila wasn't sure what she saw first. Was it that the door was open? Or that her eldest son was standing in the doorway? Or was it his look of shock? Or maybe she'd noticed the pretty sixth form girl gathering her shoes in the hallway? Or was it the way her son's lips were moving, echoing the words being spoken behind her? She turned in a daze back to Debbie.

"You deserve some happiness, Camila."

"She's right," said her son again, "you deserve to be happy, Mum."

Camila tried to focus. "Michael, what's going on? What are you doing? How long have you been standing there? Why aren't you at school? Is that why you're shocked? Why do you look shocked, Michael?"

"My mum's in love with a woman. But it's fine."

"Hi," whispered Cassie as she tried to scuttle out of the house.

"Wait, what are you doing? Where are you going?" Camila watched the girl move quickly across the pavement. "Debbie, you can go home now," she said, conscious of the audience.

"I was just saying I'm happy for you, you deserve some happiness."

"She's right, Mum," said Michael again.

"Cassie wait," snapped Camila. "Debbie, please, thank you, but goodbye now. Michael, can we take this inside?"

"We need to talk, Mum," said the deep voice.

"I'm not in love with a woman, I was just seeing how it sounded."

"Not about that."

"Cassie, can you please come back in?"

The girl spoke up quickly. "Michael, wait, I've changed my mind, please don't say anything."

"You two, what's going on? Debbie will you PLEASE just go home."

"Forget it, Mum," said Michael, reaching to grab his own shoes before shoving them on and chasing Cassie out onto the street, clumsily kissing Camila on the cheek as he passed her. "Happy for you. Harriet's nice."

"Michael, wait!"

"Teenagers," said Debbie with a sigh.

"What's going on, Debbie? Do you know anything? Michael, PLEASE?" she shouted as the pair hurried away.

"Julie's told me bits," said Debbie, shrugging at the fast-moving teenagers. "I think Cassie's having some problems. But whatever it is you're in the clear. Kids' dramas are always much bigger than ours. He didn't bat an eyelid."

Camila paused for a second. "Neither did you, Debbie." She shook her head. "Julie's said something to him as well, hasn't she?"

"People aren't stupid."

Camila looked at the woman who'd been fretting over a job on a bacon butty van whilst blaming her husband's impotence on everything other than a simple medical condition.

"And you don't have to worry about your Ethan, he's like you in that way anyway."

"In what way?"

"Well he's gay."

"What? What are you talking about, Debbie?"

"Your Ethan, he won't be bothered that you're in love with a woman; it'll make it easier for him to open up."

"Open up about what? And I'm not in love with a woman."

"You said you were."

"Is he in love with a boy? Ethan? My Ethan?"

"Why are you asking me? I don't know anything." Debbie shrugged. "Julie's the one who'll know."

"Bloody Julie. Where the hell is she?"

"That's why I came round. Don't you remember? What's going on with you, Camila? You seem frantic. You have to be careful with that, it can lead to issues like my old man's."

Camila turned her back on her neighbour and walked into her house, shutting the door hard before leaning against it, trying her best to compose herself and focus on what was happening. She'd only nipped home for a change of clothes. They were going to spend the afternoon rehearsing for the live show with different focus groups pitching as many questions as possible their way so they'd be prepared for anything on Sunday evening. She'd been told to wear what she'd be wearing on the day so she'd feel comfortable and at ease. Camila shook her head. How could she possibly feel at ease knowing her eldest son was embroiled in some sort of drama with a girl two years older, not to mention that her youngest son had suddenly turned gay. She shook her head. No, he wasn't interested in boys. He was interested in his technology. But what if the boys were on that technology?

Camila sighed. So what? As long as he was happy. She managed a smile. Michael had said he was happy. Happy for her and Harriet. Happy that she was happy. But was she happy? Right now she had no clue what emotion was coursing through her body. Maybe this was just how it felt when you were living the high-powered, working woman lifestyle? You just had to focus on the here and now and deal with issues as they arose. She nodded. That's what she'd have to do as she was expected back in the office in half an hour. Harriet had said someone would dress her, but Camila knew the only way she stood any chance of composing herself throughout a live episode would be if she felt comfortable and the new power suit she'd bought with last week's pay cheque made her feel fantastic.

Pushing herself away from the door, Camila went upstairs. One day at a time, one issue at a time, focus on the now, and the now was the show. Upping her pace, Camila grabbed hold of the top of the bannister, quickly clearing the final step, not noticing the small square instruction leaflet lodged between the carpet and the skirting board, somehow separated from its pregnancy testing kit.

CHAPTER THIRTY FIVE

To say the remainder of the week had been chaotic was a huge understatement for Camila who by ten to eight on Friday evening was collapsed on her lounge sofa, third glass of prosecco in hand. Chaotic, however, was the word she had plumped for.

"But you're all sorted now?" asked Julie, dressing gown and slippers on, settled in for the evening even though Camila was expecting a house full of people to arrive any minute.

"Well, each entrepreneur's business plan had to be in by the six p.m. deadline today, but we did it."

"Let me bloody guess, chaotically?"

"Don't take the Mickey."

"I'm not but you've used that word in every bloody sentence so far."

"Because it's been chaotic! Do you have any idea how much work's gone into all this?"

"You just file a patent claim. It's not that hard."

"The rest of it. It's like the grand finale of *The Apprentice*." Camila paused. "Actually, it's like the interview section as well where the contestants hand in their business plans to Lord Sugar and get grilled on absolutely everything. That's how Sunday night's live final's going to play out. Obviously tonight's show and tomorrow night's show is all the pre-recorded fly-on-the-wall stuff."

"I can't believe you're going to be on bloody TV."

"I'm not sure I'll be on tonight. Tonight will be all the stuff from the start where the entrepreneurs are introduced and they explain their new businesses."

"Isn't that what the whole show's about?"

"It's about what you have to do to get a business off the ground."

"Is your business off the ground?"

Camila smiled. "It's flying and I honestly think we've got a great chance of winning this."

"How do they decide?"

Camila adjusted her position on the sofa. It was nice to be able to clarify everything in her head one final time. Plus she'd not seen Julie all week and was pleased she'd opted for the interested questioning approach instead of the sulky left out approach as was often her style when Camila did things without her. For example, Julie was never fully interested in the weekends away Camila had with her sister Polly and her nieces and nephews, or the times Camila decorated a room in her house without using any of Julie's people or products; but Julie didn't do it to be intentionally mean, she just loved being at the centre of everything. Camila smiled. "You get to vote, Julie. You get to decide. Yes, there's a panel of judges, but there's also a viewers' phone-in that's taken into account."

Julie groaned far too dramatically. "God! Like *Strictly Come Dancing* then? That's always a bloody fix. Some votes from the public and some from the judges and nobody knows who scored what or why."

"Voting opens as soon as tonight's show starts."

Julie groaned again. "So it's just a reality show then?"

"It's not. It's a business competition."

"But there'll be people playing the sympathy card and others playing the fauxmance card."

"What do you mean the fauxmance card?"

"To get votes." Julie nodded. "Now get the door, that was the bell."

Hauling herself from her seat, Camila shouted to her children. "Five minutes, it's starting." She heard Michael's grunt of recognition first. He'd been in his room with Cassie, no further development in their hush-hush behaviour even though she'd tried to corner them both at different intervals during the week. It was feasible that the two teenagers could sense she didn't actually have time to talk at the moment even though she was professing the importance of taking time to listen and not judge, but neither had opened up. Just like Ethan, also upstairs on his technology, but definitely not messaging boys, because even though her conversation with him was short it was also crystal clear. She'd started off by sitting him down and telling him she was involved with Harriet in a romantic capacity, to which he'd replied: "Kinda gross, but kinda cool." She'd then latched onto this, following up with: "Just like it's cool if you want to start dating boys or girls, whatever's your fancy." To which he'd simply replied: "As if." Now whether that *as if* was about dating boys or dating in general she didn't know, but at least her youngest son was still at that: "I hate girls, and maybe even boys too, stage." It was fine, she had reasoned. Ethan wasn't the priority right now. The priority was the show.

Pulling open the door, Camila was looking forward to seeing Harriet's smiling face. Everything had been fine over the past few days: they'd been bogged down by work with very little time to address the love issue. Harriet had simply apologised and told Lydia to take out the footage before declaring she'd wait as long as she needed for Camila's feelings to catch up. Camila had known in that instant that it wasn't about her feelings having to catch up, it was about her feelings having to slow down and classify themselves, order themselves in a way, because her head and her heart were all over the place, a swirling mess of confusion.

"We brought Lambrini!" wailed Debbie from two doors down, her impotent husband, Roy, standing behind her. "We got it free with the curry we had last Wednesday, didn't we, Roy?" she continued, bustling her way into the house. "One of Julie's deals. She told us if we spent twenty pounds at Dildishad we'd get a free bottle. I bet you like Dildishad, don't you, Camila. Hey, Roy, do you get it? Dildi-shad? Dildo-shad!"

"Debbie, my children are home."

"Julie told me you'd told them. Come on, Roy, what are you doing standing there? Your legs stopped working as well, have they? He does have his issues, doesn't he, my Roy?"

The man spoke up. "We've not been invited in yet."

"Julie invited us! Party at the TV star's house!"

"I'm not on tonight's show."

"It's fine, we're coming round tomorrow night as well and Julie says we can watch the final from here too."

Camila didn't react even though her houseful was meant to consist of her children, Harriet and Julie; not Debbie, and not Debbie's impotent husband and their plastic bottle of Lambrini from the dildo-shack.

Following the couple into the lounge, Camila turned as the bell rang again, smiling instantly at the thought of Harriet. It was like this, she had found, any downers she experienced were made instantly better by Harriet. Her neighbours from two doors down gatecrashed her house party, Harriet's presence made it better. The focus group gave her a hard time, Harriet's discreet hand squeeze made it better. Deana took the huff because she wasn't given a presenting task in the live shows, Harriet's public reasoning and justification in front of the team made it better. That's why she hadn't risen to her neighbour's intrusion, or let it get to her that Julie had taken over the evening plans. Harriet was coming and that was all that mattered.

"Harriet," she said, before realising it was actually a very pretty young man standing on her doorstep.

"Stereotypical."

"Pardon?"

"Stereotypical."

"I thought you were someone else. Can I help you?" Camila heard the racing of feet behind her before feeling the rush of air that had come down the stairs like a wind tunnel.

"Harry!" gasped her youngest son. "Come in! This is my mum. Ignore her, she's going through some stuff."

"I'm not going through anything thank you very much."

"Debatable," continued Ethan, before pulling his friend into the house. "We're watching it in the lounge so you'll have to excuse my mum's weird friends, but her girlfriend, the star of the show, she's coming too which is quite cool."

"Sister," nodded the pretty boy towards Camila.

Camila frowned. Who the hell was this? She looked at her son's enthused face before noticing that his hands were technology-free.

"You're more than welcome," she said with a smile before peering out of the front door, hoping for a glimpse of the person who could bring calm to her being. She stayed in the doorway for a minute or two. It was strange how Harriet could do that, calm her but at the same time excite her and make her nervous. Harriet could give her butterflies and fluster her, but when they were together it was as if a serene tranquility descended upon her, making everything feel just perfect. It felt right when they were together. Weird, but right. Sighing, she closed the door and shouted once more up the stairs. "Michael, Cassie, it's starting."

"We've just come down," came the deep voice from the lounge.

Camila tutted at herself. She'd found this happening more often too, drifting off into a daydream, unaware of her surroundings, and it had been at least ten years since the boys had been able to come down the stairs without her hearing the school pictures rattling.

"It's starting, Mum," said her eldest once more.

Camila walked through to the lounge. Every single sofa seat was taken and there was barely any floor space left either. "I'll get a chair from the kitchen," she said with a nod.

"That's the door," shouted Julie once more, her pink dressing gown and sofa sprawl putting her right in the centre of everything. "Can't get up, sorry."

"It's fine," said Camila, not wanting anyone else to greet her girlfriend. She smiled. That's what Ethan had just called Harriet. Her girlfriend, and it had sounded so natural coming from her son's mouth... which was actually one of the strangest things ever. Everyone seemed to be so cool with it apart from her. But was she actually cool with it? Or was she at least becoming cooler? Maybe on an ice cube level she was currently a snow cone, firmer and cooler than a slushee, but not quite block of ice like yet. "Harrie—" she started, before noticing the blue uniform and blue cap.

"Dominos delivery," said the man.

Camila looked at the tall pile of boxes before widening her arms as they were thrust her way. "Do I need to pay for this?"

"You paid on the app. Have a great evening."

Camila tried to nod over the top of her arm-full before staggering into the lounge. "Go and close the front door, please," she said to Ethan before passing the pile of pizza boxes to Julie.

"I can't, I'm squashed in with Harry."

Camila looked at the pretty young man who was indeed sitting very close to her son. "I'll do it," she said.

"Plates too," ordered Julie. "Food's up, everyone, this is on me."

Camila almost fell over. She'd assumed Julie had asked one of the boys for her Just Eat login as Julie never paid for anything, certainly not real brand pizza. "Thanks, Julie," she said, genuinely meaning it. Looking around the room, Camila smiled. Yes, this wasn't planned and, yes, the person she really wanted to be here hadn't arrived yet, but this felt warm and fun and she felt special.

"Can I have a glass for my Lambrini?" asked Debbie.

"Grab me and Cassie a can of pop too, would you, Mum?"

"I only drink water," said Harry. "It's good for the skin."

"I'll have a water too then," said her youngest who'd never requested a plain water in his life before.

"Sorry and I need the loo," apologised Roy, trying to make his way through the melee without treading on anyone.

"She can't bloody do that for you too!" wailed Julie.

"You might have to hold it though," laughed Debbie. "It's so limp it almost shoots backwards."

Camila coughed. "Roy, would you like—"

"No I bloody wouldn't! I'm fine and will you keep your bloody mouth shut, Debbie."

Camila coughed again. "I was going to ask if you wanted some wine."

"He can't," continued Debbie, "it's a cause of his—"

"AND WE'RE ON!" said Camila loudly, pointing at the television before nipping to the kitchen for drinks, plates and chairs. She sat down just in time to see the end of the opening credits. Harriet's face flashed up with her full name glittering underneath. Smiling with pride, Camila couldn't help but wish Harriet were here.

****

The first episode really had been fantastic so far. Usually when she was watching something with Julie, Julie would talk the whole way through, but tonight Julie had been glued to the screen, just like Ethan who would often gravitate back to his technology and Michael who would reach for his dumbbells and start lifting those instead of watching the show. The fact there wasn't enough space for that didn't matter as everyone in the room had been hooked. The programme was really well polished and slick and there wasn't too much repetition which was often the case in real life documentary and reality shows: *'Earlier in the show we met, Sheila, struggling with her weight.'* Or: *'Let's go back and find out how David's wound is healing, here's a reminder of what happened to David.'* It was as if programme makers had suddenly become very lazy, repeating footage under the guise of a recap that had been shown only ten minutes earlier. Or maybe they felt their audience were stupid and had forgotten about Sheila's sixty stone frame or David's anal fissure. Either way the programme makers of *Budding Businesses* had got it spot on, maybe because they predicted the viewing audience was slightly more intelligent if they were interested in the topic of business, or maybe it was simply because of the huge amount of footage that had to fit into the two one-hour shows because that's all the three months had boiled down to: Three months' worth of fly-on-the-wall footage from four different businesses condensed into two hours; there obviously wasn't room for any of those annoying recaps.

Camila smiled. Harriet's segment was about to come on. The show had started with all four entrepreneurs in the same room as the rules of the competition were outlined. There had been some friendly banter between them all which set the tone for the programme. Here were four people who'd already been successful, fighting for the ultimate entrepreneur crown. The show had then focused on Barry Maddison from Maddison Computers, whose new business was a shopping app that searched clothing stores a bit like USwitch or GoCompare searched for insurance, or OnTheBeach searched for holidays, but instead, a search for "black dress" gave you all the black dresses currently on sale in the UK. Cassie had immediately tutted at the idea, saying you'd never sift through that many dresses, but as Barry's segment was finishing up popped a glimpse of tomorrow night's episode and someone on his team said exactly the same thing and the problem looked like it would be solved.

Oliver James from the restaurant chain had been up next introducing his new paleo snack café. He intended to rival the likes of Starbucks and Costa with healthy paleo snacks instead of muffins and cakes, but the majority of his segment was spent debating whether or not there was an actual call for such a place. It was a bit like a vegan café. It might work in the centre of London but the notion of franchising it to places like Doncaster or Copeland in Cumbria where the obesity rates were the highest in the UK seemed rather ridiculous. Oliver James, however, was insisting it was places like these where his café was needed the most. Camila had felt it was a bit like trying to serve fruit in a fish and chip shop, but then the snap shot to tomorrow night's programme came on showing a pop up paleo café in both of these cities with lots of customer's crowded around the counter. Michael had instantly said they must have been giving the food away for free, and that paleo food tasted like sawdust anyway and he should know as he'd tried everything that was meant to be healthy.

Next up was Jill Masters from Jill's Gyms. She was starting up a new cosmetics treatment spa where instead of going for a weekend of massages and pool relaxation you went for a weekend of Botox and fillers. The whole spa day theme was the same with robes and slippers, but instead of swimming in a pool, you'd relax in a snug as your face recovered from the needles or your legs recovered from the lipo. Julie had thought it a good idea as had Debbie, both declaring it the new place for hen parties and birthday treats, the only issue being the cost as addressed in the segment. But everyone in the room had gasped when the snapshot to tomorrow night's show was shown with official looking people in suits advising Jill on the legalities of running such a place without actual doctors present, and if actual doctors were to be employed the whole cost of the business would skyrocket.

"If they can get that ironed out, they've won," announced Julie.

"Ironed out like those faces," added Debbie. "Did you see those women?"

Cassie spoke up. "It only takes a one-day course to become a qualified Botox practitioner. We learnt about it in our ethics class. It has to be prescribed by a doctor, nurse or dentist, but anyone can train up to give the actual injection."

"You can't train up to give lipo though, can you?" said Julie. "And what else are they going to offer at this cosmetics spa? It's looking too similar to the stuff that's already out there, if you ask me."

"We'll find out more tomorrow," said Camila, "and then on the live show I'm sure they'll have full details of all the treatments available. Basically by Sunday night we need to present our up-and-running businesses. Remember this was all filmed ages ago. They'll have solved all these issues by now."

"Is yours up and running?" asked Debbie, biting into another slice of pizza, having already guzzled all of the spicy meatball one after reminding Roy spicy food was a trigger for his issues, and moving onto Cassie's margarita leftovers which Roy was also not allowed.

"Watch and see, we're on now," said Camila. It was strange hearing Harriet talk about their business before she'd even met her, because that's what it felt like, their business. It was their baby. Hers and Harriet's. They were the ones presenting together on Sunday and, yes, while Brett and Geoff would be doing a bit of talking it was her and Harriet running the show: it was their presentation. Deana had been tasked with making sure all the other elements ran smoothly, the television advert they'd taken it upon themselves to make, the website that would showcase their site, the actual live footage from the new business base that had actual real live workers ready to complete the process of idea conception to product creation once people's ideas started to roll in… and Camila honestly believed the ideas would roll in once viewers could see how the Technology Box had developed. She smiled. Harriet was being endearing on the screen, not rising to the interviewer's questions about why she was involved in the programme, simply saying you can rest when you're dead. Camila smiled again. That's probably where Harriet was now: not dead, but tied up with some other interview or one of her other businesses because she never stopped and it was something she wouldn't want to change about her. This was Harriet. This determined, focused, tenacious, head strong woman holding court on the screen was her Harriet.

"She's blown you out then," announced Debbie. "Julie said she'd be here. It's the only reason I came round. I wanted a selfie with her."

"You came for the bloody pizza," said Julie.

"Shush!" said Camila, wanting to pay full attention to the section of the H.I.Pvention story she hadn't been privy to. Deana and Harriet were with a couple of other people she didn't recognise thrashing out business ideas and it was revealed that H.I.Pvention was actually Deana's brainwave. Yes, the group had reached the conclusion together, but Deana had been the first to suggest a business for individual inventors. Camila felt guilty. No wonder Deana had felt completely hijacked by her sudden arrival, not to mention the way she was being hailed as the hero. Trying to re-focus, Camila watched as Brett and Geoff were introduced, hand-picked from H.I.P Marketing for the skill sets they could offer the new business. What was fascinating was all the footage from outside of the floor five work space showing a team of people searching for suitable business premises, another team building the website, a team of lawyers working on the legalities of the business and the contracts the inventors would have to sign, and it was like Harriet had said, they didn't need an actual invention to show that this was a good business model.

"I like this business, Mum," said Ethan with a nod. "It might not be as cool as the cosmetics spa or as universal as the shopping app, but you've got a solid business plan."

Julie laughed. "She hasn't got anything, she's not bloody in it!"

"I wasn't expecting to be in tonight's show."

Julie continued. "Oooh look, they're all getting frustrated that they can't find an idea."

Camila watched as Brett ripped up a patent drawing on the screen, smiling at the familiarity of the sight. "But you're all privy to the fact that they do," she said with a smile.

"Julie told me about your box," said Debbie. "We haven't got kids what with Roy's problems so we're not going to buy it."

Camila stared at Julie. "I told you not to go into detail about it."

"Debbie's not going to sell her story!"

"She tried," said Roy, "but the paper said they weren't interested."

"He's lying!" gasped Debbie.

Roy shrugged. "I'm not."

"Is that the door?" said Julie. "Get the door would you, Camila? I think Harriet's finally here."

Camila shook her head. "I'm not missing this bit, even for Harriet. It's the snippet from tomorrow night's show. I think I might be on it! Cassie could you could go, please?" Peering around the girl who stood up without question, Camila re-focused on the screen. And yes! There she was! Smiling in front of the nation. Her. Camila Moore.

"It's you!" screamed Julie.

"You look good, Mum," added Michael.

"Shush, shush, shush!" said Camila, pointing at the TV as she shook with excitement. They were playing the section where Harriet was introducing her, reeling off the monologue about Camila's arrival: "*Is she my trump card? Has she been up my sleeve? Is she the ace in my hole?*" Camila smiled, suddenly gasping as the footage cut to the words: "*She's my lead inventor. My soulmate. I've fallen head over heels in wild, passionate love with her. I love you, Camila, and I want the whole world to know.*"

"That's been cut down!" cried Camila. "That's out of order! That's out of context! That was meant to be cut!"

"Out in the bloody world now though!" said Julie with a tut. "Knew you couldn't trust her. Bloody fauxmance at its finest right there."

"Mum?" said Ethan. "You said it was nothing serious."

"And Dad's not going to be happy," added Michael.

Debbie joined in. "Boys, your mum loves her too, she told me at the start of the week. Hasn't she told you yet? Julie, did you know?"

"Of course I bloody well knew," said Julie.

The cough came from the lounge doorway. "Hi, everyone," said Harriet with a smile. "Sorry I'm late to the party."

CHAPTER THIRTY SIX

"Why are you still smiling?" snapped Camila.

"You said you loved me! Admittedly you've not directed it towards me yet, but you've obviously said it to that woman who had pizza on her chin."

"That was Debbie and I didn't." Camila sighed. The evening had descended into utter chaos. Julie had told Harriet she was playing the fauxmance card to which Debbie said it didn't matter as people would definitely vote for Harriet now that they'd seen her vulnerable side. Julie had then tried to explain that this was what a fauxmance was before Ethan had asked his mother in front of everyone if she loved Harriet back, to which the room fell silent and Camila told everyone to go home or go to bed. Michael had then asked if Cassie could stay the night, to which Camila had replied '*Of course not.*' It then transpired, however, that Julie had let Cassie stay the night when she'd been in charge of the boys so it made no difference if she stayed again now, to which Ethan then asked if Harry could stay which caused a scream of '*Not a chance!*' from Camila, who was only now starting to realise how that must have looked given the fact that Ethan had had many male friends stay over in the past. Now, however, with this new found sexual ambiguity hanging over his head it was a definite no, but she hadn't wanted to give this as a reason so she'd had to throw all her dummies out of the pram and kick everyone out apart from her own flesh and blood and Harriet who was still standing here, smiling.

"Why couldn't Ethan's friend stay?" asked Harriet.

"I don't want anyone staying. In fact, I'm not even sure I want you here."

"The boys said I could stay the night."

"Yes, they said that as a bartering tool to make me give in to them."

Harriet shook her head. "No, they're cool with it. They said I could stay. I'm going to stay. Is that okay? It'll be nice to wake up together and have breakfast together, then maybe we can have a day date before tomorrow night's show? I've got a few interviews to do but they're on the phone, in fact I bet the magazines will want to talk to you too."

"What are you doing, Harriet?"

"Planning our weekend. Yes, most of the interviews and interest will come on Monday morning after the grand finale so we'll have to keep our schedules free, but I think tomorrow could be quite a nice day."

"I mean you're completely ignoring what's just happened. You've told the world that you love me."

"And you've told Debbie."

"I haven't! And you said it would be cut."

"Lydia's a producer. At the end of the day they'll show what's good for the ratings."

"So you used me?"

"No. Ask her yourself. I told her to cut it. But maybe it's better now that it's out there."

"I don't want it out there."

"Why not?

"Mick. My boys. My family. My friends. My sister's tried to call me fourteen times already and my brother's even sent an email; he never emails."

"Your boys are fine. They're the important ones." Harriet tried to reach out for Camila's hand. "What's worrying you?"

Camila stepped back at the contact. "You've taken everything away from me, Harriet. All ownership of who I am. I should have been the one to address this *if* and *when* I wanted to."

"It's happened and we need to move on."

"It's really that simple for you?"

"I'm sorry, but what more can I say? I asked her to cut it. I'm just happy that you told Debbie you loved me."

"I didn't tell bloody, Debb… you know what, I think I've had a busy week and I need an early night."

"They said I could stay."

"I don't want you to stay."

Harriet nodded. "Okay. I'm sorry, I really am, Camila, but I meant every word I said. I love you. I'm in love with you. I know things are hectic with the show but it doesn't change how I'm feeling. You know where I am and I'll see you on Sunday morning for the rehearsals, if not before."

Camila watched as Harriet made her way out of the lounge. Should she follow her? Should she stay strong? Was she being stubborn to spite herself? Her boys had given Harriet permission to stay, even after she'd said no to their requests for evening company, and that was huge. That was momentous. She stepped out of the lounge and looked to the front door: that opportunity had just disappeared. Camila kept her feet planted. She couldn't go running after Harriet, she needed time to absorb all of the chaos and sort out a solution. There were phone calls to make, apologies to give. Her sister would be so cross that she was suddenly a lesbian without informing her. She wouldn't understand that Harriet was just a person she'd fallen in love with. Camila threw her hand to her mouth. There it was again.

"You should go after her, Mum," said Michael from the top of the stairs. "You've been a different person these last few weeks."

"Quite literally," muttered Camila.

"I mean it. You've been an actual person, not just my mum."

Camila turned towards her son and started to climb the stairs. "You're a good man, Michael, and I love you lots, but this is all a little too complicated to explain to you."

"I have my own complications going on."

"You want to talk about them?"

"I'm not allowed."

"Says Cassie?"

"It's her secret."

"Secrets aren't good."

Michael laughed. "Says you. Everyone thought you were a boring housewife. Not anymore."

"Oh, is this just really awful?"

"No, Mum, it's magical."

****

Padding down the stairs the next morning, Camila was still smiling at her eldest son's words. He'd been pretty much monosyllabic for the past three years yet last night he'd been profound. '*Magical*,' he'd said, and that was exactly what the past few weeks had felt like. Yes, it hadn't convinced Camila to race after Harriet, but it had ticked the box that her boys were okay. She smiled. They were more than okay. They were mature and thoughtful and most importantly they wanted her happy. Whether Harriet could make her happy was still up for internal debate, but she knew this internal debate, in its simplest form, was just overthinking: She was being too technical in her need to categorise what was going on. She needed to stop worrying and go with the flow even though her sister didn't agree, and neither, it transpired, did her sister's friends who'd apparently been on the phone airing their concerns. Sexuality was serious, apparently, and not something you should play around with. Camila felt a rush of arousal: Harriet could play around with her sexuality in any way she wanted.

As she descended the final step, Camila noticed a piece of cardboard halfway through the front door's letter box. Was it hate mail? The only person she needed to deal with was Mick, but her sons had said he was on a booze cruise to Calais with Jackie and wouldn't have watched the show. But Camila wasn't stupid, someone would have helpfully messaged him, and like Ethan and Michael had announced last night, it was the ultimate kick in the teeth for any man – his missus leaving him for another woman. The fact remained, she reminded herself, that she hadn't left Mick, he'd left her and she was free to see whoever she chose. The public announcement that she'd chosen a high-flying famous female entrepreneur probably wasn't what he'd been expecting, but it wasn't his business all the same.

Freeing the cardboard from the slot, Camila laughed. It wasn't from Mick, or any other hater, and she felt ashamed that the idea had even crossed her mind as everyone's response had been positive, mostly. She smiled at the handwritten note, Harriet's writing.

Treasure hunt, it said. *The first clue is on your car window.*

Camila laughed again; not very cryptic. She tiptoed down her driveway. It was early and not many people on her estate were early risers, plus everyone was used to seeing Julie in her dressing gown so the sight of her barefoot and in pyjamas wouldn't shock, even if the pyjamas were a rather silky new set she'd bought for Harriet's benefit. Grabbing the damp bit of cardboard clamped under the windscreen wiper, Camila felt her heart flutter.

I love you, be at my house at two.

Again, not very cryptic or even very treasure-hunty, but fun. The note was fun. Turning the cardboard over, Camila recognised the corner section of a famous shoe logo. Harriet must have grabbed whatever she could find in her car last night, which would have been a posh shoe box. She was definitely the type of person who carried a spare set of shoes and spare set of clothes in her car rather than reams of paperwork because Harriet was an electronic organiser. It was always the things that took effort and initiative that meant more and, yes, while ripping up a shoe box and scribbling a couple of lines might not seem like much, it was. Harriet could easily have driven home and ordered flowers. A grand gesture that actually took little more than a click of a mouse and money. Flowers weren't impressive anymore. Hand-written messages on make-shift notes were though. Camila groaned at herself. Why was she being so rose-tinted? Harriet was naughty and she was still cross with her.

Camila paused. But what if it genuinely wasn't Harriet's fault? What if Harriet had genuinely asked Lydia to cut it? Wasn't it wonderful that she had declared her love in the first place? Wasn't this the big romantic happy ending people dreamt of? Camila gasped. What if Harriet had meant two a.m.? She'd obviously left the note last night: *be at my house at two*. Had she been setting up for some big sex fest? Dashing back inside, Camila found her phone. *2.00p.m.?* she texted.

Harriet was quick to reply. *Obviously 2.00p.m. I don't try and apologise for my mistakes by offering up a 2.00a.m. booty call. But if it crossed your mind I'll remember it for next time.*

Camila smiled. Harriet had signed off with a wink. Was she winking that there'd be a next time? Another miscommunication to sort out? Or was she being cheeky? Either way it was light-hearted and fun, a lot like their relationship to date. Would it always be this way or would things suddenly get heavy? Sighing, Camila knew she was the one complicating matters. She'd read a quote from an author somewhere that went: *Just always be honest about your feelings. If everyone did that then the world would be a much simpler place.* The quote had stayed with her. This ideal that you'd always be open about your feelings: the good, the bad, the scary, the dangerous; and, yes, it was an ideal as you couldn't always be honest. She thought for a moment; or could you? Wasn't that the whole point of the author's quote? What would she say to Harriet if she had the nerve? She'd tell her that her heart was fluttering. She'd tell her that she made her feel confused. She'd tell her that she loved spending time with her. But most importantly she'd tell her that the love announcement was too soon.

Camila nodded. That was it. That was the issue. Her unease was centred around how Harriet could have fallen so fast. It was responsible for the sprinkling of doubt in her mind about what they actually had and where they might actually be going. But what if Harriet had simply been following the theme of the quote? What if Harriet was living life the way the author said life should be lived? Grabbing the moment. Feeling the feelings. Articulating her thoughts. Camila knew what she had to do. She had to write a letter. She'd articulate everything that way, even if only for the simple reason of getting her thoughts out there and ordered.

****

Having given the boys their breakfast and checked for a final time that they were okay with Harriet's public announcement last night, Camila sent them on their way to the gym and the library, requesting that whatever their afternoon plans were they be back in time for the show at half seven. Both had groaned and asked if they could watch it at friends' houses instead because another evening of Debbie, Roy and Julie wasn't their idea of fun. Camila had agreed to keep in text communication and make a decision later on, secretly wondering if she could get out of another houseful herself. Maybe it would go well with Harriet at two? Maybe they could watch it there, just the pair of them all snuggled up? She stopped herself; Harriet's only television was in her office so they wouldn't be snuggling, they'd be sitting on chairs, or maybe leaning over the desk. Camila let her mind wander for a moment before tapping her pen on the table.

She was sitting in her kitchen with a pad of A4 lined paper in front of her from the stash in the homework cupboard, the place where they tried to keep all things that usually went missing: the Pritt Stick, the Blu Tack, the Sellotape, the scissors, the paper clips and the pens that actually worked. She wrote the first line:

For Harriet, but also for me.

I don't know if I'm going to give you this, but I want you to hear it. Maybe I'll read it aloud to you. That would be strange wouldn't it? But most of our relationship has been strange. Imagine if my parents hadn't christened me Camila Uma Moore. We'd never have met. Imagine if the pink-haired punk, now in the focus group, hadn't gone to the toilet when she did, you'd never have seen me through the screen wearing that mesh outfit. Imagine if I hadn't come to your office and agreed to eat Thai. Imagine if we hadn't made each other laugh? Imagine if I hadn't felt the chemistry. Camila paused. She had felt the chemistry. She'd felt the chemistry from the start.

I want to be honest with you, Harriet. The chemistry threw me. The feelings threw me. Obviously not enough to make me stay away, but you have to understand that this is all new to me. I know we live in a day and age where sexuality isn't important and you can be fluid without anyone seeming to mind, but I've been with one man for my whole life. This is a big change for me. A big deal. I wish I could jump head first into whatever this is that we're doing, and I have to admit that I have been, mostly, but there's something niggling me and I'm not sure what it is. Is it because I'm new to this? Is it because this seems too good to be true? Is it because I'm not sure I fully trust you?

Camila put down the pen. There. That was the issue. She shook her head. She couldn't give this to Harriet. Yes, it was the truth but sometimes the truth hurt. If Harriet was genuinely in love with her then that would hurt her, and she didn't want to hurt Harriet.

I'm going to keep writing just to clarify everything in my mind. I'm not giving you this letter but I think I need to hear it for myself. I'm not sure if I trust you, Harriet. You've not done anything to make me doubt you, but the odd comment about your past and your other women, or "projects" as they've been called, are playing on my mind – again not enough to make me stay away, but it's there, niggling me. Maybe I don't want to let myself believe? Maybe I don't want to let myself fall? Maybe this is me in self-protect mode saving myself from any future heart ache? But, Harriet, I'd rather go there with you and have that heart ache than not go there at all. I want you. I want to be with you.

There, she'd said it. In essence the theme was: I want you, but I don't trust you. Camila gasped. How awful. But wasn't it like that in all relationships at the start as you tried to get to know the person? Weren't all motives questioned? You wondered whether that person was simply trying to take you off the market because their rival had declared an interest in you? That's what it had been like with Mick: did Mick really want her or did he want her to get at Robert Puckett? That's what she'd questioned back then so why was this questioning any different?

Okay, maybe it's not about your motives. Maybe it's more about the element of surprise. I'm surprised that you like me. You can have any woman you want, Harriet, yet you say you want me. I find that hard to believe. I have nothing to offer you, apart from my body.

There, she'd said that too. Was this just about sex? Thinking back to all the laughs they'd had and the conversations they'd enjoyed, Camila realised it wasn't just about sex.

That's wrong of me. I know we have more than great sex. We have a connection. A connection that I've not felt before. Maybe this is it. Maybe this actually is true love and I'm shocked because it's so overwhelming. I get excited when I see you. I think about you when you're not here. I dream of a future together. What it would be like. Where we would live. And see, look, it's me running away with myself. Maybe I'm holding back because I'm scared of scaring you off? The bottom line is, I really like you. I really really like you, Harriet, and I want to see where this goes.

There. That was the conclusion. Yes, this was new. Yes, this was confusing – not because Harriet was a woman, but because there were feelings involved that she'd never felt before.

I think I might give you this letter after all. It's the truth. It's my truth. Maybe once you've read it you can tell me yours?

CHAPTER THIRTY SEVEN

Camila watched as Harriet placed the letter on the duvet. They were in Harriet's bed in her apartment, both fully clothed, sitting propped against the headboard. She'd arrived as requested at 2.00p.m. to find another bit of torn cardboard from the shoe box stuck to the front door. To get in to the apartment complex she'd first had to prove who she was to the security guard at the security barrier who'd ticked her name off a list before allowing her to park in the CCTV monitored basement. She'd then ridden up in the lift that only worked once she'd swiped the security pass that the security guard had given her before alighting at Harriet's floor whose access door only opened once she'd inputted the personalised code Harriet had texted her, and then, and only then, did she have access to Harriet's front door, so it made perfect sense for the treasure hunt to start there otherwise a whole host of people on CCTV security duty would have been privy to her peculiar behaviour… and Camila knew her behaviour had been peculiar with excitable hops and giggles as she dashed around figuring out the clues. The first clue that had been stuck to the front door had said: *My feelings aren't a crook, go and look in a cook book.* Camila had knocked on the door but when there was no answer she'd tried the handle and crept in. There had been soft music coming from somewhere and a wonderful aroma of something cooking but there'd been no sign of Harriet so she'd read the clue once more and gone to the kitchen. If this had been her treasure hunt she'd have put something like: *My love's abound where recipes are found.* Or: *I'm not a deviant, my love's the ingredient.* But instead Harriet had just told her to go and look at the cook books which had made her laugh, just like the next clue had made her laugh even more: *My love's not grotesque, go look on my desk.* And even though it hadn't taken much figuring out it still felt exciting to dash into Harriet's office and scan the workspace for the next scrap of cardboard. Having got it out from under the keyboard, Camila had groaned. They'd got steadily worse: *I love you, now look in the loo.* "Oh, Harriet," she had shouted, "this is so crazy." And child-like and pure. Harriet had obviously just continued to rip apart the shoe box and write whatever clue had come into her mind, but the fact remained that she'd taken the time to set this up.

Camila had groaned as she'd read the next clue: *You're not a project. I'm where we have sex.* Not only had that piece of cardboard been trapped between the toilet seat and toilet lid, but it hadn't even properly rhymed. Having left the clue on the side of the sink and washed her hands, Camila had walked into the room where Harriet had first taken her lesbian virginity. She'd shivered as she had done every time she'd entered the space since, remembering how overwhelmed she'd felt with the pleasure she and Harriet had shared. Only this time it hadn't been a shiver of anticipation or remembrance, it had been a shiver of yearning… and of acceptance. Harriet had been sitting, fully clothed, on the bed, with two final bits of cardboard stuck to the wall behind her. On one it said: *Believe* and on the other it said: *Me.* Camila had covered her mouth with her hands at the shiver of shame that ran through her. In that moment she'd suddenly realised how much effort Harriet had made to prove her feelings… and, yes, while a ripped up shoe box wasn't like she'd written a love song or dedicated a novel to her, it was an effort she shouldn't have had to make.

Looking down at the letter that Harriet had now dropped onto the duvet, Camila wondered how they'd got to this point where Harriet had actually read the three rambling pages of unorganised thoughts. She'd decided on the way over here that it was best not to share it, but Harriet had ended the treasure hunt with the words: "I love you, Camila," to which Camila had replied: "And I think I might love you too." This had then led onto a discussion about why there was any thought involved in the declaration and the letter had been produced.

"It's quite brutal," said Harriet, fingering the hand-written pages once more.

"It wasn't meant to be. I was just trying to be honest."

"About my lack of honesty?"

"Honest with myself mostly." Camila paused. "And I shouldn't have questioned you. I understand that now." Turning to look again at the scraps of cardboard stuck to the wall, Camila smiled. "I do believe you."

"Why now?"

"Because you did this."

"It's hardly momentous." Harriet took Camila's hand and pulled her off the bed. "But this is," she said, leading them to a room at the back of the apartment.

Camila gasped as the door was opened. She'd only glanced into the space once before. It was a room possibly sold as a small dining area or snug, but one that Harriet had been using for storage, only now it had a luscious Persian rug on the floor and tall pot plants of different colours, shapes and sizes crammed into the rest of the space. She turned first to the lady palms and moth orchids – ones she recognised – before eyeing a whole host of colourful plants that she couldn't name. "What *is* this?" said Camila, unsure where to look next.

"I've brought a beautiful outdoor picnic indoors. It's miserable today but I wanted to romance you. I had these plants shipped in and I've been cooking all morning." She smiled. "Scraps of cardboard aren't love, Camila. This is love." Harriet moved them both into the room. "I've even got butterflies."

"So have I."

Harriet laughed. "No, literally, look." Harriet pointed at a brightly coloured butterfly as it took flight.

"What the bloody hell!" gasped Camila. "They're everywhere!"

"Beautiful aren't they. Just like you."

Camila ducked as a large-winged creature fluttered her way. "That one's definitely a moth!" She ducked again. "I don't think I can relax in here! They're everywhere!"

"Sit down. If you stay still they might land on you."

"I don't want them to land on me!"

"Let me change the music. I want this moment to be perfect." Harriet moved to the corner of the room and fiddled with the stereo.

"Panpipes?" Camila frowned at the wispy tooting notes. "You want me to sit on a rug in a room full of plants and butterflies and listen to the panpipes?"

"It's romantic, sit down, I'll bring the food in."

"No! It'll attract them!"

"Attract who?"

"The mini-beasts intent on landing full-winged on my face." Camila fanned away a large spotty flutterer.

"Careful, I had to sign a strict waiver about my intentions."

"Your intentions with the butterflies?"

"Yes. No cruelty. No sticking pins in them and making a collection. Butterfly releases are all the rage. We can open a window and let them go but I wanted you to enjoy them first."

"I'm enjoying the idea. Really lovely of you."

Harriet nodded. "I did think about getting birds, doves maybe, but they might have felt a bit cooped up in here."

"Unfortunately I feel a bit cooped up in here."

"Oh, Camila, I want you to feel loved."

"I don't. I feel anxious and these pan pipes aren't helping. They're tooting out the Titanic theme tune. Listen. Titanic via panpipe."

Harriet tilted her head to the side. "I think you're right. I do like this track though."

"But it's not very romantic. It's the moment before the ship sinks."

"Yes, but the panpipes make it sound beautifully haunting."

"Can we go back into your bedroom?"

"No. I'm bringing the food in. Sit down. I won't be a minute."

Camila followed Harriet's departure with her eyes before daring to look at the luxurious rug. There were three butterflies resting on it, one spotty, one stripy and one blue. They all looked dangerous. She glanced around at the set-up. Yes, it was pretty and yes it must have taken a lot of effort to arrange but Harriet would have had help moving the storage boxes and setting out all the plants, not to mention someone to release the however many hundred butterflies into the indoor jungle. She stopped. Harriet hadn't had to do this. She hadn't had to do any of this. Whichever way you looked at it, this was effort on a monumental scale. "I should have just told you I believed you," said Camila quietly, knowing that she was going to have to edge her way onto the rug. It was like all those times that Michael and Ethan made cakes or biscuits at primary school. You knew they'd be full of other children's dirty nail prints and coughs and sneezes, not to mention table grit and possible nose picks, but you had to sample them all the same and act like they were the most delicious thing you'd ever eaten.

Bending under a low-hanging leaf of an oversize Monstera, Camila decided she'd be best to crawl over the rug, using her hands to clap any landed butterflies away. On all fours she blew at a particularly stubborn red and black beast that wasn't moving, only to gasp in shock as it fluttered straight at her face. She coughed, almost inhaling it. "I can't do this!" she squealed, grabbing hold of her knees and rocking herself on the spot.

Harriet spoke from the doorway as she presented a large wicker picnic basket. "I've got food. Home made."

"That's lovely, but I almost swallowed a butterfly."

"You can't. I had to sign a waiver."

"It wasn't deliberate!" Camila continued to rock, her eyes darting around every time she sensed movement. "I appreciate what you've tried to do here and it really is lovely but—"

"So sit back and let's eat."

Camila reached out and slammed her hand on top of the picnic basket as it was lowered onto the rug. "Don't open that!"

"I have homemade falafels and pork pies. I even made a quiche."

"Is this a joke, Harriet?"

"Oh gosh, what now?"

Camila shook her head. "I can't do this. I'm really sorry, I just can't do this. I thought I might love you, but now I'm not sure again because I'm all anxious and jittery."

"I can collect the butterflies up if you want?"

"You have a net?"

"The guy gave me some nectar. They're attracted to it. I was going to see if you wanted to hold out your hand and feed them."

"No chance."

"It's very popular at weddings apparently."

"We're not getting married."

"I didn't say we were. Honestly, Camila, why can't you just relax and go with things?"

"I don't know." Camila swiped again at the big spotty butterfly that wouldn't leave her alone. "I would love to sit next to you with a beautiful homemade picnic in an indoor butterfly sanctuary and declare my love, but it's just not happening."

"You shouldn't have to force it."

"Says you, creating an indoor butterfly sanctuary and homemade picnic."

"Because I love you."

"Well that's nice, but I don't need all this."

"So what do you need? You don't believe me when I tell it to the nation, you don't believe me when I scribble it on a shoe box, you don't even believe me when I do something like this."

"I think I do believe you, Harriet, I just question how you know it for sure."

"It just hits you, Camila. Love hits you."

"And when did it hit you?"

Harriet shrugged. "Honestly? When I saw you through that window in your mesh outfit."

"That's ridiculous." Camila shook her head. "That can't be true. We hadn't even spoken. You didn't even know me."

"Love just hits you and you know when it's there because you feel its full force right here in your heart." Harriet smiled. "I feel its full force right now as I watch you anxiously rocking."

"That's not love."

"It is for me."

"No. Love's a serious declaration. It's a promise."

"Maybe the saying it part is, but the feeling it part certainly isn't. Love's an emotion, Camila, not a word. It can't be categorised. It's different for everyone. Yes there are obvious signs like feeling addicted to the person, wanting your friends and family to like the person, missing the person when you're apart, celebrating the person's triumphs." Harriet laughed. "Look at you nodding!"

"Because I agree with all of those things, I feel all of those things."

"Yet you don't feel love?"

"I can't categorise that as love I guess."

"Well I'm not here to convince you. Love's about trust, Camila. If you think about it, you never truly know what's going on in someone's mind or someone's heart. It's not like a novel where you usually hear both sides of the story. In real life you just have to take the person as you find them, as you see them. I just hope you can see me for who I am. This is me, Camila and this is my love, and yes love's different for everyone: For some people it's a feeling or a moment, or a look or a word, or an action, or sometimes it can even be a loss. I just want to enjoy what we've got now and see where it goes."

Camila nodded. "Me too. Can it go to the bedroom as these butterflies are freaking me out?"

Harriet laughed. "Oh, Camila, that right there is real love."

"Where?"

"Here, in my heart, I feel it." Harriet slammed her fist against her own chest. "It just hit me right then."

"NO!"

"Yes! You're funny and it makes me love you even more!" Harriet hit her chest even harder.

"NO!" gasped Camila once more.

"Yes! This is my love!"

"NO! YOU JUST SQUASHED THE BIG SPOTTY ONE!"

CHAPTER THIRTY EIGHT

Standing in front of the panel of judges, Camila looked across at Harriet and shared another smile. The past two days had been full of fun times and laughter. Yes, the big spotty butterfly had disintegrated on impact and the picnic had deteriorated into utter chaos with three of the tall pot plants falling over in a domino effect as both women recoiled in horror at the fatal squashing, but once they'd escaped from the panpipe playing jungle they'd managed to enjoy an afternoon of giggles and wild sex with neither feeling the need to readdress the love issue. Camila had concluded to herself that not all stories needed a definitive ending. There didn't always have to be a moment where everything came together. Sometimes things just carried on, in exactly the way Saturday night's show had depicted her and Harriet's relationship. They hadn't shown a moment where Camila had responded to Harriet's declaration; instead the programme makers had been clever in their manipulation of the footage showing scenes of the pair sitting close and laughing together or leaning over a patent drawing as if in a conspiratorial lovers' chat, even though these scenes were filmed before Harriet's actual declaration. It was as if the programme told the story without actually saying the words, and maybe that's what she'd chosen to do with Harriet. Her actions showed love even if she didn't have the nerve to declare it. And whether it was about having the nerve or whether it was actually about the reality of meaning the words, she still wasn't sure, but she'd decided to just leave the internal debate well alone.

She smiled again at Harriet. It was almost their turn to present. The live studio audience and viewers at home were being shown the television commercial for H.I.Pvention. Last night's show had introduced their Technology Box idea and walked viewers though the different stages of production from idea creation, their eureka moment, to prototype, the box now sitting on the desk in front of the judges. Both Ethan and Michael had chosen to watch that episode at friends' houses so Camila had made insincere apologies to Julie and Debbie and stayed to watch it with Harriet. Once home, however, at just gone ten, she'd been met with a houseful. Julie and Debbie were still there, her sons had returned with their friends in tow and the evening had ended up quite late and raucous. It was nice though with everyone on an excited high. Julie didn't seem too angry she'd been ditched, lording over Debbie that she had access to Camila's house whenever she wanted and yes they could invite more of the estate round to watch tomorrow night's final which had then caused Michael and Ethan to bagsy the sofas for the friends they'd said they'd invited who definitely deserved seating priority.

This chat had then escalated into the option of a street party with screens outside relaying the live show as it seemed clear that Camila's idea was going to win and yes while it would take Camila an hour to get back from the studio, people would party on until she came home to a hero's welcome. She was a star, they kept saying, and she was going to win, they insisted. Michael and Ethan had spent a huge amount of the evening showing her things on their phones trying to explain how she and Harriet were trending on Twitter and how the early polls were showing H.I.Pvention had already won, but it all seemed a little premature for Camila who, standing now in front of the judges, knew nothing was decided until it was decided. They were the last business to make their spiel and the three other entrepreneurs had all done a wonderful job. It was obvious that each of their businesses would be a success regardless of whether they won the show or not. Yes, Jill Masters had received a huge grilling about the ethics of her cosmetics spa, with the suggestion that it may encourage low self-esteem amongst young women who were made to feel lacking in their own skin, but Jill's response that young women should treat themselves *because* they were good enough elicited a cheer from the audience which seemed to encourage further her theme of: if a woman feels empowered by surgery let them feel empowered.

Camila had been sitting in the green room with the other entrepreneurs during Jill's live spiel and was unsure what she thought about it. It was all too easy to cheer along with a live audience, but in reality how many mothers and daughters would be sitting at home watching the show wishing that lip plumps and cheek fillers weren't even a thing, let alone an easy-access product that young women were encouraged to get together and just do. Likewise, the nods of approval about the paleo food samples handed out to the panel of judges, the audience and the green room by Oliver James seemed encouragingly positive, but how many people sitting at home watching the show with their fast-food takeaways would actually vote for a café that sold cold-pressed, date-and-prune-heavy health bars?

The presentation that Camila had liked the most was Barry Maddison's. His clothes shopping app was simple, useable and low-cost, but the judges seemed to have a huge issue with the fifteen copy-cat apps developed already since Friday night's show. Camila didn't seem to think this was a concern and completely accepted Barry's claims that these impersonators didn't matter as he'd be the market leader. Camila remembered nodding at this point. She trusted the brands, as did most people, and if Barry's brand was the brand she remembered then that's the brand she would use. Whether she'd actually bother to download a clothes shopping app was another matter entirely, but she liked Barry and if she were voting he'd be the entrepreneur she'd choose, second to Harriet of course.

Standing that little bit straighter as their commercial came to an end, Camila understood that the game was wide open. Yes, after last night's show she and Harriet seemed to be leading the audience vote, but these things could fluctuate and there were four judges to contend with. The programme makers had pitched the audience as the fifth judge, so at least two of the real life judges sitting in front of them right now would have to vote for their business to guarantee a win. She eyed them all carefully, wondering which one to smile at. No one looked her way, they were all too busy eyeballing Harriet. Maybe they were wondering why Harriet had a helper as none of the other entrepreneurs had presented with someone by their side. Obviously they'd used people in the same way she and Harriet had used Brett and Geoff to explain the intricacies of the business, but this final grilling session had been completed by each entrepreneur alone. Camila glanced at her boss. Was Harriet still playing the fauxmance card? If that was the reason for the huge audience vote, then it made sense to remind the judges of their love interest: a vote for the business means a vote for true love. Camila stopped herself, she was past all this now, she'd put it to bed. Harriet wanted her here because she knew the Technology Box better than anyone else.

"Right," said Claude Grifton, the judge who seemed to appear on every single reality competition going, best known for his bald head and bulldog attitude. "That advert's all well and good. It's just a shame you can't deliver on your promises."

Harriet didn't falter. "We've shown with the production of the Technology Box that we can. H.I.Pvention will see your idea though from concept development to product creation."

"No, you won't."

Harriet nodded. "We will. You have children, don't you, Joanne?"

Camila smiled. Very clever. Harriet had redirected the focus onto the softest judge, Joanne Thomas, the tall blonde who'd built her success on interior design.

"I'm sure your children would benefit from the Technology Box. All children would. All families would. We created this." Harriet stepped forward and lifted the box from the judges' desk. "We designed this. We developed this. We produced this. We've shown that H.I.Pvention can be trusted with your ideas."

Claude slammed his fist onto the table. "No, you cannot! You haven't even got the patent!"

"The patent claim has been filed," continued Harriet. "Full patent approval takes years."

"One query to the patent office," shouted Claude, "that's all it took!"

"You've lost me," said Harriet, lowering the box but still managing to keep her cool even through the nervous gasps from the audience.

Camila looked at Harriet. Harriet had explained there would be dramatics and that the judges would try and needle out all of the business's weak points, but the other entrepreneurs hadn't received anything even remotely close to this onslaught. It reminded her of an episode of *The Apprentice* where a candidate was simply told to "Get out," because they'd lied on their CV; no opportunity to explain, just thrown out in disgrace.

"GET OUT!" shouted Claude.

"Excuse me?" Camila hadn't realised she'd spoken until she noticed the two cameras closing in on either side. She froze as the bald bulldog's eyes narrowed her way.

"Your idea, wasn't it?"

Camila nodded. "Yes, it—"

"NO, IT WASN'T!" The angry bald man lifted a piece of paper from the desk. "One call to the patent office and I discover that your lauded Technology Box will never come to fruition."

Harriet took over. "It will. It has. It's here." She held the invention towards the camera. "The Technology Box is just an example of what we can do for you at H.I.Pvention."

Claude roared. "If you can't even perform a patent search then your business is dead in the water. No inventor should trust you. Now get out of my sight. There's nothing else to discuss."

Harriet continued. "We do know how to perform a patent search and we have performed a patent search." She nodded. "The patent's filed."

"FILED TOO LATE!" Claude's bald head was sweating. "One phone call and I discover a replica patent was filed two days earlier."

"That can't be right," continued Harriet. "There's absolutely nothing like this on the market and there are no patents pending for any similar technology."

"See for yourself," said the judge, thrusting the piece of paper their way. "My colleagues on the panel have their own copies."

Judge Joanne shook her head. "I must say it's very disappointing, Harriet, and very out of character."

Claude sneered. "Maybe if you'd spent more time focusing on the business instead of your little romance then this would never have happened."

Camila moved to Harriet's shoulder, reading the print as quickly as she could.

"Oh, Camila," said Harriet, slowly shaking her head.

Camila continued to scan the words, not quite sure of what she was reading but very aware of the gasps coming from the audience.

"Oh, Camila," said Harriet once more, "how could you?"

"Tell her you love her!" shouted someone from the crowd. "Whatever's happened love will pull you through!"

Claude addressed the camera. "For the benefit of the people at home, a little romance is all well and good but this is a business programme. H.I.Pvention failed to spot an identical patent that had been filed just days before theirs. They ploughed on with prototype production, even daring to present this idea as their own. Imagine if you were an inventor using the services of H.I.Pvention. Either there's a leak in their system or they'll knowingly have you paying to produce a prototype that will never legally be yours due to their inability to perform a proper patent search. Whichever the case, this whole thing's a shambles."

"You need to tell her you love her!" came another shout from the audience.

Harriet handed the paper to Camila before nodding at each of the judges in turn. "I'm sorry for wasting your time. Good luck to the other entrepreneurs; I'm bowing out of the race."

"Harriet, wait." Camila had no clue what the paper actually meant.

The audience continued to shout: "Tell her you love her! Just tell her you love her, Camila!"

"You can't bow out of the race," announced Claude. "But I can safely say your business won't be getting my vote."

"Nor mine," added Joanne.

The two other judges were silent, probably well aware that this tension was television gold.

"Harriet, wait!" Camila tried to ignore the growing audience chants as she ducked in front of the camera that had followed Harriet's walk away from the judges' table. "What have I done wrong?"

"Not in front of the cameras."

"You told me you loved me in front of the cameras!"

Harriet planted her feet at the side of the stage. "I'll happily make a fool of myself personally, but not professionally. You've made a fool of me professionally, Camila."

"What?" Camila squinted at the bright light that suddenly shone out from the third camera that had chased them to their current position.

"How could you do this to me?" whispered Harriet, trapped in by the wide lenses.

"Do what?"

"She's your friend."

"Who?" Clutching onto the piece of paper, Camila felt her fingers suddenly balling around the line she'd read at the bottom of the page: *Patent filed by Mrs Julie Biggs.* "Oh, Harriet! No! I didn't know!"

"I think we should call this a day."

Camila watched open-mouthed as Harriet headed backstage taking two of the three cameras with her. Standing still, Camila turned at the tap on her shoulder. The host of the live show who'd been interviewing the entrepreneurs once they came off stage was suddenly by her side.

"Do you think Harriet means your personal relationship or your professional relationship?"

"What?"

The microphone was thrust into Camila's face. "Harriet. She just said she wanted to call it a day."

Camila shook her head. "She can't! I love her! I don't want to lose her!"

The whoops from the audience were deafening.

Camila continued, talking fast and frantically. "My friend's an idiot, she's stolen our idea, but we can file a patent dispute. I know all about patent disputes. I've learnt everything we might ever need to know about patents in case something like this ever happened. We can file an interference claim and there'll be an oral hearing. The Technology Box is H.I.Pvention's idea and even if for whatever reason we lose the patent the business is still a wonderful business.

Harriet's a wonderful entrepreneur and I'm just sorry for any disrepute I've brought her way."

The "*aaaaaaahs*" from the audience were heartfelt.

"Vote for her. Vote for H.I.Pvention. Vote for the business model, which is good." Camila took hold of the microphone and turned to the camera, staring straight into the lens. "I know I've lost Harriet's vote, but that doesn't mean she should lose yours." She sighed. "I'm sorry, everyone, I need to go home."

CHAPTER THIRTY NINE

Pulling into her driveway, Camila realised she'd just driven the longest journey she'd ever driven in total silence. Yes, the television studio was only an hour away but she always had the radio playing in the car. She wasn't even one of those people who needed to turn down the volume to park. She loved the music and the chat, but this evening she'd chosen to drive in total silence, just in case Harriet called, which she hadn't. Everyone else who'd ever received her phone number had though, with some names flashing up on the screen that she didn't even recognise, the strangest call coming from the gutter man who'd over-charged her two years ago to clean out the gutters. There was no way he was calling at ten p.m. on a Sunday evening to offer his services. He was probably, like all the others, calling to have his five minutes of fame in front of his mates at the pub no doubt: *I cleaned that woman from the telly's gutters once; let me call her up and tell her what a fool she's made of herself on national TV*, or something like that. Camila realised she'd never know as she hadn't answered the call, or any of the other calls, her excitement at the burst of ringing instantly dissipating every time she saw it wasn't Harriet's name flashing up on the screen.

Harriet had disappeared. Camila had tried her best to find her, but Deana and the team were freezing her out, the only person seemingly willing to talk to her was the live host who kept thrusting the microphone her way but she didn't want to play any more of this out in front of the audience. She'd said her piece, she'd made her plea, there was nothing else she could do now apart from drive home to where she belonged. She was meant to wait around and do backstage chats and analysis during the half hour break before the results were announced, but there was no way she could go out on stage for the final segment of the show only to be told that they'd lost because of her.

Turning off the ignition, Camila felt her anger flare once again. Julie bloody Biggs. Throwing open the car door, she jumped at the thundering cheers of whoops and applause, her lounge window dancing with the brightly lit silhouettes of people hurling themselves up and down. She gasped as her phone rang in her hand. Was it Harriet? Had they won? Why was everyone cheering? Had Harriet redeclared her love live on TV? Had she forgiven her? She looked at the screen, ready to swipe right. Great Uncle Mac. Camila frowned at the flashing name on the display; she'd thought he was dead, as he certainly hadn't called her in over five years.

"Camila!!!" screamed Julie, dashing out of the house and onto the driveway with her arms flailing, flanked by Debbie, Roy, Michael, Cassie, Ethan and Harry not to mention half the estate who seemed to be piling out of her house. "That was me! I won that for you!"

Michael enveloped his mother in a huge hug. "You did it, Mum, you won! Me and Cassie are so proud of you."

"You're so cool," squealed Ethan. "Harry says you're cool too!"

"You bloody owe me," shouted Julie. "Terry! Pop another champers! Let's have a bloody street party! Roy, go turn the stereo on in my van, let's get this celebration started!"

"What's going on?" shouted Camila over the noise, shocked to see Julie's old man Terry for the first time in however many weeks.

"You won!" Julie grabbed Camila by the arms, jumping her up and down. "H.I.Pvention won! You got the audience vote and two of the judges' votes! You won! Your plea won it and you only made that plea because of the cock-up with the patents and that was me! Without me you'd never have won! I make money with the Technology Box, you make money because you won! I've already phoned the papers; they'll be round in the morning! We're all winners! Bloody chars!"

Terry thrust a flute of Champagne Camila's way. "We call this the Lamborghini champers, don't we, Jules. You're a bloody sort, Camila. Things have been on the up for us all since you went and turned gay!"

Camila tried to focus but was too distracted by the loud music that suddenly started blaring out from the bacon butty van and the crowd of people dancing around on her driveway. "Lamborghini Champagne? Her car? Harriet's Lamborghini?"

"Chill bloody out!" shouted Julie over the din. "It's all come together. You won! I bloody won! It was my bloody idea after all."

"To steal her car?"

"No, not the car! I only tipped off Terry and he tipped off Jack the Trader and he tipped off his men from Leyton and we all won. You won, Camila! Why aren't you smiling?"

"You think the Technology Box was your idea?"

"It bloody well was and that firm Patent Reg are fab. I'm not sure if H.I.Pvention could go up against them actually, but the whole thing's all smoke and mirrors anyway isn't it, you said so yourself. It's like *The Apprentice*, you're only bloody pretending to start these businesses."

"This is Harriet's life!" shouted Camila. "This is my life! You've ruined my life, Julie, and it wasn't your idea anyway."

Terry reached out and grabbed the glass of Champagne back from Camila. "It was her bloody idea and the people at Patent Reg filed the patent for us. We got all dressed up and everything didn't we, Jules."

"It was so easy." Julie lifted her glass in a cheers motion. "I don't know what you've been moaning about. I only had to talk them through the idea and they did the rest."

"It wasn't your idea!"

Julie gasped. "It bloody well was! I said: How about you invent something that allows kids a certain number of hours on technology a day."

"And then I invented it! Harriet invented it! H.I.Pvention invented it!"

"You mean H.I.Pvention that was that Deana woman's idea? You've got form with this, Camila."

Terry threw his arm around his missus. "End of the day, we've got the bloody patent!"

Julie shook him off and continued. "Camila, if that curveball had never come your way you'd never have done your plea and it was your plea that won those two judges over. It's not about the Technology Box after all, you said that yourself, it's about the business and the business has won."

"But I've lost, Julie. I've lost Harriet, can't you see that?"

"Oh, you never bloody knew if you wanted her in the first place, all your to-ing and fro-ing. If you actually loved her you'd know."

"I know!" shouted Camila over the loud music. "I know now! It's the thought that I've lost her that makes me realise I love her!"

"That's not bloody love."

"It is for me."

"Hardly very bloody romantic though."

Camila pulled her neighbour away from the noisy van and onto the street pavement. "Sometimes there isn't that one magical moment of knowing," she said. "Or even a momentum of magical moments or lovely experiences that make you realise you're in love. Sometimes it's the shock that you've lost someone, and I've lost her, Julie. I've lost Harriet."

"No, you haven't. She was just on the TV saying she loved you. She obviously saw your spiel from the stage."

"What?" Camila gasped out in shock.

"Dedicated the bloody win to you, didn't she?"

"Did she?" Camila grabbed hold of Julie's arm. "Did she really?"

"Of course she bloody well did. Does this mean we're friends again? Can we go closer to the van? I love it when the music's pumping."

"Oh, Julie, what am I going to do with you?"

"Let me have the patent?"

"No chance! We'll be filing a patent dispute in the morning and we clearly have all of the evidence to support our claim that it was our development."

"But it was my idea! I sat there and came up with it when you were pissed off at Ethan and his obsession with his handhelds." Julie pointed. "Ooooh look, now he's got a new hand to hold. And anyway, if you're filing a patent dispute in the morning it means you're still at H.I.Pvention so I maintain my point: it's all worked out for everyone involved." Julie flung an arm around Camila's waist.

"Look at everyone, all these happy people, everyone's dancing, and would you just look at your son and his new handheld."

Camila watched her youngest who was indeed smiling widely as he held the hand of his pretty friend Harry.

"And Michael too. Look at him. Wait, who's that?" said Julie. "What's going on?"

Camila followed the gaze to her eldest child.

"It's bloody Bill Stevens," Julie was shouting. "Bill! Bill! It's Cassie's dad. Why's he pushing your Michael? Terry, come here! Quick, do something! Roy, get involved! Break it up! What's going on?!"

Camila ran past Terry who was shaking his head and saying something about not getting involved with a boxer. "Do something!" she shouted, before charging into the man who was tall enough and muscular enough to make her eldest actually look like a child again. "Stop it!" she shouted. "What are you doing?! Roy, come and help me!"

"Your son, is it?" shouted the man as he held Michael in a head lock.

"Let go of him! He's only fifteen!"

"Excuse me," said Roy, "I think you should let go of him."

"Says who? You? Standing there holding your bollocks. Why are you holding your bollocks?"

Debbie chirped up. "He has his issues, does my Roy. He won't want them getting knocked and you're a boxer aren't you? He'll be concerned. You're concerned, aren't you, Roy?"

"He only runs the bloody boxing club," said Julie. "He's not a boxer himself. Now what is it, Bill? Calm down and tell us what's happening."

Camila continued trying to free her son's head. "Let go of him. This is private property."

"Property that belongs to me too," said the voice behind her.

Spinning around as she released her grip on the big man's bicep, Camila saw Mick standing next to her car.

"Doesn't look like you've been doing very well without me, does it, Camila. What's going on, everyone?"

"Your son, is he?" said Bill with a growl, still not releasing his choke hold.

Mick nodded. "He might have gone a bit off the rails with me being away and all that, but I'm back now and I'm here to sort everything out. Camila, whatever this is, I forgive you. You've made a fool of yourself on the telly but I'm putting it down to a mid-life crisis. I had one with Jackie but it's over now. Let's forget all about it and move on. Everyone, if you could go home. This is my home. Mine and Camila's. We'll sort out whatever this is and we'll see you all soon."

No one moved apart from Ethan who released his friend's hand.

"I've seen it already, son," said Mick, "and I'll be sorting that out too. Honestly, Camila, is there anything you haven't screwed up?"

"Me, Mick? How dare you? I'm happy. For the first time in a very long time, I'm happy."

"You don't look it, love. You've got one son in a headlock, one doing something I don't even want to discuss and a friend who's still fucking you over."

"It was my idea!" shouted Julie.

"Whatever." Mick turned to the crowd once again. "Will you all just piss off?"

Still no one moved apart from Bill Stevens who finally released Michael and pulled the boy up by the back of his shirt. "Tell him, mate. Give your dad something else to add to his worries."

Michael rubbed his neck. "I don't know what you're talking about."

"SHE'S PREGNANT," shouted the man, pointing his finger at his daughter. "You got my daughter pregnant. She's the head girl and she's pregnant!"

"Oh Julie!" gasped Camila. "You let her stay the night!"

The gasp from the crowd of people huddled on the driveway almost rivalled the one elicited from the live studio audience earlier on when Claude had made his announcement.

"Camila, you silly cow," said Mick. "Look what happens when there's no man in the house. You need me, you all need me. We'll sort this out, mate," he said, nodding at Cassie's dad. "We'll give you some money from her Technology Box invention. We're going to be minted. We'll support your girl."

Terry stepped forwards. "The Technology Box idea's ours. Mine and Julie's. No offence, mate, and it's nice to see you back and all that, but we filed the patent first. We'll be the ones making the money."

Mick shook his head. "Didn't you watch the results? That Harriet bird just said it was my Camila's idea. She said Camila was the reason they'd won the show and that Camila was the reason they'd win back the patent."

Camila smiled. "Did she really say that?"

"Does no one care that my kid is pregnant?" shouted Bill in frustration.

"These things happen, Bill," said Julie. "We'll all rally round."

"I can't believe you, Michael," said Camila, shaking her head, "after everything we've spoken about."

"It wasn't me, Mum."

Debbie snorted. "Well it certainly wasn't my Roy, was it, dear?" She addressed the crowd. "He does have his problems does my Roy."

Bill pointed his finger at Camila and Mick. "Your boy has made my girl pregnant."

"I'm not pregnant by him, Dad!" Cassie was shaking her head. "He's only fifteen. He's my friend. He's been helping me with my school work. He's been good to me."

"Now *that's* my son," said Camila.

Bill growled. "That twat of a head boy then? Was it him? Was it? Was it?"

Cassie nodded.

"That posh fucker? Goddamn it. He lives on that new estate down the road, doesn't he? I think I'll go and pay him a visit instead," he roared. "No harm meant," added the man with his own brand of sincerity.

Camila watched as half the crowd followed Bill Stevens: an angry mob intent on revenge, or entertainment. She turned to Cassie. "Are you okay?"

Cassie sniffed before managing a smile. "If I end up like you then I will be."

Camila laughed. "Like me? Look at me. Look at this mess. Are you sure you haven't got anything to do with this, Michael?"

"Of course not, Mum."

"Your son's the one who's got me through it all," said Cassie. "You should be really proud of him." The pretty girl nodded. "And you'll sort all this out."

"No, I will," said Michael, stepping up to his father and looking him dead in the eye. "Do one, Dad."

Ethan stepped forward too and raised his chin. "Yeah, do one."

Neither boy smiled nor flinched as their father half-laughed, half-flexed his shoulders.

"That's a nice way to speak to your dad." Mick looked at Camila, his face flushed with a shade of pink somewhere between anger and embarrassment. "Is this how you're bringing them up? No respect for their father?"

Camila shrugged, "You have to earn respect Mick, that's what I've taught them."

Mick stared at her and then at the stony-faced boys, then at his ex-neighbours – all watching with quite a bit of interest and not a lot of sympathy.

"You know what," said Mick, "I'm going to leave you lot to it. I might have been a bit proud of you, Michael, if you'd got your bird pregnant." He stared at his youngest son. "But as for you, mate, your mother's obviously rubbed off on you too much already."

"Good," said Ethan, "I'd like that, because she's perfect. She's happy and I'm happy and we're all happy."

"And you're happy with Jackie," reasoned Camila, wanting a quiet and amicable end to this scene.

"Kicked me out, didn't she?"

"You can stay with us," offered Terry, puffing out his chest.

"No, he can't," said Julie promptly. "Me and Camila are patching things up. I don't want you and Mick causing us problems."

Camila sighed. Was this her life? Was this her worth. These people. Was she silly to think she could ever escape any of it?

"I don't think so, Julie," she heard herself saying in an unusually firm tone. "You've gone too far this time." She turned away from her ex-best friend's gaping mouth. Throwing her head back she closed her eyes and was immediately hit in the face by a huge rain drop.

"Rain dance!" screamed Julie, as she spun away from Camila, trying to grin and look like nothing had happened. "Turn the stereo up louder!"

Camila stayed where she was, the pumping music from the van and the noise from the suddenly hammering rain drowned out by the "whop-whop" sound of a low-flying helicopter.

Cassie shouted into Camila's ear. "Go and say 'yes' to Harriet."

Wiping the rain from her face, Camila frowned up at the flashing navigation lights in the sky above them. "What?"

"You're a strong woman, Camila," said the girl. "If I end up like you then I'll know I've done well. You've been an inspiration to me and your boys are a credit to you."

"Is that the bloody media?" screeched Julie, pointing up at a helicopter that was circling their street. "They said they wouldn't come till tomorrow. Bloody hell, Camila, we need to get our stories straight. I'm having the patent, right? But they're not seeing me like this all soaked to the bone, I need to go and get changed!"

Camila shook her head. "You heard me, Julie. There isn't a story to get straight. You're not getting the patent. I can't be friends with you anymore. No more crap bargains, no more bullying, no more walking all over me. We're done. I'm done."

"You don't mean it," Julie said, trying to grin.

"I do, Julie. I really really do."

Cassie grabbed her arm. "It's Harriet," she whispered into Camila's ear as she peered up into the rainy sky. "And you're going to say yes to her, Camila." The girl smiled. "I do English Lit; we're studying contemporary romance."

"That's not Harriet and there's nothing to say yes to."

"There is. It's Harriet in that chopper, it says 'H.I.P' on the side, I saw it clear as day. You need to say yes to believing. Yes, to just going with it. Yes, to the unknown. I've learnt that from you, so have your boys. That's what I'm going to do. Come on, you can't let me down. You're my heroine."

Camila laughed shakily and wiped more rain from her face as they watched the helicopter's lights descend further. It was hovering above the playing field behind their estate. It was going to land.

"Let's go and see who it is," shouted Harry, grabbing hold of Ethan's hand and splashing through puddles as they darted off towards the playing field.

"She's come to swoop you up like Richard Gere, only she's so cool she's not bothering with a limo." Cassie shrugged at Camila's surprised expression. "That's how I'd write it anyway."

Camila shook her head, causing rain to fly in all directions. "Life's not like that. There aren't any final scenes like there are in books or the movies. Life just goes on. You just figure it out. You don't get that one moment of magic."

"But what if it's there?" said Cassie, as she smiled over at Michael. "Shouldn't you rush towards it and grab it with both hands?"

Camila gasped as she visualised her favourite ever scene from a movie. Her feet started to move of their own accord and suddenly she was splattering through puddles, the spray glittering in the street lights and soaking her to the skin. As she got to the playing field she saw the helicopter's skids settling on the grass and its side door opening. Ethan and Harry were leaping up and down waving and hollering.

"It's her, Mum, it's her!"

Camila's heart began to beat faster as the chopper's rotors slowed. Racing across the grass, she saw Harriet jump down from the open door. She was running towards her. They were running towards each other. Meeting in a swirl of rain on the white chalked halfway line of the football pitch, both women peered at each other in the gloom. At that moment the helicopter's spotlights snapped on, turning the playing field into a brilliantly bejewelled fairyland of gently falling rain. Harriet reached out for Camila's hand. Camila took it between both her own. Whether it was colder than hers, she couldn't tell, but the warmth in Harriet's eyes as rain trickled down her cheeks made the night feel like a warm one in July.

"It's pouring," Harriet said softly, smiling at Camila.

"Is it still raining? I hadn't noticed."

Harriet threw back her head and laughed. The sound made Camila's heart turn a full somersault and she allowed herself to move into Harriet's beckoning arms.

"Let me ask you one thing," said Harriet. "Do you think... after we've dried off, after we've spent lots more time together... you might agree—"

Camila gasped. "You know it! You know the *Four Weddings* scene!"

Harriet looked sheepish and nodded. "So... do you think...?"

"I do!"

The cheering from the neighbours gathered at the edge of the football pitch and the whooping of her sons barely got through the sound of the rain and Camila's beating heart as Harriet took her wet face between wet hands and kissed her. Just like in the movies.

THE END

About the author:

Lambda Literary Award finalist, Kiki Archer is the UK-based author of nine best-selling, award-winning novels. She was position 51 in the Guardian newspaper's Pride Power List 2018 and position 18 in the Diva Pride Power List 2017.

Her debut novel But She Is My Student won the UK's 2012 SoSoGay Best Book Award. Its sequel Instigations took just 12 hours from its release to reach the top of the Amazon lesbian fiction chart.

Binding Devotion was a finalist in the 2013 Rainbow Awards.

One Foot Onto The Ice broke into the American Amazon contemporary fiction top 100 as well as achieving the lesbian fiction number ones. The sequel When You Know went straight to number one on the Amazon UK, Amazon America, and Amazon Australia lesbian fiction charts, as well as number one on the iTunes, Smashwords, and Lulu Gay and Lesbian chart.

Too Late... I Love You won the National Indie Excellence Award for best LGBTQ book, the Gold Global eBook Award for best LGBT Fiction. It was a Rainbow Awards finalist and received an honourable mention.

Lost In The Starlight was a finalist in the 2017 Lambda Literary Awards best lesbian romance category and was named a 'Distinguished Favourite' in the Independent Press Awards.

A Fairytale Of Possibilities won Best Romance Novel at the 2017 Diva Literary Awards and was awarded a Distinguished Favourite in the New York Big Book Awards.

Kiki was crowned the Ultimate Planet's Independent Author of the Year in 2013 and she received an honourable mention in the 2014 Author of the Year category.

She won Best Independent Author and Best Book for Too Late... I Love You in the 2015 Lesbian Oscars and was a finalist in the 2017 Diva250 Awards for best author.

Kiki's 2018 ended on an incredible high winning 'Best Author' at the Waldorf's star-studded Diva Awards.

<u>Novels by Kiki Archer:</u>

BUT SHE IS MY STUDENT - March 2012

INSTIGATIONS - August 2012

BINDING DEVOTION - February 2013

ONE FOOT ONTO THE ICE - September 2013

WHEN YOU KNOW - April 2014

TOO LATE... I LOVE YOU - June 2015

LOST IN THE STARLIGHT - September 2016

A FAIRYTALE OF POSSIBILITIES - June 2017

THE WAY YOU SMILE - November 2018

Connect with Kiki:

www.kikiarcherbooks.com
Twitter: @kikiarcherbooks
www.facebook.com/kiki.archer
www.youtube.com/kikiarcherbooks
www.instagram.com/kikiarcherbooks

L - #0054 - 201218 - C0 - 210/148/16 - PB - DID2397223